RALPH WILDHAWK;

OR,

Alone Among the Brigands.

BEAUTIFULLY ILLUSTRATED.

COMPLETE.

LONDON :
" BOYS OF ENGLAND" OFFICE, 173, FLEET STREET, E.C
AND ALL BOOKSELLERS.

RALPH WILDHAWK;

OR,

ALONE AMONG THE BRIGANDS.

"THE ENRAGED MOTHER DREW A PISTOL AND SHOT THE BRIGAND DEAD."

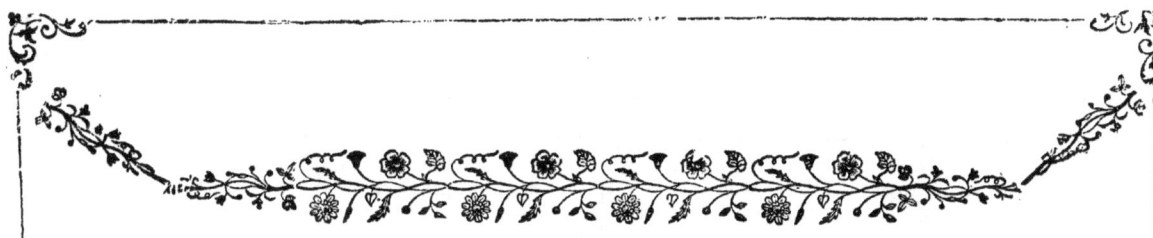

RALPH WILDHAWK;

OR,

Alone Among the Brigands.

CHAPTER I.

THE "SIGNOR CAPITANO."

"BRIGANDS! fudge! Go where I will, I hear nothing but rumours of the banditti, and their horrible atrocities ; but though I have travelled through well-nigh every pass and defile in the Abruzzi, I have never been molested."

The words were spoken by a tall, handsome, dark man, loosely wrapped in a long, black cloak.

He stood leaning with folded arms against the sign-post of the tavern, at Terracina, the last town in the Roman territory, and on the high road to Naples.

The man to whom he was speaking was Nicolo Pizani, whose name figured on the tabard, as the keeper of the way-side albergo and post-house.

He was a short, pursy, red-faced man, girt with a white apron, from which depended a jingling bunch of keys, while on his close crop of black, crisp hair was perched a cap of red cloth of the jelly-bag pattern,

Nicolo stared at the dark, sinister, but strikingly handsome face of his strange guest, with a half-doubting expression, and turning out the palms of his hands, he shrugged his shoulders with a true Italian gesture.

"*Corpo di Baccho!*" said he, "then your excellency may account yourself most fortunate, for few travellers escape the robbers of the Abruzzi, especially since the daring Marco Bravo has taken command of the robber band."

"Marco Bravo," repeated the stranger, raising his broad, black eyebrows, "and pray who is he?"

"*E il diavolo!* He's the devil," returned the host, lowering his voice almost to a whisper. "We all fear him. You know he succeeded the notorious Alessandro. Surely you have heard of him?"

"Oh, yes," replied the other carelessly. "I remember hearing him spoken of in Rome ; he was lately killed in a desperate battle with the dragoons, somewhere in the neighbourhood of Frosinone. Is it not so?"

"It is so," was the reply. "If your excellency will step this way I will show you his head ; the authorities have had it stuck up on the Appian Way, as a warning to his fellow monsters."

"*Andiamo!*" said the other, coolly, as he lit his cigar. "Let us go and look at this brigand's head."

The host led the way across a patch of greensward, and descending a rocky bank, they came upon the old Roman road.

After proceeding about a hundred yards, the innkeeper stopped and shuddered.

"*Eccolo!* there he is," said he.

Fixed in the ground stood a tall iron stake, surmounted by an iron cage, through the bars of which grinned a human skull.

A large carrion crow had perched itself on the branch of a tree near the robber's head, and at their approach, flapped his great black wings, and rising lazily in the air, flew off, but alighted at a short distance.

"So that is the head of the famous brigand chief Alessandro?" said the stranger, blowing a long whiff of blue, curling smoke on the calm summer air.

"*Sicuro,*" returned the host; "it is hard to believe that a man could follow a career that would lead to such an end as that."

"I don't know that, *amico,*" was the reply. "A soldier stands in constant peril of his life.

"If this fellow had not the wit or the good fortune to keep his head upon his shoulders, it cannot make much difference to him what was done with it after it had been taken off. 'Tis all the fortune of war."

Then, clapping the host on his broad shoulder, he added gaily—

"But come ; let us go back. I have had a long walk, and I am thirsty. We must crack a bottle together—a bottle of your best Lachryma Christi."

Nicolo's face brightened up.

He rubbed his chubby hands, and gave a chuckling laugh.

"Signore," he answered, "you shall have some of the finest vintage. The grapes were pressed in the year of the great earthquake. San Gennaro! what a not summer that was!

And, talking about brigands, it was in that year that my nephew, Giovanni, was captured, and held to ransom by Alessandro and his gang of brigands."

"The young man I saw standing at the door of the inn—was it he?"

"Oh, no, signor. That was my new servant, Pepe, a quiet, civil, ready fellow enough, but one I don't seem to take to," replied the host; "he is so silent and reserved—his manner is dark and mysterious."

The stranger laughed.

"Who knows?—he may be in league with these dreaded brigands."

Nicolo rolled up his eyes and uplifted his hands.

"The saints forbid!" he fervently ejaculated. "If I thought so, I would soon bundle him out neck and crop, or hand him over to the soldiers."

They had by this time reached the inn.

A grave-looking waiter, bronzed almost to the complexion of a mulatto, received them on the lawn.

"This is Pepe," whispered Nicolo.

"*Basta!*" returned the guest, "I don't like the look of him, I warrant you."

The landlord shrugged up his shoulders and looked unutterable things.

Meanwhile, the servant and the stranger exchanged significant glances.

They twisted their eyes to the left and gave a slight toss of the head upwards.

This they did unobserved by the innkeeper, who, in fact, had entered the house in order to procure the wine.

"Pepe," said the stranger.

"Signor Capitano," replied the other, saluting with the deepest respect.

"This Englishman whose arrival at the inn is expected—who and what is he?" questioned the signor capitano.

"He is a great English milordo," answered Pepe, "reported to be immensely rich."

"Good," returned the stranger. "By whom is he accompanied?"

"There are five—the milordo with his son, and his secretary: the two latter both very young men, mere boys, in fact, and his niece, a charming signorina. They are attended by two servants, man and maid."

"Good. Who are the postillions?"

"Pietro and Guiseppe."

"Good again; they are both of our band. Have the travellers much baggage?"

Pepe clasped his hands in rapture.

"Cospetto!" he exclaimed, "the lady's portmanteau is as big as Noah's ark, and the milord has a small iron chest, no doubt containing cash or jewels."

The stranger nodded his head approvingly.

"Do they carry arms?"

"Yes, signor capitano, rifles and pistols, and the men seem determined fellows, likely to give trouble. Those Englishmen are very devils to fight."

The stranger uttered a low, contemptuous laugh, and cocked his steeple-crowned hat fiercely upon his brows.

"I hate the English!" he said. "But have you a note containing the names of the party?"

"Yes, signor capitano," replied the other. "It was supplied me by Padre Antonio, the confessor of the band. He met the party at an inn in Albano."

"Well?"

"The good father has been in England, speaks and writes the language like a native, while his mild, benevolent smile disarms suspicion. He came here yesterday and told me that the English milord made him a handsome present."

"The padre is a valuable man," returned the stranger.

Then he held up his finger.

"Zitto! hush!" said he. "Here comes the landlord."

Nicolo now appeared with a bottle of wine, which he set upon the table.

At his approach Pepe moved away from the strange guest, and pretended to busy himself in dusting the table and arranging the chairs.

Meanwhile, the stranger stood gazing upon the exquisite scenery.

The inn, which was situated outside the walls of the city, commanded a magnificent prospect of the Mediterranean Sea.

It was backed by the picturesque old town, and the lofty, snow-capped mountains.

Terracina is the last town in the Roman territory.

The innkeeper set the bottle and glasses upon the table, and sent Pepe to fetch a loaf of bread and a water-melon.

The guest flung down a gold piece, and laughingly refused the change, stipulating only that the waiter was to have a piastre as his fee.

Nicolo was more than ever delighted with his guest.

He poured out the wine and drank his health.

The stranger took a deep draught and smacked his lips.

"This is indeed excellent," he said. "And so this was made in the year of the great earthquake?"

"It was, signore," replied the innkeeper.

"But what were you telling me about your nephew, Giovanni? A light for my cigaret, Pepe. Thank you. Where is the youth at present?"

Nicolo shook his head and heaved a deep sigh.

"He is gone to the mountains, signore."

The stranger started and stared in well-feigned surprise.

"To the mountains!" he responded. "You never mean to say that he has joined the banditti!"

"Yes, signore, it is so."

"But what motive had he for taking such a desperate step?"

"Why, you see, signore, poor Giovanni fell in love with my daughter Lisetta; but she preferred another man, one Giffone, a vine-dresser.

"The rivals met. A quarrel ensued. In the heat of passion my unhappy nephew drew his stiletto, and stabbed Giffone to the heart."

"*Che disgrazia!*" returned the stranger. "What a misfortune."

'It was indeed, signore. The poor lad was very useful to me, and I still bewail the loss of his services."

"And you have never heard any tidings of him since he joined the band of brigands?"

"No, signore—never," was the mournful reply.

"Poor Giovanni! Up till the time of his making that fatal mistake, he always detested the brigands, by whom he had once been carried off, when they gave him a great fright."

"Was his ransom paid?"

Nicolo laughed.

"No, signore," he replied. "He was rescued in a most gallant style by his mother and his elder brother. It was a capital joke."

"Pray let me hear the story."

"It happened in this way," resumed Nicolo. "There was about that time a band of brigands that infested the passes between this town and Fondi, under the command of a ferocious scoundrel named Crocco.

"My nephew had gone up the mountains to take an eagle's nest for an English traveller then staying at this inn, when he was captured by the brigand gang.

"The usual message was sent down from the hills. The brigand chief must have one thousand ducats by a certain day, or the life of the boy—he was only twelve—would pay the forfeit."

"No doubt the poor mother was distracted."

"Yes, poor thing; she was my own sister—a woman of determined spirit," rejoined Nicolo.

"She had another son, Andrea, a young fellow of perfect pluck, though his face was as smooth as the face of Apollo.

"Him she dressed carefully as a peasant girl.

"Having appointed to meet the robber chief in a certain spot, she took up two hundred ducats, and a present of cakes and fruit, the 'peasant girl' going with her as a guide.

"Well, signore, on reaching the place, they found the scoundrel waiting, with the captive lad, bound hand and foot, beside him.

"My sister first ascertained by cunning questions that the man was really alone, and then offered, with many supplications, her money, and the present of cakes and fruit.

"The villain took the latter, and munched while he counted out the ducats.

"Then, with a fierce oath, he said it was far too little—that she must go back and send enough to make up a thousand, or the head of the lad would be sent down to her without delay.

"While the woman clung supplicatingly to his knees, the disguised peasant suddenly flung a grip of iron round the robber's arms.

"As the fellow was thus pinioned, the enraged mother drew a loaded pistol and shot the brigand dead.

"Andrea and his mother lost no time in liberating the lad.

"Nor did they forget to cut off and wrap in a cloth the head of the chief, and as a reward of three thousand ducats had been set upon this article, they made quite an excellent day's business of it, on arriving safe and sound at Terracina."

"Bravo! a capital story," rejoined the guest. "Let us drink the health of your brave and clever sister. But, hark! who comes?"

Crack—crack—crack!

The cracking of whips, the rattle of wheels, and the clatter of horses' hoofs now proclaimed the approach of a carriage.

Nicolo instantly started to his feet.

"Holy Virgin!" he exclaimed, "it is the English milord and his party. I did not expect them so soon."

Then he bustled towards the house, bawling at the top of his voice—

"Lisetta—Pepe—Tomaso, turn out! Body of Bacchus! are you all asleep? The calash and six horses are here, and nothing in readiness. *Via scampa!* Turn out, you lazy drones!"

CHAPTER II.

RALPH WILDHAWK.

THE vetturino, or travelling carriage, was a very grand affair, drawn by six horses.

The postillions, thick-set, swarthy, black-browed fellows, were dressed in very quaint but smart liveries, blue jackets with facings of gold lace, cocked hats edged with gold lace, leathern breeches and enormous top-boots.

They brandished short-handled whips, with long, knotted thongs, which they cracked with tremendous energy.

Nicolo, with his pretty, arch-looking daughter, Lisetta, and his servants, Pepe, Tomaso, and Filippe, hastened to hand down the weary and dust-covered passengers from the vehicle.

To prevent all needless mystification, we will give a brief description of each of the members of the travelling party.

First, then, there was the English milord, whom the simple Italians regarded as at least a prince of the blood, but who was in fact a rich country gentleman, holding the rank of baronet—Sir Raymond Mortimer.

He was a tall, stately, and somewhat stern-looking man.

He wore a long grey riding-coat, top-boots, a cocked hat and sword, a dress somewhat old-fashioned for the period, which, we may hint to the reader, was that of the early part of the reign of our King George the Third.

His son, Edmund Mortimer, a tall, sprightly youth, very handsome, with blue eyes, but of a somewhat cruel and sinister countenance.

He was over-dressed in the latest fashion of the day.

He wore a dove-coloured coat with silver, filagree buttons, red-heeled shoes, a steeple-crowned hat of the newest mode, and a cravat of the finest lace, fastened with a diamond brooch of great value.

Ralph Wildhawk, about two years older than Edmund, was a fine, manly, but rather gloomy-looking lad.

He was nominally secretary to the baronet, but in reality had been brought up as companion to Edmund, and was dressed in a plain, but neat suit of brown cloth, which, however, fitted his perfect figure to admiration.

Violet Melville, the neice and ward of the old baronet, was a charming young girl, with blue eyes and golden hair, and an expression of mingled sweetness and intelligence, quite irresistible.

Of the two servants, one was the lady's maid, Matilda Sparkes, a pretty, but sentimental-looking nymph, and Joe Moody, a short, sturdy, morose-looking fellow, of clumsy gait and stolid, taciturn demeanour.

As the travellers descended from the carriage, the signor capitano watched them with furtive but keen scrutiny.

As his gaze fell upon the lovely face and form of Violet Melville, the colour mounted his olive cheek, and his dark eyes sparkled like black diamonds.

"What innocence and beauty," he murmured. "*Cielo!* what a prize."

Nicolo and his adherents now ushered the party into the inn with all pomp and ceremony.

The signor capitano stood near the door, and politely raised his hat as they passed him.

Violet blushed and curtsied.

The old baronet bowed sedately.

And Edmund gave a cool, supercilious nod.

The youth, Ralph Wildhawk, lingered for a moment, his dark eyes resting with a fond, dreamy gaze upon the exquisite scenery.

The Italian stepped up to him, and bowed with a smile of recognition.

"Your servant, signore," he said, very quietly; "I fear you have forgotten me."

Young Wildhawk started, gazed at the man earnestly, and instantly extended his hand.

"No, by Heaven!" he exclaimed, smiling radiantly; "you are Monsignore the Count Di Ancona, whom I had the honour and good fortune to meet in the Colosseum at Rome. I am glad to see you again."

"The pleasure, I am sure, is mutual," was the softly-spoken reply; "I shall not forget the delight it gave me to witness your enthusiasm at beholding, for the first time, those stupendous ruins."

"Indeed, monsignore; I believe that scene made a deeper impression upon me than anything I have yet seen in this land of wonder and beauty," replied the youth. "As I stood in the arena, I could almost realise those terrible combats in which the gladiators shed their blood like water, to gratify their tyrant's lust of cruelty, and where so many Christian martyrs gave up their life for their faith."

"You speak with enthusiasm," replied the other smiling; "but *figlio mio*, when you become as old as I am, or indeed, if you stay long enough in Italy, you will think but little of these things."

Then changing his tone, he asked carelessly—

"And pray, signore, had you a safe and pleasant journey from Rome?"

"Why, but indifferent," returned the boy-secretary; "in the first place, we were assailed by a tremendous thunderstorm, and were forced to take shelter in the caverns among the rocks, then twice the calash broke down, and the horses bolted, while all along the road we were subjected to a thousand petty annoyances. The tavern-keepers are harpies, the peasants all beggars, and our postillions little better than brigands."

"Brigands!" repeated the count, with a slight start; "what makes you say that?"

"They are such scowling, sulky villains." returned the youth; "that Guiseppe is the worst of the two —a very wasp."

"Have a care, *amico*," returned the count, significantly touching the silver hilt of a dagger in his belt; "such wasps bear stings, and if provoked, don't scruple to use them; this Guiseppe may be a disguised brigand."

"If he is, I care not; but hang such a knave." returned the youth, with a deep-toned laugh of disdain; "his insolence is only equalled by his incapacity. He knows as little about the management of a horse as I do of an elephant."

The count laughed,

"You English lads pique yourselves on your skill in horsemanship," he said; "but when you get to Naples, you will admit that what our vetturini lack in skill, they make up in force; like Jehu of old, they drive furiously."

Then he changed the subject, and reverting to the brigands, he asked whether Ralph Wildhawk had heard any fresh rumours of them while on the road.

"Surely monsignore has heard of the last exploit of the notorious brigand Marco Bravo?" asked the young Eglishman in surprise."

"The news has not yet reached Terracina," was the calm reply.

"Is it possible? Why, the country rings with it," answered Ralph. "It appears that there has been a desperate encounter between the banditti and the troops. Marco Bravo defeated the soldiers with great slaughter, and took prisoners their captain, two ensigns, and twenty or thirty of the men. Was ever heard the like?"

"*Diavolo!*" said the count; "he is a splendid scoundrel."

"True, he is no common man," replied Ralph Wildhawk; "I wonder what he is like?"

"An ugly little fellow. with red hair, a hunched back, a mouth like an ogre's and a distracting squint," returned the count with a low, chuckling laugh.

"Is it so?" rejoined Ralph, innocently; "I have heard a very different account of him. He has been described to me as tall, dark and handsome, with an eagle eye, and a commanding figure; indeed if I may say without offence, some such a person as your excellency."

The count bowed deeply.

"*Perdone,*" he laughed, "you do me too much honour."

"How I should like to see him," exclaimed Ralph, fervently.

"Would you really?" laughed the count. "Maybe your wish may be gratified before you have time to repent it, but you had better keep out of his way if you can."

"A brigand's must be a strange, wild life," murmured Ralph, reflectively; "replete with romantic adventure, to perch like an eagle in his eyrie among the snow-capped summits of the mountains, to swoop down upon the valleys as a bird of prey swoops on his quarry, to win all by the strong hand and the subtle brain. There's a weird charm about such a life, that appeals to the imagination."

"*Cospetto!* My young enthusiast, we shall have you running off to the mountains," laughed the count; but in sober truth, would you not like to lead a powerful banditti?"

"God forbid!" was the fervent reply. "All brigands are villains and deserve death; romance is one thing, reality another. Rather than adopt a career of crime, pillage, and bloodshed, I would be cut into a thousand pieces."

"But that's an ugly alternative, my good young friend," returned the strange count, looking keenly at the lad; "let us pray that your resolution may never be put to the test."

"Amen, with all my heart," said Ralph.

Joe Moody now came out.

"Master Ralph," he said, in a grumbling tone, "the supper is waiting; Sir Raymond is calling for you; but perhaps you prefer supping off the picturesque, and inhaling the mountain air. If so, take your fill of it. For my part, since I came into this accursed country, I have acquired such an appetite that I could eat husks with the prodigal son. But Lor' knows what horrible stuff they have set before us now. They gave me some eels—I should like to see their skins—snakes, as sure as Newgate."

"Well," returned Ralph; "I am as ravenous as any famished wolf in the Apennines; let us go in."

Then turning to the count, he added—

"Monsignore, you will not refuse me the pleasure of introducing you to my fellow travellers."

"Nothing would afford me greater satisfaction," replied the count, with another stately bow; "I have for some time desired to make the acquaintance of Sir Raymond."

So saying, they entered the passage at the end of which was the dining-room, Tomaso and Lisetta lighting the way before them with wax-candles.

Joe Moody stood on the doorstep, gazing after them, his brow lowering with sullen distrust.

Presently he was startled by hearing some one sigh deeply.

"Oh, 'evins!" lisped a female voice.

Joe Moody turned sharp round.

Beside him stood Matilda Sparkes, her eyes upturned, her hands clasped.

"Hilloa! is it you, 'Tilda?" he asked gruffly; "troubled with the nerves again. Pray don't let's have any 'sterics, there's a good wench, leastways, not till after dinner. Take a noggin of gin, that'll revive ye."

"What a 'ansome man," sighed Matilda.

Joe grinned complacently, and rubbed his chin.

"Well, so, so," he chuckled; "I wonder 'Tilda, that with your desarnment, you did not find that out long ago; you never mentioned it afore to me."

"The dark-orbed Italian; the mysterious being."

"The what, 'Tilda!" said Joe, with surprise.

Matilda clutched him by the wrist, and continued in a melodramatic whisper—

"Joseph Moody, lend me your ears."

"All right, if you won't pull 'em."

"Have you not observed a shade of profound melancholy upon his noble countenance? Depend upon it, that man fosters a secret scorpion in his adamantine 'art."

Poor Joe was thunderstruck.

"Pooh! what are you driving at, who are you talking about?"

"Joseph Moody, you have no soul."

"Well, that's a heathen remark, anyhow," grumbled Joe; do you want to put me on a level with the dumb beastes?"

"On a level with the earthy clods, the stocks and stones that have no sentiment, Joseph Moody; did you not observe that remarkable man?"

"Who—what—when—where?"

"The dark-eyed Italian stranger that was conversing with Master Ralph?"

"Yes, dash him! I observed him," growled Joe; "and I mean to keep my eye on him, I promise you."

"I strolled out here for a moment, to drink a balmy breath from yonder orange groves, and revel in this lovely moonlight, and to catch ——"

"A confounded cold in your nose."

"When my gaze encountered the gloomy glance of this inscrutable man," Matilda lisped, "and at once I felt convinced, that like the hero of the Castle Spectre, he has a weight at his heart, and a searing brand on his brain."

"Why didn't you lend him your smelling-bottle?"

"I couldn't help feeling for him; depend upon it, Joe, he is wronged, he has committed some delightful crime; perhaps has killed some rival in a duel."

"Suppose now," returned Joe, "he should turn out to be a disguised brigand, and carry you off to the mountains?"

"How delicious, how romantic!"

"Fudge! I'd soon be after him," growled Joe, and hurried into the house.

CHAPTER III.

THE HOST AND HIS GUESTS.

SUPPER over, the party of English travellers strolled forth into the lovely garden behind the inn, a very Paradise with its wealth of flowers.

Above them stood the town of Terracina, situated on a steep elevation, crowned by an ancient monastery, and higher still, upon the very summit of the magnificent rock which overhangs the town, the ruins of the Gothic palace of Theodoric.

Beyond the inn was a fine detached mass of rock rising above the road.

It was formerly inhabited by a hermit whose cell could be descried about half way up its side.

The roads at the base of this rock are washed by the waves of the Mediterranean.

Ralph Wildhawk had introduced the Count Di Ancona to Sir Raymond and the rest of the party.

Sir Raymond greeted him with stately politeness, and invited him to supper.

The count accepted the invitation with easy self-composure.

Violet Melville was charmed by his amusing talk, and laughed and blushed at his well-told anecdotes, or listened, with intense interest, to his appropriate quotations from the Italian poets.

Suddenly Sir Raymond remarked with some abruptness—

"I remember the Count Di Ancona. I met him on my last visit to Naples about five years ago; it was during the minority of King Ferdinand, when the kingdom was governed by a regency, presided over by the Prime Minister Tanucci. The count I knew was an old man, and must have been your father."

"It was so, signore." replied the Italian. "My father has been dead about three years. The news of his death came to me whilst I was staying in Paris."

Then dexterously changing the subject, he proposed that they should take a stroll into the garden and enjoy the delicious coolness of the evening.

Leaning against the porch was a guitar, which the count took up and carelessly ran his fingers over the strings.

Violet asked the fascinating stranger for a song.

The count complied without hesitation, and in a fine voice he sang a simple but pathetic love ditty, which elicited the most rapturous applause.

Young Edmund Mortimer alone of the party did not appear to entertain a very favourable opinion of the stranger.

He held himself aloof. and his countenance betrayed his jealous anger.

The song was scarcely ended when was heard the cracking of whips, the galloping of horses, the barking of dogs, and a hubbub of voices.

"What means all this commotion?" asked Sir Raymond.

Then, turning to Pepe. the waiter, he bade him go and see what was the matter.

As Pepe passed the count on his way to execute the order, he made a peculiar sign by twitching back his thumb.

The count gave a slight nod.

Quick and trivial as was this exchange of signals, it did not escape the observant eyes of Edmund Mortimer.

"That Pepe appears to be a sharp fellow, count," he remarked; " he understands your slightest gesture."

The count laughed.

"Oh, yes," he said. carelessly; "I know how to manage these rascals."

A man now came rushing out from the inn. his manner betraying the wildest excitement.

It was not Pepe, however, but Nicolo, the innkeeper.

"Holy Virgin!" he exclaimed; "a vetturino has just arrived with accounts of fresh exploits of that dare-devil Marco Bravo."

"I have no patience to listen to such stories," returned the English baronet. "Why is such a villain allowed to ravage the country with impunity? Are the authorities asleep, or do they connive at his rascalities?"

"Who knows?" rejoined the count, shrugging his shoulders. "But I have heard that even in England the roads and waste lands are infested by highwaymen, who rob belated travellers, and sometimes go so far as to stop the mail-coaches."

"Humph!" muttered the Englishman, not liking to have the tables turned thus upon himself.

"But the brigands, good Nicolo?" put in Ralph Wildhawk. "What have they done now?"

"What have they done, signore?" reiterated the host. "They have waylaid and attacked a party of travellers near Itri, consisting of a French marquis, his wife and two daughters, and a polish Jew, a travelling diamond merchant, and besides taking an enormous booty in money, watches, jewellery, and dress, it is expected they will exact an extravagant ransom."

The count's eyes sparkled, and he drew a deep breath.

"San Francesco!" he exclaimed. "what a haul, and at one cast of the net! But say, Nicolo, did Marco Bravo command the robbers?"

"Monsignore, no," replied the innkeeper; "I am given to understand that the chief was absent on some other expedition; the band, on this occasion, were led by one of his lieutenants, named Stromba."

The count smiled and gave a chuckling laugh.

"What, Maffeo?" said he.

The innkeeper stared in surprise that one who professed himself a stranger in these parts should know the brigand's full name.

"Yes, Maffeo Stromba," he said rather brusquely.

"I have heard of the fellow," said the count. "His brother Filippo was taken on the Roman frontier and sentenced to the galleys for life. And pray, did the brigands get off safely with their plunder and prisoners to the mountains?

"Yes, tell us that," continued the count.

"Signore, there is more behind," was Nicolo's reply.

"A party of the brigands lingered on the road to cover the retreat of their companions. This party was attacked by a troop of dragoons sent in pursuit of the brigands; four of their number were killed and two taken prisoners—the one a mere youth, the other an old man, who they say is mortally wounded. The worst of it is they are bringing them here."

The count turned slightly pale.

"Hark ye, my worthy Nicolo," he said. slipping some gold pieces into the landlord's hand. "One of the brigands, you say, is wounded to death?"

"Yes, excellency."

"It is a pity that the poor wretch should perish without receiving absolution. Send for a priest."

"A priest!"

"Yes. Send at once."

"But signor——"

"A priest!" returned the count, his mellow accents deepening into a perfect growl. "Inhuman as you are, would you have this wretched sinner—and we are all sinners, Nicolo—perish unshrived?"

"Heaven forbid!" returned the innkeeper. "To hang a man is one thing, to consign him to purgatory is another. Your excellency is right; we must have a priest."

"The monastery is within half an hour. Send one of your servants for a friar to shrive the dying man."

"I will send Pepe."

"Not Pepe; we shall want him. Send Tomaso for the priest."

Pepe, the mysterious waiter, now brushed past the count.

"*La forza*," he said in an excited whisper. "The soldiers will soon be here."

"I know," returned the count in an undertone. "Keep quiet ; nothing can be done to-night.

"To-morrow then, with the band ?"

"Yes, to-morrow at sunset."

"The place, signor capitano ?"

"The Devil's Gorge," whispered the strange count ; "remember."

CHAPTER IV.

"VIVA MARCO BRAVO !"

NEAR and louder came the sounds of the approaching cavalcade, the clatter of hoofs, the jingling of arms and accoutrements, the occasional blast of a trumpet, and the deep roll of kettle-drums.

"The soldiers, the soldiers," was the general cry.

The whole party of English travellers, with the Italian count and the people belonging to the inn, turned out to witness the arrival of the soldiers with their brigand prisoners.

A stirring and picturesque spectacle met their view.

Although the moon had risen, a red streak still glimmered in the west.

Winding down the rugged mountain path, defiled a troop of well-mounted dragoons, in showy uniforms, to the number of about two hundred ; after them came a large body of carabineers on foot.

In the centre of their line four men carried a litter made of boughs, on which lay rigidly extended the form of the wounded robber.

Close behind walked the other prisoner, a tall, handsome youth.

His arms were pinioned but he walked between his guards, each of whom carried a loaded firelock on his shoulder, with firm, defiant step.

Upon reaching the inn, the captain called a halt.

He threw himself from the saddle, and advanced towards the party gathered at the door.

He was a smart, well-set, dashing young fellow, and wore the superb uniform of the papal dragoons.

Upon seeing him, Sir Godfrey's face lit up with a smile of recognition, and he held out his hand.

"Captain Lanfranco, you are very welcome," he said. "While we were at Rome, you promised me an escort, which in my folly and impatience I refused."

The captain heartily shook hands with the English nobleman, smiled and nodded familiarly at Edmund Mortimer and Ralph, and bowed with deep respect to Violet Melville.

"I told you, signore, that the roads and passes were infested by the accursed brigands," he said. "I must congratulate you upon having thus far escaped them, in which you have been more fortunate than other travellers by the same road as that you traversed."

"We have heard of their misfortune," said Violet, with a shudder. "It is very dreadful, I trust, Signor Lanfranco, that you will be able to let us have an escort as far as Naples."

"Signora, be assured I and my men will not leave you until you have reached a place of safety," returned the captain, "but first of all I must dispose of my prisoners for the night."

"Let your gallant fellows lack nothing that can be procured at the inn, or indeed the town itself," said Sir Godfrey. "It is needless to say that I will most cheerfully bear all expenses."

The captain was about to make some civil reply, when he was interupted by a loud scream.

Everyone turned in the direction from whence the cry proceeded.

They beheld Lisetta, the innkeeper's daughter, clinging about the neck of the young brigand.

"Giovanni !" she shrieked. "Oh, my poor Giovanni."

Nicolo came up wringing his hands, and looking as pale as a sheet.

"Jesu Maria !" he exclaimed. "Oh, signor captain, your prisoner is my wretched nephew, Giovanni."

"I am sorry to hear it," replied the officer, coldly, "but you must be aware, my good Nicolo, that the law is no respecter of persons. Your nephew is a brigand, and has outraged the laws of his country."

Then turning to one of the soldiers, he said, curtly—

"Sergeant, on your life look to your prisoners. They must be secured for the night. But in the morning I will send a detachment to convey them to the Castle of St. Angelo."

"And, signor captain, what will be their fate ?" asked Nicolo, in a quavering voice.

"Death," was the stern reply.

"Oh, signor captain, but my nephew is so young."

"Young in years, but old in iniquity," said the captain. "Stand aside, my good Nicolo. I do but discharge my duty. You must find me some place where I can secure the prisoners till the morning. But beware, no tricks. Your life, man, upon their safe keeping."

Nicolo groaned and buried his face in his hands.

"Remove that poor girl," said Captain Lanfranco, pointing to Lisetta, who still clasped the young brigand, while she leaned her head upon his breast and sobbed convulsively, the guilty, but not unfeeling youth trying to soothe her by murmured words of endearment.

With gentle force the soldiers unwound her white, shapely arms from the prisoner's neck, and drew her away.

Giovanni gazed after her, his fine, black Italian eyes brimming with tears, his swart but handsome features beaming with passionate affection, his lip twitching with suppressed anguish.

Poor Lisetta caught his agonised look, and uttering an hysteric cry, she sank back in the soldiers' arms and fainted.

With womanly, instinctive sympathy, Violet Melville sprang to the side of the unhappy girl, and placing her arm round her waist, with the assistance of one of the serving maids, supported her into the house.

"And now, good Nicolo," said the captain of dragoons, "show me where I am to confine the prisoners for the night."

"Every chamber in the inn is occupied," returned Nicolo, in a tearful voice, "but at the end of the garden is a shed where they can remain till the morning."

A soldier stepped up to the officer, and saluted.

"Captain," he said, Michael Conaro, the elder prisoner, is dying fast. He appears to be at the last gasp."

The Count Di Ancona, who stood near, gave a start, and with a sigh, muttered to himself—

"Michael Conaro, the oldest and wariest in the band. Ah, that's bad."

"Bring the litter this way," said the captain.

The four men bearing the wounded brigand came forward, and gently deposited their burden on the ground.

Meanwhile, guided by the innkeeper, and under guard of the sergeant and four of the carabineers, Giovanni was led through the house and across the gardens to a large, strongly-built shed.

With trembling fingers, Nicolo turned the key in a heavy padlock, and threw open the door.

A soldier, with a loaded carbine, was posted as sentry at the door, under instructions to shoot the prisoner if he made the least attempt to escape.

"Sergeant," said the young brigand, in an imploring tone, "you see it is all over with me, that I have not the slightest chance of escaping; for pity's sake release my hands; the cords are tied so tight that they eat into my flesh."

The sergeant took him roughly by the shouldder, and turned him round.

It was plain that the wretched lad had not exaggerated the state of affairs; his hands were quite black, and swollen to twice their natural size.

The sergeant drew his sword and cut the bonds.

Giovanni gave a moan, half pain, half ecstasy of relief.

Then he blew upon and chafed his swollen wrists, and stretched his benumbed arms.

"A thousand thanks, signore," he gasped, while his dark eyes melted with gratitude.

"Il povero!" murmured the innkeeper. "He must be hungry after his long and painful march. Have I your permission, gallant sergeant, to bring the poor lad something to eat and drink?"

The sergeant gave a gruff assent to this request.

Nicolo hurried into the inn, and presently returned with a loaf of bread, some cheese, and a dish of macaroni, to which he added a bunch of dried grapes, and a bottle of the excellent wine of Fondi.

The sergeant then turned out Nicolo and his servants, closed the door upon the prisoner, took possession of the key, fixed and locked the padlock.

"Attention," he exclaimed, addressing the sentry.

The man raised his hand to his cap.

"Let no one go in or out without a pass from the captain," said the sergeant. "Keep a strict watch over your prisoner."

While this was passing, the travellers and the soldiers had gathered round the dying brigand.

The priest knelt by his side, and holding the crucifix to his lips, exhorted him to repentance.

The Count Di Ancona pushed his way through the throng, and stationing himself beside the dying man, gazed down upon his bloodless face in gloominess and sorrow.

He was a fine old man, grey-haired and majestical, with a high, bald forehead, and features of classic faultlessness; though his brow and lips wore a certain aspect of sternness, there was little of that brutal ferocity in the expression of his countenance that one would expect to find in a man whose life's career had been one tissue of crime.

His arm was in a sling, and his brow was swathed with a bandage stained with the oozing blood.

His heavy lids unclosed, and feebly lifting himself upon his unwounded arm, he glared around him with bloodshot eyes.

"Ah, misericordia!" he gasped, huskily. "Acqua, water—water for love of the Blessed Virgin—one draught of water!"

Ralph Wildhawk, who stood near, ran into the inn, and was the first to bring the dying wretch what he craved so piteously.

Stooping down, he placed a cup of wine and water, cooled by mountain snow, to his scorching lips.

He tried to express his thanks, but the words would not come, but died away in a hollow gurgling of the throat.

"Repent, my son, while there is yet time," said the priest. "The mercy of Heaven is measureless; the tears of true penitence will wash away the foulest stains of guilt; by the interception of the holy saints you may yet be snatched like a brand from the burning."

"Ah, Padre Dominico, is it you?" the brigand said, faintly. "Pray for my soul; Marco Bravo has promised to pay a thousand ducats for masses; he never breaks his word."

"Think not of him, my son," replied the monk. "He is the child of Satan."

"He was my capo, my chief," replied the robber, sullenly. "Tell him that it was not my fault that the band suffered loss; it was an infame, a treason, and Giraldo Monti was the traitor; upon his head be it. Tell the chief; he will not forget, he will avenge me."

"He will," muttered the Count Di Ancona, placing his hand in the brigand's.

Conaro clutched his hand and glanced up into his face with a wild, scared expression.

Then, catching the meaning of the other's rapid look, the dying brigand glanced about him upon the assembled company.

"The signor was an old master of mine before I went to the mountains," he said, in a calm, thrilling voice. "Bend down your ear, signor, my breath fails; I have a message for my friends, ere I depart."

The count stooped over him, and they exchanged a whisper.

A bright smile flickered over the face of the dying brigand.

" *Viva* Marco Bravo !" he shouted, and tried to wave his hand, but fell back.

The old brigand was dead.

CHAPTER V.

THE COUNT AND THE PRIEST.

THE corpse of the brigand, covered by a cloak, was removed to one of the outhouses of the inn. A sentry was placed at the door.

As for young Giovanni, as soon as he had finished his supper, he threw himself down upon his pallet of straw, and pretended to sleep.

It was not, however, the peril of his position or the terror of impending death that kept the young robber from his repose, but Pepe had made him a signal which he well understood, and he lay watching in the hope that some attempt would be made for his rescue.

Yet there appeared but little chance of escape, for while the main body of the soldiers bivouacked by the sea-shore, the captain, with several of his subaltern officers and about twenty of his men, agreed to pass the night in the arbours of the garden,

Tired by their day's journey, the English travellers retired to rest, but not so the Count Di Ancona.

Remarking upon the beauty of the night, and saying that he had no inclination to sleep, he threw on his cloak, and taking his walking-stick, he proposed accompanying Fra Dominico as far as the gates of Terracina.

"The night is so fair," he said, " and there is a little matter upon which I should like to consult your reverence. The fact is, a relative of mine is desirous of entering your holy order. I should esteem it a personal favour if you would give me your advice in the case."

The monk did not appear to much relish this proposition.

"There will be time enough, my son, to consider this business in the morning," he replied. " I shall return at matins to visit the unhappy prisoner and try to bring him to a sense of his awful position ; I have an order from Captain Lanfranco which will procure me admission to him. I shall afterwards be entirely at your service."

"With pardon, reverend father," replied the count ; " by the first peep of dawn I must be on my road to Naples, whither I am called by urgent business that will brook no delay. Come, father, permit me to be your companion as far as the gates of Terracina."

Captain Lanfranco here interposed.

" If you are determined to venture forth at this untimely hour," he said, " let me advise your excellency to take some of my men with you as a body guard. You may be sure that the brigands are not far distant ; it is always their policy when one of their gang is taken to make a capture by way of reprisals, in the hopes of obtaining their comrade's release by an exchange of prisoners."

The count laughed, and by way of reply flung back his cloak, and disclosed his belt, which bristled with daggers and pistols.

" You see, captain, I am not unprepared for an encounter," said he ; " and I am one who cannot brook constraint. I am willing to accept any risk rather than be fettered in my movements."

The captain shrugged his shoulders, and turned away.

" Come, Padre Dominico," said the count ; " one nip of Rosalio and we will make a start."

Nothing loth, the good priest drank a deep bumper of the cordial, and then taking up his staff, declared his readiness to set out.

Behind them lay the town, most picturesquely built between the rocky wall and the sea.

Behind it towered, dim and vast, the snow-capped mountains.

Along the sea-shore the soldiers had lighted fires, around which they were gathered in picturesque groups, some laughing, and jesting, others gambling with cards, many stretched upon the ground in every attitude of repose.

The monk and his companion toiled up the rugged mountain path.

The honest Fra Dominico from time to time cast a furtive, uneasy glance at his companion, much wondering that he did not open up the business upon which he had seemed to be so intent.

The poor priest began to feel frightened and uncomfortable.

The count's manner was completely changed.

They had now entered a narrow, winding passage between two high and rocky banks, covered with thick shrubs and bushes.

Here the monk paused, and touched his companion's arm.

" My son, we are drawing near to the city gates," he said. " If you have anything to say to me, do not lose time, as I am anxious to get back to the monastery in order to request our reverend superior to perform a midnight mass for the soul of the dead brigand."

The count started from his reverie.

" I crave your pardon, father," he said. " I was lost in thought ; but now I am all attention."

" Good, my son," returned the priest ; " but first, let me ask you, who is this person who desires to renounce the world, its passions and temptations, and take upon himself the vows of poverty, chastity, and obedience to the austere rules of our strict order."

The count put on an air of mock gravity.

" To tell you the truth, holy father," he answered, with a deep sigh, " 'tis myself who am the penitent ; myself who, forsaking the world and its vanities, would don the cowl and cassock of a friar."

" Holy Saint Dominic !" returned the priest, holding up his hands in amazement ; " can it be possible ?"

" Not only is it possible," rejoined the count, " but such is my zeal and earnestness that I must at once assume the priestly vestments."

The monk shook his head.

" That cannot be, my son," he answered ; " you must first be accepted by our superior, then you will have to pass your novitiate, after that——"

" Good father, such procrastination suits not my impatience," said the count, laughing. " Now—to-night—this instant I must become a monk, and, therefore, I will make bold to borrow your robe, while you shall take my cloak in exchange."

With this, he made a snatch at the priest's garment, but the monk sprang back, and held up his staff.

"Monstrous," he exclaimed; "what do you mean? Count Di Ancona, are you beside yourself, or have you taken too much wine?"

"Come, father, do me this favour," returned the other; "lend me your robe until to-morrow. Nay, do not look alarmed; grant me my trivial request, and you shall never have cause to repent of the good-natured action."

But the priest looked horror-stricken.

"Profane scoffer, rather would I perish," he exclaimed. "If this is a jest, it is a most unseemly one. I pray you let us part here; the distant clocks are striking twelve. I am willing to pardon and forget the follies of this night. Benedicite, my son; I wish you good-night."

He turned, and waving his hand, walked off at as rapid pace as his age and corpulency would allow of.

The count strode after him.

Before they had got many yards further, the count stopped and cast a wary glance about him.

Then he gave a long, low, peculiar whistle.

At the signal, five men, dressed as peasants, with sheep-skin jackets, galligaskins, and steeple-crowned hats, sprang from behind the rocks.

They were all armed to the teeth.

Four of them surrounded the priest, and levelled their carbines at his head, while the fifth, his gun on his shoulder, stepped up to the count, and saluted him in military fashion.

Upon finding himself thus beset, Fra Dominico uttered a yell of dismay, and would have taken to his heels, but two of the men seized him by the collar, and the other two menaced him with their weapons.

"Hold him fast," said the count.

"Shall we bind him, signor capitano?" asked one of the ruffians, showing his white, dazzling teeth in a broad grin, while he produced a coil of rope from his capacious pocket.

"No need," replied the count; "use the reverend father with all gentleness."

"Release me, ye villains," blustered the priest, in mingled rage and alarm, "or I will have you excommunicated—banned by bell, book, and candle."

Then turning to the count, he added, fiercely—

"What is the meaning of this outrage? Who are you that dare to lay sacrilegious hands upon a priest of the holy church?"

"Reverend father," said the count, doffing his beaver, "I am Marco Bravo the brigand!"

The startled monk uttered a cry of consternation.

"Do I confront that villain?" he exclaimed, after a moment's pause, during which he had recovered his courage and presence of mind; "that robber and assassin, outlawed alike by God and man."

"Spare your breath, good father, for those who tremble at the curse of their fellow-sinners, which I do not," returned the brigand chief, sternly.

Then seeing that the priest's words were not without their effect upon his superstitious followers, for they relinquished their hold, and devoutly crossed themselves, he added mildly—

"Dismiss all fear, good father; I am incapable of injuring the defenceless and benevolent, and trust me, despite a rashly-spoken word, I deeply revere your sacred vocation, so much so," he went on, laughing, "that I intend to assume the cassock this very hour myself."

He made a sign to his men, who at once began disrobing the luckless friar, who seeing that resistance was useless, with a groan resigned himself to his fate.

While this was going on, Marco Bravo took off his cloak and handed it to one of the brigands.

He then divested himself of his coat, but retained his belt with its armoury of knives and pistols.

"Romano," he said to one of the brigands, who was engaged in stripping the monk, "search for a pass in the handwriting of the captain of dragoons; the good father has it concealed in his bosom."

The man handed him a slip of paper.

"Here it is, signor," said he.

"Good," said Marco Bravo. "Now assist me to put on this sheep's clothing."

The men obsequiously obeyed.

In a few moments the brigand had donned the priest's robe.

The cowl was pulled over his head so as to hide his features, the hempen girdle fastened round his waist, and the rosary and crucifix attached to it.

Upon seeing their chief so effectually disguised, the brigands burst into a merry laugh.

"Thou sayest well," cried Fra Dominico, grinding his teeth. "Thou art verily and indeed a wolf in sheep's clothing."

"Is it so?" laughed the robber; "then I shall make the better monk, for cowl and cassock, like charity, cover a multitude of sins. How do I look Generoso?"

The tall, handsome fellow to whom he addressed himself, and who appeared to occupy a higher grade than his companions, answered with a cheery laugh—

"But fold your hands across your breast thus, and bend your eyes upon the ground, and the disguise is complete. Diavolo! never before, captain, could I appreciate the saying that dress proclaims the man."

Then stooping upon his knee, he added, with mock humility—

"Your blessing, holy father."

Marco Bravo hit him a crack on the head with the rosary.

"No profanity, you dog," said he. "Respect my holy office."

The poor scandalised monk held up his hands, and groaned in spirit.

"The cup of my iniquities is full," he gasped out with a shudder.

Marco Bravo was about to make some scoffing retort, but warned by the sullen, disaffected looks of the three brigands, he checked the impulse.

"Come, we are wasting time," he said briskly. "Now comrades, attend to my orders."

The men nodded assentingly.

RALPH WILDHAWK. No. 2 "BOYS OF ENGLAND" EDITION. PRICE ONE PENNY. PUBLISHED AT 173, FLEET STREET, E.C.

"'HOLD HIM FAST,' SAID THE MYSTERIOUS COUNT."

" Conduct the father to the little cavern half a mile on the road to Fondi. You know the place?"

" Yes, captain."

" Keep him safe, and remain there till I join you. One of you must keep a sharp look-out and in case of an alarm, make your escape into the mountains."

Then, addressing himself to the priest, he added—

" I owe you a bag of ducats to be expended in masses for the repose of the soul of poor Michael Conaro."

The monk did not make any reply.

" Stay you behind, Generoso," said the chief to his lieutenant; " I shall require you."

The four brigands shouldered their muskets, and led away the priest, who had enveloped himself in the chief's mantle, and stalked between his janitors in sullen silence.

Generoso remained beside his chief in an attitude of respectful silence.

Marco Bravo kept silent till the brigands and their captive were out of sight; he then turned to his subordinate.

" Generoso," he said, a dark frown clouding his brow, " that last affair was managed very clumsily; Giovanni is a prisoner, and in Michael Conaro I have lost one of the best and bravest of my band."

" Pardon, signor," replied Generoso, " no blame attaches to me; the fault lies with the goat-herd, who betrayed us for the sake of the reward."

Marco Bravo's countenance expressed the subdued fierceness of a devil.

" His doom is sealed," was his bitterly-spoken reply. " I will make of him a terrible example to all who dare so much as dream of playing me false. But let that pass now; it is with me a principle never to abandon a comrade in distress; we must rescue young Giovanni."

" True, captain," answered Generoso; " but the task is a difficult one."

" I do not deny it," returned the brigand chief; " but I have ever found Giovanni brave and faithful. I will save him at any cost."

Then after a few moments' reflection, he looked up, and asked abruptly—

" How many men have you brought, Generoso?"

" Twenty, signor."

" Good; half that number will suffice," rejoined Marco Bravo. " Where are they concealed?"

" In the vaulted galleries of the ruined palace of Theodoric," said the robber.

" Very well," replied his chief. " Now listen to me, Generoso; the hut in which Giovanni is confined is situated at the end of Nicolo's garden; behind it is a deep ditch. Take five of the men, and post them there. In this disguise I shall obtain admission to the prisoner; keep close in the ditch, and when I give you the signal, assist me with as little noise as possible to remove some of the boards through which we may get the prisoner out."

" But the noise, signor," objected the man; " we should alarm the sentry."

" Tush! I will manage that," returned the brigand. " Do you be there to second my efforts, and all will go well."

" But you run a terrible risk, captain."

" I accept the peril," answered Marco Bravo. " No more words; post five of the men in the little wood that skirts the rock on which the city stands. Let them there await our coming."

" I will not fail, signor," replied Generoso; " and for to-morrow is it your intention to stop the party of English travellers on their road to Naples? The milordo, they say, is immensely rich."

" My brave Generoso, there is one thing I should like to do."

" And what is that, captain?"

" Listen, Generoso," answered the brigand chief; " there is in the train of the English nobleman, a youth who acts as his secretary; his atrocious name is Ralph Wildhawk. Bah! what a barbarous jargon these English call a language. Now the lad I speak of is a fine, high-spirited, and ingenuous youth, to whom I have taken a great liking. I should like much to carry him off; he is swarthy and dark-eyed —odd to say, much resembling La Catarina, our widowed chieftainess, and speaks our language fluently. He is snubbed by milordo's son and heir—a sorry cur—and I believe, with a little persuasion, he might be induced to join our band."

Generoso did not appear to approve of such a remarkable proposition, for he shook his head.

" Ah, signor, beware what you do," he answered; " these foreigners are never to be trusted; and above all an English boy. It will be an evil day when one of them is allowed to become one of us."

Marco Bravo turned a scowling look upon him.

" Silence," he said. " I am your chief, and know best what is for the interest of the band. Who shall dispute my will?"

Then he went on in a milder tone—

" Enough, Generoso, it is time we parted. You understand my orders?"

" Yes, captain, perfectly."

" Good, then, addio."

" Addio, signore."

Bowing with great reverence, he walked away and soon disappeared.

The brigand chief, Marco Bravo, lingered a moment, and then strode off in the direction of the roadside inn.

CHAPTER VI.
THE ESCAPE.

MEANWHILE, Giovanni lay upon his straw pallet, intently listening to every sound.

He had seen and recognised Marco Bravo, and more than that, Pepe had made him a familiar sign by which he was made aware that an attempt would be made for his deliverance.

He tried in vain to sleep.

But now he felt it impossible to keep his eyes shut.

His heart ached with remorse, his brain was afire with a thousand burning recollections of guilt and misery that almost drove him to despair.

At last, unable to control himself, he sprang up and paced up and down the narrow confines of his prison house.

He tried to encourage himself by putting on an air of bravado, and whistling a robber song.

It was useless.

"What a miserable wretch am I?" he murmured, wildly wringing his hands. "I thought when I first ran away to the mountains and joined the banditti, that I should soon make a fortune, and be able to take my dear Lisetta to some place of refuge far away."

"Lisetta!"

The name touched a tender chord in his heart, and his eyes overflowed with tears.

The clocks of the city began to strike.

He counted each stroke, till the last boom died away in hollow echoes, reverberated from the enclosing mountains.

"Twelve," muttered the young brigand.

The clatter of arms was heard without, and the gruff voice of the sergeant challenging the sentinel.

"They are changing guard," said Giovanni to himself. "I wish it were all over. To be hunted down like a wolf, to die with my fangs in the throats of the bloodhounds, that were a reasonable death, not unexpected. but this horrible confinement. Oh, it drives me mad."

The time wore on.

Tramp, tramp, tramp. The monotonous and untiring footfall of the sentinel seemed to fall on the captive's heart like the toll of the death-bell.

A footstep was heard approaching, and then a whispered conversation was heard without.

Hark!

It is the voice of Marco Bravo, the brigand chief, he hears—then Pepe's.

Giovanni's heart fluttered with the hope of escaping from a brigand's death.

"Courage, Giovanni," he cried, placing his hand on his heart; "be brave, man. Marco Bravo is near, and I shall yet escape."

The next moment he was startled by hearing the deep voice of the sentry cry—

"Stand on your life! You cannot pass here."

"What, old comrade, have you forgotten me?" asked the unseen person.

"It is Pepe," said Giovanni, recognising the voice. "He is talking to the sentry, and now they are laughing together. Good, here's a crevice through which I can see them. Brave Pepe! The sentry is drinking."

"Another glass, old comrade," said Pepe's voice. "The morning breeze from the mountains is biting cold, a dram will do you good."

"My head is weak, Pepe," answered the soldier. "A very little takes effect on me, especially since I got that deep cut on the sconce in a battle with the brigands of the Abruzzi."

"This I remember, comrade, that when I was in the army, you could drink deeper than any of us," laughed Pepe. "If the Rosolio is too strong for you, take a pull at this bottle of Fondi; that cannot hurt you."

"Well, well, comrade, just one glass. Your health."

"And yours, Jose mio; here's to pleasant memories of old times."

"Ah, Pepe, we have had many a jolly carouse together," laughed the soldier. "You could sing the best song and tell the merriest story of any man in our regiment; we were deucedly sorry when you gave us the slip."

"But you won't betray an old comrade?"

"Basta! what do you take me for?" replied the soldier, gruffly; "only I must say, Pepe, that I should have thought a smart, dashing fellow like yourself would have chosen some more manly occupation than that of drudge at a common wayside albergo."

"Oh, for that I am well enough," returned Pepe, carelessly.

"But come now, old comrade, I have a slight favour to ask you, and one that you must not deny me."

"Humph, I don't like the beginning," grumbled the soldier; "it can't be money you want."

"Bah! money galore," chuckled Pepe, taking out a canvas bag, and chinking it temptingly in the other's ear.

'I've money to spare, and money to spend,
And money at need to lend to a friend.'

"And that's a rhyme for you. Here, old comrade, don't be afraid to speak; if you want a handful of ducats, you have only to say."

"Body of Bacchus, you are a trump, Pepe," replied the soldier, delighted; "and if you will lend me a few carlini, I shall be grateful."

"Well, here are ten golden pezze, will that do?"

"Per Bacco! you are indeed a right good comrade," replied the simple fellow.

"Don't mention it," returned Pepe, "I can get plenty more. And now about the favour I have to ask."

"Well, what is it?"

"I want you to let me have a peep at the prisoner. I have a message for him from his uncle, Nicolo. I won't stay a moment."

"Maldito!" growled the soldier, "is this your friendship? You want to tempt me to a breach of duty, knowing right well that if I listened to you, I should be tried at the drumhead, and be shot within the hour. Here, take back your money and make yourself scarce, or by my father's head, I will drag you before the captain, and denounce you as a deserter and a spy of the brigands."

"Don't be a fool, comrade, don't be a fool," returned Pepe, trying to appear calm. "I am sure you are not the man to serve an old comrade such a scurvy trick. What is the lad to me? Don't I tell you that I am but doing my master's bidding? The old man is well-nigh distracted with grief at his nephew's position."

"Come, now, Pepe, is this the truth?"

"The truth! Che demonio, do you suppose that I am going to be made the cat's-paw to drag the chestnuts out of the fire for another's benefit? Not I."

"Stay a moment, Pepe," cried the soldier, beckoning him to come back. "What was this message?"

Pepe returned with feigned reluctance.

"Oh, it was harmless enough," he said. "I was only to ask the boy if anything could be done for his comfort, to promise him on the part of his uncle that no money should be spared to procure the best advocate in Naples to conduct his defence at the trial."

The good-natured soldier evidently began to relent.

"Now, look you here, Pepe, yonder comes the good priest, Fra Dominico; he, I know, has a pass to see the prisoner. You shall go in with him, but if you stay longer than three minutes, or attempt to play any tricks on me, by the Holy Virgin, I will put a bullet through your body."

"Never fear, I shall only be too glad to get the business over," replied Pepe; "you may as well accompany me and witness the interview."

"I warrant you I mean to do so," returned the soldier.

At this juncture, the tall, slim figure of a monk came gliding towards them.

The soldier started.

"How is this? That is not Dominico," he muttered.

The priest now came up, and gravely bowed his head.

"Good morning, my son," he said, in a deep, sepulchral voice. "Where is the prisoner? I have a written order of admittance."

"Very good, father," returned the soldier, rather doubtfully; "but I thought it was Fra Dominico that I was to pass."

"Fra Dominico is indisposed," returned the monk. "I have been sent as his substitute."

"Well," said the soldier, "let me look at the order."

The monk handed him a slip of paper.

"That is right," said the sentry, "I know that cross; it is the captain's mark, but as to the writing, I am no scholar. Pepe, you can read, here, tell me what it says."

Pepe took the slip and read as follows—

"To the sentry in charge of the prisoner, Giovanni Pizano.

"Admit the priest to your prisoner. He may remain with him for half-an-hour, but no longer.

"(Signed) JULES LANFRANCO,
"Officer in command."

CHAPTER VII.

THE ESCAPE.

"GOOD," said the soldier, "this will do. One priest will serve as well as another."

As he finished speaking, he put the key in the padlock.

"Pepe," said the monk, in a low voice. "Where's your stiletto?"

"I have it here," returned Pepe, touching the haft of a long knife stuck in his girdle.

"Be ready and strike deep."

The soldier threw open the door.

"Come, Pepe," he said, "as you want to speak to the prisoner, you must be quick about it, for the time is short."

The disguised monk, Marco Bravo, made a sign to Pepe.

Pepe turned white, but nodded in acquiescence.

The soldier entered the hut, and took up the lamp from the table.

The light of the lamp filled the place, and fell upon Giovanni, who had curled himself upon his pallet of straw, and pretended to be asleep.

Giovanni roused himself, and sat up rubbing his eyes, and yawning heavily.

"Get up, lad," said the soldier, "here is a good priest, who comes to hear your confession, and to give you absolution, and Pepe too is here to bring you a message from your uncle."

The monk took the lamp from the soldier's hand, and replaced it on the table.

"Rise, my son," he said, "I may not remain long with you; let us not waste time."

Then he whispered to Pepe—

"Now's the time; strike home."

Pepe drew his stiletto, and crept behind the soldier. A quick flash, and his arm descended.

The brigand had struck the knife to the haft, between the shoulders of the sentry, who dropping his musket, staggered a few steps, and fell to the ground.

"Jesu Maria! I am stabbed," he groaned. "Ah, cursed treachery."

"Presto! quick, Pepe," cried the brigand chief. "Press your hand over his mouth, put an end to him at once."

Again Pepe's knife descended on the poor soldier.

"He's gone, captain," was the reply.

"Stiff and stark," replied the brigand chief, with perfect coolness. "Neatly done, Pepe. But, faugh! How he bleeds. The place reeks like a shambles. Luckily his cloak is red, and the stains will be less visible."

As he spoke, he stooped over the body of the murdered man, and loosened his mantle.

"Here, put it on, Pepe," said he. "Take his shako, and his musket, and mount guard at the door until I call you."

Pepe, with a pale face, threw the cloak over his shoulder, put the hat on his head, and shouldering the musket, stepped out of the hut, and paced slowly up and down before the door.

Marco Bravo then made a sign to Giovanni for him to keep perfectly quiet.

The youth stood transfixed, gazing upon his chief with awe.

Marco Bravo tapped at the wall.

"Companions," whispered a voice outside.

"Companions" has ever been a recognised password among the brigands, and is so to this day.

"Loosen and remove these boards," said Marco Bravo. "Is all safe?"

"Yes, signore."

"Quick, then."

A crashing noise was heard as the robbers pulled out the rotten boards, causing the rusty nails to start.

"Zitto, quiet," whispered the chief, savagely; "are you mad? Less noise."

The men murmured a promise of obedience, and removed two of the boards with as little disturbance as possible.

"Softly, softly," entreated Marco Bravo. "One more, and it is done."

Another board was ripped away, and a gap appeared, through which glared the fierce countenance of Generoso.

"Now," said the chief to Giovanni, "creep through."

The youth threw himself upon his hands and knees, and forced his way through the aperture.

The brigands gripped him with a firm grasp, and helped him to descend into the dry ditch.

Marco Bravo then stepped to the door.

"Come, Pepè," he said. "You must escape with us to the mountains. Take care. I am going to put out the light."

But the warning came too late.

The noise made by Generoso and the rest of the brigands in removing the planks from the wall of the hut, had attracted the attention of some of the soldiers who were in the garden.

Several of them pointed towards the hut, and shouted to the sentry to look to his prisoner, while others, seizing their arms, came rushing towards him.

Thoroughly alarmed by this movement, and excited by the stern, commanding voice of his chief, Pepe darted into the hut, and hastily clapped to the door behind him.

This he did in the full expectation of a shower of bullets being sent after him.

At the moment of the entry of Pepe, the brigand chief extinguished the light.

In the dark Pepe stumbled over the body of the poor soldier, whom he had so treacherously murdered.

The gun slipped from the brigand's grasp, and striking against the table, went off with a loud report.

"Idiot!" growled Marco Bravo, "what have you done? You have ruined all. Quick, man, for your life."

While he was yet speaking, a shout of consternation arose from the soldiers.

Bang, bang!

A volley of musketry cracked on the still night air, the bullets whizzing through the door and walls of the hut.

One shot passed so near to Pepe's head, that it brushed his cheek, causing the blood to flow.

Pepe, however, contrived to gain the breach in the wall, and escaped into the ditch beyond, and joining the other brigands in their flight, rushed off in the direction of the mountains.

Meantime, the soldiers, several of whom carried lanterns, had pushed open the door of the hut.

The sergeant, his drawn sword in one hand, and a horse-pistol in the other, was the first to enter.

Upon seeing the body of the unfortunate sentry lying weltering in his blood, the sergeant sprang backwards.

"*Gran Dio!*" he exclaimed. "Treachery and murder. The sentry is killed."

"Yes, sergeant," rejoined one of the men, holding aloft the lantern, "and the prisoner has escaped."

A rapid glance round the hut sufficed to show them how the brigand had effected his escape.

The table lay overturned, while at the back of the hut several planks had been ripped away, making an aperture sufficiently wide for a man to pass through.

"It is plain that this is a case of confede-racy," said the sergeant. "He must have been assisted from someone outside. Has anyone entered the hut to-night?"

"Only a priest, sergeant," replied the dragoon. "He had a pass signed by Captain Lanfranco."

The sergeant bade a man run and tell the captain what had happened.

Then turning to the others, he added—

"Quick, my men, let us at once go in pursuit of the brigands. We may yet overtake the scoundrels, and avenge our poor dead comrade."

The men gave a growl of fierce assent, and cocked their muskets ready for action.

The sergeant dashed through the opening in the wall, the rest following as fast as they could.

Led on by the sergeant, the soldiers entered the narrow passage between high banks, that we have lately described as having been traversed by the disguised Count Di Ancona, and Fra Dominico.

They hurried up this slope at the top of their speed, for they had discovered footmarks and occasional spots of blood, and knew that the robbers must have taken that direction.

Behind them they heard the galloping of horses' feet, the clanking of arms, and the buzz of voices.

"Forward, my brave fellows," cried the sergeant, waving his sword. "If we can overtake them before they reach the bridge that spans the mountain torrent, we shall capture or kill some of them at least; don't let us allow the captain to snatch from us the laurels within our grasp. If we recapture the prisoner, we shall be rewarded."

The men responded with a shout of applause.

"Hurrah!" they cried. "Death to the brigands!"

They hurried on.

"Halt," shouted the sergeant. "Look yonder, there, among the olive trees, I see dark figures gliding swiftly; they are making for the bridge."

The men looked eagerly in the direction in which he was pointing.

The figures of several men were seen rushing along, but, as though catching sight of the soldiers in pursuit, they turned and plunged deeper into the grove.

"Steady, men. Present arms—fire!" shouted the sergeant, setting the example by discharging his pistol at the grove.

The men levelled their muskets and blazed away at random.

The brigands responded to their volley with a derisive cheer, and fired a volley in return; several of the soldiers were wounded, but only slightly.

The defiant attitude of the brigands, however, only served to exasperate their pursuers more.

"On to the bridge," shouted the sergeant. "Avenge our dead comrade!"

The men hurried on, cursing the robbers, and breathing vows of the direst vengeance against them.

As they ran, they reloaded their muskets.

They had not proceeded far, before they were

"PEPE DREW HIS STILETTO, AND CREPT BEHIND THE SOLDIER."

overtaken by Captain Lanfranco and his troop of cavalry.

Beside the captain, and mounted on a fiery black horse, rode young Ralph Wildhawk.

"The cursed assassins, where are they, sergeant?" shouted the captain, who fairly trembled with rage and vexation.

"Yonder, captain," replied the sergeant, pointing with his sword. "They are skulking through the olive grove."

"Ten thousand curses," growled the captain, through his clenched teeth. "If they gain the bridge that crosses the torrent, we shall lose them."

He had scarcely finished speaking when two sharp cracks, which sounded like pistol shots, were heard from a little distance.

"What does this mean?" said the captain, in bewilderment. "Those shots are not fired in our direction and can't be meant for us."

"Perhaps, captain, some of your troop have taken another road, and so intercepted the villains," suggested Ralph Wildhawk.

"It cannot be so," returned the officer. "I don't know what to make of it, unless it be some trick to throw us off the scent, but that we will soon discover. Forward, men."

They spurred their horses, the mounted dragoons soon outstripping the men afoot, though the latter raced after them as fast as they could.

They turned the angle of a rock, and, to their immense astonishment, beheld a man standing in the middle of the road.

His hat was off, and his hair streamed on the morning breeze.

His back was towards them, and he appeared so intent upon some mysterious object, that he showed no signs of being aware of their approach.

As they drew near, they saw him raise his arm, and deliberately fire down the road, in the opposite direction to that from which they were advancing.

"It is one of the brigands," shouted the captain. "Fire upon him."

But Ralph Wildhawk reined round his horse in front of them.

"Hold, gentlemen, for Heaven's sake, don't fire," he shouted. "That man is no brigand, but the gallant Count Di Ancona."

CHAPTER VIII.

A CHALLENGE.

RALPH WILDHAWK was right; it was, indeed, no other than the Count Di Ancona.

He had now turned round, and picking up his hat, he walked to meet them, with his habitually easy and graceful stride.

"The count," exclaimed Lanfranco. "Is it possible?"

"Yes, it is the count, who, thanks to the presence of mind of this kind young Englishman, is able to answer for himself," returned the other, laughing gaily. "*Diavolo!* he has extricated me from a confoundedly awkward predicament, for I was fixed between two fires."

"But in the name of wonder," asked the astonished captain of dragoons, "at whom or what were you firing?"

"At the brigands, of course."

"The brigands," ejaculated the captain, and the young Englishman in the same breath. "Have they passed this way?"

"Yes, and what is more, captain, your prisoner has escaped, for I saw him amongst them. I recognised the lad at once."

"I know it; he has escaped by the connivance of the people at the inn and the help of some of the members of his band," replied the captain.

"Most likely," answered the count, with provoking indifference. "For I saw that rascal servant of old Nicolo's—what was his name?"

"Pepe," half shrieked the excited dragoon. "It is quite true, he has left the inn; no doubt he was a brigand spy."

"Count, did you notice whether there was a priest with them?" asked Ralph Wildhawk.

"A priest," said the other, after a moment of reflection. "Yes, now I recollect there was a sort of monk with them, but I don't believe he was any more a priest than I am myself."

"What was he like?"

"Oh, a slim, agile fellow," replied the count. "He certainly wore a monk's robe loosely thrown about him, but beneath it I observed that he had a belt full of pistols and daggers. He seemed to take command among the rest, for he shouted his orders in tones of authority."

"It must have been the brigand chief, Marco Bravo himself," exclaimed Lanfranco.

The count laughed heartily.

"I should not wonder at all if such should be the case," he answered. "For a more dashing-looking fellow I think I never beheld in my life."

"But you, count, what brought you here?" asked young Ralph.

"Oh, my brave boy," replied the count, shrugging his shoulders; "my legs, I suppose. Have you forgotten that I accompanied the worthy Fra Dominico as far as Terracina gates, feeling inclined for a moonlight stroll?"

"True, and I warned you not to go," replied the captain.

"You did, signore," answered the count, "and I heartily wish I had taken your advice. Look, here's some proof of what I say."

He held up his hat, in the crown of which there was a hole through which a bullet had passed.

"What, then, the scoundrels fired upon you?" said Ralph Wildhawk.

"*Sicuro.* As I was returning, the whole party came rushing past, along the top of the rocks; when they saw me, they shouted to me to stop; of course I took no heed of their challenge, so they fired. See, there's blood on my cloak."

"Good Heaven, are you wounded?" cried Ralph Wildhawk.

"It is a mere scratch," returned the count. "But it irritated me and I fired after the knaves, and I hope I hit one or two of them."

Then turning to the captain, he added in a sarcastic tone—

"Does it not strike you, signore, that we are losing valuable time in explanations that might well be deferred till a more fitting opportunity?"

"*Maldito*, yes," growled Lanfranco, with a start, causing his charger to rear and plunge. "The brigands, which way did they go?"

"They clambered these rocks like mountain-goats," returned the count, "and made straight for the ruined palace of Theodoric up yonder."

The captain muttered an oath.

"We must dismount," he growled, "and follow them on foot ; our horses will be useless."

He threw himself from the saddle.

His men did the same.

"I must not allow you to run into needless danger, signore," said the captain, addressing himself to Ralph Wildhawk. "I pray you stay here with the men I must leave in charge of the horses, until our return."

But Ralph Wildhawk sprang from his horse.

"Do not think it, captain," he said, eagerly ; "this is a fine adventure, and I mean to see it out, even at the risk of my life."

The count laughed and clapped him heartily on the shoulder.

"Bravissimo," he said, "spoken like a lad of mettle. I am glad to see you show such spirit."

"We Boys of England are not deficient in pluck," said Ralph. "But what are your intentions ? Do you propose to return to the inn or to accompany us?"

"To go with you," answered the count. "Besides, I owe that rascal Marco Bravo a grudge for his insolence and audacity, and nothing would give me greater pleasure than to put a bullet through his scheming brain."

"Away, then !" cried the captain. "Your peril be upon your own heads."

"Follow me," returned the count, briskly ; "I will lead the way."

As he spoke, with an activity that excited great admiration in the beholders, he sprang up the rocks, and made towards the grim old ruin. Soon they found themselves on the verge of a tremendous precipice.

Ralph Wildhawk gazed around him with awe and wonder upon a scene more savage and desolate than he had ever before witnessed.

Rocks upon rocks.

A chaos of huge, black, threatening forms lay scattered or piled around.

Just below them the ground broke off into a precipice.

Ralph Wildhawk was surprised to see an immense black vulture perched on the summit of a neighbouring rock, his bare, grey neck contrasting strangely with his jetty body.

To the eyes of Ralph Wildhawk he seemed to stand the height of a man, but this must have been illusive, yet he certainly was far superior in size to all of his species the young Englishman had seen elsewhere.

As he was not one hundred yards from them, Ralph Wildhawk drew his pistol, and crept nearer to secure his aim.

The count, however, stepped up to him, and caught him by the arm.

"Do not fire," he said. "In the first place the report would give the brigands intimation of our whereabouts, and in the second, it is a pity to waste powder and shot which you may presently want for better game."

"You are right, eccelenza," returned Ralph Wildhawk. "Carried away by a thoughtless impulse, I did not consider that."

So saying, he at once replaced the pistol in his belt.

Meanwhile. the huge bird opened his wings, and wheeled down majestically into the valley, uninjured.

Ralph now uttered a sudden cry of alarm, and pointed to a dark object lying among the heath, close to the margin of the precipice.

"Look yonder, signore," exclaimed Ralph ; "what is that ? It looks to me like the prostrate body of a man."

"No doubt one of the brigands," replied the count. "Perhaps killed in the last skirmish with the soldiers. That may account for the presence of the foul bird you wanted to shoot just now."

Captain Lanfranco and his men now came up.

They found a brigand lying upon his back, his face ghastly pale, and the blood streaming from a wound in his left side.

His eyes were closed.

He was quite unconscious, and evidently dying from loss of blood.

The rough soldiers shook him, and with brutal imprecations questioned as to what had become of his comrades.

For an instant the dying man unclosed his glazing eyes, and stared at them with a wild, vacant stare, at the same time muttering some articulate sound.

Then he made a feeble attempt to raise his hand to his brow, as though to make the sign of the cross, but his arm sank limp and powerless by his side. Then his jaw fell.

The death rattle convulsed his throat.

His head dropped backwards, and he died.

"There's one rascal the less," said the count, looking grimly down upon the pallid face of the dead brigand. "I would give something to know that it was a bullet from my pistol that had settled his account."

"You seem much embittered against these bandits," said Ralph, adding with a sigh— "Poor devil ; he may have had some soft spot in his nature. Perhaps he has left parents, a wife or sweetheart to mourn for him."

"Aye, and comrades to avenge him," muttered the deep voice of the count.

"That is the worst part of the case," rejoined Ralph. "One deed of bloodshed leads to another. You Italians carry a vendetta through generations. I must own I think you too revengeful."

Captain Lanfranco now interposed, urging them to hasten on.

They recommenced their toilsome and perilous march, having covered the body of the brigand with a cloak, and leaving it for after removal.

The wind now freshening to sudden blasts, seemed to howl defiance, and the clouds rising from the valleys, threatened to overwhelm them.

Ralph was perched on the verge of a tremendous precipice, sinking many hundred feet beneath him.

On approaching the brink, he was pulled back by the count.

" Do not venture so near," said the Italian. "I must warn you that gusts of wind often sweep these heights with such fury, as to carry one over in an instant."

They then drew near a ravine, down which dashed a waterfall in foamy thunders.

Built on a ledge of the precipice was a sort of platform of rough-hewn logs, and on the opposite side of the gulf appeared a similarly constructed landing stage, but the wooden bridge which should have connected them was gone.

Upon seeing this, Captain Lanfranco threw himself into a terrible passion.

All the furies seemed to seize him.

"This is just what I expected," he said, with an oath. "The villains have cut away the bridge, and it is impossible to follow them any further."

Then, turning upon the count, he said—

"This is your fault. Why did you bring us by this route? Had we pushed on to Itri, we might have stolen a march upon them."

"My fault?" was the placid reply. "Signore, you must recall that remark."

"I will not recall, and maintain it is the truth," retorted the other, hotly. "Why did you delay us when we first encountered you?"

"I delay you!"

"Yes, with your balderdash and braggadocio, your wire-spun stories about your own heroic conflict with the brigands; but for that hindrance, we should by this time have overtaken Marco Bravo and his band. This miserable affair may prove my ruin. I shall be tried by court-martial, and perhaps cashiered; but what is that to you?"

"Captain Lanfranco, I must not allow you to talk in this strain to me," replied the count, with perfect composure. "You must remember that it was I myself that warned you that you were wasting time in asking me so many idle questions—I that urged you to hasten the pursuit. I can make every allowance for your chagrin at this misadventure, and should there be an inquiry, if my testimony in your favour will be of any service, you are most welcome to it."

The captain only made a gesture of contempt, and turned sullenly away.

The blood rushed to the count's bronzed cheek, and his eyes flashed.

He strode after the enraged officer, and laid his hand upon his arm.

"Captain Lanfranco," he said, in a grave, impressive tone, "you have insulted me. Are you willing to make an instant apology?"

"Never!" returned the other; "but if you seek satisfaction, I am ready, now, on this spot, to fight with you; see, my sword is ready, count."

And the brave captain drew his sword, ready for contest.

The count laid his hand upon the hilt of his sword, but the next moment bowed with stately politeness.

"You shall hear from me again," he said.

The captain waved his hand.

"To-morrow I shall be at Naples," he replied. "Send to, or come to me at the castle of St. Elmo, and doubt not you will find me ready to cross swords with you, sir count."

CHAPTER IX.

THE BRIGAND'S WAGER.

RALPH WILDHAWK thought it time to interfere, to prevent the quarrel proceeding to extremities.

"Signori," said he, "these recriminations, as it seems to me, are quite uncalled for. The person who is really to blame is the treacherous priest who visited the prisoner."

"I gave the pass to Fra Dominico," replied the captain. "The man who came in his place was, no doubt, an impostor, perhaps a brigand in disguise."

"I should not wonder if the murderous villain were none other than Marco Bravo himself," rejoined Ralph Wildhawk.

"But then, what has become of the good padre?" laughed the count.

"You should know best," said Captain Lanfranco, "you were the last man known to be in his company."

"True," was the cool reply; "I left him about a hundred yards from Terracina."

"Villain," said the captain, unsheathing his sword, "I believe you are in league with the scoundrels, and am half inclined to run you through the body."

He pointed his sword to the count's body.

"Not now, signor, while we are surrounded by your soldiers, but remember, we meet again."

"Well, this Marco Bravo must be a daring villain," said Ralph, to change the subject.

"Diavolo, you are right," answered the count; "but then the brigand chief is such an ingenious rascal. By-the-bye, do you remember how he, singly, robbed thirteen persons?"

"No," replied Ralph Wildhawk; "but I should much like to hear the story."

"Well, I will recount it," answered the count; "it will serve to beguile the tedium of our journey back to the inn; and I think it time we were on the march."

Captain Lanfranco muttered a gruff consent, and the party commenced descending the mountain.

"And now for my story," said the count, taking Ralph by the arm. "You must know that there is a large gang of brigands in the Abruzzi mountains, under the command of a notorious man, named Pescatore."

"I have heard of him," replied Ralph Wildhawk. "He is second in infamy with Marco Bravo himself."

"Bah!" rejoined the count, contemptuously, "there is no comparison between the two men —not to rob the devil of his due, however, for it cannot be denied that Pescatore is as brave as a lion; but then he lacks the finesse, the insight of his rival."

Here the count paused and lighted a cigarette, and then resumed—

"It seems that Marco Bravo and Pescatore met together at a certain tavern which they frequented. Naturally enough they compared notes, and related their exploits. Pescatore began to brag how he and his band had attacked the palace of a wealthy noble, the Prince De Santa Croce, and carried off the whole family to the mountains, and how he had afterwards defeated the troops that were sent to rescue the captives."

"There he lied," put in Captain Lanfranco, brusquely; "I led the troop. We shot ten of his rascals, and took five; we should have caught him and the rest, but were misled by false information brought us by the goat-herds of the mountains."

"What would you have, signor capitano?" rejoined the count, shrugging his shoulders. "I tell you the story just as it was told to me."

Captain Lanfranco cast an evil glance towards the count.

"With the signor capitano's indulgence, I'll go on," continued the count, with a smile of provoking suavity. "Where was I?"

"Pescatore was boasting of his daring deeds," supplemented Ralph Wildhawk.

"*Sicuro*," returned the count; "now Marco Bravo, feeling rather piqued at being outdone by his rival, offered to bet that he would, without the assistance of a single follower, rob the diligence that plies between Naples and Terracina."

"Of course, Pescatore accepted the bet?"

"He did, signor," replied the count; "and lost; for note how Marco Bravo won."

The count laughed long and heartily.

"Cospetto, it was good fun," said he; "Marco hung up a number of hats and cloaks among the bushes on the wayside, with poles projecting, which, as it was dusk, looked like men drawn up with guns presented. Then he fastened a cord right across the road. The diligence soon came rattling along, and the horses encountering this obstacle were, of course, thrown to the ground. All was terror and confusion. Then Marco sprang out from the bushes, and planting himself in the middle of the road, shouted, as if to his followers—

"' *Attenti, figliuoli!* Attention, my lads, but do not fire till I give the word.'

"Then, doffing his hat, he politely requested the passengers to deliver up their purses, watches, and jewels, threatening an instant volley if they did not comply. The travellers were all so completely taken by surprise, and so glad, moreover, to be let off thus easily, that they obeyed without a moment's hesitation, and the contents of their pockets were quickly handed to the captain of the formidable band, who, in return, assisted to raise the struggling horses, and with great urbanity, wished them a pleasant journey, and dismissed them on their way, rejoicing that they had met with no worse treatment."

Ralph Wildhawk could not help laughing heartily at this droll anecdote.

"What a pity that such a man should so abuse his talents," he said. "Who knows what honour he might have achieved if he had entered the army, and have displayed his abilities in the cause of patriotism?"

They had now reached the valley where their horses had been left.

At the count's request, one of the troopers was ordered to dismount, and lend his horse to the Italian noble.

The count and the captain of dragoons behaved towards each other with studied courtesy; nevertheless, they exchanged a glance which conveyed very plainly the real state of their feelings.

They had not forgotten the challenge which had passed between them, and were determined to carry out their quarrel to the bitter end.

The sensation caused at the inn was tremendous when the dragoons returned without a prisoner.

Nicolo, poor fellow, had much ado to conceal his exultation at his nephew's escape, while Lisetta put in an appearance; and though she still looked pale, she seemed radiant with happiness.

Meanwhile, Captain Lanfranco held a court of inquiry in the principal room of the inn.

The absence of Pepe provoked great suspicions, and poor Nicolo was almost frightened out of his wits when the officer told him flatly, that as the man's master, Nicolo ought to be held responsible for his conduct.

Nicolo protested that when taking the man into his service, he had received from him a letter of recommendation from one of the most respectable hotel-keepers in Naples, and that before the events of last night, he had never detected anything in his behaviour that could provoke the slightest suspicion in regard to his honesty.

The Count Di Ancona now came to his host's rescue.

He pointed out that the brigands had many spies and agents, not only among the peasants and shepherds of the mountains, but also among the *veturrini*, or postillions, and the servants employed at the various hotels and taverns along the high road, and that it would be very unjust if honest people, who might chance unwittingly to engage their services, should be called to account.

Hereupon, Captain Lanfranco turned rather fiercely to the count, and asked, in a tone of passion—

"Who are you, sir, that takes the liberty of interfering in this matter? You may be a spy yourself, perhaps, notwithstanding your gay appearance. Let me have your papers for examination."

With infinite coolness the count drew a bulky pocket-book from his pocket, and, with a smile, handed it to the officer.

The captain of dragoons ran his eye over the papers, and could find no flaw in them: they were properly viséd and authenticated by the stamps and signatures of the government authorities, and the description perfectly tallied with the bearer.

Under such circumstances the captain had nothing else to do but to return the pocket-book, not knowing yet what to think of the strange man.

It was determined at this council that the sergeant and a small detachment of the men should be left at the inn until orders arrived from head-quarters for the further attack on the brigands.

Sir Raymond Mortimer chafed grievously over the delay caused by the startling reports that the brigands would most likely attack him and his friend near the Devil's Glen.

RALPH WILDHAWK No. 3 "BOYS OF ENGLAND" EDITION. PRICE ONE PENNY. PUBLISHED AT 173, FLEET STREET, E.C.

"'YOUR ORDERS, SIGNOR CAPITANO?' SAID THE BRIGAND."

But, of course, after all that had happened, it was not practicable for them to set out without an escort.

The count promised to accompany them on their journey.

When the council broke up, the count walked out of the inn and stood before the door, lounging and smoking, and apparently watching with interest, the manœuvres of the military, and the arrival of different wayfarers at the inn.

Amongst many of the peasantry on their way to market were two mountain shepherds, driving a flock of sheep and goats.

They were wild-looking fellows from the Abruzzi, dressed in a picturesque costume—they each carried a knotted stick, and a long crook, and were attended by several dogs, of a remarkably fine breed, being rather smaller than our Newfoundlands, and snowy-white in colour.

Bold and faithful, these wolf-hounds are in great request among Abruzzesi shepherds. On account of the wolves that frequently descend from the mountains and commit serious ravages, they are obliged to keep great numbers of them.

The shepherds say that two of them "of the right sort," are a match for an ordinary wolf.

The shepherds, with their flock, stopped before the door of the inn, the animals crowding round an ancient cistern to drink, and their keepers calling for bread and cheese and a bottle of Fondi wine.

The count regarded the two men searchingly for a moment or two, and then, stepping from the door, addressed one.

" Be cautious, I may be watched. Speak low. What have you done with the priest ?"

The man grinned, and touched his hat.

" We have him safe, signor capo," he replied. "Not far from hence—when are we to release him ?"

"Not at all," answered the count, thoughtfully ; " no, it won't do. If he returns to the monastery, he will tell the particulars of his capture, and the news will reach Naples soon enough to spoil my plans ; carry him off to our mountain glen, but treat him well."

"Yes, signor," answered the man, "but are we to make an attack on the English party as you proposed ? The band is ready."

"No, I have changed my mind," replied the count ; "the escort is too strong, the attempt would cost too much ; nevertheless, tell Generoso to post a force of at least forty men in the Devil's Gorge. Whether they will be wanted or not, depends entirely upon circumstances."

The man touched his hat and promised obedience, and the count re-entered the inn.

CHAPTER X.

FAMILY EXPLANATIONS.

BEFORE the inn, a scene of bustle and excitement preceded the departure of the travellers.

While the dragoons were forming single file, Nicolo, Lisetta, and the servants attended the English guests to their carriage.

Meanwhile, the grooms and postillions were engaged in putting to the horses, a task of no small difficulty, and even danger.

They were all Poledri—colts, or very young horses, hot, wild, vicious and almost unbroken ; but for spirit, wind and speed, they were very astonishing creatures.

With four of these snorting, neighing, kicking and biting equine devils, the task of putting to was tremendous.

The postmasters generally kept these poledri in store for the English.

"For," said they, "your Milordo always likes to go fast, and he knows what horses are."

Sir Godfrey Raymond Mortimer—the baronet had two Christian names—and his fair young ward, Violet Melville, got into the vetturino, while the two servants, Joe Moody and Matilda Sparkes, took their places in the rumble.

As for Edmund Mortimer, Ralph Wildhawk, and the Count Di Ancona, they mounted on horseback to ride beside the carriage.

Captain Lanfranco put himself at the head of his troop, and the order to march was given.

With a cheer from the bystanders the cavalcade started.

Ralph Wildhawk found in the Italian count a most amusing and delightful companion, and listened with eager interest to his anecdotes, or laughed merrily at his sallies of wit.

At length the count stopping short in the midst of a story, looked curiously up into the bright open face of the frank English lad.

"By the way, signore," he said, "I should like to ask you how it is that you, who have never been in Italy before, speak our language so well."

Ralph flushed with pleasure as he replied—

"I am much honoured by the compliment you pay me."

"Via ! It is no compliment at all," replied the count. "I give you my word I never before heard an Englishman speak Italian with such fluency and perfection of accent as you do."

"At any rate, that is not wonderful," answered Ralph, in a softened voice, "considering it is my mother-tongue."

The count started.

"Is it possible ?" he exclaimed ; "you astonish me."

"Still, it is true," replied Ralph. "My mother was an Italian."

"And your father ? He, of course, was an Englishman."

"Yes," was the reply. "I am of humble parentage, and what advantages of education and position are mine, I owe entirely to the kindness of my honoured patron."

"You act as his secretary," said the count. "I am aware of it—I was so informed by Sir Mortimer's son."

"Did he tell you so ?" returned Ralph, a shade of vexation crossing his face, while his eyes flashed rather angrily. "He always takes care to explain our relative positions to everyone he meets. Bah ! It does not matter. My story is a very short and simple one, but if you care to hear it, I will tell it you."

"Nothing would give me greater pleasure," answered the count.

"Well then, signore, I must inform you that in his younger days, before his marriage, Sir

Mortimer, as you call him, was as fond of travelling as he is at this day," continued the youth. "He visited many foreign lands, and in all his excursions was attended by a brave and faithful body-servant, named Wildhawk. While in Italy, Wildhawk married Maria Monti, a Neapolitan girl, the daughter of respectable parents. I am their son, and bear my father's name, Ralph Wildhawk.'"

"Then in point of fact you were born in Italy?" said the count.

"It is so, signore," replied Ralph. "But I was still a mere infant when my parents with Sir Mortimer returned to England. My father was promoted to the position of land-steward, and I was brought up on the estate. My mother never could speak English very well, and we always talked Italian. Of my father I knew little, for he died when I was very young."

"And your mother, is she alive?"

"Alas, no, monsignore," replied Ralph, with a deep sigh. "I lost in her my best and dearest friend, five years ago."

"And had your parents no other children besides yourself?" asked the count.

"None," replied Ralph; "I am their only child. But to return to Sir Mortimer; soon after his return to England with my father and mother he married a rich heiress—a very beautiful and high-born young lady, by whom he had one son."

"Edmund Mortimer, of course."

"Yes, monsignore. Soon after the birth of Edmund, my patron, with his beautiful young wife, took a tour upon the Continent. They arrived at Naples."

"Well?" said the count, growing deeply interested. "What followed?"

Ralph cast a quick glance around to make sure that he was not overheard, and then lowering his voice, replied—

"At Naples Lady Mortimer died suddenly and under mysterious circumstances."

"How mysterious?" queried the count, lifting his black brows; "was there any suspicion of foul play?"

"I cannot tell you much about the sad affair," answered Ralph; "the subject is strictly ignored and forbidden, but a dark rumour reached England that the lady had been murdered."

"Santa Maria!" ejaculated the count; "murdered!—by whom?"

"By an Italian woman, whom Sir Godfrey Mortimer had made love to before his marriage, and who stabbed her rival to glut her thirst for revenge."

"Cospetto! By no means unlikely," said the count, "my countrywomen are as vengeful as Medea if once their jealous passions are aroused. But your Italian mother, did she never tell you the truth concerning this terrible report?"

"She grew very angry with me when I questioned her about it," was the reply; "declared that it was utterly false, that Lady Mortimer's sudden death was occasioned by heart disease, and she commanded me never to mention the subject in her presence again."

"So then I suppose you and young Edmund were brought up together as foster-brothers?"

"Not exactly so," replied Ralph. "I re-mained at home. I did not go to Eton with Edmund, but was sent away to a lonely village in Cornwall."

"There is one question I would ask you, amico mio," said the count. "Were you at home, or at school, at the time your mother died?"

"No, signore, I was then away in Cornwall," answered Ralph, "and knew nothing of my mother's illness and death, until I was sent for to attend her funeral. It has always been a source of the keenest regret to me that I was not by her bedside to catch her last breath and receive her dying blessing."

The count put his forefinger between his knitted brows, and thought for awhile—

"Strange," he muttered to himself, "strange, if my half-formed suspicion should prove true, after all."

"But the full name of your patron?" he asked.

"Sir Godfrey Raymond Mortimer; some call him simply Sir Godfrey, others style him Sir Raymond."

"Indeed!" said the count, musingly.

Then he said briskly—

"Excuse the remark—but there seems to be little love lost between you and your patron's son and heir. The young milordo appears rather reserved and haughty for one of his age, not to say a trifle insolent and overbearing."

"Oh, Edmund is a good fellow at heart," replied Ralph; "he, as you observe, is the heir apparent, while I am but a poor secretary."

"He appears to pay great attention to the signorina," continued the count; "are they engaged to one another?"

"No, I believe not," replied Ralph, drawing a deep breath. "They are both so young; no, there is no decided engagement between them —not yet—not yet."

The count observed how the poor lad's voice trembled as he spoke, and how he changed colour. The count smiled grimly.

"Hark! What is the meaning of this flourish of trumpets?" cried Ralph.

The bugle of the dragoons was sounding a long and loud challenge, that made the neighbouring rocks and woods reverberate.

"That means that we are approaching Fondi, our next stage."

As he spoke, the cavalcade turned a corner of the road, and the town appeared in sight.

Fondi is a dirty and miserable town of five or six thousand souls.

The general appearance of Fondi, and the wild costume and sinister countenances of the inhabitants sufficiently confirm the ill repute it has borne for many centuries.

It is called the robbers' nest of the frontier. No two towns of Italy have contributed so many daring men to the army of brigands, as Fondi and Itri, and the traveller will be hardly at a loss to recognise in their present population abundant evidence that the hereditary spirit wants only the opportunity to prove by practice that it is not extinct.

Here the baggage of our travellers and their passports were examined.

The search was very rigorous.

At length, however, they were suffered to pass.

They stopped at an inn, called the "Locanda Barbarossa," of which we shall have more to say in the ensuing chapter.

CHAPTER XI.

THE BRIGAND MARCO BRAVO.

THE inn at which our travellers stopped to rest and change horses was called the "Locanda Barbarossa."

The count took the landlord of the inn apart, and held a long and private conversation with him.

After partaking of some refreshment, the travellers prepared to resume the journey, as the English baronet was all impatience to reach Naples as soon as possible.

"Oh, signore," said Violet, to the count, "what a piece of good fortune it is that we are under the protection of the gallant Captain Lanfranco and his men. The landlord of the inn, who it appears can speak English a little, has been terrifying my maid with more stories about the dreadful brigands. He says, too, that one particular ravine that we shall have to pass on our way to Itri, is notorious as being the haunt of Marco Bravo's gang, and is known far and wide as 'The Brigands' Glen.'"

"Have no fear, signora," replied the count, "with such an escort we may set all the brigands of the district at defiance; and of this you may rest assured, that should you ever encounter Marco Bravo, you would receive nothing but the most considerate and respectful usage at his hands."

"Heaven forbid I should ever have occasion to put his courtesy to the test," she answered, with a visible shudder.

Then she added, with a bright blush—

"Monsignore, I have a great favour to ask of you."

The count's eyes sparkled, and he bowed profoundly.

"Signora, trust me, I can conceive no greater happiness than the honour of serving you, even at the cost of my life," he answered, in his soft Italian.

"I thank your excellency," she replied, with some coldness; "but my request is but a simple one, and in granting it you will be performing an act of kindness none the less appreciated because it is easy. I want you to reason with Ralph, I mean with Mr. Wildhawk, over whom I know you have great influence."

The count's black brows met in a dark, sudden frown, but his countenance immediately cleared, and he answered in his suavest accents—

"Indeed, signora, I am afraid you overrate the estimation in which I am held by this young gentleman. Yet so far as lies in my power, I shall be proud to serve one who finds an advocate in yourself."

"Oh, signore, you must tell him not to expose himself so rashly to danger," she replied, with suppressed eagerness; "he is so brave and headstrong, has such a passion for adventure, that at times I really tremble for his safety. When Captain Lanfranco and his men went in pursuit of the escaped brigand, I tried in vain to dissuade him from accompanying them, and I have heard him say that like

another Salvator Rosa, he should delight to mingle with these picturesque banditti, study their character, and make sketches of their forms, their dress and customs, and their romantic haunts."

"Did he say that?" replied the count. "His wish may be gratified sooner than he looks for, but *Corpo di Baccho!* what a droll idea."

"Is it not absurd?" returned Violet, with a light laugh. "These were his exact words— 'Nothing would please me better than to spend months with these picturesque vagabonds, to throw myself upon their hospitality, and be alone in the brigands' glen.'"

"Ha, ha, ha! excuse my laughing, Madonna mia," replied the count, "but the fancy is so odd and original; so thoroughly English—well, I will do my best to divert him from a freak as perilous as it is eccentric."

"By so doing you will earn my deepest gratitude," said Violet, rising.

"This most enviable youth appears to have aroused a feeling of interest which many others would give worlds to inspire," he said.

"Why should I deny it?" she answered, with a rich, rosy blush, but a frank smile. "Ralph is esteemed by all who know him— but hark, monsignore, the postillion's horn is sounding."

"Come, Violet," cried Sir Mortimer, putting his head in at the door, "the carriage waits."

"I am ready, sir," replied Violet.

Advancing to the count, she held out her hand.

"Monsignore, I rely upon your promise," she said.

The count bent low, and kissed the little white hand with as much reverence as if he were paying homage to a queen.

"Signora," he said, "I live only to execute your orders."

Violet rewarded his gallantry with a grateful smile, and swept from the room.

"She loves him," muttered the count, between his clenched teeth. "The worse for him; the worse for them both. This English girl is altogether bewitching; she must be mine! I will proceed cautiously, however; I must keep my disguise a little longer—besides, there is my quarrel with the insolent captain of dragoons, that has to be settled—no, I will waive my purpose until we get to Naples, and then I will do such a deed as shall make the whole peninsula ring with the name of Marco Bravo."

Thus communing with himself, he strode forth from the inn.

He found that Violet had joined her uncle in the carriage, while Edmund Mortimer and Ralph Wildhawk had already mounted their horses.

The count sprang into the saddle, while Captain Lanfranco gave the order to march, and the cavalcade moved on.

They passed on their road the remains of numerous Roman tombs, immense circular masses on a square base, remarkable objects which marked the grand style of architecture peculiar to the ancient empire.

At length they reached the Brigands' Glen, or, as it is sometimes called, The Devil's Gorge.

It was a rough and dreary pass, leading to the miserable town of Itri.

It wound up the mountains amidst scenes of forbidding and lonely aspect, which seemed, both by the natural formation of the country, and by the facilities of escape from one frontier to the other, peculiarly fitted to be the haunt of brigands of both states.

Here Captain Lanfranco called a halt—and then with a strong detachment of his brigade rode forward to scour the country, in order to ascertain that there were no robbers lurking in ambush.

With his usual impetuosity Ralph Wildhawk accompanied the soldiers, and the count, casting a significant look at Violet, dashed after him.

Winding in and out amongst the rocks, and leaping their horses over bush and briar, the dragoons beat about in search of any lurking foe.

The soldiers, scattered abroad, peered into every nook and corner likely to conceal a skulking desperado, but their search proved fruitless.

Ralph Wildhawk, with all the keen zest of a Boy of England, kept close by the captain, and with pistol in hand, looked searchingly about him. All at once Captain Lanfranco turned his head, and asked abruptly—

"Where is the Count Di Ancona?"

Surprised at the question, Ralph looked for the count, but he had disappeared.

The fact was, that taking an opportunity when his companions were intent upon the search, the count had turned the rein and riding down a narrow and precipitous path, entered a little valley cumbered with rocks and overgrown with heather and brushwood.

Here he checked his steed and looked behind to see that he was neither followed nor observed. Then he gave a low, peculiar call.

At the signal a score of heads were raised above bush and briar, and a man in a handsome and picturesque costume, carrying a long carbine on his shoulder, sprang up from the dry bed of a torrent and came running towards him.

He stopped, breathless from his sharp run over the rough ground, and made a military salute to the count.

"Your orders, signor capitano?" said the brigand.

"*Scampa via!*" replied the count; "hear me, good Francesco. The travellers must be allowed to pass. We are not strong enough to risk a conflict with a whole brigade of dragoons; besides, I have altered my intentions."

Francesco bowed, then turning round, he made a motion with his hand, at which his comrades crouched down behind the rocks and whin-bushes, leaving the valley to all appearance void and lonesome.

"Does the signor capitano accompany the travellers to Naples?" asked Francesco.

"Yes," returned the count. "To-night we shall sleep at the next stage—Itri, and to-morrow at sunset we shall reach Naples. The next day, do you with Generoso and a dozen picked men enter the town disguised as zingari (gipsies) and take up your abode in the usual quarter; do you comprehend?"

"Clearly."

"Good, tell Generoso to dress himself in a suit of livery, such as is worn by the servants of the real Count Di Ancona, and attend me at my hotel in the Strada Di Toledo."

"I will not fail to do your bidding, signor."

"And now, Francesco, make haste to conceal yourself, for I hear the sound of horses' hoofs; the soldiers are approaching."

The brigand bowed, shouldered his carbine, and re-entering the dry bed of the mountain torrent, vanished from sight.

The count then turned his horse and galloped off to meet Ralph Wildhawk and Captain Lanfranco, who now came riding into the valley.

"Well, gentlemen," he said, smiling and lifting his hat, "what success?"

"We could find no trace of the brigands," replied Ralph, "and fear your excellency has met with no better success."

"No," the count answered, "either the rascals are overawed by your strong force, or else the brigand chief, Marco Bravo, is away."

Suddenly Ralph caught hold of the captain's arm, and, pointing upwards, exclaimed—

"Look, captain, is not that object on the mountain-top a brigand? See, he is bringing his carbine to his shoulder."

The captain looked upwards. The next moment the report of a gun echoed through the mountains.

The count seemed annoyed, and a fierce glance passed over his face.

Then, suddenly looking at the captain, he exclaimed—

"That man on the mountain top can be but a simple hunter. A brigand would have comrades. But, come, we have yet a long, rough road to traverse e'er we reach Itri."

The bugles then sounded a recall, and the soldiers with Captain Lanfranco and his companions returned to the carriage.

Once more the cavalcade started on its way.

The road, descending a hill, passed through some lovely country, diversified with vineyards and forest trees.

When the party arrived at the squalid little town, they were forced to put up with what wretched accommodation its solitary inn could afford.

With abject servility the innkeeper welcomed the great English milord and his train, and ushered them into the best room.

It was a large dreary chamber, wainscoted with dark oak, but miserably furnished.

One thing, however, struck the visitors with admiration as soon as they entered the door.

It was a fine portrait of a very lovely woman, in the bloom of womanhood, with noble features, splendid black eyes, and a wealth of raven hair.

The portrait, drawn by a master hand, appeared to stand out from the canvas.

It was a half-length figure, the boddice of bright scarlet, tastefully embroidered with gold thread.

It was a glorious picture.

Upon entering the room, Violet descried it at once, and cried with a burst of enthusiasm—

"Oh, uncle, look what a splendid picture!"

"Where, child?" asked Sir Raymond.

OF "RALPH WILDHAWK."

"THE HUGE, UNGAINLY BRUTE RAISED HIMSELF ON HIS HAUNCHES."

Then, his eye catching the painting, he staggered back, and turned pale as death.

Recovering himself, he turned abruptly to the innkeeper, who stood beside him, bowing and fawning.

"Whose portrait is that, and who painted it?" he asked, in a husky voice.

"Highness," replied the man, bowing low, "it is the portrait of La Catarina."

"La Catarina," gasped the baronet; "and pray who is La Catarina?"

"So please your excellency, La Catarina is, or was—for awhile ago there was a vague rumour of her death—the wife of a notorious brigand, who once commanded the band now under the leadership of Marco Bravo. The fellow was executed. I saw him die, and he was a brave man. His head is exposed to this day in the wayside near Terracina, the scene of one of his most atrocious crimes."

"His name?" asked Sir Raymond.

"Mazzaroso."

Sir Raymond uttered a faint sound, but controlled himself by a violent effort.

Meanwhile Ralph Wildhawk had come in, and his attention was instantly riveted by the picture.

"Are you, too, struck with admiration by this noble work of art, Mr. Wildhawk?" asked Violet Melville, softly. "Is it not a beautiful face?"

"Yes," replied Ralph, drawing a deep breath, and speaking in a tone of abstraction. "Yes, I have seen that face before."

The baronet started.

"Where, sir?" he asked, rather sternly.

"I cannot tell," replied Ralph. "It may be only in my dreams."

"Pshaw!" retorted Sir Raymond, "mere sentimental nonsense; this peerless creature was the vile paramour of a bloodthirsty brigand, nothing else. So much for your romance."

Ralph's eyes flashed, but he checked the angry retort that rose to his lips.

"But uncle, perhaps she had been cruelly wronged," rejoined Violet; "or clove with womanly devotion to a guilty love."

"Divine!—clove with devotion to a guilty love. Oh, Joseph," whispered Miss Matilda Sparkes.

"Fudge!" growled Joe Moody, to whom the remark was addressed. "I'll warrant the jade sold him to the runners and went to see him hung."

"Well, we'll speak of this again," returned Sir Raymond. "But now let us think of supper. Let us have some refreshment before we retire, for we are weary."

The innkeeper bowed and retired.

When the remainder of the travellers had gone to rest, the baronet, lingering in the state-room, and ringing for the servant, bade him send up his master.

When the innkeeper came in, Sir Raymond looked at him sternly.

"I wish to bid you a price for your picture," he said; "but no chaffering. Accept or refuse my offer as you will. I shall give no more than what I think in itself an extravagant price. I will give you a thousand pounds for the picture."

Though staggered at the mention of a sum so enormous, the Italian's avarice was aroused. Had he been offered a million, he would have wanted more.

"A thousand guineas? Ah, your excellency, that is a considerable sum," he answered, "but I doubt if it would repay me for the falling off of my trade, that would follow the loss of such an attraction to my customers."

The English baronet, who had his cheque-book in his hand, quietly closed it, and put it back into his pocket.

The Italian was greatly terrified at the thought of letting such a splendid opportunity slip through his fingers.

"My lord, you shall not be crossed in your wish upon any consideration," he said eagerly. "The painting is yours; here, Cicco," he shouted to a dirty-looking servant, "take it down and pack it up carefully, and let it be placed with the rest of his excellency's baggage."

The baronet smiled grimly.

The Count of Ancona had been a silent, but attentive observer of this little scene.

When it was concluded, the count walked out into the stable yard.

Here he encountered a swarthy, evil-looking fellow, engaged in tossing straw upon a dung heap.

"Companion," said the count, stepping up to him and touching him very lightly on the arm.

The man started violently.

Then leaning upon his dung fork, he stared up at the count in astonishment.

Then as the count gave a peculiar fillip with his fingers, a broad grin lit up the ostler's face, and his black eyes twinkled.

"Holy mother," he exclaimed; "it is the signor capitano. Your orders?"

"Hark ye, Benito," replied the count, with a smile; "the English milordo has just paid a thousand guineas to your master for the portrait of La Catarina."

"In gold, signore?" questioned the man.

"No, he has given him a cheque upon his bankers at Naples," replied the count. "Find out when your master goes to cash it, and let me know."

"I will, captain," answered the man, "The English noble is very rich, I suppose?"

"As rich as Plutus," answered the count, "but it shall go hard but we will lighten him of some of his load."

CHAPTER XII.

THE DUEL.

IT was towards evening, two days later, when the brigand, Marco Bravo, still disguised as the Count Di Ancona, accompanied by his lieutenant Generoso, in a rich livery, walked along the shores of the glorious Bay of Naples.

Fishing boats were drawn up on the shore, and the idle sailors were leaning in the half shadow which they afforded.

For some time the count walked on, lost in thought, his eye bent moodily on the ground, paying little heed to his companion.

At length he broke the silence.

"Now, tell me, Generoso," he said, "what news of the man that keeps the inn at Itri, of whom the English noble bought the portrait of La Catarina? Have you secured the fellow?"

"Yes, captain," returned Generoso. "I left the management of that affair to Stromba and Pietro ; they waylaid the man somewhere between Moladi Gaeta and Sant' Agata. He has been carried off to the mountains."

"It is well," replied the brigand chief. "Demand two thousand piastres as his ransom, and if it is not paid, whip off his head and stick it up as a sign-post before his pig-sty of an albergo."

"It shall be done, captain."

"But about the thousand guineas he received from the milordo—have you got them?"

"To the last broad piece, besides a bag of piastres he had on his own account."

"*Bravissimo!* not a bad stroke of business, was it?"

"By no means, signore," answered Generoso, laughing. "But may I ask, signore, what are your intentions with regard to the English travellers?"

Marco Bravo paused in his walk and regarded his companion with a peculiar and triumphant smile.

"*Attenti*, my good Generoso," he said, chuckling ; "I intend to astound them by what the French call a *coup de théâtre*, literally so."

"But how, signore?"

"Never mind for the present," answered the brigand chief ; "I have as yet but half formed my plans. Meanwhile, I have to settle a little affair of honour."

"*Corpo di Baccho!* it is with that burly captain of dragoons, is it not?"

"Even so."

"I feared as much," returned Generoso, in a tone which implied vexation. "Ah, signor capitano, let me implore you to take care of your life ; remember how precious it is to us all. Think of the band."

"I trust I shall bring no disgrace upon the band, my cautious Generoso," replied the other, "and I feel sure that I shall come off safely."

"But reflect, signor, this Captain Lanfranco is the best swordsman in Rome or Naples."

"That remains to be seen," returned his chief, dryly. "I have had some practice."

"Your skill and experience in fencing are not to be denied," replied Generoso. "But at such a time as this even a slight wound might disconcert our best-laid plans."

"Fear you not for me," replied his leader, with confidence ; "I shall know how to take care of myself."

"And when is the duel to be fought?"

"To-night."

"Diavolo! And where?"

"We are not more than a hundred yards from the appointed spot."

Generoso looked carefully round, and then lowering his voice, said excitedly—

"Listen, signor, I can make things right, and save you from all risk."

"What do you mean?"

"Let me conceal myself behind a rock, and as soon as you cross swords with the soldier, I can make a bound from my hiding-place and give him his quietus with six inches of cold steel."

His chief frowned darkly.

"Dog! do you dare to propose such a base and cowardly deed to Marco Bravo?" he growled.

"*Via!* if you attempt to interfere, I will kill you on the instant. Foot to foot, and hand to hand, I will cope with him alone. Yes, be assured but one will leave the ground alive."

They had now reached a little sandy inlet of the bay, sheltered on all sides landward by high rocks, and in every respect suited to the fell purpose on which the brigand was intent.

At the entrance of a narrow way between the rocks which led into this sequestered niche Marco Bravo stopped.

"Remain here, Generoso," he said. "Should I fall, I command you upon the terrible oath you swore at your initiation to make no attempt to avenge me ; let Lanfranco go free— never molest him—he who slays me in fair and open fight is not an object for revenge."

Generoso muttered a reluctant consent, but inwardly resolved to follow his own course.

"Now hide yourself," he said, "I shall rejoin you presently."

So saying he passed through the rocky passage into the little creek.

Captain Lanfranco stood by the margin of the sea, smoking a cigarette, and gazing dreamily across the glistening waters at the distant scar of Capri that rested like a cloud upon the horizon.

Upon hearing the crunching sound made by the footfall of his approaching foe upon the crisp sea-sand, Captain Lanfranco turned hastily.

The adversaries confronted each other with steadfast looks.

They lifted their hats, and bowed with sedate courtesy.

"I crave your pardon, Captain Lanfranco," said the count, in his blandest tones, "that I am a few minutes behind time, but the fact is, I was detained in the city by some acquaintances whom I could not shake off."

"Apology is needless," answered the officer, with equal politeness ; "I myself have also been hindered and have but this moment arrived."

The count smiled.

"I thank you for your consideration," he said ; "but since we are met, it may be as well that we should waste no time."

As he spoke, he threw off his coat and drew his sword.

Captain Lanfranco bowed slightly—so they stood stripped to their shirts, each grasping the hilt of his slim rapier, and regarding the other with a steadfast look.

"Before we take our ground and cross swords," said Captain Lanfranco, "there is a question I would ask of you."

"Indeed," replied the other calmly. "Since the secret cannot remain long in your keeping —for I shall recover it—I have no objection to gratify you upon the subject to which I know you are about to allude."

"Are you so confident?" returned the soldier, with a faint smile. "Do not forget that a proud spirit sometimes precedes a fall. You cannot be ignorant of the fact that I have never met my match in an affair of this sort."

"I am aware of that," answered the other,

"and esteem it both an honour and a piece of good fortune that I am here to measure swords with so redoubtable an antagonist. But your question, signor?"

"You are not the man you pretend to be." said Captain Lanfranco; "you have assumed the name and title of the Count Di Ancona for some nefarious motive."

"You are not mistaken," replied the disguised robber.

"You are then——"

"The brigand chief, Marco Bravo!"

"By Heaven! I am but little surprised at this confession," replied Captain Lanfranco. "I have for some time suspected the truth. But the letters and passports you showed me had all the stamp of authenticity—you must have obtained them from some accomplice attached to the government."

"Not so," returned the brigand, "the letters and passport were perfectly genuine documents, belonging to the real Count Di Ancona, now a captive in the hands of my band."

"Marco Bravo, you are a genius!" returned the captain. "It is a pity that such brilliant talents as you have displayed throughout your career should be so wretchedly misdirected."

Then, as he took his place and advanced his sword, he added sternly—

"After what you have said, you will clearly understand there can be but one issue to our contest."

"Assuredly," answered the brigand, with unmoved composure, "our duel is à l'outrance one or both of us must fall. So much the better—the higher the stake, the more exciting the game."

With that, they crossed swords.

For some time they played with each other, testing each other's skill.

Marco Bravo, being what he was, a splendid villain, and a man of iron mould—was like all who are truly courageous, collected and prudent—he fenced as he would have played a game of chess, more for the pride than the profit of victory.

Captain Lanfranco could scarcely repress an exclamation of astonishment at finding himself matched against such a formidable adversary.

From the time when he accepted Marco Bravo's challenge, he had made light of it, fancying himself more than a match for any swordsman in Italy.

Now, however, he discovered his mistake; still he did not for one moment despair of the result of the conflict.

Long impunity, with self-esteem, supported him; he felt sure that he would conquer.

Still he fought very warily.

Presently, believing he perceived his advantage, the soldier made a fierce lunge, but the brigand was too quick for him, and parried his rapid thrust with consummate dexterity.

They lowered their weapons, glaring upon each other with that wild, fixed expression that did not exactly bespeak mutual hatred, but a grim determination on either part, to kill or die.

Again they crossed swords and attacked each other fiercely.

The captain of dragoons, by a masterly feint, succeeded in betraying Marco Bravo into laying himself open to a deadly thrust.

Then rushing swiftly in, the captain lunged and passed the lithe blade of his rapier through the fleshy part of the brigand's left arm.

Marco Bravo smiled grimly and nodded his head as much as to acknowledge "a hit; a palpable hit," but then he set his white teeth and made his black brows meet in a thunderous frown.

"Captain Lanfranco!" cried the brigand chief, "your time has come."

Then, with a furious, overbearing rush, the brigand darted in and plunged his sword to the hilt through the soldier's breast.

With glazing eyes the brave Lanfranco let fall his sword, clutched the air, and as Marco Bravo drew out his reeking blade, the noble soldier fell flat on his back and with a sigh expired.

"Diavolo, I am sorry for this wound," said Marco to himself, as he clutched his left arm with his right hand, transferring the sword to his left. "Tsa!" he went on, drawing the air through his clenched teeth and grinning with pain, "this is confoundedly unlucky; still, it might have been worse than it is. At least, I have proved myself a better swordsman than the brave Captain Lanfranco."

He drew out his handkerchief, wiped the blood off his sword, and returned it to his sheath.

Then he gave a low whistle.

Generoso sprang out from behind a rock and approached his chief.

Marco Bravo turned towards his follower, a grim smile curling his thin lip.

"Soh," said the brigand chief, "I am not dead yet, amico."

"No, signor capitano," returned the other; "but you have got a bad hurt. I fear. Let me look at your arm."

"Only a flesh wound," replied Marco Bravo; "but it is rather provoking, as my English friends may ask questions it will be extremely awkward for me to answer."

"For all that I think, signor, you may account yourself fortunate that it is no worse," was Generoso's answer; "the dragoon fought like ten devils."

"True, amico; it was the sharpest action I was ever engaged in. The captain was a brave man," said Marco Bravo.

"From my hiding-place behind yonder rock, I watched the contest narrowly," rejoined his follower. "More than once, when I saw you hard pressed, I had much ado to restrain myself from sending a bullet to cut short the struggle; I could have done it nicely, as the captain's back was turned towards me. However, I remembered your orders."

"You did well, Generoso," said the brigand chief, with a nod of approval. "I would not have missed this experience for more than I can tell. Hereafter, I shall feel myself invincible."

"Well, captain," rejoined Generoso. "Do you not think it is time we should be returning to the city? If any of the fishermen should come along and surprise us, the consequences might be unpleasant."

"You are right, Generoso," answered Marco

Bravo ; " I am thinking what we shall do with the poor devil."

" Throw his body into the bay."

" No, no," returned Marco Bravo, shaking his head. " His body would float, or might be dragged up by some of the fishermen. Let me see."

Marco Bravo pondered a moment.

" First we will search his pockets for any papers he may have about him," said the bandit captain. " They perhaps may guide me in my future proceedings."

He turned to the corpse of the dead soldier.

He lay rigid, his white face upturned to the moon, which poured a flood of spectral light upon the stern, handsome features, causing the glassy, blindly-staring eyes to glisten in an awful manner.

The fresh, bluff breeze stealing landward from the sparkling bay, stirred his crisp raven hair, and caused his scarf to flutter idly.

The fierce crimson splash upon his left breast, showed up in dread contrast with his drift white linen.

His long, slim rapier lay gleaming at his side.

For some time the two bandits gazed down in gloomy silence upon the dead man's face.

Generoso sighed, devoutly crossed himself, and under his breath, muttered a prayer for the repose of the departed.

" Bah !" said Marco Bravo, rousing himself and stamping his foot. " He was a brave fellow, and met his death like a man ; I will pay masses for him. Wake up, Generoso," he added, giving his man a sounding slap on the shoulders. " One would think you were a child that had never looked upon the face of death before.

" Go, fetch me his jacket and capote, that he has left so neatly folded on the sand-bank yonder."

Generoso started from his moody reverie, and hastened to execute his chief's order.

He brought the cloak and richly-laced coat of the young soldier, unfolded them and handed them to Marco Bravo.

" These may be useful at some time or other," said the brigand chief, spreading the cloak smoothly out upon the sand.

Then he proceeded to rifle the pockets of the coat. The first thing he found was a gold watch, which he handed to Generoso.

The brigand examined it attentively, weighed it in his hand and then, with a grin of satisfaction, slipped it into his pocket.

Marco Bravo then handed Generoso a purse.

" It is not very heavy," he remarked.

" No, signore, but there is a diamond brooch that sparkles in his cravat," rejoined his confederate. " And a signet ring upon his finger."

" You had better take them, whilst I overlook these papers," replied Marco Bravo, with perfect calmness.

Generoso knelt down beside the corpse.

He unfastened the glistening ornament from the neck cloth.

Then, not without a shudder, he drew the ring, which was set with a blood-red ruby, from the stark, dead finger.

Suddenly his eye caught the golden glim-

mer of something that lay upon the dead man's breast, and was visible through a rent in the shirt.

He made a greedy clutch at it.

In doing so, his hand came in contact with the icy-cold, clammy flesh, and he uttered an involuntary cry.

"*Che demonio !*" growled Marco Bravo, looking up from the papers and frowning, " what is the matter now ?"

Generoso hung his head, ashamed of this momentary weakness.

" *Cospetto*, signore," he answered with a forced laugh, " I was a little startled at finding this handsome toy attached by a gold chain round his neck."

" What is it ?"

Generoso handed it to him.

" It is a locket," said the brigand.

" *Per Baccho !*" he exclaimed, in admiration, " what a lovely face."

Upon opening the locket, he found the finely-executed miniature of a girl of surpassing loveliness.

Around the portrait was entwined a braid of glossy dark hair.

Upon turning to the reverse of the locket, Marco Bravo muttered with a start—

" Lucia Di Carrara ! Can it be possible that the contessa, a lady belonging to so high and proud a family, could have lavished her affections upon a poor captain of dragoons ?"

He then placed the locket round his own neck.

" Lucia di Carrara," he mused. " I once thought to make her my prize, but now I have no care for aught in life but to win my beautiful English signorina."

Then shaking his head, as if to dismiss such light thoughts from his mind, he went on perusing the papers.

" These letters are from her," he said. " Wild, youthful, gushing with hope and tenderness—one, two, three, six, a seventh, the last—pah !"

He let it fall from his fingers, it fluttered to the ground, wet with blood.

" This was nearest his heart," gasped Marco Bravo, stooping and picking it up.

Then he went on with his examination.

He found a little note book, containing bills and receipts, cards of invitation and other private papers, and at last he came to an official document, stamped and sealed.

" This is of importance," he said.

Then, touching his confederate on the shoulder, he continued—

" Look here, Generoso."

" Well, captain."

" Here is a letter from General Gonzalvo, granting Il Capitano Lanfranco twelve days' leave of absence, together with his passport."

" *Bueno*," rejoined the other, rubbing his hand. " That will be useful."

" Yes," said the brigand chief, " and, best of all, it will give us time. Lanfranco disappears, what has become of him ? Oh, he has obtained twelve days' leave of absence to visit his sweetheart, who resides in Genoa—ha, ha, ha !"

Generoso shuddered at the harsh, grating laugh with which his chief finished his heartless speech.

"Twelve days," continued the brigand chief, speaking to himself, rather than to his companion. "That will give me ample time to carry out my project; let me see, which of our men belong to his troop?"

"Pavone, captain," replied Generoso; "I met him this morning; he appears very miserable and discontented."

"Why so?"

"He prefers the free mountain life to the discipline of the camp and barrack," answered Generoso. "Some time ago he was flogged at the halberts for a slight offence."

"Ha, what might it be?"

"He was engaged in digging a trench for the new fortifications at the castle of Saint Elmo, when a surly sergeant struck him across the shoulders with a cane."

"What, struck Pavone!" returned Marco Bravo. "He must have been either a great fool or a bold fellow, that sergeant. But what did Pavone do?"

"Why, you see, signor *mio*, at the moment poor Pavone had no other weapon to revenge the blow but the spade he carried," answered Generoso. "With that he made a dash to fell his tyrant to the earth, but his comrades interfered and overpowered him. He was afterwards tried for the attempt to assault his officer, and for the offence received a hundred lashes."

"Diavolo!"

"He asks you to avenge him, Signor Capitano."

"His request is reasonable," answered Marco Bravo, with a cruel smile. "This concerns the honour of the band. Tell him to send me the name of his persecutor, and I will take care to have him captured, and for every lash Pavone suffered, a dozen shall be inflicted; the wretch shall be flayed alive."

"He will be pleased, signore, to find you so prompt to avenge his cause," answered Generoso. "But he bade me to petition you to relieve him from his present irksome and dangerous position. He stands in constant peril of his life. Should it be discovered that he is in league with brigands, he would be at once tried and executed."

"Tell him that he shall shortly be recalled," answered Marco Bravo, "and that he shall receive a handsome reward for his prudence and fidelity."

"Trust me, captain, such good news will afford him great comfort."

"Meanwhile, he must be patient," the brigand chief went on to say, "for I have some delicate business for him. He must give it out that Captain Lanfranco has departed for Milan, and that he—Pavone—carried the captain's trunk to the post-house whence he started. He must also let me have early information of the intended movements of his regiment."

"I will take care to convey your orders, captain," returned Generoso.

"It is well," answered Marco Bravo. "And now let us dispose of the body."

He placed the jacket with the pocket-book containing the letters in the cloak of the luckless officer, and tied the whole in a bundle.

Then he and Generoso set to work with their swords and hands to scoop out a deep hole in the sands.

This work took them some time.

When it was completed, they lifted the corpse and placed it in the trench.

They covered it over with sand.

Then they stamped it down, and left the ill-fated duellist to slumber in his unknown grave.

CHAPTER XIII.

THE English baronet, Sir Raymond Mortimer, whose great wealth and political interest were well known in the highest circles of Neapolitan society, was everywhere received with the greatest respect.

He, his son Edmund, and the fair Violet Melville were presented at court, and invited to all manner of balls, routs, and pleasure excursions.

A score of the gay youths of the Neapolitan nobility paid court to Edmund Mortimer, and led him into a round of dissipation, to him as novel as it was delightful.

He tasted of every pleasure that wealth and rank could supply, he kept late hours, dressed sumptuously, drank hard and played deep.

Indeed, he seemed to have acquired a sudden and violent passion for gaming, and spent night after night at the gaming-table.

As yet, he had not suffered any loss through this new and perilous habit, but on the contray, had won heavily, having an unusual run of luck.

As for Ralph Wildhawk, his position was soon discovered by the time-serving guests.

But Ralph cared not one jot for this.

Proud, high-souled, and of independent spirit, the brave young Englishman held all sycophants, however high-placed, in the heartiest scorn.

One thing, however, caused a wide gap in Ralph's peace of mind.

For days he had not seen nor heard anything of his engaging friend, the Count Di Ancona.

"He is the only one among these people who seems to court my friendship, and appreciate my feelings," he said to himself. "I wonder what has become of him."

Then the recollection came back to him of the count's quarrel with the captain of dragoons, and the subsequent challenge.

Ralph's thoughts dwelt on the Count Di Ancona.

"With the count," said Ralph to himself, "I feel that I could face to the death even the brigand chief, Marco Bravo, or any of his desperate mountain band."

Ralph made his way to the public gardens, where he met several of Captain Lanfranco's military friends.

He at once inquired the whereabouts of the captain.

"Captain Lanfranco," said the officer, "has obtained twelve days' leave of absence, and has gone to visit his friends at Milan."

Ralph thanked them for the information they had given, and made his way to the count's residence.

Upon reaching the Count Di Ancona's hotel, Ralph met Generoso on the threshold.

The brigand still wore the livery of a servant, and upon seeing Ralph, he bowed with obsequious politeness.

The young Englishman inquired after the count's health.

"His excellency has been confined to his room by a slight accident," replied the valet; "but he gave me orders to announce you, signor, whenever you did him the honour to call; his excellency will be very much delighted at your visit."

"Thanks," replied Ralph, "pray conduct me to his room at once."

"This way, signor," replied the valet, bowing.

He ushered the young Englishman into a splendidly-furnished apartment.

The Count Di Ancona reclined upon a couch beside a large open window, that commanded a glorious prospect of the Bay of Naples.

He was reading a newspaper, and smoking a cigarette.

Ralph started at seeing how pale he looked, and that he wore his left arm in a sling.

With an easy, graceful air, the count rose to receive his visitor.

"You are most welcome, signor," said the count, with a cordial smile; "I was just thinking of you; indeed, it was my immediate intention to despatch my servant to your hotel to apprise you of the little accident which has confined me at home for the last few days. But I suppose that Generoso has told you all about it."

"Excuse me, your excellency," returned Ralph, shaking him by the hand, and gazing in his pale face with genuine solicitude, "your man only mentioned a slight accident. I trust that you do not make too light of it, and that it is really nothing serious."

"Oh, no," replied the count with a careless laugh; "it was but a fall from my horse. Fortunately no bones were broken; still, my arm was much cut and bruised, and I lost a good deal of blood."

Then, after a pause, he asked, with abruptness—

"By the bye, signor, have you seen anything lately of Captain Lanfranco?"

"No, excellency," replied Ralph; "but about an hour ago I met some of his fellow officers in the Villa Reale."

"Yes," rejoined the count, hastily, "and could they give you no account of his whereabouts?"

"They told me that the colonel of his regiment had given him twelve days' leave of absence, and that he had set out for Milan to pay a visit to his family."

The count walked up and down the room, and seemed lost in thought.

Then he said, suddenly—

"It is as well so; in twelve days I have no doubt I shall have recovered from the shock I have sustained. It will be time then to meet him. Meanwhile, signor, should any of his friends ask questions about me, pray bear me witness that I am temporarily disabled."

"I trust you do not allude to a few hasty words that passed between you on the occasion when we were in hot pursuit of the escaped brigand," replied Ralph; "I am sure your ex-cellency is too liberal, too generous to take account of a hot speech spoken in a moment of irritation."

"You forget, signor," he replied, gravely, "I made every allowance at the time, but Captain Lanfranco persisted in his unmanly and insulting conduct—nay, gave me the lie to my teeth."

"Still, your excellency, he has had time to reconsider and regret his hastiness," returned Ralph; "and I have no doubt he will be found willing, nay, eager to retract his ill-advised speech."

"I hope it may prove so," answered the count. "I am by no means of a vindictive temperament, and shall be glad enough to retire from a quarrel, dishonouring to both parties, if I can do so with propriety."

"I am right glad to hear you speak with such good sense and feeling," answered Ralph.

"Well, well, let us talk of something more pleasant," rejoined the count. "How have you amused yourself since last we met?"

"I have enjoyed myself beyond measure," was the enthusiastic reply.

"But what do you think of our idle, worthless lazzaroni?"

"The happy, picturesque vagabonds, I almost envy them their lot," replied Ralph.

The count laughed.

"Since you are so fond of the vagabond picturesque," he said, "should you like to disguise yourself after the style of the Arabian caliph, and study the humours of the lowest classes?"

"Nothing in the world would give me greater pleasure," answered Ralph; "it was but this morning while walking along the Marinella, I saw a party of those strange people whom you call Zingari, and we in England speak of as gipsies. They were dancing, fiddling, and telling fortunes; I was wonderfully amazed by their curious performances."

The count's eyes flashed, and he started as though struck by a sudden thought.

"Did you see amongst them one girl—a dancer—a girl of the rarest beauty of form and features?"

The colour mounted Ralph's cheek, as with a slight laugh, he answered—

"I saw the girl you mention, signor count, and I confess she deserves your praises; she is quite a paragon of beauty, whose loveliness is equalled only by her wit and vivacity."

"*Diavolo!*" returned the count, shrugging his shoulders, "do you mean to say that you spoke to her?"

"Indeed, I did," was the answer; "and was charmed with her shrewd replies. She even looked at my hand and told me my fortune."

The count bit his lip.

"And what sort of future did she prognosticate for you?" rejoined the count, in a calm and even tone.

"I am sorry to be forced to acknowledge that her predictions were not so favourable as I could wish."

"She warned me that I was on the eve of meeting with a disastrous adventure."

RALPH WILDHAWK No. 4 "BOYS OF ENGLAND" EDITION. PRICE ONE PENNY. PUBLISHED AT 173, FLEET STREET, E.C.

"'CAPTAIN LANFRANCO HAS OBTAINED TWELVE DAYS' LEAVE OF ABSENCE,' SAID THE OFFICER."

"The little vixen," laughed the count. "Oh, beware of her, *amico,* for she is a very syren."

"She seems to me to be a very sensible and amiable girl," replied Ralph, rather hastily; "and bears a stainless reputation."

"That is true, and she well deserves it," answered the count, nodding assentingly. "The fair name of Zara is untarnished by the breath of scandal."

Then he added in a serious tone—

"Woe to the rash fool that dares to speak slightingly of her virtue, for she has powerful friends."

"At court?"

"Why, yes, at court," returned the count, smiling. "At the court of her royal brother, Isaco Il Nero, the King of the Zingari."

"Then she is a princess," was the laughing reply. "I am glad of that for her sake."

"A princess," returned the count, "I warrant you as proud of her lineage as any Guelph, Bourbon, or Hohenzollern that sits on an European throne. She claims descent from the Pharaohs of Egypt, and, as I have already told you, her brother is king of the gipsies."

"A king of shreds and patches, I'm afraid," said Ralph.

"As for that, his patch-work cloak and paltry regalia adorn a monarch that, amongst his own subjects, is more powerful and despotic than many a potentate robed in velvet and ermine."

"Is it possible?" replied Ralph.

"I will give you a case in point," rejoined the count. "What I am going to tell you happened about a twelvemonth ago.

"There was a poor devil in Naples, one of those *improvisatores,* who gain a livelihood by amusing our indolent, pleasure-seeking populace with impromptu songs and recitations. It seems that he fell violently in love with La Zara, and not being able to keep the secret of his passion, went about everywhere singing her praises in songs of his own composing. Now, whether the king of the Zingari was disgusted at the badness of the poetry, or the presumption of the poetaster is more than I can tell; but one thing is certain, that the poor troubadour was found drowned in the bay."

"But might he not have met his death by accident?" asked Ralph.

"Who knows?" replied the count, smiling grimly; "but as he had between his shoulders a wound some six inches deep, the case looked just a little suspicious."

"Well, I should like to see and know more of these singular people," said Ralph Wildhawk.

"Your wish shall be gratified," returned the count. "I am well acquainted with Isaco, and shall be happy to present you to his Egyptian majesty. To-morrow evening, if you are still so disposed, we will go thither in company."

Ralph expressed his willingness, and inquired whether the count had engagements for the present evening.

"Yes," said the count; "I have an appointment to meet some friends at the Casino Reale."

Ralph changed colour, and a shade of vexation crossed his face.

"That is the celebrated gaming-house, is it not?" he asked.

"Yes. Do you play, signor?" rejoined the count.

"Never!" returned Ralph, with some vehemence. "In the first place, I am too poor to be able to afford losses, and in the second, I consider winning at games of chance but an ill means of gaining gold."

"Well said," returned the count. "You speak very wisely. For my own part, I care little for play—or, at least, deep play. Still, I am under a kind of necessity to visit such places as the casino, where I meet so many friends."

Ralph Wildhawk paused a moment before he replied.

He was thinking of his foster-brother, Edmund Mortimer, and it occurred to him that if he (Ralph) were to visit the gaming-house, he might find an opportunity of talking to him, and persuading him to struggle against his vicious and dangerous propensity.

"I should like to visit the casino," he said. "It is well to see life in all its phases. If agreeable to you, I will go with you to-night."

The count shook his hand with much warmth.

"I am quite delighted at your promise," he said. "Where shall I meet you?"

"Where you will."

"Let it be here, then, at about seven o'clock."

Ralph bowed in acquiescence.

The count showed his white teeth in a cordial smile, again shook his hand, and rang the bell.

Generoso, with great ceremony, ushered him to the door, and dismissed him with the politest of bows.

"He has a good heart," muttered the youth, as he trudged along through the bustling streets of noisy Naples. "I would that there were more like him."

Meanwhile, the count was thoughtfully pacing up and down his sumptuous apartment.

"Generoso," said the count, laying his hand on his confederate's shoulder when the other returned, "we are playing a bold game."

Generoso looked grave and shook his head.

"Too bold—too rash, signor capitano," he answered; "we cannot keep it up much longer. We must get back to the mountains."

The disguised brigand laughed.

"Tush!" said he. "Fortune favours the bold."

Then, after awhile, he said—

"Tell me, Generoso, how do you prosper in your love-making? Does your pretty little Zitella—I forget her name—show any signs of relenting?"

Generoso burst into a fit of hearty merriment, and gleefully snapped his fingers.

"Matilda *mia.* Ah, how beautiful, how witching she is!" he answered. "Give me an English girl for a sweetheart, the world over."

"It is strange that the murky island of Britain should produce flowers of such loveliness," returned the count. "I have seen many fair women in my time ; but even in my dreams, have not formed a conception of such fresh, sweet beauty as that which adorns the peerless English signora, Violetta."

"I fear, signor, the *bionda*—the fair-haired belle, has stolen your heart," replied Generoso. "But, if what her maid tells me is true, you have a powerful rival in the young secretary."

"I know it," returned the chief, frowning darkly, "and I am sorry for it. I have taken a great fancy to the lad, and would not willingly do him harm ; but should he dare—but we will not think of that. If anyone can lure his affections from their present object, it is the dark Zara the Zingara."

"Ah, captain, captain !" remonstrated Generoso. "More women — more women ! It is not well. Woman is the mother of mischief."

"Granted, since such fellows as you and I, Generoso, are our mothers' sons," returned the brigand chief, smiling like a demon. "But to business. What kind of girl is your Matilda, and when will you visit her again ?"

"I am to visit her to-night. I am going to play a serenade under her window," returned Generoso.

"Ha, ha, ha ! pray do not frighten her," laughed the count ; "and take care your sweet voice is not mistaken for the howl of a stray wolf, which it so closely resembles. Still, I am glad of what you tell me. Ply her well ; use all your arts to win her confidence, for in her we shall find a most valuable ally."

"Good, signor," returned Generoso, bowing to his chief.

CHAPTER XIV.

HAVING an idle hour or two to pass away, Ralph Wildhawk amused himself by strolling through the crowded streets, taking mental notes of all he saw.

Upon reaching the gates of the hotel, he saw, standing in the carriage drive, a cumbrous and richly-gilded chariot, drawn by four magnificent horses, the coachman and footmen attired in gorgeous liveries.

As he approached, Violet Melville and a young lady he had never seen before, tripped down the steps together.

She stepped lightly into the heavy chariot, the door was clapped to, and the stately equipage got into motion.

The Italian lady waved her laced handkerchief from the window to Violet.

When the carriage was gone, Ralph mounted the steps, and entered the vestibule.

Violet lingered as if willing to speak with him.

Ralph reddened.

He raised his hat, and bowed with grave courtesy, but his eyes spoke that which his lips dared not utter.

Violet blushed, and gave him her hand.

"You have been playing truant of late, Mr. Wildhawk," she said, smiling sweetly.

Wildhawk stammered something about engagements, and added that he had just returned from visiting the Count Di Ancona.

"I am glad that you are on such good terms with the count, for he appears to be a gentleman of honour and refinement," said Violet. "We miss him very much."

Ralph Wildhawk informed her that the count had met with a slight injury through a fall from his horse.

Violet expressed her regret at the count's mishap, and then added quickly—

"There is another of our friends whom we have not seen for some time. Captain Lanfranco. Have you heard any news of him?"

Walter felt surprised, and a qualm of doubt and uneasiness caused him to start.

"Captain Lanfranco," he repeated. "Why, yes, Miss Melville, I made some inquiries about him of one of his fellow officers, whom I met in the Villa Reale, who informed me that he had obtained a furlough to visit his friends at Milan."

Violet's face cleared.

"I am glad to hear that," she said, "for the sake of the lady who has just bid me adieu."

"The beautiful lady whom I saw enter her carriage just now ?"

"Yes. Is she not lovely, and so Italian ? I am quite enchanted with her," returned Violet, warmly. "Do you know who she is ?"

"A lady of high rank, I should think."

"Indeed she is, and nobly sustains her exalted position," answered Violet. "The young lady you saw is the Contessa Lucia Di Carrara."

"I am not surprised," rejoined Ralph. "But I think you said you were glad to hear tidings of Captain Lanfranco for her sake. Are they relations?"

Violet blushed deeply, and hung her head.

For awhile she preserved an embarrassed silence, and side by side they mounted the grand staircase.

Violet paused on the landing, where there was a little conservatory, one mass of bloom and verdure.

"Perhaps you have not heard," she said, "that the contessa is much attached to Captain Lanfranco, though her family disapproves of her marriage with him, and wish her to form an alliance with the Prince Di Santa Croce."

Ralph Wildhawk trembled in every nerve, and his voice grew husky as he replied, in a low voice—

"I think I can guess their objection against the gallant soldier. He is poor, and connected with no great family."

Violet raised her eyes to his.

"You have guessed right," she answered, in her softest accents.

"And, Miss Violet, do you blame her for not acceding to the wishes of her friends, for not enslaving herself to a man she cannot love, who, though not so rich or high-born as herself, is a gentleman and a devoted lover ?"

"I blame her ! No, indeed," replied Violet, with generous warmth. "No true woman would barter away her heart and hand for rank or gold."

Ralph listened to these words in breathless rapture, and was about to make some ardent reply, when a door opened with a jar.

"Ralph," said a harsh voice. "I am glad of your return. I need your assistance."

Sir Raymond stood near them, a frown on his brow.

Violet uttered a faint cry, and instantly hurried away.

Ralph bowed coldly.

"I am at your service, Sir Raymond," he said.

"Then come with me to the library. I wish to confer with you on business of importance."

CHAPTER XV.

MATILDA SPARKES sat by the open window, gazing at the moon.

The romantic Matilda was very fond of moon-gazing.

She and Joe Moody had been supping together in a little back room of the hotel, overlooking a small but lovely garden.

She had risen from the table after partaking of a repast that would scarcely have satisfied a hungry sparrow, and leaving Joe still in the midst of his attack upon a round of beef, had posed herself in a graceful attitude.

After some moments of silence, broken only by the clatter of Joe's knife and fork, she uttered a loud exclamation.

"O Hitaly !"

Joe was so startled, that he let fall his knife and fork, and gaped at her in speechless amazement.

At length, after a struggle, he gasped out—

"No, don't, 'Tilda ; no 'sterics. I can't and won't stand 'em."

"The moon, Joseph, the Hitalian moon," cried Matilda, in ecstasy ; "the bright, beautiful moon ! the sight of its splendour always affects me."

"So it do most lunatics," growled Joe, "and I see it's at the full."

"I'd rather be a lunatic, divinely mad, than such a dull, grovelling lump of ignorance as you, Joe ; there now," retorted Matilda, snappishly.

"You're wery welcome to the preference, I'm sure, 'Tilda," answered Joe, drinking off about a pint of mulled wine at a draught.

"You're always a-trying to wound my sensitive feelings," whimpered Matilda. "You're a brute, Joe."

"I aren't much of a judge of poetry, 'Tilda," was the grave reply, "but that 'ere remark is neither perlite nor poetical."

Matilda tossed her pretty head in polite contempt, and then turning her back to him, once more fixed her gaze upon the brilliant orb of night.

"Oh, that I had wings, that I could fly," murmured Matilda.

"You couldn't fly without 'em, 'Tilda," replied Joe, with a grin ; "though I really wonder that you haven't 'em."

"Why, Joseph ?" asked Matilda, turning round to him with an encouraging smile.

"Cos you're a goose."

Matilda stamped her foot, and once more turned her back upon him.

"I suppose you thought I was going to say cos you were an angel," returned her tormentor, with a provoking leer. "Not for Joseph. I never knew but one female as was an angel, and she was an old lady as was deaf and dumb,

and paralysed. She died unmarried at the early age of seventy, and left all her fortune to her butler, an old fellow servant of mine."

Matilda bounded from the window, and placed herself before him.

"Now, Joseph, will you look me in the face ?" she said, imperiously.

"With all my 'art," returned Joe. "I was always fond of pretty picters."

Matilda's wrath was at once appeased. She blushed, and turned aside her head.

"Joseph, you're not quite such a brute as you pretend to be," she answered. "You can talk sense when you like. Now do you really mean to say that you see nothing beautiful in this glorious Hitalian land ?"

"In course I do," replied Joe, slapping his thigh, "when you're before me."

"Don't be nonsensical, Joseph," simpered Matilda ; "but tell me, what do you think of the Bay of Naples ?"

"There's some fine fish in it, I dessay."

"But Vesuvius ?"

"Smokes a good bit."

"The olive and the vine ?"

"Olives are only fit for pigs, but the wine is certainly first-rate."

And as if to emphasise this opinion, he filled a tumbler full of Rosolio, and gulped it down without winking.

"And the fire-flies, Joseph."

"And the fleas, Matilda—oh, Lor' !"

"Well, Joseph, but if you don't like the country, what do you think of the people ?"

"I'd rayther not express my opinion, 'Tilda," returned Joe ; "I object to using strong language before ladies."

"But the men, what gallant, handsome fellows they are ! How many of them have such glorious black eyes."

"They should all have black eyes, the dirty vagabonds, if I had my way," growled Joe, squaring his fists and dealing a fearful blow at some imaginary object.

"And the women ?"

"Oh, Matilda dear, they're ducks."

"Oh, indeed, Joseph ; and I'm only a goose.'

"Only a goose ; why, a goose is a much bigger and finer bird than a duck, any day, and nicer eating," replied Joe. "Now don't get into 'sterics agen, 'Tilda, my dear, but just look at that—what do you call it ?" and he pulled a Neapolitan coin from his pocket.

"Why, I think they call that a grano," she replied. "But why do you ask me ?"

"Now, just tell me, 'Tilda, how many of these 'ere paltry things do it take to make one English shilling ?"

"I don't know," replied Matilda ; "ever so many—there's no counting them."

"And there's no counting how many pretty Italian girls it takes to make up the sum of beauty in your own lovely self, my ducksy 'Tilda," returned the gallant Joe.

There was a smack—two smacks, one a little louder than the other.

"For shame, Joe."

Joe put on his hat, and took up his stick.

"I tell you, my dear," he said, "that for beauty, you beat the best on 'em a hundred to one. So now, I'll bid you good-night, and I hope as you'll dream about me."

"Where are you going, Joseph ?"

"I shall just take a turn in at the wine shop, and crack a bottle with some of the English couriers and walets; though, Lor' knows, I'd sooner be enjoying myself at the ' Pig and Whistle' over a long clay, and a pot of heavy wet."

Matilda held up her hands in righteous indignation, while Joe, with a laugh, put on his hat, and snatched up his walking-cane.

"Be careful, Joe, that you don't run against any of those daring brigands," cried Matilda.

"Brigands," said Joe; "I should like to see the Italian brigand that would stand up before Joe Moody's English fists."

And Joe hurried from the room.

Matilda reseated herself by the window.

The moon was shining brightly, rendering every object in the small garden distinctly visible.

Just opposite to the window at which Matilda was sitting, there was a little shed in which the gardener kept his tools, and against it there leant a long ladder, used in pruning the orange trees, or gathering the fruit; a little further on a fountain flung its diamond spray into the air.

"Was there ever anything so lovely ?" murmured Matilda. " It reminds me of the balcony-scene in Romeo and Juliet—but, ah, me ! where is the Romeo ?"

As the words passed her lips, her ear caught the sound of an approaching footstep.

"Gracious goodness !" exclaimed Matilda, "it's a man."

She beat a hasty retreat from the window, and crossing the room, laid hold of the handle of the door.

Her steps were arrested when she heard the twang of a guitar.

" Oh, Hevins," she exclaimed, " there's someone going to serenade me. How delicious. Whoever can it be ?"

She crept back to the window, and concealing herself behind the curtain, peeped cautiously out.

" Be still, my palpitating buzzom," she muttered. " Bless my life, if it is not the count's gentleman, Signor Generoso."

Then a loud, rough voice commenced singing about as melodiously as an average night raven.

Generoso, however great his other accomplishments, was not born under a rhyming star, so being unable to improvise verse from his own pure brain, he contented himself with singing a homely ditty, primitive in its style and expression, but a great favourite among the common people.

This is a literal translation—

> " Thou art good, thou art fair,
>   Thou art loving and free,
>   Thou seemest a bride,
>   I am dying for thee.
>
> A beauty so rare
>   Ne'er saw I till now ;
> Or a woman so dear,
>   Or so lovely as thou."

Of course, this amorous ditty being couched in choice Italian, the romantic Matilda did not understand a single word of it, but she was none the less, perhaps all the more, enraptured.

"Divine," she murmured ; " oh, that I could speak the charming language. Shall I—shall I give the poor fellow one word, one smile of encouragement ? It were heartless to refuse."

She returned to the window in a flutter of joyous excitement.

Upon seeing her, he showed his snowy teeth, laid his hand upon his heart, and blew kisses from the tips of his fingers.

"Ah, *signorina, carissima, inamorata,*" he murmured, sweetly. "Ah, so lovelier, meese. Peak at *povero* Generoso ; he for she die for love."

"Alas, poor creetur," sighed Matilda, "can you bestow your affections upon a poor, simple maiden such as I am ? Oh, Romeo, Romeo ! wherefore art thou Romeo ?"

"Ah, ah ! Romeo, *buonissimo.* Me Romeo am no toder—Romeo only, *divina* Julietta," returned Generoso, quite astonished at his own eloquence and proficiency in the English tongue. " I Romeo, she ze *divina* Julietta ; read dere, *anima mia.* All come from ze *cuore,* ze—ze inside of me."

And he thumped his breast.

"Read ; me play *la musica,* so long Meese Matilda read."

With that, he tossed a bouquet of flowers up to the window.

Matilda caught it up in breathless trepidation, and found inserted among the flowers a dainty little note.

With trembling fingers she eagerly broke the seal.

She read as follows—

"To Miladi Matilda Sparxa."

"My lady," gasped Matilda ; "he takes me for a lady of title. But I always had such an air of distinction. I have often been told so."

Then she continued reading—

"Matilda, one adored, your servant of love to thou dies all the time. Little children no more like *confetti* and sweetness-stuff, more so as Generoso wish at kissing thy lips made of honey. No stop, but fly with Generoso, marry Generoso to the church. Most affectionate husband *amoroso* he some time be. Fly always—run away, bella Matilda. *Addio, mille* —tousands kiss."

"Beautiful," sighed Matilda, "most beautiful. This is the nat'ral and unaffected pathos of feeling ; and considering he's Hitalian, so well worded. Poor fellow."

Meanwhile, Generoso was strumming away at his guitar like mad, and making night hideous with his screech-owl serenade.

"Gracious goodness." exclaimed Matilda, "but I must not let him make such a desperate noise—I should say, harmonious discord. We may be discovered, betrayed, and all will be lost."

She went back to the window, and made a sign to him to leave off playing and shouting.

Immediately Generoso threw down his mandoline.

Then he ran and fetched the ladder before mentioned, and adjusted it to the window.

He mounted the ladder.

Matilda gave a slight shriek.

With a loud oath, a man sprang over the wall, and seized the guitar, which Generoso had left in the gravel path. Crash !

"RALPH DREW HIS SWORD AND GAVE CHASE."

The mandoline descended on the devoted head of poor Generoso.

The luckless Italian uttered a yell of pain and fury, and stumbling backwards, rolled down to the foot of the ladder.

It was Joe Moody who had committed the sudden and unlooked-for assault upon the gallant serenader.

On his way to the wine shop, he had to pass under the garden wall, and while doing so, he caught the twang of the mandoline.

"Take that, Signor Generoso," growled Joe, brandishing the splintered instrument over the prostrate musician ; "you smirking blackguard, get up, and stand before Joe Moody, and mind your nose."

Generoso rolled over on the gravel path, and then springing to his feet, uttered a savage oath, and whipped out the stiletto which he kept concealed under his coat.

"I will have your life, English dog !" roared the Italian.

Generoso made a dash at Joe.

But Joe was too quick for him.

Whirling round the mandoline, he struck the knife from Generoso's hand.

The Italian stood bewildered.

Deprived of his weapon, he knew not what to do.

"Now, then, you vagabond !" shouted Joe, sparring with his fists, and throwing himself into a fighting attitude. "Come on, and see what Joe Moody from England will give you."

But Generoso, though a daring brigand, did not understand this kind of warfare.

He stood irresolute, putting up his fists in an awkward manner, and retreating step by step.

Joe waited a moment or two, with the chivalrous intention of allowing his adversary to plant the first blow.

Generoso, however, contented himself by raising first one elbow and then another, as if to ward off an attack, during which movements his fierce black eyes roved restlessly round in search of the stiletto.

Seeing this, Joe made no more ado, but let drive at him with such energy and effect that the Italian was driven back under such a shower of well-directed blows ; at last he lost his footing, and stumbling over the marble edge of the basin of the fountain, fell souse into the water.

Meanwhile, Matilda had raised the house by her frantic screams.

Joe dragged the half-drowned Italian and shook him till the moisture flew about in spray, as from a trundled mop.

Then flinging him off, he stood with clenched fists, glaring upon him.

"Why, you darned, smirking, 'sinwatin, catgut-strumming, maccaroni-eating, barber's monkey, get up, and show fight like a man !" roared Joe. "Do you s'pose that you can come here with your inveigling ways to captivate my Matilda, and as I'm a-going to take it easy ? I defy you, you Judas's chariot ! Come on."

The Italian now stamped and foamed with passion, and flinging himself upon the Englishman, began clawing, biting, and kicking, until at last Joe got his head into chancery, and then the brigand received from Joe's fists something that he never forgot.

Of course, all this disturbance had thoroughly alarmed the inmates of the hotel, who came running out with lights and such weapons as came readiest to hand to quell the tumult.

With shouts, curses, screams, and gesticulations, the servants flung themselves upon the infuriated combatants, and dragged them asunder.

As for Matilda, the cause of all this disturbance, she had fainted in the arms of the corpulent man-cook, who looked dreadfully scared and puzzled as to what to do with his fair burden.

When the clamour was at its height, a peacemaker appeared upon the scene.

It was no other than Violet Melville, who, attended by two tall lackeys, who bore stout cudgels in one hand, and lanterns in the other, now entered the garden.

Upon seeing the ludicrous figure cut by the half-drowned Generoso, and the fighting attitude of Joe Moody, whom the others could hardly restrain, Violet could scarcely refrain from laughing.

However, she soon composed her countenance.

"What is the meaning of this disgraceful scene?" she asked. "What, you, Joseph? What have you been doing to this poor man ?"

"Miss Violet, what business has he to come here with his caterwauling, a-trying to delude the hearts of respectable English females ?" returned Joe, bridling up. "Such a outlander as is wery little better than a Red Injun."

"*Eccelenza*, no hear dis John Boule ; ros bif !" replied Generoso. "He von *porco*, what you call pig brutal. I make *la musica* for Miladi Matilda, he gib me grand *colpo*, one knock wid mandolina ; me lose stiletto or else kill him, *ma la vendetta*. Ze vengeance, wait some no time ; ze vengeance !"

And drawing his finger across his throat, to indicate what he would do to Joe, on the first favourable opportunity, he scowled like a demon and hurried off.

"If that feller's not a brigand, may I die in my shoes ; here, come back and have it out !" shouted Joe, shaking his fist at the retreating figure.

"For shame, Joseph," cried Violet.

Then turning to the maid servant, to whom the cook had resigned the insensible Matilda, she said—

"Carry the poor silly girl into the house."

With that she left the garden, accompanied by the servants.

"We shall be murdered in our beds by such assassinators, unless we keep our eyes open," growled Joe, as he sullenly moved off. "But I think I've given the vagabond one lesson in the use of the English fives."

CHAPTER XVI.

THE Count Di Ancona, accompanied by Ralph Wildhawk, sallied forth just after sunset, and they made their way towards the Casino De Toledo, the gambling house which Ralph knew to be the favourite resort of Edmund Mortimer.

The count still looked pale and haggard, and carried his arm in a sling.

"I had the pleasure, this afternoon, of catching a casual glance of a very lovely lady as she was getting into her carriage," said Ralph.

"Indeed!" replied the count. "Do you know her by name?"

"Yes, she had been visiting Mistress Violet Melville," returned Ralph, "who informed me that her visitor was no other than the famous beauty, Lucia Di Carrara."

The count paused in his walk and gave his companion a half-startled look.

"The countess in Naples," he exclaimed, in a tone of surprise.

"Are you acquainted with her?" asked the young Englishman, steadily returning his glance.

"But slightly," returned the count.

While they were thus talking, they passed beneath the shadow of one of the numerous churches that adorn the city.

All at once Ralph felt a snatch at his watch-chain.

Instantly the dark figure of a man darted out from the black shadow of the church and crossed the road in the full flood of the moonlight.

"I am robbed by that man, but he shall not escape me," exclaimed Ralph.

Then he drew his sword and prepared to give chase to the thief.

But the count interposed.

"Hold," he said. "Do not follow him; he will lead you into some of the purlieus of this dangerous quarter, where you may be beset by his confederates and perhaps murdered. Such things have been done before now."

Then to Ralph's astonishment the count rushed away at the top of his speed in pursuit of the robber.

"And he will endanger himself for my sake, but it is so like him," muttered Ralph; "but this must not be."

With hastening pace he followed the count.

The count stopped in the middle of the road and uttered a peculiar cry.

At the sound the thief halted abruptly, and turned his head.

The count beckoned to him to come back.

The fellow had drawn his stiletto, but at the signal he instantly replaced it in his belt and sullenly returned.

He looked at the count with an air of curiosity.

"Companions," he said, rubbing his right thumb on the palm of his hand.

"Aye, companions, you dog," growled the count, in a tone of piercing sternness. "What do you mean by robbing my friends, and that, too, in my company?"

The man looked frightened and confused.

"Pardon, signore," he replied, bowing with the profoundest respect, "I did not know you, it was so dark in the shadow yonder. Pardon my mistake."

"Give back your plunder," replied the count.

The man, who, though a bold-looking fellow, appeared to be all in a tremble, instantly returned the watch to the count.

The count handed it to the astonished young Englishman.

Then frowning fiercely at the thief, the count waved his hand.

"*Via scampa!* be off," he said, "and beware, you rogue, to be more careful for the future."

Apparently only too glad to be released, the man instantly took to his heels, and was out of sight in the twinkling of an eye.

The count laughed heartily.

"You see, I understand these scoundrels," he said, turning to Ralph. "You see how obedient they are to a word or look."

"It is wonderful," returned Ralph. "But whence do you derive this mysterious influence over such lawless vagabonds?"

"Mysterious," repeated the count, still laughing; "I can easily explain the mystery. I know all their signs and passwords."

"And pray, where did you obtain knowledge which it appears you can put to such useful account?" replied Ralph.

"Oh, I am one of the initiated," replied the count.

He paused beneath a lamp, and turning up the cuff of his sleeve, showed a peculiar hieroglyphic mark, tattooed upon his arm a little above the wrist.

"Look at that," he said.

"What does it mean?" asked Ralph.

"It means," replied the count, smiling grimly, "that I belong to the right honourable and most ancient order of beggars and brigands."

"And by whom were you invested with such a high order of merit?" asked Ralph, feeling a little uncomfortable.

"This talismanic symbol was imprinted upon my arm at the command of his majesty, Isaco Il Nero," replied the count. "He who bears it can walk through the lowest slums of this den of thieves with impunity."

"You amaze me," said Ralph.

"But you have promised to introduce me to your royal friend and patron, the king of the gipsies," rejoined Ralph.

"Yes, and what is even better, to the beauteous princess, his sister Zara," returned the count.

"Meanwhile, let me give you a bit of advice, O disciple," continued the count, in the same easy strain.

"From the moment he lands here, till he quits the place, a foreign traveller should always carry his handkerchief in his hat, his purse in his breast pocket, and his watch well secured with a strong guard; for the pickpockets of Naples are the most expert in Europe."

Ralph laughed.

"I shall not forget to take your hint, monsignor," he replied, "but here we are at the casino."

The gambling-house, a very handsome structure, stood in the middle of the Via De Toledo.

"How I hate these places," muttered Ralph; "they are the devil's traps to catch the thoughtless and unwary. I feel it my duty to wile Edmund away from the brink of the dread precipice on which he stands."

They entered.

The count gazed about with an easy assurance, and smiled benignantly, every now and

then lifting his hat to some of the most distinguished-looking persons in the crowd.

It appeared somewhat strange to Ralph that the people thus saluted did not return the compliment.

Ralph, being of a free, out-spoken temperament, was about to make some remark upon this curious circumstance, when his attention was suddenly attracted to a tall, slim, handsome young fellow who stood leaning against a pillar, his hands thrust deep into his pockets, and his eyes gloomily fixed upon the ground.

"There is Edmund," muttered Ralph to himself, "and to judge by the expression of his face, I doubt not that he has lost heavily."

"Go and speak with him," said the count, "but if you please, excuse me just for five minutes. Yonder I see my old friend, the Prince Colonna; I will shake hands with him and return to you upon the instant."

With that he smiled and bowed, and strode away.

Ralph looked after him in some anxiety and soon descried him deep in conversation with an elderly man, very showily dressed.

Thus left to his own resources, Ralph felt a little vexed and angry.

He walked up to Edmund and touched him on the arm.

The young gentleman started irritably, and glanced at Ralph with a half-savage glare.

"What, you here!" he exclaimed with an ill-natured sneer; "you are about the last person I should have expected to meet in such a place as this."

"But I am not here to play," replied Ralph, mildly.

"How then?" was the sharp response. "As a spy, I suppose—a spy upon my actions?"

Ralph's cheek flushed crimson.

"I am here in company with my friend the Count Di Ancona," he replied quietly.

"The count! pshaw!" was the contemptuous reply.

This was too much for Ralph.

"The count——" he began.

"Is a man of the world, which you are not, Master Ralph," rejoined Edmund, with a provoking air of superiority. "Now, look here, you say you come to the casino as a spectator, and not to gamble; is that so?"

"I have told you," replied Ralph, coldly.

"All the better for you," growled Edmund, sulkily, turning upon his heel.

"Stay a moment," returned Ralph, laying his hand upon his arm, "you are out of spirits; have you had bad luck?"

"Bad luck!" returned Edmund with a bitter laugh. "The devil's own run of ill-luck; why, I have lost—but what matters it to you how much I have lost? But if I had but a few loose guineas to set upon my cast, I am sure my luck would turn, and I should be sure to redeem my losses."

"Say you so?" said a voice close by his ear. "The prince is ready to give you your revenge."

It was the count who spoke.

With noiseless step he had crept up to them.

Young Edmund's eyes sparkled and his cheek burnt.

The count placed a purse in his hand.

"Here are a hundred ducats," he said; "I never bring more lest I should be tempted to play high."

"But the prince just now refused to play with me any longer," replied Edmund; "he declares that it goes against the grain to take advantage of such ill-luck as mine has been this night."

The count laughed heartily.

"The prince has become mighty conscientious all at once."

Then tapping the young English gentleman on the shoulder, he added dryly—

"Depend upon it, *amico*, he knows that you have come to that turning point when luck must change, and he dares not give you your revenge."

Then taking both Edmund and Ralph by the arm, he led them towards the gaming-saloon.

"*Andiamo*, let us go," said he; "let us play high. Believe me, fortune favours the bold."

So saying, he led them into the splendid apartment where such vast sums of money were lost and won.

There were many women of rank and wealth present, who seemed to be playing with more desperate ardour than the men.

Players alone were allowed to be seated.

Near the end of the table the Prince Viconti stood looking on with sparkling eyes and folded arms.

The count came to the side of the prince, and whispered in his ear—

"Companions."

The prince started and turned round.

The count whispered something in his ear, whereupon he left the table.

After the pair had conversed together for a few moments, the count returned to Edmund Mortimer.

"My dear young friend," said he, "I have arranged your little affair with the prince, who expresses his readiness to play with you again."

As he spoke, he placed a well-filled purse in Edmund's hands.

"Take what you want," said he; "but having recouped yourself for your losses, do not play any more, at least, not to-night."

Edmund cordially thanked the count for his kindness, and eagerly promised to abide by his advice.

The infatuated young gamester recommenced playing with increased ardour and excitement.

As the count had predicted, Edmund's luck changed, and it mattered not whether he put his money down on the black or red, he was sure to win.

At last, with a chuckle of triumph, he swept a pile of gold, silver, and bank notes into his hat.

"Ah, monsignore, you are indeed my benefactor," he said, turning to the count. "You see I am already in possession of sufficient funds to repay your loan."

"*Assai*, enough," rejoined the count. "Fortune is but a fickle jade; tempt her no farther, It is time to leave off playing."

Edmund looked vexed and disappointed.

"What will the prince think of me ?" he asked.

"I shall think that you act very sensibly by taking the count's advice." rejoined the prince. "We shall meet again on some other occasion, when, since I am the loser, I can take my revenge."

Casting a long, lingering look at the table, Edmund bowed to the prince, wished him a good evening, and suffered himself to be led away.

Upon his departure, the count took Ralph's arm, saying—

"By the way, I have a startling bit of news for you. Edmund Mortimer has discovered our gipsy princess."

Ralph started.

"Zara !" he exclaimed.

"Zara. I am given to understand that the foolish young man has presented her with a pair of emerald bracelets that cost a thousand English guineas."

"And did she accept them ?"

"Did you ever know a woman, especially one of her race, who could refuse a present of jewellery ?" laughed the count.

"I am sorry to hear it," rejoined Ralph.

"Think what you please," returned the count. "But be sure of one thing, Zara dares not offend her royal brother by refusing a costly gift, come from whence it will."

The count then stepped up to Edmund, shook hands with him, and took his leave of them both.

Upon reaching the hotel, they found Joe Moody standing in the hall.

He held in his hand a red morocco case, which he was contemplating with a puzzled expression of countenance.

"Well, sirrah, what have you there ?" asked Edmund, brusquely.

"Something for you, Master Edmund," replied the servant, with a stiff bow.

"For me ! What is it ?"

"A queer affair altogether," replied the man, bluntly. "About half an hour ago, a strange, wild-looking fellow, as dark as a mulatto, called at the hotel. I thought he came with an eye to the forks and spoons, and had half a mind to kick him out. He asked for the young milordo. I told him your honour was from home. 'When your master returns, said he, 'give him that and tell him that the next gift he may be fool enough to send to the same quarter, will be brought back with less ceremony,' and making me a low bow, behold ye, he stalked off with the air of a prince."

Edmund's cheek flushed crimson.

He took the case from Joe.

He touched a hidden spring and the lid flew open.

A pair of bracelets were disclosed, sparkling with jewels.

"The devil," gasped Edmund, biting his lip. "The proud little minx has sent me back my present. Well—well, by-and-bye I shall find some means of——"

Then breaking off abruptly, he turned to Joe.

"What sort of man was he, do you say, that brought this ?"

"A swarthy fellow, with a eye as wild as a hawk's, and long ringlets like a woman's ; I

should take him for a gipsy, or some sich vagabond."

"It must have been Isaco Il Nero," muttered Edmund ; "I will make him pay for his insolence."

And thrusting the case in his pocket, he mounted the stairs.

Joe Moody looked after him with a grim smile.

There was a throb of exultation in Ralph's heart.

"I am glad, I am very glad that the beautiful girl named Zara has acted with so much propriety," he soliloquised. "No good could have come to her from friendship with Edmund, of that I feel sure. My friend the count formed an unjust estimate of her character, and I am glad to find him wrong for once in his life."

CHAPTER XVII.

AFTER leaving the two young Englishmen, the Italian count walked off in the direction of the Villa Reale.

He had not proceeded far before he encountered a tall, handsome cavalier, enveloped in the ample folds of a long black cloak.

This person stopped directly in the count's path and eyed him curiously.

"Body of Bacchus !" he exclaimed with a ringing laugh, "how very fortunate."

The count started back, and instinctively clutched the hilt of his rapier.

"What an admirable disguise," cried the man, who accosted him. "Yet it is not sufficient to deceive me. I know that I have the honour of addressing the illustrious Marco Bravo."

And once more he laughed loudly and merrily.

A sickly pallor overspread the brigand's face, and he cast a startled—a guilty look around him.

"The Count Beltrani !" he ejaculated, then he went on in a low, hurried voice—" prudence, monsignore ; do not speak my name aloud in such a public place—a jest to you may be death to me."

The count looked highly amused.

"I know—I know," he said, nodding his head assentingly, "I will be more discreet ; and now vouchsafe me your attention, signor—what must I call you ?"

The brigand smiled grimly.

"I am for the present the Count Di Ancona, but ever your excellency's most humble servant."

Again his interrogator laughed most immoderately.

"Excellent," he cried, clapping his hands ; "you are a great man, signor capitano, but how comes it that even you, with all your daring, can venture on such a bold impersonation ?"

"The count is my prisoner."

"Then you must cut his throat," was the cool reply. "For I lost a heavy stake to him, and owe him more money than I care to remember."

"SHOT THROUGH THE HEART, THE POOR SOLDIER REELED AND FELL."

Marco Bravo laughed.

"I think your excellency would prefer paying your own debt than his ransom."

"What, you brigand, I suppose you mean to ask something tremendous?" rejoined the young noble in the same light and mirthful strain.

"Fifty thousand piastres," was the cool reply.

"Ye gods! what a rapacious scoundrel!" exclaimed Count Beltrani. "Fifty thousand piastres! 'Tis the ransom for a king. But come, you rogue, you don't really mean to say that you expect to be paid such an exorbitant sum as that."

"It all depends upon whether the prisoner considers his life worth the price."

"But if his friends refuse to send the money—what then?"

"It will be the worse for the count, that's all," returned the brigand. "Unless within three months the ransom be paid to the last *grano*, I shall send the count's head as a keepsake to his friends."

"Friend Marco, it seems to me you are a most atrocious scoundrel," retorted the young noble; "but for all that, I have always found you a very serviceable fellow, and I am about to entrust you with a commission of more than ordinary delicacy. I cannot tell you how pleased I am to have met you so opportunely, for I require your immediate services—come this way."

And stepping out in front, he walked rapidly onwards. The brigand followed him.

The fact was the robber held the young count in profound respect.

He had always found in him a liberal paymaster and a faithful protector.

Beltrani had frequently employed the robber chief and his gang in affairs—to say the least, of a rather questionable nature, and as yet they had worked in great harmony together.

The Count Beltrani paced on till they reached the church of St. Paolo, and followed by Marco Bravo, entered its beautiful cloister.

Pausing here, the count took a miniature from his neck, and showed it to Marco Bravo.

"Do you recognise this portrait?" he asked.

A slight tremor ran through the brigand's nerves, and he changed colour.

"Certainly," he replied, with as much composure as he could command; "it is a likeness of the beautiful Lucia Di Carrara."

"Very good, I am glad you know the lady; you will find your task the easier," rejoined the count. "I love the beautiful Carrara, but women are capricious and she does not favour my suit, nor do I stand high in favour with her relatives."

"You have a rival, perhaps?"

"You have guessed rightly," answered the count. "Lucia has formed a romantic attachment for one Captain Lanfranco, a beggarly officer of dragoons far beneath herself in birth and station."

"You wish him to be removed."

"Thank you, I can take care of him," replied Beltrani, tapping the hilt of his sword, "but I am determined to get the lady into my power, and force her into a marriage."

"How can I assist your excellency in the matter?"

"You must carry her off."

The brigand nodded.

"I will do my best," he answered. "But you must tell me in what manner I am to proceed."

"Let me see," he said, touching his forehead reflectively, "it must be done three days hence. Of course it must not appear that I had any hand in the business."

"I understand that, your excellency," returned the brigand.

"The countess will leave Naples for her villa at Sorrento, on the seventeenth day of the month—now this is the fourteenth, so you will have ample time to make your preparations."

"Then I suppose I and my band are to stop her carriage, and carry her off by force of arms?"

"Just so," replied the count. "But mind, there must be no disguise; you and your troop must be dressed in your brigand costume, and it must be given out that she has been robbed and plundered by the banditti."

"And whither are we to take her?"

"To your fastness in the Brigands' Glen," answered the count. "There you must treat her with all gentleness and respect, but hold her in safe keeping until I send you further orders."

"Of course she will not travel without an escort."

"No, but as the roads between Naples and Sorrento are open and considered safe, her escort will consist of only fourteen dragoons, besides her servants and postillions," answered the Count Beltrani. "Will you undertake this enterprise?"

Marco Bravo replied—without hesitation—

"I will."

"You are a fine fellow," replied the count, slapping him on the shoulder, "and now as to the terms?"

"It is a difficult business," returned Marco Bravo. "I cannot ask less than three thousand piastres, and as the dragoons will no doubt offer a desperate resistance, I must have five hundred piastres for each of my men that may be slain in the engagement, and fifty apiece for those who are wounded."

"Re—— friend Marco, you have no conscience," rejoined the count, "but as a lady is in the case, we will not chaffer about money matters. Only do your work in a prompt, masterly style."

"You shall have no cause to complain, I warrant you," answered Marco Bravo.

"Then it is a bargain," rejoined the count. "Your hand upon it."

The two scoundrels shook hands in the most cordial manner, and parted.

Marco Bravo hastened home, to find Generoso with his face bound up.

Marco stared at him in astonishment, and asked what was the matter.

Generoso, in doleful tones and with many a bitter oath, related the misadventures that had befallen him on the occasion of his first attempt at winning the heart of Matilda Sparkes, the pretty maid of Violet Melville.

When he went on to tell how the mad Englishman, as he styled Joe Moody, had broken the guitar over his head, and had afterwards "boxed" him, the brigand chief burst into shouts of laughter.

Not pleased at finding his sorrowful tale met with so little sympathy, Generoso became frightfully enraged, and swore the direst vengeance against Joe, swearing he would stab him the first time he crossed his path.

But Marco Bravo frowned, and shook his head.

"You must pocket your wrongs, for the present, at least, my good Generoso," said he. "Your enemy will soon be our prisoner, and you may then do what you like with him."

He then proceeded to give his confederate an account of his chance meeting with his patron, the Count Beltrani, and the result of their interview.

Generoso listened with sparkling eyes, and rubbed his hands at the prospect of doing a good stroke of business.

"We have stayed too long here," said Marco Bravo. "Courage is one thing, mere rashness another. If it had not been for this cursed wound, all would have been accomplished. Well, for a day or two, I must get back to the mountains, then I will return, and work out my plans with regard to the young Ralph Wildhawk and La Zara.

"But that reminds me, the term of Captain Lanfranco's leave of absence will be up to-morrow, and inquiries will be set afoot in regard to his delay in reporting himself; that must be looked to. Report himself; no, that he never will do again, unless his ghost walks from his deep grave."

And the brigand smiled grimly, as he thought of the dead young captain of dragoons.

CHAPTER XVIII.

A CARRIAGE drawn by four horses, with two mounted postillions, was stationed at the door of the villa in which dwelt the lovely Countess of Carrara.

The escort of dragoons had not yet arrived.

The countess sat at an open window that overlooked the courtyard.

She was dressed in travelling costume.

Her maid, a very pretty girl with fine dark eyes and luxuriant black hair, entered the room.

"Bianca," said the countess, turning quickly towards her, "I thought I heard the sound of horses' feet, and the jingle of arms. The escort, is it come?"

"Signora, the dragoons are approaching," replied the girl. "I saw them from an upper window, galloping along the Marina."

Lucia blushed.

After a moment's hesitation, she asked, somewhat hurriedly—

"Bianca, do you know who is in command?"

"Yes, signora," she replied; "they tell me that a young lieutenant named Bassano has taken the place of Captain Lanfranco."

"Why so?" returned Lucia, looking mortified.

"I understand, signora," replied the girl, "that Captain Lanfranco has outstayed his leave of absence, and that his comrades are becoming rather uneasy about him."

Then seeing the deadly pallor that overspread the face of her young mistress, Bianca was frightened, and rushed to her side.

"Pardon, signora, I have distressed you," she said; "I ought not to have told you this idle story. It is but three days since Captain Lanfranco's leave expired, and a thousand things may have happened to prevent his return."

Lucia sighed deeply, and pressed her hand to her bosom.

"I wish the journey was over, and that we were safely arrived at Sorrento."

"Courage, signora," replied Bianca; "the road is a pleasant one, and with such a strong escort of soldiers we stand in no danger of being attacked by the brigands."

"No, that is true," replied Lucia. "By the way, the brigands have been very quiet lately; we have not heard of any more exploits of that terrible Marco Bravo."

"It is reported, signora, that the brigand chief, having gained an immense fortune by plunder, has thrown up his command, and has left the country."

"Let us hope the report is not too good to be true," answered her mistress. "But, hark! the soldiers are come, and we must be ready for the start."

The stirring blast of a bugle, and the trampling of horses' feet was now heard in the courtyard below.

A few moments later the countess, with her maid, got into one carriage, while the retinue filled another.

Lieutenant Bassano and his men saluted, the cavalcade got into marching order, and moved off.

The road from Castelamare to Sorrento is one of the finest drives in the kingdom.

About two hours after the Countess Di Carrara with her train had set out from Naples, a party of well-armed men might have been seen descending this mountain path.

They numbered forty besides their leader, and were without exception fine, handsome, athletic fellows.

They were, in fact, the flower of Marco Bravo's band, whom he had selected for this daring and important expedition.

They wore a kind of uniform or costume, which was very rich and picturesque.

Marco Bravo was distinguished from the rest as well by his splendour of attire as by his bold, commanding demeanour.

When they had reached an opening in the rocks which hemmed in the narrow mountain path, Marco Bravo called a halt.

The best trained soldiers could not have obeyed the order with more promptitude and dexterity.

The whole troop stopped as one man.

The place where they were standing commanded a most magnificent prospect of the Bay of Naples, and a remarkably fine view of Mount Vesuvius.

Below them ran the white road we have described.

Marco Bravo leaned upon his carbine, and gazed eagerly along this causeway.

Then he turned.

"Where is Generoso?" he asked.

"Here, captain." replied Generoso, stepping out from the ranks.

"And Stromba."

"Here, captain."

The burly, ferocious-looking ruffian thus summoned came lumbering to the captain's side.

"Now listen to your orders," said the brigand chief.

The men touched their hats, and stood silent and attentive.

"The carriage will pass in less than an hour's time," said Marco Bravo. "We must get ready for action. You, Generoso, with a dozen men, will place yourself on the other side of the road, taking care to keep well under cover of the rocks and bushes. Stromba, with twelve men, will post himself in the rear so as to cut off their retreat, while I and the rest will approach from the front."

Having issued these commands, the brigand chief took care to make sure of their being properly carried out.

The several sections of the band went their separate ways.

Marco Bravo then clambered to the top of a mass of rock, from which point he could see for a considerable distance.

In a few moments the brigands had concealed themselves so effectually that not a vestige of them could anywhere be seen.

Marco then turned to his own detachment.

He made a gesture to them to follow him, and strode off through a beautifully-wooded ravine that led down to the road about a quarter of a mile nearer to Sorrento.

Marco Bravo turned and addressed Pepe, who walked close behind him.

This rascal will be remembered as the traitor servant who had assisted at the escape of the young brigand Giovanni Pizano from the inn at Terracina.

"We shall not have much trouble in this affair," said the brigand chief, "for the Count Beltrani has given a hint to some of his creatures among the men of the brigade to show but slight resistance, and then to take to flight."

"And who commands the soldiers, signor capitano?" asked Pepe.

"A lieutenant named Bassano, in the place of Captain Lanfranco, who has mysteriously disappeared," was the reply.

"And is this officer in the plot?" asked Pepe.

"No," replied Marco. "He is quite ignorant of what is to take place, and I make no doubt will fight bravely," adding, with inconceivable coolness—"You are a good shot, Pepe; the best in all the band."

The fellow grinned with gratified vanity at a compliment coming from such a high quarter.

"I understand you, signore," he replied. "I will take care and not miss my mark."

"Good." replied Marco Bravo, "and now let us conceal ourselves. Giovanni." he went on, speaking to the young brigand who had escaped from the inn, "post yourself on yonder rock, and give us a call when the right moment comes."

The youth hurried off to obey the order, while the rest hid themselves among the bushes and rocks, and kept the most perfect order and quietness.

In suspense and excitement, they lay flat on their faces listening for Giovanni's signal.

Half an hour passed away in this manner, when from the distance was heard the swift clattering of horses' hoofs, accompanied by the rumbling of carriage wheels.

"They are coming," whispered Marco Bravo; "look to your arms and be ready, comrades."

There was a gruff murmur of assent.

It was followed by an ominous click-clicking as the men cocked their muskets.

"Pepe," continued the brigand chief, "do you creep forward and take your position amongst yonder bushes; you know what to do."

"Yes, signore," replied the other, and he silently moved away with his musket ready for use.

He had not been gone an instant before Giovanni gave a peculiar cry, exactly like the scream of an eagle.

"Now is the time, men," said Marco Bravo, in a low tone. "Follow me."

He emerged from the bushes and walked straight into the middle of the road, his men crowding after him.

He led the way down the road to meet the carriage, which was surrounded by a troop of dragoons in gay uniforms and splendidly mounted, their weapons glancing in the sunshine as they came dashing towards them.

The brigands drew themselves up in the centre of the road, Marco Bravo boldly taking his place in front of them.

"Aim at the horses," said the brigand chief, "and when they fall, rush in and do the rest with your clubbed muskets and stilettoes."

He then stepped forward and levelled his gun at the soldier who rode foremost in the cavalcade.

"Halt!" he shouted, in a stern, commanding voice that would have become a general on the field. "Halt, I say; or advance at your peril."

The soldier in advance was for a moment so struck with astonishment, that he pulled up his horse.

So sudden and unexpected was the act, that the whole train was thrown into confusion, but the brave fellow at once recovered his presence of mind.

A single glance sufficed to assure him of the character of the men he had to deal with.

Uttering a bitter oath, he unslung his carbine from the saddle-bow, and fired point blank.

The bullet passed through the crown of the brigand's hat, knocking it off his head.

Without a second's hesitation Marco Bravo returned the fire.

Shot through the heart, the poor soldier reeled in the saddle and dropped heavily to the ground.

The high-mettled charger, relieved of his load, and snorting with rage and fear, came rushing down like a thunderbolt upon the little group of brigands.

They opened their ranks to let him pass,

and with head erect, dilated nostrils, and streaming mane, he dashed through their midst with the sweeping speed of the whirlwind.

Screams from the female servants in the second carriage were now heard soaring shrilly above the deep-toned curses of the troopers.

Though for a moment checked and thrown into disorder, the dragoons rallied.

The lieutenant came galloping to the front.

"What does this mean?" he shouted, fiercely. "Who has the audacity to impede our march?"

"One who commands the road," answered the brigand chief, laughing.

"And who are you?" demanded the lieutenant.

"Marco Bravo."

"You daring scoundrel," retorted the lieutenant, "you have gone a step too far; your life shall pay for your villany."

And drawing a horse-pistol from his holster, he took aim at the brigand, but before he had time to draw the trigger, a sharp report resounded from a bush on the rocky bank to the left, followed by a puff of white smoke.

The lieutenant uttered a groan of mortal agony, and fell over his horse's head, crashing to the ground—a dead man.

The horse would have darted away, but one of the soldiers caught it by the rein.

"Bravo, Pepe! good shot," chuckled the heartless brigand chief. "Now, comrades," he went on, turning to his men. "Now do as I told you; present, fire!"

At the word, the robbers blazed away, killing and wounding the horses, and then rushing in, attacked the disabled troopers with blind fury.

Clubbing their muskets, they beat them down, then drawing their stilettoes, stabbed them.

While this was going on in the front, shots and shouts were heard from the rear, while the brigands in ambush on either side of the road opened a murderous fire.

Then Marco Bravo and his immediate followers rushed in, and a hand-to-hand encounter ensued.

Though one of the robbers was killed and several others wounded, Marco Bravo's band soon gained the mastery.

The struggle was short, but terribly sharp while it lasted, but several of the dragoons, with a promptitude which was, to say the least, suspicious, turned their horses' heads in the direction of Castelamare, and dashed off in full retreat, the brigands doing little to stop their flight.

Marco Bravo now stepped up to the side of the carriage, removed his hat, and bowed with the grace of a veteran courtier.

Though terribly alarmed, and white as marble, the brave young countess maintained perfect composure.

"If your purpose is to rob us, Marco Bravo," she said, coldly, "deserted by our faithless and cowardly escort, we have no power to resist your will, but if one spark of manly feeling lingers in your breast, deal gently with my poor, frightened servants. Trust me that you will gain more by moderation than violence."

"Eccelenza, do not give yourself one mo-ment's uneasiness," replied Marco Bravo. "My purpose is neither plunder nor violence. Give your servants to understand that nothing more is required of them than to follow my directions, and all will be well."

Lucia glanced rather contemptuously at the pack of women who rode in the next carriage.

Bianca, who was by her side, though trembling violently, was almost as calm and collected as herself, but the others were screaming, fainting, or wringing their hands, and calling frantically for aid on all the saints in the calendar.

The conduct of the men was even worse.

Several of the lackeys lay crouched together under the carriage, or the bellies of the horses, while the postillions had dismounted, and passively surrendered themselves to the brigands.

"Go," said Lucia, to the brigand chief. "Go, and, if you can, do something to pacify those poor, distracted creatures."

Again Marco Bravo made a deep obeisance.

"I am your servant in all things, eccelenza," he replied. "I will go upon the instant, but first I must request you to descend from your carriage."

Lucia bowed haughtily.

"I have no choice but obedience," she answered. "Come, my poor Bianca."

With that she stepped down from the carriage.

The trembling maid followed the example of her brave young mistress.

Marco Bravo consigned the charming pair to the charge of Generoso.

He then went to the other carriage, and by mingled threats and persuasions obtained something like order.

He then returned to the countess and Bianca.

"Signora," he said, "my object is to remove you to an asylum where you will be secured against the machinations of your enemies."

"My enemies," repeated the countess, in utter astonishment.

"I speak but truth, signora," answered Marco Bravo. "You have secret enemies who have concocted a plot for bearing you off, and immuring you in a convent, but a nobleman of great distinction, an unknown but powerful friend, has taken this strong measure to frustrate the vile conspiracy; nothing but good is intended towards you."

"What nobleman, what friend?" exclaimed Lucia, more than ever bewildered. "I must say, Signor Bravo, that he takes a most extraordinary way of displaying his good will."

"I am not at liberty to mention his name," answered the brigand.

Then glancing around—

"But time is precious," he said. "It is time we were on our way."

"And whither will you take me?"

"Eccelenza, to a place where you will be received with the honour due to your rank," replied Marco Bravo; "but it will be quite impossible for me to allow so large a retinue to accompany you, therefore be pleased to select one or two of your attendants to go with you."

Lucia hesitated.

Her lips quivered, and she turned deadly pale and faint.

"To go alone, and with such wretches as these. Horrible!" she murmured, "but rather so than expose these poor girls to peril for my sake."

"Time presses; have you decided?" said Marco Bravo.

"Yes, I have decided," she answered, with forced calmness. "I will go alone."

Bianca threw herself upon her knees, and clasped her arms about the waist of her fair young mistress.

"Never, signora," she sobbed. "I will never leave you."

Lucia stooped and kissed her on the forehead.

"Go, my kind Bianca," she replied. "You will serve me best by returning to Naples, and conveying the intelligence to my friends of what has befallen me."

"I would rather die at your feet," returned the faithful girl. "Do not drive me away."

Lucia remained silent.

She could not bear the thought of being left in the hands of the surrounding desperadoes without one female companion, and yet she was loth to involve Bianca in her own trouble. Marco Bravo soon put an end to the controversy.

"You are a brave and faithful girl," said he, "and you shall have your wish. Eccelenza, I have determined that your maid shall accompany you."

"Thanks, many thanks, signore," rejoined Bianca.

Marco Bravo and his followers now bestirred themselves, and prepared for their long and difficult tourney.

The carriages were rifled, and while some loaded themselves with trunks and other baggage, others picked up their wounded comrades, and bore them in their arms.

The postillions were directed to remount the horses and all the servants of the countess, except Bianca, were told that they were free to return to Naples.

They scrambled pell-mell into the carriage, while the postillions cracked their whips, lashed their horses into a tearing gallop, and dashed off as if the devil were behind them.

The brigands witnessed their precipitate departure with a derisive cheer and shouts of laughter.

"Via! on to the mountains," was now the word of command.

"To the mountains!" reiterated the countess. "Surely you do not think that we poor women can endure the toil and fatigue of such a journey?"

"Patience, signora," returned the brigand chief. "At a little distance we have surefooted mules in readiness, and a few hours' ride will bring you to your destination. Do me the honour to accept my arm."

But Lucia shrank from him with a shudder of horror and loathing.

"No," she said, "if I need assistance, I will accept it only from this youth, who being the youngest among you, is, I trust, less deeply steeped in crime."

And she lightly placed her gloved hand upon the arm of Giovanni Pizano, whose black eyes flashed and white teeth glistened in a smile of delight at such a preference.

"As you please, eccelenza," returned the brigand chief, bowing coldly. "Generoso, do you escort the Signora Bianca."

Generoso advanced.

"Now," cried Marco Bravo, "onwards to the mountains."

CHAPTER XIX.

MARCO BRAVO leading the way, the brigands with their fair captives, finally came into a pretty and romantic little glen.

Here they came to a halt.

The men carrying the wounded and the baggage had gone on before.

In the little gorge they found a number of mules, several of which were gaily caparisoned, and furnished with side saddles, such as ladies use in riding among the mountains.

Lucia Di Carrara was mounted upon one mule, with Giovanni for her guide, and Bianca upon another in the charge of Generoso.

For a long time they proceeded in perfect silence.

But an hour having passed away without any alarm of pursuit, they grew more confident, and beguiled the tedium of their journey with merry songs and jests and careless laughter.

Marco Bravo kept close by Lucia.

For another hour they continued ascending a narrow pass, which was severe work for the more heavily-laden mules, as the path was in many places very rough and rocky.

After a laborious progress of some miles, they reached a sort of tableland near the head of the pass.

On this elevated spot they halted to rest and refresh themselves.

They found the rocky ground made a harder couch than the two delicately-nurtured ladies had been used to.

By the direction of Marco Bravo this was soon remedied.

The brigands set to work in cutting down with their knives a sort of broom, which they found growing in the neighbourhood, and which, spread under their cloaks, made a very good seat for the ladies.

Then one of the mules was unpacked, a wine-skin opened, and rations of coarse bread with pieces of dried kid's flesh were served out among the men.

Marco Bravo endeavoured to prevail upon the ladies to partake of some choicer viands brought for their especial use, but they both declined, pleading want of appetite.

They drank, however, a little of the wine mingled with a hornful of clear water from a neighbouring spring.

Lucia would not even take this from the hand of the brigand chief, but only from the youth, to whose protection she had entrusted herself.

This rebuff seemed to give extreme mortification to Marco Bravo.

He bit his lips, and a sullen frown overcast his dark but handsome countenance.

Bianca perceived this change in his manner, and grew alarmed for the consequences.

After a struggle with herself, she determined to remonstrate with her young mistress.

"Pardon, dear signora," she whispered, "but I feel it my duty to entreat you not to give offence to that terrible chief. Consider that we are entirely in his power, and that we ought to do all we can to conciliate, rather than offend him."

"I do not dispute the truth of what you say, my good Bianca," replied the countess. "But towards this man I feel an aversion I cannot describe."

"The feeling is very natural, eccelenza," answered her maid. "Who that has heard of the numerous and shocking atrocities committed by this dreadful man, can regard him with anything else but abhorrence?"

There was a strange, thrilling tone of deep meaning in Lucia's hushed voice as she answered quietly—

"No, no, Bianca; there is more in it than mere general hatred of his crimes. I feel as if he were some dark and powerful agent, sent to work me ill, as though his hand were stained with the blood of someone very dear to me."

"But, Madonna *mia*, you know that it is not so, and must therefore try and efface the impression from your mind," argued Bianca. "At least, disguise your sentiments until we are out of his grasp."

"Your advice is good, and I will try to follow it," replied the young countess, smiling faintly. "But I fear I shall find it a difficult task. Oh, if the good and brave Captain Lanfranco was here to aid me, I should be safe."

Marco Bravo now came up and announced that the time had come for renewing the journey.

Lucia Di Carrara rose and bowed a dignified assent.

"We are ready," she said. "But, pray tell me, have we a long journey before us? We are already very much fatigued."

"We shall arrive at our destination an hour before sunset," replied the brigand chief.

He strode away to bid his men prepare for a fresh start, and the two ladies remounted their mules.

They occasionally met with wandering shepherds, feeding their goats and sheep, from whom they sometimes got a supply of goat milk, which was very acceptable.

Upon meeting with one large party of them, Marco Bravo called a halt, and entered into a long and eager conversation with their *capo*, or head man, a venerable old fellow, with a silvery beard, fine aquiline features, and quick, penetrating eyes.

After leaving the shepherds, our travellers crossed the open valley, and again for some hours wound up a steep and rugged path between two lofty mountains.

Here they met with two brigands belonging to the band, who were posted on a high rock as scouts or sentinels, to give notice to their comrades in their fastness beyond of the approach of any enemy or wayfarer who might come near.

Upon seeing them, Marco Bravo uttered a wild and curious call, exactly like the cry of a wolf.

This the sentinels at once responded to by a similar noise.

Then trailing their long muskets, the picturesque-looking rascals came bounding like antelopes down the rocky path, the feathers in their steeple-crowned hats fluttering in the keen, fresh mountain breeze.

The greatest joy was displayed at this meeting by both sides.

But this joy was soon changed to grief, as their wounded comrades were borne along, writhing, moaning and praying.

They stamped their feet, tore their black hair, gnashed their teeth, and poured out a volley of anathemas against the cursed *soldati* who had wrought the mischief.

More than one of the villains fingered the hafts of their long knives, and cast evil glances at the two pale and trembling captives, as if they could hardly restrain themselves from falling upon them and quenching the thirst for vengeance in their innocent blood.

But Marco Bravo quickly put a stop to these hostile demonstrations.

"*Attenti!*" he shouted, in his sternest and most imperious tones. "Comrades, to order."

There was immediate silence.

It was wonderful to observe in what thorough control the brigand chief held his wild and lawless followers.

"Pietro," he said, turning to one of the sentinels, "is all well?"

"All is well, signor," returned the man.

"And everything in readiness for the reception of our distinguished guest?"

"All is prepared, signore; the apartments in the old tower are fitted up in a manner fit for the reception of a princess."

"Very good," replied the brigand chief. "And what women have you brought to attend upon her excellency?"

"Maria, Marta and Giugletta."

"I approve the choice," replied Marco Bravo. "Forward!"

The party then moved on again.

Marco Bravo came to Lucia's side and doffed his hat, as he always did when addressing her.

"Signora, we have arrived at our journey's end," he said.

"I am right glad to hear that our journey is over at last, for I and my poor Bianca are half dead with fatigue."

"A few steps further, and then repose," answered Marco Bravo, cheeringly.

Having passed through a narrow passage, between two walls of rock, they came upon a circular plain of some extent, just as the sun was setting.

In the midst of this plain, was reared a picturesque martello tower.

Upon approaching this stronghold of the brigands, a stirring scene was presented.

In the barrack-like courtyard were a swarm of fine-built, swarthy, black-eyed fellows.

Some were grooming the mules, others furbishing up their weapons, others again casting bullets.

Nor was the presence of the fair sex wanting to enliven the scene.

Fine, well-formed women all of them, these

brigandesses ; many were young and extremely pretty.

Not one of them but wore a crucifix and one or two relics, while all wore stilettoes, and some even pistols thrust through their silk sashes.

Upon seeing the approach of the chief, bugles sounded, and the *zampoyna*, or native bagpipe, droned out its note of welcome. Then the rocks and crags around re-echoed the stirring shout—

"*Viva* Marco Bravo !"

The brigand chief stopped short in the middle of the square, and drawing himself up to his full height, gazed around him with majestic mien, his dark eyes flashing with pride and exultation.

He took his hat from his head, and made a stately bow.

Every hat was off in an instant.

"*Victoria! Victoria! Eviva* Marco Bravo !"

In this way Marco Bravo and his train proceeded slowly to the entrance of the martello tower.

The ladies were received by three pretty, gaily-dressed lasses, who stood on the steps curtseying with deep respect.

These damsels led the way into the gloomy building, the two captives following.

Marco Bravo was himself about to enter the old tower, but Lucia Di Carrara waved him back.

"Leave us to ourselves now, signore," she said ; "we are quite out-worn, and long for repose. To-morrow, if you wish to see me, send me word, and I will receive you."

"Be it so, eccelenza," replied the brigand chief. "*Santa notte*, I wish you good repose."

With this the brigand retired.

The two girls, faint and weary after their long and toilsome journey, partook of a light repast, after which they immediately retired to rest.

Despite the danger and uncertainty of their position, they were so out-worn with fatigue that they both enjoyed a deep and refreshing slumber.

The next morning they rose hurriedly, and glanced at each other with blank faces, for it was some time before they could realise their situation.

"Bianca, there is one resource left me," answered the countess. "I can die !"

"Dearest signora," returned Bianca. "Do not let us abandon hope ; we may yet find some opportunity for escape."

She had scarcely finished speaking, when a sound of footsteps was heard in the courtyard.

The countess shuddered.

"Look, Bianca," she said, in a hushed and terrified voice. "Tell me what is passing."

Bianca ran to the window.

"Holy Virgin !" she exclaimed, "it is a poor old man the wretches are dragging along—he wrings his hands, and his looks betoken the extreme of fear—what will they do with him ? Surely their purpose is murder."

"Come away, Bianca—come away," replied her mistress. "Do not look upon such horrors."

The two girls, enfolded in each other's arms, cowered together in a corner of the room.

Then was heard the sharp crackle of musketry.

The countess and her attendant clung close to each other, not daring to breathe the suspicion that was uppermost in their minds.

But in a few seconds the firing ceased, and all was still again.

The countess then finished dressing, and the pair descended to the apartment below.

Here they found the breakfast set out, and Giovanni Pizano bustling about the room, dusting and arranging the furniture.

He appeared to be installed in the post of footman or waiter.

When they came in, he was humming to himself some wild robber-song, in a clear and superb tenor voice.

He started upon perceiving the ladies, broke off his song, and saluted them with a profound bow.

"Giovanni," asked the countess, who turned as pale as death, "what was the meaning of the noise of guns we heard just now ? Tell me, has murder been done here ?"

The youth's dark cheek grew sallow, and he shrugged his shoulders.

"Do not ask me, eccelenza," he replied. "It is better for you not to know—you will get used to such sounds ; they are of everyday occurrence."

"Do not refuse to answer my question, I implore you," returned the countess ; "let me know the worst."

"Well then, signora, since you will have it so," answered Giovanni, with another shrug, "one of the prisoners, whose friends—poor devils—have neglected to pay his ransom money, has been shot ; his head will be sent to his wife, who lives at Monteleone. You see, eccelenza, Marco Bravo is a stranger to mercy."

"Horrible !" gasped the countess. "Ah, my poor Bianca, how deeply I regret having so meanly taken advantage of your fidelity and devotion ; but if my prayers can move the hard heart of the brigand chief, I will obtain your liberation."

"Do not think of it, signora," answered the faithful girl ; "I will live or die with you ; but you, Giovanni, will you not aid us to escape from this den of murder ? It cannot be that you are as yet steeped in crime so deeply as the wretches your companions."

Giovanni held up his hand.

"*Zitto !*—hush !" said he, in accents of alarm. "These very walls have ears."

"But gold," urged the countess. "I am rich, and if you could but manage our escape, and fly with us, I would supply you with ample means to leave the country, and to spend the rest of your life in peace and comfort."

"No, signora," he replied in tones of respectful firmness, "it cannot be ; I must not—I dare not listen to such suggestions. You know not Marco Bravo ; his lynx-eyed vigilance watches over us all. None can escape him."

And so saying he hurried from the room, as though frightened by what had already passed between them.

He did not appear for the rest of the day.

The hours wore wearily and sadly on.

The countess was in despair.

"My last hope is gone!" she murmured. "A faint, wild idea flashed through my brain, that in that lad, Giovanni, we might find a friend, but it is plain that he stands in such awe of the terrible Marco Bravo, that we can expect no help from him."

But Bianca seemed disposed to take a more favourable view of the case.

"All is not over yet," said she; "we will try him once more; he is young and impressionable. and I do not despair of success."

During the day, the two fair captives sat by the window, watching the movements of the brigands.

Night fell; the captives had received no visitors, nor were they in any way disturbed; they retired early to rest, wondering and fearing what the morrow might bring forth.

CHAPTER XX.

THE bold and exciting exploit of Marco Bravo and his band, which we have to relate in the following chapter, is strictly founded on fact, and will give a startling proof of the pitch of audacity reached by the Italian bandits a few generations ago.

But first we must return to our English travellers for a moment.

Ralph, thrown upon his own resources, found the time hang heavily on his hands.

Then came the startling rumour of the capture of the Countess Di Carrara.

When this news was confirmed by the ignominious return of the military escort, of the carriages, and the servants, a profound sensation prevailed.

All the nobility were furious, and railed bitterly against the weakness and inefficiency of the police, who were unable to prevent such audacious outrages being perpetrated within a few miles of Naples, and in the open day.

Ralph Wildhawk was for taking the matter into his own hands, and of organising a corps of volunteers, who might pursue the robbers to their mountain fastnesses and exterminate the whole herd.

Meanwhile great surprise was expressed at the protracted absence of Captain Lanfranco, and fears were entertained that some sad mishap had befallen him.

About this time, the celebrated dancer, Zara, was performing at the theatre at Castellamare, and nightly attracting crowded houses.

Young Edmund Mortimer seldom failed to attend the theatre.

He had conceived a violent fancy for the beautiful dancing girl, and tried every means he could think of for obtaining an interview with her. But he constantly met with repulse.

Sir Godfrey and his family visited the theatre on the occasion of the first performance of a new opera.

There was a very distinguished and brilliant assemblage.

Every part of the house was thronged to overflowing.

Violet Melville looked her loveliest, in her elegant and becoming costume, and seemed radiant with happiness, her cheek clear and rosy, and her lips bright as a child's.

Ralph Wildhawk kept close by her side, from time to time bending over her, and carrying on the conversation in an undertone.

Sir Godfrey was preoccupied in holding a profound political argument with an Italian minister, whose breast was one blaze of stars and orders.

As for young Edmund, he was equally absorbed in conning the play-bill, and counting the moments until he should see his adored one.

"This is the first time you have seen the famous Zara, I believe?" said Violet.

"On the stage I have never seen her perform," answered Ralph, "but I saw her dance in the Villa Reale, during the carnival."

"I know," rejoined Violet, smiling; "I have heard her strange, romantic story. They say she is a mere Zingara, a gipsy, but is acknowledged to be the most beautiful woman in Naples."

"The most beautiful Neapolitan," replied Ralph, in a quiet tone; "but not the most beautiful lady in Naples."

"Now you meant that for a compliment," returned Violet, "but I am not to be caught by such extravagant flattery."

Then she added, quickly—

"Look at Mr. Mortimer, how glum he looks, and yet he seems to anticipate an evening of pleasant amusement."

Before Ralph Wildhawk had time to reply, the musicians entered the orchestra.

They looked white and scared, but scarcely anyone noticed this.

They took their places, and played the overture.

They played it, however, so badly, that the Italian audience—and the most illiterate Italian is a keen judge of music—hissed.

"This is a bad beginning," muttered Ralph Wildhawk.

Even Sir Godfrey Mortimer started and stared in surprise, while the Italian noble with whom he was conversing, put his fingers in his ears.

"Tsa! this is abominable!" he said, holding up his hands, and shaking his hoary head. "Corpo di Baccho! what can it mean? I never heard them play so badly."

There was a breathless hush of expectation.

By-and-bye the curtain rose.

The scene presented on the stage was a dark wood

The stage itself was crowded by a throng of men, dressed in the picturesque brigand costume, and armed with stilettoes and long guns.

The audience took little notice of this, and they thought it belonged to the action of the play.

But what they did observe as being remarkable, was, that all the men wore masks.

Presently there entered a tall, finely-dressed figure, apparently the captain of the band.

In one hand he held a drawn sword, in the other a pistol.

He was masked like the rest.

Advancing to the footlights, he made a low bow to the audience.

"Ladies and gentlemen," said he, in a clear, ringing voice, that made itself heard in every part of the house, "most of you have frequently assembled here to witness many mimic scenes of life ; among the rest, there is one, a drama depicting the vicissitudes of brigandage. Ladies and gentlemen, I am about to treat you to a little of the real thing ; I am sure all lovers of truth and fact will enjoy this novelty."

A buzz of consternation ran round at this extraordinary address.

Many of the audience, struck with alarm, rose from their seats, and appeared to be about to hurry from the theatre.

Then the stern, clear voice of the brigand chief rang out his orders to his men—

"*Attenti*, comrades. Present !"

At the word, the muzzle of every gun was directed at the audience, so as to sweep the house.

"Keep your seats, ladies and gentlemen, I beseech you," continued the brigand chief, in the same loud, bold tone. "The least movement made towards departure will oblige me to give an unwilling order to my men ; they are good marksmen, and will pick off the first man that attempts to rise ; so as you value your lives, remain where you are."

There was a dead silence. Then looking round, he cried in a loud, ringing voice—

"I am Marco Bravo !"

There was something so impressive in the cool, matchless audacity of the transcendent rascal, that the people were overawed.

No one seemed to have the power to speak, or even to move ; they all seemed suddenly struck into stone as by the power of the fabled head of Medusa.

At the same time, the brigands on the stage stood as motionless as statues, their muskets aimed at all parts of the house.

At length, Marco Bravo sheathed his sword, but kept the pistol still grasped in his left hand.

Then, followed by Generoso, Stromba, and about half-a-dozen more of the brigands, he left the stage, followed by his guard, who shouldered their muskets, and marched in military order. The bandit chieftain visited the boxes, the pit, the galleries, every part of the house, collecting money, watches, jewellery, swords, and mantles.

When Marco Bravo entered the box of Sir Godfrey Mortimer, all rose to their feet.

Ralph Wildhawk and Edmund Mortimer clapped their hands to their swords.

At a gesture from their chief, the brigands levelled their muskets at the heads of the two young men.

The victims of the well-arranged and audaciously-executed plot perceived at once that they were entirely at the mercy of the villains, and that resistance was quite hopeless.

So without further parley they removed their watches, drew the rings from their fingers, and purses from their pockets, and placed them in the bandit's hat.

Ralph Wildhawk, in his turn, took off his watch and rings, and with an air of contempt, held them out to the masked robber captain.

"Not from *you*, signore." responded the bandit, bowing him off ; " Marco Bravo does not rob or injure his friends."

Ralph Wildhawk started, and looked hard at the speaker, whose voice sounded so familiar in his ear.

Then his cheek flushed with shame and anger.

"The worst injury you could do me I should hold pardonable in comparison with your insult, in classing me among the friends of the outlawed wretch you name," retorted Ralph, sternly. "If you are indeed Marco Bravo, you are well aware that I never saw you, or spoke with you before, and let me add that whenever or wherever we may meet on equal terms, I shall think it my duty to risk my life in ridding the earth of such a miscreant. There, robber ! Treat me as the rest ; I scorn your forbearance, and will receive no favour at your hands."

So speaking, he flung the purse at the brigand's feet.

Marco Bravo laughed heartily.

"As you please, signore," he returned, shrugging his shoulders. "The world has wronged me, and I owe it nothing but hatred and defiance. I spurn its laws, and I am as lawless in my attachments as my enmities. I will not touch your money ; take it back, and let me warn you that friendship is rare and never to be despised ; that the day may not be far distant when you will be glad to rely upon the aid even of——"

"Who ?" cried Ralph.

"Marco Bravo !" replied the brigand.

All were astonished at this strange speech, and Ralph Wildhawk murmured to himself—

"That voice ! that voice ! Where have I heard it before ?"

Violet Melville had instinctively crept to the side of the object of her secret passion.

With that forgetfulness of the presence of others, common to those in love, Ralph Wildhawk passed his arm around the fair girl's waist, and clasped her tightly.

With violent trembling, she disengaged herself, and offered her money and trinkets to the bandit.

"No, signora !" returned the brigand chief, "your beauty is your ransom ; I will accept nothing but the rose that you wear upon your breast ; I will keep it as a memento."

Violet instantly plucked the flower from her bosom, and held it towards him.

Marco Bravo advanced to take it, when Ralph Wildhawk struck him back with a violent blow.

"Traitor ! idiot !" hissed the brigand, all his passions roused ; "ungrateful as you are, you shall die for this."

Quick as thought, he drew a dagger from his sash, and rushing upon Ralph, would have stabbed him to the heart, had not Violet thrown herself between them.

Meanwhile, one of the brigands presented his musket at Ralph Wildhawk.

He would have fired, but Marco Bravo, recollecting himself, rushed upon the man and struck the musket up.

" Bang !"

It went off in the air.

The ladies in the theatre shrieked, the men fingered their sword-hilts, but Marco Bravo maintained a perfect calmness.

In a moment, he seemed to have recovered his good humour.

" Enough !" he said, laughing. "As master of the situation, I can afford to be magnanimous. I forgive you, signore—and so *addio!*"

He bowed himself out of the box.

Very soon after, he and his men left the theatre.

Then followed an outburst of long pent-up wrath and excitement.

The men, who had showed themselves the greatest cowards while the brigands were present, now raved and swore vengeance against the robbers, and boasted of the mighty deeds they would have performed if they had only been supported by the others.

The Italian noble in the box with Sir Godfrey, sat for some time petrified with astonishment, his hands wandering idly over his breast, from which the daring robber had cut away every one of the stars, crosses, and other decorations.

At last he appeared to collect his scattered senses, and then burst into a torrent of invectives.

He at once sent for the manager, who was brought in, limp, tottering, and looking the impersonation of abject fear.

The diplomat stormed at the poor fellow, and accused him of being an accomplice of the brigands.

The manager utterly denied this, and stated that about an hour before the time for commencing the performance, a number of masked and well-armed ruffians burst in at the stage-door.

They took possession of the green-room, the dressing-rooms, and every other portion of the theatre behind the scenes, seized manager, musicians, actors and actresses, and presenting their loaded muskets at their heads, and using the most horrible threats, compelled them to obey their orders.

Not content with this, they despoiled the actors and actresses of their money and jewellery, sparing only La Zara, whom they treated with the greatest respect, and cleaned out the treasury.

They then confined the luckless players in the green-room, setting a sentinel at the door, with orders to shoot down any of them who made the slightest attempt at escape.

The musicians were then sent into the orchestra, while a brigand was posted for raising the curtain at the right moment.

The musicians were threatened with a volley of shots if they gave the least signs of an intention to warn the audience of the catastrophe that awaited them.

Such was the manager's story.

What followed has already been told.

The Italian noble did not appear satisfied with the manager's plain and truthful explanation ; and he was put under arrest and cited to appear before the magistrates on the following day.

Of course there was no thought of performing the drama which the audience had assembled to see.

They left the theatre and hurried to their homes, in a state of mind more easily imagined than described.

Many of the younger and more fiery of the men swore that they would combine and form a band, to rescue the Countess of Carrara, and exterminate the brigands.

Ralph Wildhawk put himself at the head of this movement.

He seemed to feel it a point of honour to do everything in his power to show how scornfully he rejected the robber's friendship.

The commandant of the Neapolitan dragoons took himself the command of a large body of troops, both cavalry and infantry, and at once marched off to the mountains.

When Sir Godfrey and his family returned home, Violet took an opportunity of speaking to Ralph Wildhawk alone.

" Tell me," she asked, " did you notice anything in the voice and manner of the masked brigand captain, that reminded you of someone with whom we are both of us well acquainted ?"

Ralph Wildhawk started at the question.

" I did !" a flood of conviction rushing in upon his mind ; " I felt sure that I had seen and spoken to the man before."

" And I had the same impression," answered Violet. " Who did you take him to be ?"

Ralph smiled rather painfully.

" Nay, since you give the challenge, let me ask you to tell me your own thought ?" he said.

" Well, then, I will," she replied firmly ; " I entertain no doubt in my own mind that the masked robber was no other than your amusing friend, the Count Di Ancona."

" Great Heaven !" ejaculated Ralph. " The same idea occurred to me. But yet the thing is absurd, impossible ; I saw the count's papers, and as you have yourself seen, he has been received in the highest circles, without doubt or hesitation ; still it is most strange. I would not for the world wrong a man I like so much by an unjust suspicion, yet the tone of the voice, the bearing, the dark eyes and hair, the resemblance was wonderful."

" And there is another and most important consideration that gives strength to my conviction," she replied ; " that is, the robber's openly-professed friendship for you, his absolute refusal to take your money. Supposing this Count Di Ancona to be what I think him, a daring impostor, he may yet have some sparks of humanity in him, and may have taken such a liking to you, his confiding friend and companion, that, as he said, he would not injure you.

" What should Marco Bravo the robber, the stranger, care for you whom he never saw before ? No, no, depend upon it, the count and the brigand are one and the same man."

"THE BRIGAND DREW A DAGGER AND RUSHED AT RALPH."

"It is very strange," assented Ralph Wild-hawk; "yet I am so unwilling to believe it."

At this moment, Joe Moody thrust his head in at the door.

"Pardon, Master Ralph," he said, "but here's that guitar-strumming maccaroni just come from Naples; he is all over dust and dirt, and his horse steams like a wet blanket. He brought this note from his master."

"What! you don't mean to say that it is Generoso, the count's servant?" rejoined Ralph, eagerly. "Then his master is at Naples."

"Laid up in bed from his wound, which has broke out afresh," returned Joe; "there's his letter."

"Now, Mistress Violet, what ought we to think of ourselves for our baseless suspicions of a kind and honourable man?" cried Ralph, with triumph. "My friend is innocent; this is a clear *alibi*, not guilty, honourably acquitted —hurrah!"

CHAPTER XXI.

GENEROSO was now ushered into the room.

As Joe Moody had stated, the Italian's hand-some livery was bespattered with mire, and he had all the appearance of having just come off from a long, hard ride.

Ralph Wildhawk eagerly broke the seal of the count's letter, and read what follows—

"ECCELENTISSIMO SIGNORE,—I returned to my old quarters in the Via Di Toledo, two days ago. On my road from Gaeta, my carriage was stopped by the brigands. I was plundered, and should have been carried off to the mountains, but for a timely alarm that soldiers were at hand. My wounded arm is still painful. I miss your society much, and look forward with pleasing anticipation to the time when we shall meet again; till then, *addio*.

"SILVIO DI ANCONA."

The frank, ingenuous face of the young Eng-lishman lighted up with a smile of satisfaction.

"Tell your master, my good Generoso," he said, "that I am delighted to hear of his return to Naples, and that I will do myself the honour of paying him a visit within a few days, and add that the villains who robbed him, have perpetrated an outrage here, in Castellamare, that surpasses all their former exploits."

A peculiar smile flitted over the dark, sa-turnine features of the Italian.

"I heard something of it, signore," he re-plied, "from the vetturini I met on the road; but have yet to learn the particulars."

Ralph Wildhawk then gave him an account of the affair at the theatre.

Generoso held out his hands and shrugged up his shoulders in boundless amazement at the unparalleled audacity of the brigands.

Ralph Wildhawk then dismissed him, not forgetting to place some money in his hand.

Generoso bowed, and left the room.

"I am glad of this," said Ralph, turning to Violet Melville, after the man had left the room, "and I am also glad to find that the gentry of Castellamare have resolved to make a foray among the mountains, and to crush the horde of thieves and murderers.

"I know of no man more fitting to lead such an expedition than the count himself. His cool-ness and intrepidity in moments of danger are astonishing. I am deputed to arrange every-thing, and I will propose the count for our leader."

And in his quick, impetuous way, Ralph placed himself at a table, and commenced writing.

"One moment, Master Ralph," rejoined Violet, as with a smile, she tripped to his side, "if I may advise you, I think it would be best not to act too hastily; you should, I think, first see the count."

"My life upon his faith and honour," replied Ralph, with enthusiasm; "surely you cannot doubt him after this?"

And he held out the count's letter.

"It appears genuine," she replied; "here's his crest stamped on the paper; you know his handwriting, of course?"

"Oh, yes," he replied; "I have received several letters from him; besides, was not this brought by his own man?"

"That is true," she answered, "but I do not like that Generoso; he looks sly and treache-rous."

"Most of these Italian servants appear to be artful knaves, though civil, serviceable, and intelligent," returned Ralph Wildhawk; "I have the count's authority for saying so."

Violet smiled rather doubtingly as she retired from the room.

Ralph wrote a frank effusive letter to the count, which he gave to Generoso and dismissed him. As soon as that rascal left the palace, he burst into a long and hearty laugh.

"*Corpo di Baccho!*" he chuckled, rubbing his hands, "what a genius is our captain. He carries more tricks in his bag than the fox in the fable."

After walking on for about half an hour, he stopped at a little *albergo*, or tavern, which stood by the roadside.

He entered and asked for Marco Bravo, of course, by an assumed name.

He was immediately ushered into a small private apartment, where he found his chief seated at a table with a note-book before him, in which he was making entries.

Marco Bravo received his confederate with a smile of welcome.

Generoso presented the letter to his chief.

Marco Bravo, when he read it, appeared in-finitely amused.

"*Per Baccho!*" said he, "this is a rare piece of fun, and a fine stroke of fortune. The en-terprising young Englishman, who is as brave as he is hot-headed, to appoint me commander against my own band; it is too much."

Then he sprang to his feet, and paced about in a glow of excitement and exultation.

"This caps my best hopes!" he said, "and out of it I can work wonders. But come, Generoso, let us have one cup of wine together in congratulation for our late victory, and then back to Naples, for to-night I expect to meet the Count Beltrani, from whom I am to receive money on account for the affair of La Carrara."

The wine was brought in.

When the servant had gone away, the brigands filled up and pledged each other.

"Viva Marco Bravo!" said Generoso; "see how true it is that fortune favours the bold!"

"Not always, between ourselves, *amico*," answered the brigand. "Luck has much to do with one's efforts, but one stands in great peril after making a lucky stroke. We must ensure ourselves against a change of fortune, and to do so let us be very cautious. You must not go near Castellamare until I think it safe for you to do so."

"I obey, signore," replied Generoso, "but be not too exacting. The pretty English girl draws me thither like a magnet, but you won't forget your promise, captain, when the time for the performance arrives."

"Fear you not, Generoso," replied Marco Bravo, "she shall be yours; but did you not tell me that the rich English heiress was present when you delivered my letter to the secretary?"

"She was," replied Generoso.

"And you told them that you had come direct from Naples."

"Yes, and that the vetturino was waiting for me at a neighbouring inn to carry me back to the city."

"You told them no lie there, Generoso," replied his chief, "the carriage and postillions are ready at the door. I shall muffle myself in a capote, and in this disguise have no fear of recognition, so let us make a start without further delay."

Thereupon they hurried from the inn, and getting into the carriage, dashed off at a great pace in the direction of Naples.

On the next day but one Ralph Wildhawk visited his friend the count, at his old lodgings in the Via Di Toledo.

He found that distinguished nobleman in the same luxurious apartments that he had occupied on the former occasion.

He wore his arm in a sling, and looked rather pale and haggard.

When Ralph Wildhawk came in, he rose, and greeted him warmly.

After the first salutations were over, and they had seated themselves at the window, a bottle, glasses, and box of cigars on a table between them, Ralph spoke.

His manner betrayed some agitation.

"I cannot express my pleasure at seeing you once again, my dear count," said Ralph, "but have you heard the terrible news?"

The count looked at him with a languid smile.

"I am almost tired of shocking surprises," replied the count: "what's the matter now? Some fresh villany of that rascal, Marco Bravo?"

"Oh, not that," returned Ralph Wildhawk. "Do you not remember Captain Lanfranco, the officer of dragoons who escorted us from Terracina to Naples?"

"Yes, but my remembrances of him are not very favourable," was the cool reply. "I must say I thought him a very impertinent fellow. I hear that he has deserted from his regiment, and bearing in mind the clumsy way in which he conducted the pursuit of the escaped brigand, I must confess that I consider him no great loss to the service."

"Hot words passed between you, as I witnessed, eccelenza," Ralph Wildhawk replied, gravely. "Respect his memory, for misfortune is always deserving of respect, and he was a most unfortunate man."

The count took the cigar from his lips, and stared at him in blank surprise.

"His memory," he repeated. "What do you mean? Surely you don't mean to say the man is dead?"

"Such is the fact," answered Ralph Wildhawk.

"I have not heard of it," replied the count.

"Only this morning his body was found; and it was only by the uniform it was recognized, being in an advanced stage of decomposition."

"*Per Dio!*" exclaimed the count, "is it possible? And how do they suppose that he met with his death?"

"He was foully murdered, beyond all doubt," answered Ralph Wildhawk. "His sword lay by his side, drawn, and its blade rusty with blood, while his shirt was torn and bloody where he had been stabbed to the heart."

"And his papers — his valuables — his money?" asked the count."

"He had been robbed of everything," was the reply. "It was plain enough that he had been assassinated for the sake of what he had about him."

The count rose with a stern, determined countenance.

"I'll tell you what, signore, this must not go on," he said. "It is monstrous! If this fatal affair were traced to its source, I would lay my life the culprit would be found to be Marco Bravo."

"Perhaps so," answered Ralph Wildhawk. "It is by no means unlikely that either he or some of his gang may have been the instruments, but it is whispered abroad that a very distinguished personage is suspected of having set them on."

The count turned pale, and thrust his hand into his pocket, in which he carried a loaded pistol.

Instantly afterwards the count recovered his composure, and asked very quietly—

"And who is the suspected person?"

"I do not know," replied Ralph Wildhawk, "and if I did, I should scarcely feel myself justified in mentioning his name until he was publicly accused of the crime, but whoever he be, he is supposed to be one of the numerous suitors for the fair hand of the Countess Di Carrara; it is thought that she gave her preference to poor Lanfranco, who was murdered by a rival from motives of jealousy."

A smile of such malice as might become a triumphant fiend, flickered over the count's dark, handsome face.

He seemed to be aware that his looks betrayed his feelings, for he turned aside his head.

There was a pause.

"The Count Beltrani!" he muttered. "Very probable. He is a haughty, unscrupulous, vindictive man. Well, well, signore, if you please, we will change the subject."

"With all my heart," returned Ralph Wildhawk. "To no one but yourself would I have broached it, and it is one too horrible for contemplation."

The count filled up the glasses, and drank to his friend.

"And now tell me," said he, "are you still in the same mind with regard to your romantic scheme for invading the brigands' glen?"

Ralph brightened up.

"Yes, signore," he replied, "if it meets with your approval."

"It does," returned the count. "I think it a most excellent plan. Many among the young nobles of Naples and the surrounding towns are good mountaineers, and brave as their swords; they would form a gallant band, and, I make no doubt, would effect more than a whole regiment of the regulars."

"I'm glad to hear you say so," answered Ralph Wildhawk; "I am fond of adventure; it would please me well to flesh my sword in the cause of humanity, and to approve my courage in a warfare against these mountain wolves, so I trust you will accept me as a humble volunteer."

The count smiled.

"But the matter does not rest in my hands," he replied; "I am not commander."

"Oh, but you will be—must be," rejoined Ralph. "Who so fitting as yourself for the post?"

The count laughed.

"You do me too much honour," he said, "and I must deprecate the partiality of friendship; indeed, you will find many a better man if you look about."

"Never," returned Ralph, shaking his head; "I hope you will not refuse the offer of the command."

"Perhaps not," returned the count, "if it is offered me."

"Read this," said Ralph, eagerly.

He took from his pocket a letter, signed by some of the chief nobles of Naples and Castellamare, requesting the count to lead them against the brigands.

"Well, I will consider of it," he said.

"They entreat you to accept the command," Ralph urged, "and I am commissioned to bring them an answer."

"They could not have selected a more able and zealous envoy," answered the count, smiling. "I will consider of it."

Soon after Ralph Wildhawk took his leave.

When he was gone, the count sprang up, and threw the sling from his arm.

"The old Count Di Ancona died; his son, a victim to a blighted passion, returned from abroad after a long absence," he muttered. "I, Marco Bravo, captured him; his papers, his servants, his palace are in my hands. They say I am wonderfully like him in face and features. He must die. But I am playing a dangerous game. Yes, I will consider of it."

CHAPTER XXII.

THE Countess Di Carrara and her maid, Bianca, remained prisoners for some days in the fastness of the brigands, and were not molested.

The fact was, that their two persecutors, Marco Bravo and the Count Di Beltrani, had been so occupied by their own absorbing affairs that they had not found time or opportunity to give the poor captive ladies any trouble by their unwelcome presence.

As for Marco Bravo, the events already narrated sufficiently account for his absence.

Of the Count Beltrani there is more to be said.

The discovery of the dead body of Captain Lanfranco, combined with the capture of Lucia Di Carrara, were incidents which, taken together, involved him in a rather serious difficulty.

It appeared that on the day previous to that on which Lanfranco had left the Castel St. Elmo to visit his friends, he and Beltrani had met at a certain casino, where high words had passed between them.

The quarrel seemed likely to end by a challenge and a duel, but the intervention of friends, and the consideration of Beltrani's high rank, prevented it.

Count Beltrani had withdrawn in high dudgeon, with a half-threat on his lips.

After that Lanfranco had gone away, and nothing more had been heard of him until his body had been discovered.

Of course, strict inquiry was made concerning the mysterious affair.

Beltrani, who in this case could afford to do so, demanded the most searching inquisition, and as not a tittle of evidence could be brought against him, he was in the end honourably acquitted.

Yet, remembering his former career, many people harboured dark suspicions against him, for which the proud noble cared not one jot.

Lucia Di Carrara began to look wretchedly ill.

Bianca, on her part, only sustained her sinking spirits by encouraging and caressing her beloved young mistress.

The three girls selected to wait on the countess performed their duties with diligence and cheerful good will, while some of the men, ruffians steeped to the lips in crime, showed her such delicate attentions as bringing her fruit and flowers from the plains and ice from the mountain tops.

What struck the countess as the most surprising thing of all, was the light-heartedness of the outlaws.

Young Giovanni was in constant attendance upon the ladies.

"Where is your chief?" asked the countess one morning. "Tell him that I wish to speak with him."

"Pardon, *eccelenza*," he replied, "the *signor capitano* is away, I know not where."

The countess then made another attempt to persuade him to assist them to escape.

But Giovanni was not to be tempted.

"I dare not, signora," was his conclusive reply. "If you gave me all the wealth you possess, of what use would it be to me? My life would be forfeit, and the *vendetta* would overtake me though I fled to the ends of the earth."

"But surely you cannot intend always to lead this frightful life?" asked the excited countess.

Giovanni sighed.

"Signora," he answered, "I have no choice. There is no hope for me."

"Folly," returned the countess. "You are young, and by a bold stroke you might save yourself from the consequences of past errors, and secure a bright and happy future."

Giovanni shook his head.

"I do not much care whether I live or die," he said, "but neither pardon or reward could ever induce me to betray the band."

"But do you never think of your home?" urged the countess, "your friends—the girl that you love?"

Unbidden tears bedewed the dark lashes of the young Italian.

He answered in a softened tone—

"They are never absent from my thoughts; I am always thinking of my kind uncle and of my darling Lisetta."

"I am glad to hear it," answered the fair captive; "it shows that your heart is still in the right place. And having such thoughts, why do you not try to return to them?"

Giovanni waved his hand with a gesture of despair.

"It can never be, signora," he replied, in tones of the deepest despondency; "I shall never see them again."

And as if anxious to avoid further remonstrance, he bowed, and hurriedly left the room.

The next day there was unusual bustle and excitement in the courtyard of the ancient fortress.

Lucia Di Carrara turned deadly pale, and clasped her arms about the waist of her faithful attendant.

"Bianca, it is he," she gasped; "it is the robber, the assassin, Marco Bravo—I am lost."

Bianca clasped her fair young mistress closer to her bosom.

"Courage, dearest signora," she answered, soothingly; "have no fear. It is not from him you have to fear. His employer, the Count Beltrani, would force you into a marriage repugnant to your wishes, but villain and libertine as he is, he will not dare to offer you any insult; and e're the day comes for your hated nuptials, we may find some means of escaping."

The countess burst into tears.

"Bianca," she answered, between her sobs, "I echo the words of poor Giovanni—'There is no hope.'"

The sound of a light, firm footstep was heard ascending the stairs.

"Hist, signora," whispered Bianca, trembling with fright.

"Listen, Bianca," returned the countess in a breathless voice.

She drew from the folds of her dress a long, shining stiletto.

"Look at this."

"Signora."

"Do not interrupt me; do not seek to change my resolve," returned the countess. "Do you know where I got this?"

"No, signora; but I implore you to put it away."

"Never."

Bianca tried to wrest it from her hand.

"Stand off, I command you," said the countess; "you are no friend if you would deprive me of the sole means of defending my honour."

Then after a pause she added in a hurried tone—

"I will tell you how I obtained this weapon. During one of our rides with the brigands through the mountain passes, I saw it fall from the sash of one of the robbers and bury itself among the heather; I feigned fatigue; I asked them to suffer me to rest awhile."

"I remember it," replied Bianca; "it was the last time we took a ride together; they lifted you from the saddle, and you sat down to rest on the verge of a precipice."

"It was so," returned the countess; "unseen by anyone I secured the dagger and concealed it under my mantle."

"But to what purpose?"

"To plunge it into the heart of the first villain who offers me violence, whether he be the count or Marco Bravo."

"Oh, hush, signora," replied Bianca distractedly. "Hide the weapon; someone comes."

The door opened.

A tall, majestic figure entered.

The countess and Bianca uttered a cry of astonishment. It was a woman.

A tall, fierce-looking woman, with a fierce, wild face, eagle eyes, and the dignified air of an ancient prophetess.

She was dressed in the picturesque costume worn by brigandesses, but of more costly material than usual.

A poignard glistened in her silk sash, and in her hand she clasped a long gun.

She strode towards the frightened girls.

They recoiled before her.

Bianca screamed.

Summoning courage, the countess was the first to speak.

"Who are you?" she asked. "What is your will with us?"

"Fear me not," replied the woman. "I am La Catarina, the queen of the brigands."

CHAPTER XXIII.

SEEING how the countess and Bianca shrank before her, the queen of the brigands drew back, and waving her hand with a motion, half encouraging, half contemptuous, she lowered the gun and placed it against the wall.

"Compose yourselves, I pray you," she said, mildly; "from me you have nothing to fear. I come hither as your friend, and with no other intention than to serve you."

Lucia Di Carrara flung herself at her feet, clasping her hands.

"You profess yourself our friend," she said. "If you are not deceiving us, show your goodwill by releasing us from this foul prison."

"You know not what you ask," was the cold reply: "my power is considerable, but does not extend so far as that."

"Tell me, then, who are you?" asked the countess, "and tell me what kind of influence you hold over the lawless desperadoes that they pay you such respect?"

"They fear me," replied La Catarina; "they hold me in superstitious awe, their imagination having invested me with supernatural attri-

"'I AM CATARINA, THE QUEEN OF THE BRIGANDS,' SAID THE WOMAN."

butes which, it is needless to say, I do not possess. I do not discourage their foolish belief, because it gives me power and security."

"But how came you to associate yourself with such wretches?"

"That is a long story, and a painful one," replied La Catarina. "Let it pass now."

"You style yourself their queen," pursued the countess. "How did you gain that title?"

"I am the widow of their late chief," she answered.

"Poor woman," returned the countess, "I have heard of that notorious brigand; he was captured by the soldiers, was tried, and suffered death."

"He died like a man," answered La Catarina. "Though ruthless to all others, he was kind to me. Peace be with him."

"If you are our friend," rejoined the countess, "tell us why we were brought hither?"

"Can you not guess?"

"From a hint that Marco Bravo let fall, it would appear that I am the victim of the guilty passion of a rich and powerful noble, who employed the brigands to carry me off."

"It is so," answered La Catarina; "and it is because I know it to be so, that I came hither to serve you if I can."

"You can only serve me by setting me at liberty," returned the countess, sighing. "From what motive do you take such interest in our fate?"

The fine classic face of the brigandess flushed, and her dark eyes glittered with a wild, strange light, as she replied—

"I am unwilling to raise the veil from the past," she answered; "but, as your question is a natural one, I will answer."

Then, bowing with graceful courtesy, she went on—

"I pray you, eccelenza, be seated."

The countess timidly murmured her thanks, and posed herself upon a couch.

With a queen-like air La Catarina seated herself.

For a few moments there was silence.

Lucia watched the brigand queen in fear and curiosity.

La Catarina sat, her dark eyes fixed upon the ground, as though lost in meditation.

At length, rousing herself, she spoke.

"Eccellenza," she said, a wan smile flitting across her expressive features, "I am growing old. It is hard for you, in the proud flush of youth, to judge of the sad change time makes; there is nothing so hard as to imagine what the old have been in youth. I was once beautiful, and proud, and vain withal."

"The fame of your beauty has reached me, La Catarina," answered the countess. "I have seen your portrait painted by a master hand."

The brigand queen took no heed of the remark.

"Beauty is, at the best, a fatal dower," she went on, calmly, "and ever so when it falls to the lot of the lowly born, the humble and poor; aye, it is a curse. I found it so."

She paused, and the countess shuddered at the wild, half-insane look of the brigandess.

"A cruel curse," muttered La Catarina; "I loved, and was beloved."

"By whom, La Catarina?"

"By a man of high station; he was a foreigner, an Englishman," continued the brigandess. "He removed me from the scene of what he was pleased to call my degradation. I was placed in a convent school, where I received the most careful training. He wooed me constantly and fervently till he won my heart, and I loved him as only a woman, an Italian, can love."

She stopped abruptly.

She gasped for breath, her bosom visibly palpitating, and then continued in a tone of exquisite pathos—

"Eccelenza, there was something very beautiful in the love I bore that man. I courted praise, I read my mirror, I studied night and day. In my own opinion, I was unsightly, I was a dullard, I knew no art of endearment, I had no charm of thought or speech; I hated and despised myself because—though I had all sorts of courtly minions who admired my beauty and knew nothing of the secret of my birth—because I could not be by endless grades so dear, so lovely, so accomplished as I wished to be for him. Jesu Maria! how terribly I loved, how terribly I loved that man."

La Catarina's eyes were suffused with tears, while her lips curved with scorn.

The countess looked at her in silent awe and wonderment.

"Did he abandon you?" she asked.

"We were married," she replied, "and spent together some months of happiness; then one of his kinsmen, a wealthy noble, died; my husband inherited his title and riches, and then, for the first time, he showed signs of regret at having bestowed his hand upon a poor Italian contadina."

"But he could not break the bonds," answered the countess; "you were his lawful wife."

"His wife, but he contrived to evade the law," replied La Catarina. "Wishing to get rid of me, he took counsel with one of his profligate companions, the Count Beltrani."

"Is it possible?" ejaculated the countess. "It must have been the father of the wretch who persecutes me, at whose instigation I was brought hither."

"No other; the vile son of a vile father," returned the brigandess. "Well, signora, the count discovered that the priest who had married us had been unfrocked for some shameful offence, and that our marriage was illegal. I should at once have left my false husband, but I clove to him for the sake of my child, my darling boy."

"Have you a son yet living?" asked the countess.

"No, signora," she answered, sadly. "He was torn from me, and I afterwards learned that he had died in England."

"And what became of your husband?"

"I will tell you," she replied. "Not daring openly to divorce me, the coward employed Mazzarosa and his brigands to carry me off to the mountains, and it was given out that I had been murdered. My husband returned to England, where he subsequently married another lady."

Then she paused, her dark eyes glowing, and her thin lips curled with a smile of ferocious triumph.

"But, La Catarina!" exclaimed the countess, with an involuntary shudder, "what followed?"

"He brought his bride back to Naples," she answered, "and I had my revenge."

"*Santa Maria!*" gasped the countess, "surely you did not kill him!"

"It was at her—my rival—that I struck the blow," returned the brigandess. "It was my first intention to slay them both, but my heart failed me when I heard his voice, for I still loved him. I spared him, but stabbed his mock wife to the heart, and escaped. Since then I have lived and reigned the queen of the banditti."

"Horrible," murmured the countess. "It was a fearful crime, yet I must own the provocation was great. But, tell me, did you see or hear no more of your false and cruel husband?"

"Never, signora," answered the brigandess: "he returned to England broken-hearted, and I never beheld him again."

Having thus finished the sad story of her wrongs, La Catarina rose, calm and dignified, with no trace upon her features of the emotions which had lately seemed to shake her very frame.

"I have told you thus much of my history, that you might understand why I act as I do," she said. "The fame of the kindness and charity of the noble-hearted Countess Di Carrara has penetrated even to these mountain fastnesses. I cannot promise you immediate liberation, but I will watch over your safety, and will take care you shall suffer no wrong from that villain, the Count Beltrani, whom I hate for his father's sake."

"Thanks, my kind friend, whom Heaven hath sent to protect me at a moment when I had lost all hope," replied the countess. "Oh, that I could persuade you to quit these dreadful scenes and associations. I have powerful friends, through whose influence, I doubt not, your free pardon could be obtained; then, in the peace and seclusion of a convent, you might pass the rest of your life in serene preparation for another and a brighter world."

"No, signora," answered the brigandess, "I am content to remain as I am. Among these outlaws I have found friendship, respect,—even veneration. They have pitied my sufferings, and what is more, have helped to avenge my wrongs. And so adieu for awhile. I shall remain here, that I may be ready to aid you when the hour arrives that I fear is near at hand."

So saying, she took up the carbine, and flinging it across her arm, made a stately bow and moved towards the door.

Before she had time to leave the room, young Giovanni entered, his looks betraying alarm and excitement.

La Catarina gazed upon him steadfastly with her keen, eagle eye.

"How now, Giovanni?" she asked, "what news? Has Marco Bravo returned?"

"No, signora," answered the young robber,

"but I have to announce the arrival of the Count Beltrani; he desires an audience with her excellency the Countess Di Carrara."

The countess rose in a great fright.

She flung herself at the feet of the brigand queen.

"Say I refuse to see him, good Giovanni," she exclaimed; "oh, Catarina, I throw myself upon your protection; now is the time to redeem your promise; use your power to save me."

The brigandess laid her hand softly and caressingly upon the fair girl's brow.

"Be quiet, child," she said, "and I will see what can be done."

Then, leaning upon her musket, she pondered for a moment or two.

"Tell me, Giovanni," she said, "how is the count attended?"

"By four men, signora," answered the brigand.

"He has ordered mules to be saddled and everything got in readiness to remove the countess to his villa on the road to Castellamare."

"Of course he and his men are well armed?"

"Yes, they all carry swords and pistols," was the reply.

"Listen then," replied La Catarina, with perfect coolness; "do you take care of the men; I will reckon accounts with the master."

Giovanni stared aghast.

"But, signora, you are forgetting Marco Bravo," rejoined the young brigand, in a trembling voice; "what will he say or do, if we presume to thwart his plans?"

"Marco Bravo is your chief," she answered quietly; "but I am your queen, and it was I who invested him with what authority he possesses; remember, I have gifts that proceed from a dread source, powers that can make the boldest among you crouch and tremble."

Giovanni crossed himself.

"She has the *mal occhio*, the evil eye," he muttered; "those she frowns upon sicken and perish."

Then he added aloud—

"Speak your commands, signora: if possible, I will obey them."

"Admit the count——"

The countess held up her hands imploringly.

"Oh, no, no," she gasped; "I will not see him."

"It is impossible to refuse him admission," returned the brigand queen. "but have no fear. I will be near you, and will be your safeguard."

Then addressing Giovanni, she went on.

"Give that to Rozzi, who came hither with me," she said, drawing a diamond ring from her finger; "when he sees it he will remember his oath, for he has sworn to do my bidding; tell him to seize the lackeys in attendance upon the count, to disarm and bind them, and keep them prisoners."

"Good, signora," returned Giovanni, "but I dread the displeasure of Marco Bravo, who will consider it an act of open mutiny."

"Marco Bravo will not dare to dispute my will," replied the queen of the brigands; "besides, I can explain my proceedings in a manner that will satisfy him."

Giovanni gave a shrug of resignation, unwilling enough to obey an order which he dared not disobey.

He was well acquainted with the character of the extraordinary woman with whom he had to deal, and knew that she was not to be trifled with.

"And what message am I to take to the count?" he asked.

"Tell him that the countess will receive him."

Lucia hid her face in her hands, but she dared not offer any further opposition.

Giovanni at once retired.

Grasping her musket in her left hand, the brigand queen pointed with her right to a curtain that screened the entrance of the adjoining chamber, in which the countess slept.

"I will conceal myself behind that curtain," she said; "when the count comes, he will use all his eloquence to persuade you that he has no other design than to deliver you out of the hands of the brigands, but trust him not."

"How can I trust such a perfidious villain?" asked the countess, with disdain.

"Do not go with him, whatever he may say."

"I would rather die on this spot," returned the countess, her eyes flashing.

"Should he attempt to remove you by force," continued La Catarina, "I will instantly fly to your rescue."

Bianca now held up her hand with a terrified look.

"Hush, hush," she said; "he comes."

La Catarina hastily retired to the adjoining chamber, drawing the curtain behind her.

Blushing like a rose, the countess smoothed back the tresses from her forehead and took a seat near the open window, motioning to Bianca to place herself by her side.

Immediately afterwards, the Count Beltrani entered the room.

Very handsome and dashing he looked, dressed in his rich travelling suit, embroidered with gold lace and trimmed with the costliest furs.

The count was a broad-built, dark man, with a luxuriant black moustache, a fine but sensual eye, and a most graceful carriage.

He advanced towards the countess with a well-feigned air of earnest solicitude.

"Signora," he exclaimed, "thank Heaven, I have found you at last."

The countess rose and bowed with coldness.

"I think your excellency has not found it so very difficult a business to discover my whereabout," she answered, with a sarcastic smile.

The count was taken aback; his countenance betrayed the embarassment he felt.

However, he instantly recovered himself.

"For that, signora, the news of your capture by the brigands reached Naples on the same day that the unfortunate mischance occurred," he replied quietly; "as you may suppose, the event caused a profound sensation. Troops were sent out in all directions to hunt down the brigands and extricate you from your unpleasant and dangerous position, but all their efforts to overtake the robbers proved useless."

"How chanced it then that your excellency succeeded where others failed?"

"By a most fortunate accident I discovered that Marco Bravo had carried you off to this ancient, half-ruined fortress," was the count's reply; "I have influence with the villains, for to tell the truth, their mountain retreats are so inaccessible and their powers of annoyance so great, that a weak government, such as at present rules the Neapolitan kingdom, is obliged to negotiate with the outlaws as with some hostile power."

"The more shame to the government," returned the countess, indignantly.

"So say I," rejoined the count; "had I my way, I would soon put an end to such a disgraceful state of affairs, but under existing circumstances, that is impossible."

"Well, signore?"

"I did the best I could," answered the count, shrugging his shoulders. "I knew a trusty fellow who had access to Marco Bravo; I made terms with the brigand chief, and I am here to save you, to restore you to your friends."

The countess smiled disdainfully.

"A plausible tale," she answered; "but, as I well know, false from beginning to end."

The count's cheek flushed with anger.

"Signora!" he exclaimed.

"You know I speak the truth, Count Beltrani," she retorted, with firmness; "if you doubt it, hear this. Marco Bravo himself told me that he acted as he did at the instigation of a rich and powerful employer, who paid him handsomely for his vile services."

The Count Beltrani scowled.

"Ha! the traitor," he muttered.

Then throwing off disguise, he knelt at her feet.

"Adored Lucia," he murmured, in passionate accents, "can you not forgive my bold trespass?—an act to which I was impelled by a reckless but devoted attachment. You know that I have long loved you. Pardon me, accept me, and it shall be the aim of my life to atone for the bold, rash enterprise by which I won you."

"Monsignore," answered the countess, in freezing tones, "when I rejected your suit, I did so with sorrow and regret that I was compelled to give pain to one whom I then considered an honourable gentleman. But now that you have dropped the mask, I tell you I scorn and defy you."

The Count Beltrani smiled.

"Signora, though I have taken a determined course that, perhaps, I can hardly justify to my own conscience, I have gone too far to retract," he said. "I cannot leave you here, in captivity amongst a horde of remorseless villains, from whom your very life is not safe."

"An open foe is easier to withstand than a pretended friend," answered the countess. "I would rather trust myself with these mountain wolves than with you."

Beltrani frowned.

"Your anger overmasters your discretion, signora," he answered; "but I must protect you against your own imprudence."

Then seizing her by the hand, he hurried on in a voice husky with passion—

"Lucia, have pity on me. I love you to distraction. Think how you are compromised. Look forward into the future, and reflect how happy we may be together. I have wealth and power ; I can make you the proudest lady, as you are the loveliest, in the court of King Ferdinand."

"Never !" returned the countess ; "I will die first. I hold my life and honour in my own hands. Approach me at your peril."

As she spoke, she drew the dagger from her scarf, and directed it at her breast.

The count started back.

His face became livid with rage and mortification.

"Nay, then, there is but one course," he shouted. "Since I must use force, I cannot help it. You must and shall be mine ; no other man shall claim you."

As he spoke, he bounded forward, and seizing her by the wrist, wrenched the weapon from her hand.

Lucia shrieked.

"Save me, Catarina—your promise—save me !"

Count Beltrani clutched her by the arm, and dragged her towards the door.

"Come," he said, hoarsely, "you are mine. No power on earth shall part us. Bid your maid follow ; I will save you from yourself."

Again the countess shrieked wildly.

The count's vindictive temper now got the upper hand of him, and grasping her by the arm with brutal violence, he dragged her across the floor.

Then there was a sudden flash, a quick report, and the small turret-chamber became full of smoke.

Count Beltrani uttered a yell of anguish, and staggered backwards.

He dropped heavily upon the floor.

"Accursed treachery," he groaned ; "I am murdered."

The countess and Bianca screamed with dismay.

They recoiled, and clasped in each other's arms, gazed in silent horror upon the form of the count, as he lay writhing and moaning with mortal agony.

Very calmly La Catarina stalked forward, and placing herself before the dying man, grounded her musket, and looked down upon him with the cold, impassible countenance of the executioner who watches the contortions of his victim stretched upon the rack.

The Count Beltrani raised himself upon his elbow, and fixed his bloodshot eyes upon the brigand queen ; his glance bespoke the direst hatred and thirst of revenge.

"La Catarina !" he gasped ; "murderess, 'twas you who slew my father ; you have completed your fiendish work, for I am the last of my race."

Then he eagerly waved his hands, made the sign of the cross, and called for a priest ; he tried to repeat a prayer, but the death rattle in his throat choked his utterance.

Count Beltrani fell back and expired.

The countess and Bianca stood gazing at the dead count, horror-stricken, unable to move or to speak.

At length the countess gasped in a breathless whisper—

"Wretched woman, what have you done ?"

"A good deed," replied La Catarina, with unruffled composure. "I have rid the world of a profligate miscreant, and saved you from an enemy who would have broken your heart, and brought you to an early grave."

"*Maria Madre !*" murmured the countess. "I would rather the worst had befallen me than this deed should be done. I cannot help feeling that I am an accomplice in the dreadful crime."

"Crime !" retorted the brigand queen, with quiet disdain ; "is it a crime to shoot down a wolf, or set one's heel upon an adder ? It is virtue and not crime."

"Oh, take me hence," gasped the countess ; "I cannot bear to look upon him. Ah, Catarina, the memory of this shocking scene will haunt my waking thoughts and nightly dreams. You have rendered me miserable for life."

"Is this your gratitude ?" sneered La Catarina. "If you did not need my help, why did you call on me to save you ?"

"How could I dream that you would take such violent means to save me ?"

"What other means presented themselves ?" returned La Catarina. "The greater number of the band hold their chief in such awe and respect, that I have reason to fear that even my influence, great as it is, would not have availed to induce them to assist you in your escape."

She was interrupted by a hubbub of voices.

A throng of brigands came rushing into the room.

CHAPTER XXIV.

AT the sight of the corpse of Count Beltrani, that lay weltering in a pool of blood, the brigands uttered a shout of consternation.

One of the men stepped forward with knitted brow, his hand grasping the hilt of his stiletto.

"The Count Beltrani slain !" he exclaimed. "The friend of Marco Bravo. Who has done this ?"

"'Twas I who did it," answered La Catarina, boldly.

A murmur ran through the crowd.

"Then, signora, 'tis you must answer for it to our chief," said the spokesman, in a sullen tone.

"I am prepared to answer for my actions to him you call your chief," was the haughty reply, "but I hold myself responsible to none. Am I not your queen ? Tell me, Guiseppe."

There was something so imperious in her manner, that the brigands drew back whispering amongst themselves.

"Answer me," said La Catarina.

Guiseppe shrugged his shoulders.

"We have ever paid due homage to the widow of the renowned Mazzarosa," he answered, sulkily ; "but men cannot serve two masters. The chief will be terribly enraged at what you have done."

La Catarina laughed her scorn.

"Is there one among you, Marco Bravo included, that dares dispute my will ?" she answered. "You had a brother, Guiseppe, what has become of him ?"

RALPH WILDHAWK No. 7 "BOYS OF ENGLAND" EDITION. PRICE ONE PENNY. PUBLISHED AT 173, FLEET STREET, E.C.

"COUNT BELTRANI UTTERED A YELL, AND STAGGERED BACKWARDS."

"You know well enough," he replied, hanging his head. "Poor Maffeo was taken prisoner and shot at Frosinone."

"And why did he meet with such a misfortune?" she asked, sternly; "was it not because he dared to rebel against my authority, and scoff at the powers I derive from a dread source?"

"I know not that," returned Guiseppe. "I only know that you bore him ill-will."

"Not without cause," answered the queen of the brigands. "Do you not remember my parting words to him when he started from the mountains on his fatal expedition?"

"I remember them."

"They are not easily to be forgotten," pursued La Catarina. "'*Andate in mal ora*'— 'go in evil hour,' said I, 'you march to your death.'"

"*E vero*!" murmured the brigands, "it is too true."

Then, again turning to the refractory brigand, with a smile of triumph, she added—

"Do you wish to follow your brother's footsteps, Guiseppe? Will you neglect so palpable a warning?"

"*Zitto!*" cried the brigands. "Guiseppe, do not anger her; she will cast a spell upon you, and you are a dead man."

This warning from his superstitious comrades was not without its effect upon the would-be mutineer.

His olive cheek grew livid, and his strong limbs quivered.

"Pardon, La Catarina," he muttered, with childish simplicity; "I did not mean to offend you. I own your mysterious power. Do me no harm."

"On your knees, then," cried La Catarina, waving her hand. "Acknowledge me as your queen and mistress."

Her poor, stupid dupe instantly crouched at her feet while the rest of the brigands got up a shout—

"*Viva* La Catarina!"

"It is well," she answered, coldly. "Now, remove the count's body, and let it be placed upon a bed. Send a trusty messenger to Marco Bravo to acquaint him with all that has happened."

"It shall be done, signora," rejoined the brigand.

"And now," continued the brigand queen, in the same authoritative manner, "get mules ready, and select a dozen men to accompany these ladies to the Convent of Pozzano."

This order met with general disfavour.

There was a shout of consternation.

"Release the prisoners!" they exclaimed, "we dare not. It is impossible."

Many dark and threatening glances were cast upon the unhappy captives, while several of the desperadoes clutched the hilts of their stilettoes, or handled their muskets as though to suggest their readiness to kill the prisoners rather than set them at liberty.

Lucia and Bianca cowered beneath the dreadful scowls of the remorseless villains by whom they were surrounded, and seemed about to declare that they would not attempt escape, but La Catarina, by a stern look, warned them to be silent.

As for herself, the brigandess maintained her bold, undaunted composure.

In a brief speech, in which there was a strange mixture of fiery eloquence and biting satire, she played with their fears.

She told them that so long as they kept the ladies captive there was no safety for them, that troops would be sent to destroy their fortress and rescue their prisoners, that for the death of the count she would hold herself responsible, and would alone bear the brunt of the law's revenge, while she declared that Marco Bravo had overstepped the bounds of prudence, and that his rash proceeding must inevitably bring about the destruction of the whole band.

This last consideration was not without its weight with the band.

Not a few of the brigands were alarmed at the daring lengths to which their chief carried his schemes of ambition, and were not sorry to find that La Catarina had sufficient courage to put a check upon him.

At all events, they offered no further opposition to her directions.

Having thus wrung from them a reluctant consent to her plan, La Catarina lost no time in carrying it into execution.

The prisoners were to be accompanied by half-a-dozen of the brigands, in the disguise of peasants and shepherds.

Guiseppe, well-armed, took the lead of the little party.

The countess tried to persuade young Giovanni to go with them, promising to procure him a free pardon, and to supply him with a sum of money sufficient to enable him to leave the country and establish himself in a foreign land.

The brigands, both men and women, mustered in the court-yard of the old Moorish fortress to watch the departure of the fair captives thus unexpectedly liberated.

Giovanni took a respectful leave of the countess, thanking her for her generous offer, but steadily refusing to accept it.

La Catarina and the two ladies then mounted their mules, and, guarded by the brigands, set out on their journey to the convent of Pozzano.

For several hours they rode along a narrow, rugged, and perilous mule-track over the mountains.

On the way, it was agreed between the countess and the brigands, that upon their arrival at the convent nothing should be said or done to compromise the latter.

The countess, it was decided, should tell the nuns that they had made their escape from the robbers' stronghold, and had fallen in with a company of peasants that were travelling by the mountain paths to a market at Castellamare.

The sun was setting in a flood of crimson splendour, when the weary and jaded party arrived at the gates of the convent.

Upon ringing the gate-bell, the wicket was opened by an elderly, sour-visaged portress.

The countess asked for shelter, and told the tale which had been dictated to her by the brigands.

The lady superior of the convent was at once sent for.

She came, and received the countess and her attendant with the warmest hospitality.

La Catarina created a great sensation among the simple nuns, both by her picturesque dress, her noble countenance, and lofty and dignified demeanour.

Though grateful to the brigand queen for having preserved her from a fate she dreaded worse than death, the countess could hardly repress a shudder when she felt her lips pressed to her forehead.

"Accept my thanks for the great service you have done me, Catarina," said the countess; "I would to Heaven my deliverance had not been purchased at a price so dreadful. I will pray that your heart may be changed, that you may spend the remainder of your days in some such quiet place of refuge as this convent, and seek consolation for the bitter past where alone it may be found."

But La Catarina only smiled sadly and shook her head.

The brigands and their chieftainess then left the convent.

The countess at first intended leaving the convent within a few days and returning to Naples. This, however, was not to be.

The unfortunate lady was destined to receive a most cruel and unlooked-for shock.

The dreadful news reached her of the murder of poor Captain Lanfranco, to whom she was so passionately attached.

The fatal tidings were told her by a thoughtless servant abruptly and eagerly.

Upon hearing them, the countess uttered one shriek of horror and fell to the ground in a deep swoon.

For several weeks she was confined to her room, so dangerously ill that her life was despaired of.

Her reason fled, and she lay in a kind of stupor, regardless of everybody and everything around her.

Among those who came and remained by her side at this terrible time was the amiable Violet Melville, while Sir Godfrey Mortimer and Ralph Wildhawk came frequently to inquire how she was progressing.

At last the crisis came, but thanks to the youthful vigour and good constitution of the fair patient, it passed favourably.

Though wretchedly pale and woe-begone, and wearing the deepest mourning, the countess was calm and full of energy of purpose; she seemed to have set her mind upon some object which she was bound to achieve at any sacrifice.

She confided her secret to no one but Bianca; when the latter urged her to quit scenes associated with such painful memories, she answered firmly—

"No, Bianca, I shall retire to Sicily for a few months in order to recruit my strength, and then I shall return to Naples, for I have a task to perform, and when that is accomplished, I shall feel content to die."

"What task, signora?" asked Bianca.

Lucia's eyes flashed, and her lips compressed themselves as she answered, in a low, stern voice—

"To avenge the death of my murdered lover."

"But upon whom?" asked her attendant. "Whom do you suspect of having committed the fearful crime?"

"I have no doubt, but a deep-rooted conviction, that the villain who assassinated Lanfranco," she answered, "was no other than Marco Bravo, the chief of the brigands."

CHAPTER XXV.

MEANWHILE, the whole kingdom resounded with a loud outcry against the weakness and supineness of a government that could suffer itself to be set at defiance by a small band of desperate outlaws.

Ralph Wildhawk bestirred himself to organise his company of volunteers, eager to distinguish himself in a foray against such pests of society.

He sought his friend the Count Di Ancona at his residence in the Via Di Toledo, but did not find him at home.

One of the servants gave him a note, in which the count excused himself on the plea of being again forced to leave Naples for a few days, but promising to return as soon as possible, and to take a lead in the expedition against the brigands.

The fact was that Marco Bravo had become terribly enraged and alarmed when he heard of the death of his rich and powerful patron and protector, the Count Beltrani.

He hastened to the mountain fortress, and was still further exasperated at finding that the captive ladies had been suffered to escape.

He heaped all kinds of abuse upon Guiseppe, and even so far forgot himself as to offer to strike him with his stiletto.

It was only through the interposition of Giovanni and Generoso that his life was saved.

"Pardon him, signor," said the young brigand. "He was the least to blame of any. It was he who offered the greatest opposition to La Catarina, but he was overruled."

The brigand chief drew back, and though his breast still panted with rage, he returned the dagger to his sash.

Guiseppe stood hat in hand before his enraged chief, his eyes bent sullenly upon the ground, his lips curved in a sneer that betokened treachery.

Marco Bravo scowled fiercely around at his followers.

"Dolts and idiots that ye are," he growled, "will you suffer yourselves to be led to destruction by a reckless, capricious woman, whom grief and wrong have rendered half mad?"

He paused, and again turned a wrathful look upon Guiseppe.

"And you, too—you to whom I entrusted the command during my absence, what excuse have you to make for an act of revolt?"

"I did but execute her orders who is the acknowledged queen of the band," returned Guiseppe. "Warned by the fate of my poor brother, I dared not brave her displeasure. She has the evil eye; there is no resisting her mysterious power. If she puts her ban upon anyone who offends her, misfortune follows his track as surely as night succeeds the day."

"True, true," murmured the brigands; "La Catarina is not to be offended."

"Well for her that she can keep herself out of the clutches of the familiars of the Inquisition," retorted Marco Bravo, with a sneer, "since her own companions accuse her of witchcraft. I would La Catarina were here."

"You have your wish," replied a firm, thrilling voice. "I am here to answer for myself."

The crowd divided.

La Catarina, gun in hand, and with countenance as calm and composed as the face of some classic statue, stood before the astonished brigand chief.

Marco Bravo frowned and bit his lip in vexation.

Nevertheless, he bowed courteously, for there was something in the air of the brigand queen which commanded respect.

"Signora," said Marco Bravo, "I deeply regret that you have thought proper to exercise your authority in a manner so strange. The result cannot fail to be serious to us all. It was bad enough that you should have killed the Count Beltrani, on whose protection we have so long depended for security, and from whom we derived so much profit, but it was worse to let the prisoners go who, while we detained them, were our best safeguard against a host of enemies."

La Catarina smiled disdainfully.

"Signor Marco Bravo," she answered, with cool politeness, "I had a perfect right to act as I pleased in the matter."

The brigand stared at this assertion.

"If that be the case," he answered, "I have no alternative left but to resign my command."

Then, turning to his men, he took off his hat and bowed haughtily.

"Comrades," he said, "I am no longer your captain. I am sure there is not one amongst you who will not render me the justice of acknowledging that I have done my best to serve you—that I have carried you successfully through bolder, yet more prosperous, enterprises than were ever undertaken by any of my predecessors—that I have encountered the same dangers, shared the same hardships, as the humblest amongst you—have dealt fairly in the division of the spoil; in short, that I have devoted myself heart and soul to the interests of the band. I challenge denial. Farewell, then, my brave companions! All I ask in parting with you is that you will still bear me in remembrance."

This speech occasioned the profoundest amazement and consternation among the excited brigands.

As, with proud and stately step, the brigand chief turned and moved away, his followers closed around him like a pack of frightened children.

Some clutched his mantle, others embraced his knees, but all were alike earnest in displaying their unwillingness to part with so brave and distinguished a leader.

"No, no, we will never desert our noble captain," was the unanimous shout. "*Eviva* Marco Bravo!"

A subtle smile stole over the brigand's handsome though sinister features.

He gracefully waved his hand towards the brigand queen.

"Comrades, I am deeply moved by this demonstration of attachment and fidelity," he said; "but you must choose between us—one alone can command. Is it to be myself or the signora?"

The band, with a superstitious dread of the supposed mystic powers of La Catarina, stood silent and perplexed.

La Catarina burst into a hearty laugh.

"A pretty comedy, and well played, Signor Marco Bravo."

Then she paused, and resumed, in an even and conciliatory tone—

"But what is more to the purpose, you are a brave and skilful leader, whose loss would be irreparable."

This was spoken with such evident sincerity that the band were quite delighted.

"*Viva* La Catarina!" they shouted. "*Viva* Marco Bravo!"

La Catarina advanced a pace towards the brigand chief.

"Why should there be any misunderstanding between us?" she said, with a bold frankness that was very telling. "Let me remind you how after the capture and execution of the late gallant chief, Mazzarosa, I was freely elected queen of the band. As for the Count Beltrani, I had a *vendetta* against him."

Marco Bravo started.

"Is it possible?" he exclaimed; "for what cause?"

"For his father's sake," rejoined La Catarina. "He was my personal foe, a perfidious villain, who ensnared my husband and wrecked my happiness for life. With my own hand I slew the son; I glory in the deed. Were there a hundred of the serpent brood, I could crush them without one qualm of remorse."

"It is unfortunate, however, signora," was the cold reply, "that in avenging your own quarrels you should imperil the safety of the band."

La Catarina answered quickly—

"Not so, all is for the best."

Marco Bravo sneered and shook his head.

"Yet it is true," rejoined La Catarina; "mark me, signor, that man Beltrani was a man to be dreaded, most of all by yourself. He used you as a mere tool, to do his foul work; and, when he needed your services no longer, he would have thrown off the mask, and abandoned you to destruction. Let him go; if we incur some present danger through my act of retribution, what of that? Do we not ever carry our lives in our hands? Is not peril the abiding condition of our existence?"

"It cannot be denied," said Marco Bravo.

"Courage, then," rejoined La Catarina; "let us be friends; the future spreads before us clearer, safer than before."

"Enough, signora," answered Marco Bravo, kissing her hand. "I am satisfied."

At beholding this reconciliation between their admired chief and the sybil, of whom they stood in such childish awe, the brigands waved their hats, brandished their weapons and shouted vociferously.

There was but one man who held aloof, and showed no sign of pleasure.

It was Guiseppe.

He was deeply wounded by his chief's anger and menace, and resolved upon having his revenge.

"Proud as he is," muttered Guiseppe, "within a month he shall be pining a prisoner in the strongest dungeon of St. Elmo."

Harmony thus restored, Marco Bravo proceeded to unfold his schemes for the future.

The first question that arose was how to dispose of the body of the murdered Count Beltrani.

At length Generoso hit upon an expedient.

There was a hut on the mountains, belonging to a shepherd in league with the brigands, and situated on a mule track, at a few miles' distance from Castellamare.

The body was to be conveyed thither, and left in charge of the shepherd.

The man was then to be directed to convey the news to the authorities in Naples, of what the brigands had done, even at the risk of his being impressed as a guide to the Brigands' Glen.

"I have no fear," said Marco Bravo. "The man I know may be trusted."

Then he expressed a wish to see the body of the count.

He waved his followers back and entered the tower alone.

Mounting the spiral staircase, he went into the bedchamber lately occupied by the countess and her maid.

The room was darkened, for the narrow window was shaded with a striped Venetian awning, but through this the mellow light struck in, and fell upon the dead man's face.

Stretched upon the bed, cold and rigid as a marble effigy upon a tomb, he lay, the ineffably beautiful repose of death impressed upon his features.

"After life's fitful fever, he sleeps well!"

Marco Bravo stood gazing upon the inanimate form of his patron and employer, late the gayest of the gay, with a clouded brow.

"When will this come to me?" he muttered to himself. "And how? Perhaps in some hot encounter, perhaps by treachery. Let it come. It is rest. It is welcome anywhere but on the scaffold."

Then a sudden recollection flashed upon his brain.

Hard of heart as he was, he shuddered violently.

He thought of poor Captain Lanfranco as he lay upon the blood-soddened sand, his glassy eyes staring blindly upwards at the unpitying heavens.

With a forced laugh of scorn at his own weakness, he hurried from the chamber of death.

CHAPTER XXVI.

IT will be remembered that when the Count Beltrani came to the brigands' stronghold, in order to carry off Lucia Di Carrara, he brought with him four men servants.

By the orders of La Catarina, these poor fellows had been overpowered, disarmed, and kept in close confinement.

Marco Bravo directed that they should be released, and sent under an escort of the robbers, to accompany the dead body of their murdered master to its resting-place at the hut of the *padrone*, or head-shepherd, in the mountain defile.

These arrangements were strictly carried out.

In the city a court of inquiry was convened, and a company of dragoons were sent to the shepherd's hut, to bring away the corpse.

Meanwhile, Ralph Wildhawk and Edmund Mortimer had exerted themselves with success in raising a troop of volunteers to wage war with the brigands, and so many recruits hastened to join them, that Marco Bravo himself became alarmed.

"I must muzzle this young British bulldog," mused the brigand.

He pondered for some time in this vein.

At length, his thoughtful brow cleared, and he chuckled to himself at having hit upon an expedient for getting Ralph into his power.

"The young madcap; he is as simple and confiding as he is daring and adventurous," said the brigand to himself. "I will entice him to take a walk with me into the mountains, and there make him a prisoner."

The next day Ralph Wildhawk called at the count's residence, in the Via Di Toledo.

The young Englishman appeared to be in the highest of spirits.

"See, excellenza," he said, producing a notebook, "since last I had the pleasure of visiting you, no less than twenty brave gentlemen have joined our corps, and we are resolved at once to commence active operations."

"It is time something was done," rejoined the count. "What a terrible affair is this of Count Beltrani's!"

"One's blood boils to think such outrages can be possible in any civilised community," said Ralph. "But it is some consolation to reflect that the career of the villain Marco Bravo draws to a close."

"It has been long enough, in all conscience," replied the count. "And now let me beg your attention, signore, to a proposal I have to make."

Ralph bowed.

"I am all attention."

"I think the exploit I am about to suggest is just such a one as will suit your enterprising temperament."

He then took from the drawer of a bureau a map, which he spread out upon the table.

"This is a map of the whole range of the Apennines," the count explained.

He then laid his finger on a small cross, marked in red ink.

"You may be aware that I am the owner of a large farm near the town from the name of which I derive my title. I mean Ancona," continued the wily villain.

"Well, signore?"

"Now, this cross I have marked denotes a shepherd's station, and a wild and almost inaccessible gorge, known as the 'Brigands' Glen.'"

"I guess your purpose," cried Ralph, his eyes sparkling with animation; "we are to go to this shepherd's station as scouts and gather what information we can as to the whereabouts and the strength of the enemy."

" Exactly so," returned the count. " The shepherd I employ has been in the service of my family since his boyhood ; he will give us shelter, and guard our secret."

" But I suppose it will be necessary for us to assume some disguise ?" asked Ralph.

" Yes, we will dress ourselves as peasants, or mountain-guides," replied the count ; " and my man, Generoso, shall accompany us."

" It is an excellent plan," rejoined Ralph ; " but we must take care to go well armed."

" It will be prudent to do so," returned the count, " but we must be cautious ; we must, of course, leave our swords at home. For my part, I shall take a brace of pistols and a stiletto, and perhaps a carbine, which will be in keeping with our assumed character of mountaineers."

" Very good," said Ralph ; " I will go at once and purchase the necessary clothing, and will rejoin your excellency at whatever time or place you may be pleased to appoint."

" You cannot do better," the count replied. " But let me impress upon you the necessity of keeping our intentions a profound secret. Marco Bravo has his spies in all quarters, and it is scarcely safe to trust anyone."

" I will not neglect your warning."

" Agreed, then," replied the count ; " meet me here, at about this hour to-morrow."

Ralph Wildhawk gave his word to keep the appointment, and took his leave.

When he was gone, the count burst into a long and hearty fit of laughter.

" He is mine !" he exclaimed, rubbing his hands. " I will station some of my men in ambush, and secure him, and keep him a prisoner alone in the Brigands' Glen."

And the brigand smiled grimly, thinking that Ralph Wildhawk would fall into his trap.

After a few moments' thought, Marco Bravo muttered—

" But whilst I thus capture young Wildhawk, I must manage the whole business in such a manner that he shall not suspect me of treachery. I will be taken prisoner at the same time as himself, and he shall be kept in the belief that I am what I pretend to be—the Count Di Ancona."

He rang the bell.

Generoso answered the summons.

" I attend your orders, signor capitano," he said.

" Those men I sent for, Generoso," said the count ; " have they arrived ?"

" Yes, signore ; they are below."

" It is well," said the count. " Who are they ?"

" Stromba and Pietro," replied the other.

" Guiseppe has done well in sending them," said the brigand chief. " He could not have selected two better men for my purpose."

" Shall I introduce them ?"

" At once," was the reply.

The man bowed, and left the room.

Presently he returned, bringing with him the two brigands.

They stood, hat in hand, before their chief ; their eyes bent reverentially upon the ground.

" Welcome, comrades !" said Marco Bravo. " Now listen to my directions.

" I am about to play off a little stratagem, by means of which we shall secure a young fellow. the secretary of the rich milordo," said the brigand chief ; " and I shall require your assistance."

He then directed their attention to a certain point on the map.

" You see this narrow place, marked on this chart ?" he said. " Do you know what it indicates ?"

" Yes, signore," answered Stromba ; " it is the Devil's Gorge, which gives access to the Brigand's Glen."

" Right," said Marco Bravo. " Now mark well my directions. I and Generoso are to go on a hunting expedition into the mountains, in company with the young Englishman whom I intend to capture ; we shall be dressed as peasants. I will lure our man to the entrance of the gorge ; there you must lie in ambush, and at a signal from Generoso, rush forth and make us all prisoners."

The brigands grinned, and nodded significantly.

" We understand, signore," they replied. " We are to lay hands on you, as though you were a stranger, and a prize, that the Englishman may not suspect the truth."

" Precisely," answered Marco Bravo. " But more than that, you must pretend to recognise me as the Count Di Ancona, against whom your chief entertains the fiercest animosity. To carry out the farce, appear to deliberate whether you shall take my life upon the spot. Do all you can think of to hoodwink my companion."

The brigands laughed, and promised to obey these orders to the letter.

Their chief then dismissed them, telling Generoso to supply them with refreshments, and to give them such further explanations as they might require.

CHAPTER XXVII.

RALPH WILDHAWK, upon returning home, amused himself for some time in cleaning and loading his firearms, and in packing in a knapsack a few articles which he deemed necessary for the expedition.

Amongst other things he resolved to take with him, were a telescope, a compass, and a leathern flask of brandy.

It must be observed that Ralph Wildhawk was not staying at Castellamare with Sir Godfrey Mortimer and his family, but occupied lodgings in Naples.

" I will go to the opera," said Ralph to himself. " There is a new ballet to-night, and La Zara dances. It is a month since I saw the charming girl. It is well for me that my love for Violet precludes another passion, or the lovely gipsy girl might cost me a heart-ache."

Then putting on his sword, and flinging his cloak around him, he donned his hat, and went forth into the streets, always gay and crowded, in this merry capital, till a very late hour.

Ralph Wildhawk was well known to the officials of the theatre, who at once escorted him to Sir Godfrey's box.

The ballet was an Eastern spectacle, the scenery beautiful, and the costumes magnificent.

La Zara danced with more than usual grace and agility, and her performance met with frantic applause.

Ralph Wildhawk looked round the house, and was not displeased to find that Edmund Mortimer was not present.

As soon as the curtain fell, our young hero left the theatre, and proceeded homewards.

It was a glorious night, and the walls and pavements were flooded with the silvery moonbeams.

A hallowed stillness prevailed around, the more impressive from its contrast with the noise and bustle of the glaring scene which Ralph had just quitted.

He was walking leisurely along, when his startled ear caught the echo of a half-stifled shriek.

It seemed to be the voice of a woman in pain or distress.

Ralph Wildhawk paused in his walk, and listened; but the cry was not repeated.

Then he heard the heavy rumble of coach wheels.

He hurried on.

Soon the gleam of a lantern met his gaze.

He paused, and proceeded more cautiously, until he entered a small open square.

Here he found a carriage drawn up.

The coachman on the box looked anxiously behind him, while of the two footmen, one stood holding the carriage door open, while the other stood beside him, holding aloft a lantern.

Presently a group of men advanced.

The one who led the way was a tall, slim fellow; he bore in his arms a young female, thickly veiled.

He and his companions were all masked.

They approached the carriage.

As they did so, Ralph perceived that the female so far recovered as to be able to make a faint struggle to extricate herself from the arms of the masked man, who held her tight.

A gurgling cry came from her lips, but it was evident that she had no power to cry out aloud, for her mouth was gagged.

"What brutal outrage is this?" thought Ralph Wildhawk; "some poor girl they are carrying off by violence. I will defend her with my life."

He flung himself before them.

Whipping his sword from the sheath, he approached the leader, and presented the point at his breast.

"Held!" he shouted; "you shall not stir till you have unmasked yourselves, and have told for what reason this lady is thus dragged by force through the streets."

The man whom he addressed staggered back; he appeared quite thunderstruck.

Then turning to his companions, he muttered something to them in Italian.

They responded with a savage growl.

There were three of them.

The tallest and burliest of the three now made a rush at Ralph, lunging at him with his sword.

Stepping backwards, the young Englishman parried the stroke, and then, with a forward bound, passed his sword through the ruffian's body.

When they saw their comrade sink to the ground, mortally wounded, the others uttered a fierce shout, and flung themselves upon Ralph.

One attempted to seize him by the throat, but Ralph hurled him back by a blow with his fist.

His head struck against the base of a pillar, and he rolled upon the ground, stunned and senseless.

The other took to his heels, and in an instant was out of sight.

Ralph then turned upon the man who still bore the struggling girl in his arms.

"Release the lady, and throw off your mask," cried Ralph, "or by Heaven I will kill you on the spot!"

The only answer to this threat was a muttered execration, and calling upon the servants in charge of the carriage to come to his assistance, the man tried to push by.

Ralph turned pale, and lowered his weapon, for the voice sounded familiar to him.

Resolved to convince himself of the other's identity, he sprang upon him and tore the mask from his face.

Upon beholding the countenance of his antagonist, Ralph uttered a cry of horror and astonishment.

It was Edmund Mortimer.

Edmund's features were distorted, and perfectly livid with rage and mortification.

"Beware what you do, Ralph Wildhawk," he said; "I will not brook your insolent interference. Stand back, and let me pass, or your blood be upon your own head!"

"Release the lady, or you shall not pass," cried Ralph.

Their swords crossed.

Edmund thrust savagely, but Ralph only parried to defend himself.

Meanwhile Zara, for the captured lady was the young dancer, by a violent effort managed to extricate herself, and removed the scarf from her face.

She would have taken to flight, but one of the servants caught her by the wrist, and held her fast.

Edmund, who appeared to have lost all self-control, and to be intent upon killing, or at least maiming, the generous youth who had been his companion from boyhood, kept up the struggle with the bitterest determination.

Ralph had as much as he could do to save himself, and at the same time to avoid hurting the son of his employer and benefactor.

Yet he possessed the advantage of being by far the better swordsman of the two.

For some moments they fought furiously, while Zara struggled with the ruffianly fellow who held her, and rent the air with shrieks for help.

Ralph, by a dexterous turn of his sword, brought the blade against the hilt of his opponent's weapon, and with a light fillip sent it flying through the air.

It flew over Edmund's shoulder, and fell with a clash on the opposite side of the street.

At this moment a shout was heard in the distance, and a mob of men and women, bearing torches, were running towards the scene of the fray.

"Thank Heaven, here come my friends!" panted Zara.

Again she shrieked wildly.

Ralph looked round, and trembled with excitement and dismay.

"Fly!" he shouted to Edmund; "it is the gipsy band; one moment's hesitation, and you are lost."

Edmund saw his danger, and, disarmed as he was, had no alternative but to submit to circumstances.

He cast a spiteful look at Ralph.

"This is an awkward affair," he said, "but I can make it worth your while to keep it a secret. Yet, I doubt not that your high sense of honour and duty will compel you to betray me to my father."

"Perish the thought!" returned Ralph, with calm disgust. "As for your base insinuation, it does but accord with the rest of your conduct. I shall be glad enough to forget the events of this night. But escape while you can; get into the carriage, and bid your knave drive fast."

Seizing Edmund by the arm, he pushed him into the carriage, and shouted to the man to drive on.

He slammed-to the door, the footman sprang up behind, the coachman lashed the horses, and the vehicle dashed away at lightning speed.

As soon as it was gone, Zara came to Ralph's side.

Her dark, eloquent eyes beamed with gratitude.

"Signore, how can I thank you?" she said, in her softest accents, "for your brave and generous defence of me? Never shall I forget the debt I owe to you."

"Do not speak of it, signora," replied the young Englishman; "I am but too happy to have found an opportunity of serving you. But, tell me, do you know the man who has been guilty of this disgraceful outrage?"

"But too well, signore," was her reply. "He is the son of the great English milordo."

Then looking backwards at the approaching crowd of gipsies, she added, in a frightened whisper—

"I beseech you do not mention his name to my brother Isaco, who is so jealous of my honour that he would not fail to wreak dire vengeance on anyone who dared to offer me the slightest insult."

"Signora, I shall not disregard your caution," replied Walter. "But I am ashamed to know that one of my countrymen should have acted such a villain's part."

The gipsies now came rushing up, their torches flaring, and their faces betraying the utmost indignation.

At their head strode a tall, broad-shouldered fellow, with swarthy features, black eyes that glowed like living coals, and black hair that streamed upon his shoulders in long silky ringlets that a woman might envy.

He was fantastically dressed, and wore a wealth of barbaric finery, a gold chain hung round his neck, and his fingers sparkled with valuable gems.

Upon seeing Ralph, he glared at him darkly and suspiciously.

Zara saw the look, and knew its import; she hastened to explain the state of affairs.

"Oh, my brother," she said. "This brave signore has saved me from a set of ruffians, who would have carried me off but for his timely and gallant defence. Single-handed he fought against seven of them, and had you not come when you did, he must have been slain."

The king of the gipsies bowed haughtily to the English youth.

"Eccelenza, receive my best thanks for the noble service you have rendered to my dear sister," he said. "Trust me, I shall not let it pass unrecognised."

"I have done no more than anyone would have done under the same circumstances," said Ralph. "But let me advise you, Signor Isaco, not to expose your beautiful and accomplished sister to such a peril again."

"Who were the wretches that dared to attempt this act of violence?" the gipsy king asked, sternly, as he turned to his sister. "I will have justice, or if that be denied me, will take my own revenge."

"I know not who they were," she answered, trembling; "they were all masked, and wrapped close in their mantles."

"Do you know them, signore?" he asked, addressing himself to Ralph.

"They were masked," returned Ralph, evasively; "but I doubt not you will be able to discover who they were."

"Stay but one moment, signore," answered the gipsy king; "here lie two of the rascals; let us have a look at their faces."

Then he beckoned one of his men.

"Michael," he said, "give me your torch."

The gipsy placed it in his hand.

He stepped forward, and held the flaming link over the face of the man Ralph had killed.

"Remove his mask."

This was done.

The ghastly face thus revealed to the light, was seen to wear, even in death, its wonted evil scowl.

The gipsies uttered a general shout.

"It is Fontana."

"You know him then?" asked Ralph.

"Well enough," returned the king of the gipsies. "You have done well in ridding the world of one of the vilest scoundrels that ever dealt a stab in the dark; he belonged to the gang of Paolo Spadovio, a profesional assassin."

"Can it be possible that Edmund has fallen so low," thought Ralph, "as to league himself with such atrocious villains?"

The gipsy king then turned away to examine the other ruffian who, though not dead, lay a heap of senseless, bleeding humanity.

Before, however, they had time to remove his mask, they met with an interruption.

The roll of drums and the sound of a bugle were heard, and the steady tramp of a body of men advancing towards them.

"It is the patrol," cried Michael; "let us begone. If they overtake us, they may ask unpleasant questions, and perhaps put us all under arrest."

"Home then," returned the gipsy king. "Sister, lean upon my arm; fear not, the wrong you have suffered shall not pass unavenged."

Ralph was about to bid them farewell, but the gipsy king laid his hand upon his arm.

"Do not leave us, signore," he said; "should you fall into the hands of the soldiers, the result might be annoying, to say the least of it."

Ralph thought so too.

"You are right," he answered; "I do not wish to be interrogated."

"Come, then, with us," rejoined Isaco Il Nero; "while you are under my protection, no one will dare to molest you."

"I will go," said Ralph.

They then hurried off in the direction of that quarter of the city in which the gipsies lived.

They had scarcely turned the corner of the street, when there was a shout of dismay from the soldiers, which made it clear that they had stumbled upon the bodies of the dead and wounded bravoes.

Once more the bugle rang out its piercing note of alarm.

Isaco lifted his sister in his brawny arms, and the whole party hastened their flight.

Arrived at the gipsies' haunt, Ralph Wildhawk was cordially entertained by Isaco Il Nero.

The gipsy king produced some bottles of the rarest wines, and a right royal carouse ensued.

Ralph would willingly have retired from the scene of revelry, but could find no reasonable excuse for giving offence to his genial host.

He was prudent enough to abstain from drinking deeply.

He remembered what a task the morrow had in store for him.

The mirth grew fast and furious.

Songs were sung, and wild dances wildly danced by the merry Bohemians to the strum of guitars, the squeaking of pipes, the drone of the bag-pipe, and the click-clack of the castanets.

At length, however, King Isaco called for silence.

With some difficulty order was obtained.

The king then turned to Ralph, and with appropriate gravity, proposed to make him free of the gipsy band.

Ralph Wildhawk would have laughingly declined this honour, but Zara, who sat beside him, urged him by no means to refuse it.

"I pray you, signore," she said, "become one of us. If you are once adopted into the band, you will never lack friends at need. Life is uncertain, the times are troublous; you may be placed in circumstances of difficulty and danger, when the help of devoted friends may be of great value. Become a Zingaro, if only for my sake," she added, gazing upon his frank, handsome face with a pensive, but bewitching tenderness that was irresistible.

"Lovely Zara," he answered, "I shall take your counsel, and with pride and delight, join a community of which you are so bright an ornament."

Zara laughed rather bitterly, shook her head, sighed, and cast down her eyes.

"He loves me not," she mused. "Love admires, worships, but does not flatter. Yet he is my friend, and now will become even as a brother. I am glad he will join the band."

Ralph Wildhawk having expressed his willingness to be initiated into the mysteries, and to claim the rights of the brotherhood of the free Zingari, preparations were made to gratify his wish.

The initiation was performed with many curious and fantastic ceremonies too long and complex to enter into.

It was evident they were of Eastern and of very ancient origin.

The *patrico*, or priest, officiated throughout, and when all was over, he called upon Ralph to pay him a small fee.

Ralph threw into his hat quite a handful of English guineas, telling him to spend part of it in wine and food for the poorer members of the band.

This mark of the friendliness and liberality on the part of their newly-joined brother, made a very favourable impression upon the gipsy band, who one and all swore they would risk their lives in his behalf if called upon to do so.

The hour was now grown so late that Ralph became anxious to take his departure.

It was not without reluctance that his hospitable sovereign suffered him to go, sending two of his men with torches to conduct him out of the maze-like quarter into the open thoroughfares.

When he reached the door, Zara, who had very timidly followed, took him by the hand, and placed a splendid emerald ring upon his finger.

"Wear this in remembrance of the poor gipsy girl who has so much cause to keep you in dear memory," she said. in a tremulous voice. "Do not lose it, for it is a talisman; while you wear it, you are proof against the worst evil that may beset you—will triumph over all dangers and difficulties. *Addio*, signore; forget me not."

CHAPTER XXVIII.

THE next morning Ralph Wildhawk rose betimes, and prepared himself for his journey to the mountains.

He dressed himself in the picturesque costume worn by the peasants of the Apennines.

It consisted of a jacket and breeches of dark brown velveteen, a long mantle and slouched hat, gaiters and heavy boots.

In this attire Ralph looked his assumed character to perfection.

Having thus equipped himself, he wrote a letter to Sir Raymond Mortimer to acquaint him of his purpose, despatched it, and then hurried off to the Via Di Toledo to meet his friend the count.

He found him and Generoso awaiting him, ready and impatient for the start.

They were dressed in similar style to himself, and both were well armed.

The count heartily shook hands with his young friend.

"*Per Baccho!*" he said, "what a difference dress makes to a man's appearance. Capital,

capital, the mountaineer to the life. What is your opinion, Generoso?"

The fellow grinned.

"*Eccelenza!* I think with you the disguise is perfect," he answered. "No one could help being deceived by it."

"I am glad you are satisfied," returned Ralph Wildhawk; "but I am afraid that if we fall in with a party of real mountaineers, they will detect my imposture through my awkwardness in climbing."

"You awkward—you are just a little too rash, that's all," replied the count. "I remember, on the occasion of our madcap chase after the escaped brigand, your agility quite astonished me."

"And now, signore, what is your intention as regards the route we are to take?"

"I have arranged all with such prudence and precaution as I am master of," was the count's reply. "I will tell you my plans as we proceed on our way. How far has the driver agreed to take us?"

"As far as Isernia."

"That will do," answered the count; "of course, we must pursue the rest of our journey on foot."

Then he poured out three glasses of wine.

"Come, my friends," he said, "let us drink a toast to our undertaking, and then we will be off at once."

They raised their glasses, and clinked them together.

"A prosperous and successful journey," said Ralph Wildhawk; "and may it result in the capture and death of the ruffian Marco Bravo."

The count laughed.

"There will be time enough to think of that after our return," he said. "Meanwhile, let us rather wish that we may not fall into the rascal's clutches."

Generoso nodded grimly.

"Your excellency has good cause to say that," he rejoined; "for I have been told that Marco Bravo has a special animosity against yourself, and has sworn to take your life."

"Oh, the pleasant rogue," he laughed, "he does me much honour in considering me of so much importance. But, *andiamo,*" he added, clapping Ralph on the back, "let us be going."

They left the house by a back entrance, so as to escape observation, and made their way to a quiet street where the vetturino had been ordered to wait for them.

The count spoke to the driver in the dialect which is peculiar to the mountaineers of the Abruzzi.

The man, who happened to be a native of one of the mountain villages, appeared to be quite pleased at being addressed in a language familiar to him since a boy, and soon was on excellent terms with the chief of the hunting party.

They adjourned to a wine shop to drink a stirrup-cup together before starting.

Ralph was struck with admiration at the ease and naturalness with which the noble, high-born, and accomplished Count Di Ancona, adapted himself to the humble character he had assumed.

"What a capital actor he would have made," thought Ralph; "no part comes amiss to him;

he certainly can be all things with all men. He's a wonder."

Leaving the wine shop, they returned to the carriage, and got in. The vetturino mounted the box, lashed his horses, and urged on his wild career in the break-neck, devil-may-care fashion of his reckless tribe.

"We shall stop for the night at Isernia," said the count. "There is an inn there which is much frequented by hunting parties; we shall there dismiss the vetturino, and then, my friend, we must mount to the lofty fastnesses of the eagle, the izzard, and the brigand."

Ralph cast a glance at the snow-crowned peaks and glaciers of the mighty range in the distance.

The road was straight and level to the foot, and led to the lofty range of mountains which bound the plain of Solomna on the south.

The ascent began under the town of Peterano, and continued with little intermission for five miles.

At this little town, the last view over the plain is one of those rare prospects which are never forgotten by the traveller; it is, perhaps, the finest scenery of its kind in Italy.

The whole plain is spread out like a map at the foot of the pass, and the distant prospect is bounded by a long line of snowy mountains.

Another wild defile, two miles in length, brought them to a second village, placed in a deep, precipitous ravine, in one of the most desolate quarters of the pass.

The ascent which followed was very steep, and our travellers were forced to leave the carriage, and trudge on foot.

The country became wilder and more dreary than that already passed.

Our travellers stopped at a little wayside tavern, to rest and refresh themselves.

The innkeeper, a bluff, jolly old fellow, served them up a substantial repast, and a bottle of excellent wine.

After they had made a hearty meal they placed themselves at the window, to smoke a cigar, enjoy the magnificent prospect, and to taste the fresh, keen, bracing mountain breeze.

The landlord soon joined them, and soon they were chatting quite cosily together.

The host was very inquisitive.

He asked them many questions, to all of which the count gave the most plausible and truth-seeming replies.

At last, he turned the conversation upon affairs of the chase.

"Have there been many hunting-parties of foreigners and tourists, this year?"

"A good many," replied the host. "Especially those half-mad English, who will brave anything. They have thinned the game the more because they are obliged to form themselves into large parties, to protect themselves against the brigands."

"The brigands!" repeated Ralph Wildhawk. "Is it not said that the notorious Marco Bravo and his gang infest this district?"

The landlord changed countenance.

"Who knows?" he answered, shrugging his broad shoulders. "He is like a Will-o'-the-wisp, here, there, and everywhere; but, no doubt he has his favourite retreats in many parts of the Abruzzi."

A cynical leer flitted over the count's dark, saturnine features.

"But I am told he is a good friend of the inhabitants of these mountain hamlets," he said; "that he never molests you, and that, so long as you abstain from treachery, you have no cause to fear him."

"On the contrary," replied the innkeeper, looking keenly at his guest, "Marco Bravo has been a benefactor to some of our villages."

"In what way?" asked Ralph.

"About two years ago," replied the landlord, "a fearful storm threw down the walls built to retain the soil, carried away the earth and its produce, and destroyed the labour of years. As you may imagine, there was fearful distress and suffering among the peasants; not a few of them dying with hunger. It is hardly credible, but no less true, that Marco Bravo sent a thousand piastres to relieve the pressing wants of the starving wretches."

The count laughed.

"I think you have cause to congratulate yourself that you live under his reign, rather than his predecessor's. I mean the terrible Mammone."

"San Francesco! what an incarnate demon that fellow was!" exclaimed the innkeeper.

"Do you remember him?" asked Ralph Wildhawk. "I thought he lived before your time."

"No; though I was a mere child when he was taken and shot, I still remember with horror the frightful tales told by my parents and neighbours," replied the innkeeper.

He then pointed to a curiously-shaped copper vessel, much battered, that hung from a rafter.

"There is a relic of his cruelty," he said; "one of his instruments of torture."

"That!" replied Ralph, getting up to examine the object thus pointed out to him. "It looks harmless, and resembles nothing in the world so much as a copper kettle."

"You must know that what I am telling you, happened during the late war between the kingdom of Naples and the French," continued the landlord. "Mammone and Fra Diavolo, with other chiefs and their banditti, offered their swords to the king of Naples. Their offer was eagerly accepted by the king and queen, who loaded their ruffianly allies with honours, and addressed them as 'our generals, and our friends.'"

"Precious generals!" said Ralph.

"The process resorted to by the robbers for discovering the whereabouts of the peasants' treasure was a cruel and effectual one. Yonder kettle, full of oil, was set on the fire. If an unfortunate woman who protested that she was ignorant where her husband had hid his treasure, relented, and showed the place, she was not molested; but if she persisted in her obstinacy, or really did not know where it was, the scalding oil was poured upon her neck, breast, and body."

"Good Heaven! what monsters!" exclaimed Ralph, and he turned to the count, saying—"I rejoice more and more that we have undertaken to hunt down fiends who can commit such atrocities."

"You may well call them fiends, for they are the most barbarous ruffians that ever walked the earth," said the landlord.

Then he continued—

"I can assure you that many were subjected to this inhuman treatment, others were merely beaten; and there is a very worthy woman, a neighbour of mine, in this same village. who boasts to this day, that, though the ruffians stabbed her in several places, she did not betray her husband's trust."

In such conversation as this, two hours passed away, when the pretended chamois-hunters paid their score, shook hands with their genial host, and resumed their journey.

Night had closed in before they reached the base of a remarkable rocky mountain, called Monte Maggiorone, and drove their jaded horses along the rough stretch of road that led to the district of Isernia, with the snowy peaks of Matese in the distance.

They put up at an inn, called "La Posta," and, wearied out by their long and tiring journey, retired to rest directly after they had supped.

Ralph fell at once into a profound sleep; but his rest was disturbed by the most terrible dreams.

His mind was filled by the terrific images called up by the tales of the brigands he had heard during the day.

He imagined himself a prisoner in their hands; their dark, fiend-like faces scowled around him; their fists were shaken in his face, and their stilettoes flashed before his eyes.

Then he thought he was dragged away, to a dark and gloomy chamber, around which were ranged the rack and wheel, and every variety of implements of torture.

In the midst of this horrible dungeon, stood an immense cauldron, standing in the midst of a pyre of fiercely-burning coals, and throwing off a dense cloud of rolling vapour.

He thought that beside it stood the chief of the ruffian band.

As Ralph was dragged forwards, the chief, with the laugh of a demon, pointed to the boiling cauldron, and advanced to clutch his victim.

As he did so, the mask fell off his face, and Ralph recoiled with a shout of horror, as he recognised the familiar features of his pretended friend, the Count Di Ancona.

A cheery laugh rang in his ears, and a glare of sunshine dazzled his eyes.

He started up, and felt a heavy hand laid upon his shoulder.

"Basta!" exclaimed a well-known voice, "I fear you have slept but badly."

Ralph looked round, and as he recovered his scattered faculties, he perceived that it was the count himself, who sat by his bedside.

"I—I have been dreaming," faltered Ralph, confusedly, in that half-bewildered state between sleeping and waking.

"There is no doubt of that," returned the count, laughing; "and, what is more, you were dreaming out loud, for you gave a shout loud enough to bring the roof down."

"Dreaming," gasped Ralph; "dreaming horribly—most horribly!"

RALPH WILDHAWK No. 8 "BOYS OF ENGLAND" EDITION. PRICE ONE PENNY. PUBLISHED AT 173, FLEET STREET, E.C.

"RALPH BY A DEXTEROUS TURN SENT HIS ENEMY'S SWORD FLYING."

"Why, man, you tremble like a reed in a tempest; your brow is bathed with sweat, your eyes glare like a maniac's," continued the count. "Come, this will never do; rouse ye, rouse ye! one would think you had seen the devil."

"I have seen his counterpart," sighed Ralph.

"In the form of Marco Bravo—ha?"

"Even so; but, what is strangest of all. I dreamed that you, my good friend, were he."

The count gave a forced laugh.

"And even were it so, you would have no cause for fear," he answered. "Did you not tell me that Marco himself professed himself your friend?"

"My friend! Do not jest—the subject is too painful," replied Ralph. "Between me and that atrocious villain there can exist no feeling but the bitterest hatred and hostility."

"Well, well, dismiss your morbid fancies, inspired, no doubt, by the bugbear stories we heard yesterday," was the answer. "I have sent the *vetturino* about his business. The breakfast is waiting; rise, and dress yourself, for we must start early in search of the mountain brigands."

CHAPTER XXIX.

IT was a glorious morning, and as our three adventurers left the inn, the scene presented to their gaze was magnificent beyond description.

The sharp morning air blew freshly in their faces, and as they proceeded, Ralph felt its inspiring influence, and recovered his wonted spirits.

The count was more than usually animated, while Generoso, on the contrary, seemed rather downcast and anxious.

"And now tell me, signore," asked Ralph, as they strode along, "whither are we going?"

"You see that the road, descending the hill, winds down to the valley of Volturno?"

"Shall we halt at the town of that name?" was Ralph's next question.

"No, we shall turn off to the left," replied the count. "There is a narrow pathway through the forest, much used by the wood-cutters, charcoal burners, sportsmen, and smugglers. If we follow it for some miles, it will bring us to a small and lonely station, where we shall find a little colony of shepherds."

"You seem to be well acquainted with the country, monsignore," said Ralph.

"No wonder," was the careless response. "At one time I had a lodge in these parts, where, during the hunting season, I spent many pleasant days and had good sport."

"Are we likely to meet with any game on our journey?"

"Most likely, as the woods are full of wild boars, and a bear is occasionally met with."

"I hope we may fall in with one or the other," replied Ralph; "I should like to try my skill."

"I doubt not you will have an opportunity of doing so," the count replied. "We must keep our eyes open."

They now turned off by the path the count had indicated, and crossed an old stone bridge, which spanned a dark and deep chasm, from which arose the roar and rush of waters.

Ralph was enchanted with the glories of the sylvan scene.

They passed several open spaces or clearings, where the ground was cumbered with the trunks and branches of felled trees, black, burnt and charred.

The ground in these places was scorched and covered with grey ashes.

These were the spots where the charcoal burners had been at work.

Ralph kept a keen look-out for game.

Generoso, who was walking a little distance ahead, suddenly stopped.

He waved his hand to his companions.

They understood the signal.

They came to a sudden standstill.

Generoso unslung his rifle, and cautiously drew back the trigger.

Ralph and the count followed his example, and stood silent and heedful, their weapons poised in their hands.

There was a rustling among the under-brush, at the distance of about thirty yards ahead of them, accompanied by a low, grunting sound.

Presently a huge grizzly beast came darting out of the covert into the wood path.

It was a monstrous wild boar.

His small eyes glowing like burning coals, his stiff bristles set up along his huge black body, his curved and ripping tusks gleaming white through the green gloom, the ferocious brute came rushing at Generoso.

The fellow blazed away at him at random.

Whether or not his aim was true, the ponderous brute came rushing on at a rapid pace, that one would scarce expect to see in such an ungainly animal.

Generoso had only just time to spring nimbly on one side to avoid the charge.

Evidently scared, he dropped his rifle, and saved himself by scrambling up a bank by the wayside.

The brute stopped short, his little red eyes glowering upon the weapon, his snout routing the ground, then catching the rifle on his tusks, he tossed it backwards over his head; it fell on some stones, and the stock was shattered to pieces.

The count did not let this opportunity slip.

He instantly raised his rifle to his shoulders and fired.

The bullet struck the boar in the shoulder, and a stream of crimson blood welled up from the wound and streamed down his rough hide.

He was staggered for a moment, and uttered a fierce shriek of pain and rage.

Again the huge forest monster, with the stiff bristles set up along his black, curved body, and his white tusks gleaming on the ground, made a rush.

As the wild boar charged, the count turned round to climb the bank as Generoso had done.

He did not escape so easily as his comrade.

His foot caught in a ground vine, he fell and rolled half over, the brute stumbling over him, so that he narrowly escaped being ripped open.

Finding he had missed his aim, the wild beast, with a grunt of baffled rage, drew back, and was about to make another charge.

Ralph Wildhawk stepped forward.

He took steady aim.

The report of his rifle rang through the forest glades. The bullet struck him full between the eyes.

The animal stood with drooping head and blood-streaming snout.

Ralph drew his hunting-dirk, and flinging himself upon the monster, plunged in the blade, and with a powerful thrust, drove it home through the boar's neck to the very brisket.

A convulsive shiver ran through the brute's unwieldy body, the red, fierce glare vanished from his little deep-set eyes, then swaying gradually to and fro, he rolled over upon the ferny ground limp and dead.

Then Ralph ran to the count, and assisting him to rise, inquired if he was hurt.

"No, *amico*," laughed the count, stamping his feet and shaking the dust from his clothes. "Yet, had it not been for your ready assistance, I might have shared the fate of the dainty Adonis. But, *cospetto!* is this your first encounter with one of these black animals?"

Swine are generally called by the Italians *animali neri*—black animals.

"My first," replied Ralph, smiling with pardonable vanity. "I should think boar hunting, if carried on on a proper scale, must be sport royal."

Then, turning round, he added—

"Where is Generoso?"

The man emerged from between a clump of trees, and sprang from the bank into the path. His face betrayed some excitement.

"How now, Generoso?" laughed the count. "What ails you that you look so bewildered— have you not yet recovered from your fright? Come nearer, man; the brute won't hurt you. He is as dead as his great ancestor, the wild boar of Calydon."

"Oh, it's not that, eccelenza," replied Generoso, his teeth chattering, "but I'm afraid this adventure will take an awkward turn, and that we shall have to tackle worse foes than black animals."

"What do you mean?" asked Ralph.

"Why, signore, you know how I scrambled up the bank to get out of the way of the monster?" answered Generoso. "Well, no sooner had you fired your rifle, than I heard a whistle, and looking through the trees, caught sight of a rock, in an open space; on this rock there stood, as though on guard, a man; he wore a long cloak and a slouched hat, and carried a long carbine on his shoulder."

"Ha!—was he alone?" asked the count, a little anxiously.

"Yes, when I first saw him," returned Generoso. "But when you fired, he whistled, and beckoned with his hand, and he was joined by three others also armed with long carbines."

"They may be a party of hunters like ourselves," suggested Ralph.

"No, signore, for they were all dressed alike, in a half-military uniform," was the reply.

"Then they must be brigands!"

"No doubt."

"Even in that case," returned Ralph, "they would hardly think of molesting a party of poor chamois hunters, as we pretend to be."

"Let us hope not," put in the count; and he spoke rather gravely. "But, at any rate, it will be well to give them as wide a berth as possible. Did you notice, Generoso, which way they went?"

"They were not coming in our direction," replied the other; "they descended from the rock, and plunged together into the thicket."

"Let us be going," said the count, hastily; "we must avoid them, if we can. Come, signore."

"This is very provoking," said Ralph, in a tone of vexation; "I intended to have cut off this black fellow's head and have carried it with us to the next inn and got it cooked for supper; a boar's head is a dish for a king."

"There is no time to think of that now," replied the count. "Let us push forwards."

"At least I will have one of his ears for a trophy," laughed Ralph.

He cut off one and placed it in his pouch.

"Had we not better reload our guns?" he added.

"No, no; there is no time," replied the count, hurriedly. "If we are surrounded, we shall have no alternative but to surrender at discretion."

Ralph looked at him in amazement.

"This from you, count!" he said. "Why, Generoso says he saw but three of them, and therefore we are a match for them."

"Generoso saw but three of them," returned the count; "but you may depend upon it that there is a whole company of them lying in ambush somewhere near at hand."

"What is to be done?" asked Ralph. "I will not beat a retreat if there should be a dozen brigands."

"I am of your opinion that we had better put on a bold front and keep on our way," was the reply. "We must trust to our ingenuity to deceive the rascals and lead them to suppose that we are what we pretend to be, poor chamois hunters, whom it is not worth their while to meddle with."

But Generoso did not approve of this plan.

The cunning scoundrel put on an aspect of the most abject terror, so natural, and at the same time comical, that the count was forced to bite his lip to keep himself from betraying himself by a fit of laughter.

"Oh, eccelenza! let us run for it," he exclaimed, clasping his hands together. "If we fall into their hands, we shall all be murdered. The wood is thick and like a maze; if we run, we shall stand some chance of escaping."

"Bah! coward that you are," retorted the count, in an angry tone. "The bolder is the more prudent course; follow me."

The count strode forward, with firm step, but quick and watchful eyes continuously glancing to either side.

Generoso followed, creeping low, starting every instant, and ducking his head, as though he caught sight of a gun pointed at him—it was indeed "excellent fooling."

Ralph Wildhawk brought up the rear.

" I would rather die than be taken prisoner and held to ransom," he muttered to himself. " Death to me is preferable to the thought that Sir Raymond Mortimer should loosen his purse-strings on my account."

In this order they proceeded for some distance, enduring all the torments of suspense.

Yet, though they looked keenly about them, neither in advance, nor to the right hand or the left could they detect any signs of the brigands.

At length they came upon a rather wide opening in the wood, scattered over with large pieces of rock.

They paused, and breathed a little more freely.

" Perhaps, after all, Generoso was mistaken in the character of the men he saw," suggested Ralph, who was usually inclined to look at the bright side of things; " or, if not, they may have come to the conclusion that we are not the sort of folk they are on the look-out for, and so will allow us to pass on unmolested."

" Let us hope so," the count said, grimly.

Ralph now for the first time missed his rifle.

After his battle with the wild boar, he had left it propped against a tree, and the count had quietly taken possession of it.

Ralph knew that the count's own weapon was damaged, and though he thought it a little strange that he should take his, he set it down to absence of mind caused by the excitement of the moment.

Besides he still had a brace of pistols in his belt, and was fully resolved to use them, if driven to extremity.

They crossed the little plain, and were about to enter a little passage between some tree-crowned rocks, when a shrill whistle was heard.

" The brigands at last !" cried the count.

He raised Ralph's gun that he was carrying, and cocked it.

Then with a growl of rage and disappointment, he dashed it down.

" *Maldito !*" he exclaimed, savagely, " curse the piece ; it is unloaded."

As for Generoso, he flung himself upon his face on the ground, groaning with fright.

Ralph Wildhawk stood firm, his eyes steadily fixed upon the dark opening between the rocks.

He determined to fire upon the first man who should appear at the entrance.

He had not long to wait.

There was another whistle, and about twenty men, dressed as bandits, with carbines in their hands, and stilettoes and pistols in their belts, darted out from behind the rocks and from the thick cover of the bushes.

" San Francisco !" cried the count, " all is lost. We are surrounded. Take care, signore, pray, don't fire."

But either Ralph did not hear, or he did not regard this caution.

Seeing a fierce-looking ruffian approaching him, who, by some slight distinction in his dress, appeared to be the leader of the gang, he levelled his pistol and fired point blank.

The weapon was aimed full at the robber's breast, but as the smoke cleared away, he saw the man was still steadily and swiftly approaching him.

" Confusion !" gasped Ralph, " there is treachery. My pistols have been tampered with."

To put this to the proof, he fired the other, but though his aim was steady and direct, with no better result than before.

It was plain that the bullets had been drawn, and this must have been done at the tavern where they had last rested, but by whom ? He knew not what to suspect.

However, little time was allowed him for idle conjectures.

He threw aside the useless weapons, and drew his hunting-dirk.

The brigand—it was Stromba, now sprang upon him.

" Surrender !" he shouted. " If you offer the least resistance, you are a dead man."

But Ralph was not one likely to surrender so easily.

He prepared for a desperate resistance.

His only thought how to extricate himself from the clutches of the robber.

He tried to strike at him with the dagger, but the fellow slipped aside, and the blade of the weapon came in contact with the rock behind him.

It was shivered to pieces.

By a sudden exertion he freed his arm, dashed up the fellow's carbine, and gripping him by the throat, dashed his head against the rock.

The suddenness of the attack took the brigand unawares.

He staggered back, stumbled, and fell. -

Ralph fell with him, still keeping his knuckles imbedded in his throat, till Stromba's eyes started from their sockets, and his face grew black from the agonies of strangulation.

But Ralph now felt himself seized from behind.

Three men had set upon him.

One wound his arms round his body, while the other two seized his wrists.

With blows and curses, he was dragged from his victim.

A number of brigands now closed around him.

They presented their carbines at his head, and appeared to be in such a terrible rage that every instant he expected to have his brains blown out.

With an air of sullen resignation, he remained quite still, convinced that it was mere folly to contend any further with fate.

He looked round, to see what had become of his companions.

Generoso lay flat on the ground, with his face downwards, while one of the brigands had set his foot upon his back, and pointed a gun at his head.

As for the count, he had also given up the conflict, and stood silent and passive between two of the robbers, who stood beside him with the muzzles of their loaded carbines close to his ears.

Stromba sprang to his feet, and with eyes flaming with passion, was about to throw himself upon Ralph, and plunge his stiletto into his heart ; but the count stepped forward, and shouted fiercely—

" Hold, there !"

The brigand instantly let fall his arm, and stood glaring upon his intended victim with eyes that glowed with the fire of infernal passion.

Once more the ruffian uplifted his arm, but again the count's stern voice deterred him, and with a scowl of hatred, he turned sullenly away.

Ralph was as brave as man could be, and grasped in the strong clutch of the two robbers who held him, he had not blenched; still, he could not help rejoicing when the man fell back, and thrust the knife in his belt.

His admiration for the count's boldness and presence of mind was boundless.

"What a noble heart he has," he murmured, to himself; "he thought not of his own danger, but concerned himself only for me. Then, what power he possesses over these ruffians; his voice seemed to awe them as the growl of a lion would daunt a pack of wolves or jackals."

Meanwhile, the count had quietly stepped forward.

"Now then, my boys, let us come to busines," he remarked; "which of you is the captain?"

"I am the *capo*," returned Stromba, drawing himself up to his full height.

"You are Marco Bravo, I presume?" said the count.

The man grinned.

"No, signore; I am not quite so great a man," he answered. "But I command this troop, and you are our prisoners."

"Listen to me, *amico*," rejoined the count, tapping him familiarly on the shoulder; "do you not think you are playing the fools, in throwing your net to catch such poor fry as we are—only mountaineers, without a handful of *scudi* between us?"

"You lie," was the burly brigand's rough retort. "We know who you are."

He then made a sign to some of the brigands, who forcibly set Generoso upon his legs, and held him.

Then the two principal robbers, standing a little apart from the rest, held a whispered consultation together.

From time to time they darted scowling looks at the prisoners.

Then the pair of *bandito*, Stromba and Guiseppe, came back and posted themselves before the count.

"We know you," said Stromba; "you are the Count Di Ancona, and the other"—pointing to Ralph Wildhawk—"is the young English *milordo*."

The count started, but instantly regained his composure.

"*Corpo di Baccho!*" he laughed; "there must be something very distinguished in our appearance that we should be mistaken for such exalted personages."

"There is no mistake," growled the robber. "We received information of your intention, which was to come among us as spies, to find out what you could in regard to our numbers, and our whereabouts, that you might betray us."

The count waved his hand contemptuously.

"Take care that you are not disappointed," he said. "Remember 'All is not gold that glitters.'"

"We know what we are about," replied the bandit; "our chief, Marco Bravo, is never deceived. It was by his orders that we lay in wait for you. We had the minutest description of you, and are well aware that you are the men we are looking for."

Then turning to Generoso, he took him by the arm and shook him.

"Speak, you rascal," he said, "or I will have you flayed alive. Is not your name Generoso, and is not this man your master, the Count Di Ancona?"

"Most valiant brigand," whined Generoso, "his excellency is indeed the count, my master —my noble, kind master. Oh, spare his life, and mine too. I am a poor wretch whom it is not worth your while to murder. I have saved a small sum of money—it is very little— but you shall have it to the last *grano*, if you will have mercy on me."

"The execrable coward," cried Ralph, bursting into a rage; "oh, my brave count, this is worse than all. To think you should be basely betrayed by such an execrable villain!"

The count shrugged his shoulders.

"Signore, all that troubles me is that I should have been the means of drawing you into this trouble; but then, who can contend against Marco Bravo?—he is the devil."

"Do not speak so, I entreat you," returned the generous young Englishman; "I embarked in this enterprise of my own free will. But do not fear, you are rich, and even were it not so, Sir Raymond would willingly pay the ransom for us both."

Stromba frowned and shook his head.

"That cannot be," he said, addressing the count; "Marco Bravo has sworn to kill you if ever you fall into his clutches. You must prepare for death."

"Be it so," returned the count; "I would not deign to beg my life of such a villain. But I hope a better fate is in store for this brave young Englishman?"

"Oh, his case is different," replied the bandit. "Our chief will demand a heavy ransom, but if it be paid, the young milordo will be set at liberty."

"It never shall be paid," exclaimed Ralph, with vehemence. "I desire no more than to share the fate of my friend."

"Tush, tush!" rejoined the count; "your death will profit me nothing. Live and avenge me."

Stromba cast an evil look at Ralph.

"I should advise you not to make such a rash speech to Marco Bravo," he said. "Our chief is a man of quick temper, and he might take you at your word."

Then he pointed to the count.

"Guiseppe," he said to his companion, "you know your orders. Take ten of the men and escort the count to the spot where you are to meet our chief. I and the rest will conduct the young milordo safely to the Brigands' Glen."

"Stay one moment," said Ralph Wildhawk, slipping from between the two bandits who were keeping guard over him; "it is but a small favour I ask of you. Permit me to shake

"THE COUNT RAISED HIS RIFLE AND FIRED."

hands with my friend before we are finally separated."

The count made a sign with his hand at which the ruffians fell back, murmuring a sulky assent.

Ralph grasped the count by the hand, which he shook warmly.

"My dear count, what has happened is not more than what we might have expected. But trust me, I do not feel my own position, for I am a friendless fellow, and hold my life at a pin's fee. But," he said, in a low tone that bespoke genuine emotion, "I am to be confronted with Marco Bravo. If I have any power of persuasion, I will do my utmost to procure your release, and if I fail, I will rather die by my own hand than the ruthless villain should receive one penny on my account."

A slight flush overspread the count's face, and he cast down his eyes.

"Do nothing rashly," he replied. "I have little fear of Marco Bravo. His avarice will prove a stronger passion than his thirst for revenge. Besides, the band will not be willing to lose the ransom. Come what may, I am prepared, and so *addio*. I hope we may soon meet again."

Ralph was about to make some reply, but the brigands who had charge of him dragged him away.

"Forward," shouted Guiseppe, who had command of Ralph's guard; "forward with our prisoner to the Devil's Glen."

As they entered the narrow passage between the rocks, Ralph turned and waved his hand to the count, who returned the salute. When Ralph and his escort had disappeared, the count burst into a loud laugh, Generoso and all the brigands heartily joining in.

"*Diavolo!*" he exclaimed, clapping his hands. "That was well done. I have only one fault to find with the performance of our little comedy. You, my friend Generoso, rather overdid your part."

Generoso laughed.

"*Altro*, signore," he answered; "at any rate, the Englishman was thoroughly taken in. He believed my affected terrors to be genuine, and I'll warrant is thoroughly convinced that you are no other than the Count Di Ancona."

"That is true," replied his chief, nodding. "I am the veritable Count Di Ancona, and he looks upon me as a hero and a martyr. I would have it so."

"*San Francesco!* what fools these Englishmen must be," laughed Generoso.

"He is no fool," returned the brigand chief, "but a fine, open-hearted lad, whom I like very much. I wish we could enlist him in our band, but there is no hope of that. 'Tis a pity, too, for though ingenuous and easily imposed upon, he is as brave as a lion."

"I like him too," rejoined Generoso, "and here is one thing you have to thank him for. In our encounter with the wild boar to-day he saved your life."

"I shall not forget it."

"I suppose, signor capitano," rejoined Stromba, "that it is your wish that we should still keep up the deception that you are really the Count Di Ancona?"

"By all means," was the prompt reply.

"What shall we tell him in regard to your supposed capture?"

"Say that I was taken before Marco Bravo," returned the chief, "who upon seeing me got into a terrible rage and threatened my life, but afterwards relented on the promise of being paid a heavy ransom."

"Good, signore."

"And now, comrades," rejoined the chief, "I am about to engage in another enterprise that will bring an immense sum to our treasury. I shall capture the rich English *milordo*, Sir Mortimer, his son and his charming niece, and exact their weight in gold before I consent to liberate them."

The men laughed and cheered and tossed up their hats.

"*Eviva* Marco Bravo!" they shouted. "Long live our noble captain!"

CHAPTER XXX.

RALPH WILDHAWK marched along in the midst of a file of brigands, through the narrow gorge, walls of gloomy rocks on either hand.

He reflected upon all that had passed during that eventful day, and the preceding evening, when he had slept at the inn of the mountain village.

"It was there that my pistols were tampered with," he thought.

"But how, and by whom? I kept them in my belt all the evening, and did not remove them until I retired to rest, and even then I placed them close beside the pillow, within easy reach. The charge was drawn while I was asleep.

"Could it have been by the innkeeper, whose horrid stories about the atrocities of the brigands caused me to have such bad dreams?"

The more he brooded over the affair, the more puzzled he became.

"I should suspect that fellow Generoso," he mused, "only that he appeared so genuinely frightened when seized by the robbers.

"Well, it is useless to torment myself by trying to unravel a mystery to which I have no clue. I shall not be sorry to confront that extraordinary outlaw, Marco Bravo—he openly professed himself my friend. In wonder's name, what can he know of me?—what interest can he have in one who is to him an entire stranger?"

As they proceeded on their way, the brigands' manner towards their prisoner softened; they even spoke to him cheeringly.

"*Non avete paura*," said their leader. "Don't be afraid. It is only a question of money. Our captain is an honourable man, and as soon as your ransom is paid you will, no doubt, be set at liberty."

Walter thought it good policy to be on as good terms as possible with his captors, so he assumed an easy and confident manner, and asked them many questions about their individual histories.

"Was it taste or compulsion that caused you to embrace such a wretched mode of existence?" asked Ralph Wildhawk of a brigand.

"Accident, signore, pure accident," the fellow answered, with a sigh.

"As how?" questioned Ralph.

"You see, it was in this way," returned the bandit. "I am myself no mountaineer, that is, I mean, I was not one originally, for I was a fisherman, and had a boat of my own; you have heard of the great earthquake which half ruined the city (Naples) about ten years ago?"

Ralph said he had read of it.

"Well, signore, I was out in a boat with a brother of mine when the earthquake happened," continued the brigand. "The sea rose and the storm was frightful. Our boat was dashed against the rocks of the island of Ischia; my poor brother José got drowned, and I had a narrow escape of my life. I was picked up on the shore, half-drowned and terribly bruised, and was carried to a convent in the town of Foria, where I was nursed by the nuns, till by the aid of my patron, San Gennaro, I recovered my health and strength."

Here he paused, and crossed himself.

"But though recovered from illness," he resumed, "my boat, my only worldly possession, having been destroyed, I was a ruined man.

"About this time I scraped acquaintance with a Jew, and he consented to lend me a sufficient sum of money to purchase another boat, on which he held a mortgage, while he exacted such an exorbitant interest on the money that he had lent me, that I was, if possible, worse off than ever. Everything went wrong with me. After a bad season, I found myself unable to pay the interest on the loan; my boat was forfeited, and worse than that, he threatened to throw me into prison if I did not pay the interest on the debt.

"The infidel dog came to me, and when he found that I was unable to pay him, he shrieked with rage, tore his hair, cursed, and threatened me, and even shook his fist in my face, and I a good Catholic and he a black heretic! It was too much. I had never killed but one man before, and that was in a fair fight; but I could not stand an insult from a Jew, so I drove my stiletto into him, and pitched his vile carcase into the bay."

Here he stopped, quivering with passion at the recollection, while his black eyes flamed with vindictive passion.

Then he went on.

"Would you believe it, signore?" he said, with an air of disgust. "Instead of being applauded for the righteous deed, the *sbirri*, the police, bribed by his wealthy friends, came to my lodgings to arrest me; but I had timely warning, so I escaped to the mountains, and joined the band of the gallant Marco Bravo."

By this time they had reached a high elevation.

The prospect was wildly magnificent, and its effect was heightened by the varied aspects under which it was seen.

Descending into the glen, the scene grew still wilder and bolder.

Ralph gazed up the crags which topped carelessly over the very edge of the chasm, and expressed his admiration of their fanciful forms.

The brigands told him the names of these rocks which were as fantastic as their shapes, such as the "Nun," the "Cathedral," the "Bishop," the "Giraffe," the "Lion," and so forth.

"Tell me, friend," asked Ralph, as they trudged through a rocky valley that seemed interminable, "whither are you taking me? Have we much further to go?"

"*Lontano, lontano!* a long, long way," he answered, vaguely, waving his hand towards the hills. "We shall not reach the Devil's Gorge till noon to-morrow."

"Then where are we to sleep to-night?" asked Ralph.

"In a cave called the Hermit's Cell, at the end of this pass," returned Stromba. "Cheer up; you have but two miles to travel, and when we reach the cave, we shall find some comrades there who will have prepared a good supper for us, and strewn rushes for us to rest upon."

"In Heaven's name then, let us push forward," returned Ralph.

The brigands roused themselves and stepped out briskly, and in about half an hour's time reached the end of the glen.

There was here a wide gallery between two lofty ranges of rock, very similar to the pass where the brigands had laid their ambush.

Upon nearing this spot the brigands came to a standstill.

They crouched down under cover of some stunted bushes and clumps of heather.

They made a sign to Ralph to do likewise. He at once obeyed.

The brigands whispered to him to keep quiet.

Walter was surprised at so much precaution taken in such a lonely, out-of-the-world spot, especially as the brigands had told him that they were going to meet their comrades.

But he set their conduct down to its true cause, the force of habit and discipline.

Trailing his gun along the ground, Stromba crept forward on his hands and knees for the distance of about twenty yards, and then stopped.

He uttered a long, shrill, peculiar call, in striking mimicry of the cry of a prowling wolf.

The dismal "ooo-wow-wow!" finishing with a snap and snarl, was answered by a like signal from the rocks beyond.

Then a couple of tall, steeple-crowned hats were cautiously raised above the rocks.

The wolf cry was renewed.

Four men dressed in the uniform of the banditti now emerged from among the rocks and came running towards their comrade. Stromba shouted to his men, who at once sprang to their feet, and with a joyous shout hurried on to meet their companions.

CHAPTER XXXI.

THE brigands greeted each other with great cordiality, and all adjourned at once to the cave of which Stromba had spoken.

Ralph Wildhawk was so thoroughly wearied by his long and toilsome march, that he was right glad to find rest and shelter at last.

When the supper was over, they retired into the cave, having set two men, armed to the teeth, to act as sentinels throughout the silent watches of the night.

Though some of the bandits stretched themselves upon their folded cloaks in the warm blaze of the watch-fires, the greater number of them showed no inclination for sleep, but amused themselves by relating their exploits, singing love or robber songs, and playing at the game of *morra*.

This is a very ancient game in Italy.

Knives are not unfrequently drawn after a disputed game. It happened so in this case.

A tremendous row commenced, and Ralph was astonished that men could quarrel so fiercely about a cause so trivial.

Whipping out their gleaming stilettoes, and yelling mutual execrations, the two players were about to rush like tigers upon each other.

Their comrades, however, interfered.

Throwing their arms about the infuriated disputants, they forcibly dragged them asunder.

There was quite a brawl; fighting, wrestling, and swearing, the two men tried to shake of the restraining grip of their well-intentioned companions, and fly at each other's throats.

Stromba now seemed to think it high time to interfere, in order to prevent disastrous consequences.

Throwing himself between the two fellows, he drew his pistols.

In tones of stern authority, he bade them put up their weapons and shake hands.

He swore that he would blow out the brains of the first man who dared to resume the dispute.

This resolute conduct had its effect.

After a good deal of grumbling, the storm subsided, the players shook hands, and, to do them justice, in a few moments appeared to be as good friends as ever.

But the disturbance had thoroughly aroused Ralph.

Tired as he was, he felt no further inclination to sleep.

He rose, and walking to the fire, entered into conversation with the bandits.

Stromba paid him great attention, made him drink from his flask of Rosolio, and apologised for the turbulence of his men.

"I will take care, signore, that they shall not offend again," he said. "It is well for them that Marco Bravo was not at hand to punish their audacity."

Ralph smiled.

"I suppose he rules the band with a rod of iron?"

"Diavolo! yes," laughed Stromba. "But then your excellency must observe that nothing but strict discipline can keep such wild spirits in curb."

"I wonder that your leader should permit such a dangerous game to be played by such fiery fellows. If I were in his place, I should not allow it."

"The chief has expressly forbidden the game of the *morra*," replied Stromba; "and it is only in his absence that they dare to play it."

"Your chief appears to have perfect control over the band," remarked Ralph.

His thoughts wandered back to his friend the count, whose quiet, yet masterful tone he could not help, in some vague way, connecting with the power of the brigand chief.

"I know but one man like him."

"*Cospetto!* he must be a rarity; for my part, I think no one is like Marco Bravo," answered Stromba. "He leads his band as a shepherd leads his flock."

"And yet I have been told that you own another chief, or rather chieftainess," rejoined Ralph. "One you call the Queen of the Brigands—is this so?"

A strange look of awe crossed the brigand's face, and he lowered his voice.

"You allude to La Catarina?"

"True," returned Ralph.

"You see, eccelenza, she is no ordinary woman," answered the brigand; "she rules the band by a mysterious—a supernatural sway; she is what we Italians call a *strega*."

"What is that?"

"A witch, an enchantress," was the simple and evidently convinced reply.

"Trust me, a mere idle superstition," replied Ralph. "I wonder any man of common sense could allow himself to be imposed upon by pretentions as false as they are ridiculous."

"*Altro*, signore," rejoined Stromba, gravely shaking his head, "to convince you to the contrary, I have but to say that a few years ago, I saw one of these same witches burnt alive in the Mercato—the chief market-place in Naples. I shall never forget it."

Ralph shuddered, and inquired some particulars about Marco Bravo.

"What profession did your chief follow," he asked, "before he joined the banditti?"

"Marco Bravo is a man of good birth," replied Stromba. "He held a commission as a captain of dragoons in the service of King Ferdinand, and was considered the best swordsman in the army. He had a quarrel with a certain marquis about a lady; the rivals met, and Marco Bravo came off victorious, running his adversary through the body. As the marquis was his superior officer, there was a great stir made about the duel; our captain was arrested, tried by court-martial, and condemned to death. He contrived, however, to escape, and fled to the mountains."

After some further conversation of the same kind, Ralph expressed his desire to sleep.

It was a good while before Ralph Wildhawk could obtain the solace and refreshment of balmy repose.

He lay listlessly watching the strange wild scene around him.

The brigands slumbering in the lurid glare of the watch-fire, the sentinel pacing his careful beat; the dark, frowning shadows of the overhanging rocks, all combined to form a picture worthy of the savage genius of Salvator Rosa.

At length surrounding objects grew dim and indistinct, and Ralph's head sank upon his arm. He fell fast asleep.

CHAPTER XXXII.

NEAR the Largo del Mercato, the great market-place of Naples, lies a vast network of narrow streets, inhabited by the lower orders.

Through one of these close and dingy thoroughfares a tall, swarthy, sullen-looking fellow strode along.

He was wrapped in a long mantle. patched and faded from its original rich brown to the colour of dust, while his slouched hat was pulled down close over his beetling brows.

He pushed his way with morose indifference through the noisy, jostling crowds that thronged the streets.

Sometimes he would rudely push aside some laughing orange girl, who abused him roundly for his want of manners ; another time he would tread upon the corns of some lazzarone sleeping supine under a doorway, who would rise and howl out a curse against the disturber of his repose, which only met with the response of a harsh and derisive laugh.

Several of the men were so enraged at the roughness of the sour-visaged stranger, that they fingered the hafts of the long knives stuck in their sashes.

But one glance of his black, fierce eyes sufficed to cow the boldest, and the gigantic fellow was suffered by all to pass on his way unmolested.

He looked about him from side to side, as though to find something which eluded his search.

At length he stopped at the entrance of a narrow alley, to which access was given by a low-browed archway.

Passing under this, he entered a small court, surrounded by very high houses in the last stage of squalor and dilapidation.

"This is the place," he muttered ; "and now to find my man."

After a moment's hesitation, he bent his steps towards a high, many-gabled building, quaint and grim.

The ungainly structure was fronted by a heavy balcony, resting upon pillars grotesquely carved, and reached by a steep, rickety stairway.

Proceeding along the creaking platform for some distance, the stranger struck three heavy raps with his knuckles against a pair of iron-bound, fast-closed shutters.

"Who knocks?" said a gruff voice from within.

"All's well, Tomaso," replied the other.

"Who are you, since you know my name?"

"A friend."

"What friend?"

"No matter. One who brings you good news."

"Good news!" retorted the voice, in a snarling tone. "Is the devil dead?"

"No, nor Marco Bravo." laughed the stranger. "But I am a friend, for all that. Let me in."

"I warn you I am armed."

"Quite right; but keep your weapons for your enemies, and not for those who come to do you a service."

"But who are you?"

"Do you know little Cecca, who sells flowers in the Mercato?"

"Dear little Cecca ! She is the idol of my soul !" replied the voice. "Do you bring a message from her?"

"Yes, and a token besides—a little gold cross you gave her some months ago."

"Push it under the crack below the door," was the answer ; "then, if I am satisfied, I will let you in."

He pushed the little cross under the door as directed.

For a moment or so he waited very patiently.

"Open the door," he said again.

After much clashing of bolts and bars, the door was at length cautiously unclosed.

Springing in, the mysterious visitor stumbled down a step and alighted upon the shaky floor of a spacious but wretched apartment.

Nothing more squalid can be conceived than the appearance of the chamber.

The place was lighted by a dimly-burning lamp, swinging on a chain from the ceiling.

The man who had admitted the stranger into this wretched den was a wan-looking fellow, with pinched features, black, fierce eyes, and a mop of matted black curls.

He sprang back with a curse. and snatching a pistol from his belt, presented it at his visitor.

"Guiseppe Veletri !" he exclaimed.

"Michael Cornaro, it is I," returned the disguised brigand, holding up his hand. "If you fire upon me, you will kill your best friend. and, what is more to the purpose, alarm your neighbours."

"You are a spy of Marco Bravo's," returned the other, still keeping the pistol levelled at the head of Guiseppe ; "you are sent here to betray or to kill me ; but beware. Your life is in my hands."

Guiseppe threw open his cloak.

"See," he said, "I have no weapons but my stiletto. Keep your pistols; only sit down and be calm, and let us talk together, for I have much to say to you."

Michael Cornaro lowered the weapon, but hesitated a little to accept the invitation of his guest.

"First swear to me that you were not sent hither by Marco Bravo."

Guiseppe threw off his hat, and made the sign of the cross.

"I swear it. I swear that I come in good will and to do you a good turn—by the blessed San Gennaro, my patron !" was the vehement response.

"How is it, then ?"

"A motive of revenge brings me here," returned Guiseppe. "Marco Bravo is a tyrant. He has shamefully wronged me. I hate him, and I have sworn to take my revenge."

"In what has he offended you ?"

"He insulted me—struck me—would have stabbed me, had I not been saved by Generoso." returned the brigand, gnashing his teeth. "And now, if you are satisfied, give me your hand."

Cornaro replaced the pistol in his belt, but still kept his left hand upon the stock.

His brow cleared a little, and advancing, he shook hands with his former comrade.

"That's brave," said Guiseppe. "Now let us smoke a cigarito together, and if there is any wine left in the bottle, let us drink to a better understanding."

The two ruffians sat down at the table.

"THE ARREST.

Michael Cornaro poured out a hornful of the generous wine.

Guiseppe pledged him.

"*La buona fortuna*—good luck to you, comrade," he said. "I am anxious to know why you are hiding here like a rat in his hole, when you might be flaunting about the Marinella like a fine gentleman."

Cornaro ruefully shook his head.

"You think I am rich?" he said.

"Well, I don't see how you can be poor," replied Guiseppe. "A thousand piastres is a good round sum."

Cornaro clasped his hands, and shuddered from limb to limb.

"It was blood-money. Would to Heaven I had never touched it!" he replied. "Why does he not kill me at once? Why does he render my life hell upon earth—this demon, Marco Bravo?"

Guiseppe started.

"You have seen him, then?"

"No; but he haunts me like an invisible fiend," returned Cornaro. "His influence is about me wherever I go—his voice of menace rings in my ears like the first rumble of a coming earthquake."

"But as yet he does not appear to have done you much harm."

"No; that is the worst of it," was the strange answer. "I wish he would fulfil his threat and put me out of my misery."

He drooped his head upon the table and gave a deep groan.

"You astound me!" exclaimed Guiseppe. "I little thought that a spy and informer who had betrayed the band would need to petition our chief to cut his throat. I thought such a favour would be granted without the trouble of asking."

"You don't know what torments I have suffered," replied Cornaro. "There is no escape for me."

"Courage, man," replied Guiseppe. "I am come expressly to show you a way of deliverance. But drink, man, and drown care."

With a sickly smile, Cornaro stretched out his arm, and took the drinking-horn.

"Yes; I am not afraid of that," he said. "It is a bottle of Rosolio that my kind Cecca brought herself, and tasted it with her own sweet lips. It is no poison."

He took a deep draught.

"Come, now; tell me how it was you first were tempted to turn traitor?"

"Marco Bravo degraded me from my command," replied Cornaro, "and I vowed vengeance against him. Besides, a thousand piastres was offered to anyone who would betray the band. It is now many months ago since Marco Bravo laid a plan to stop the carriages of a rich English milordo."

"Yes, I know; Milordo Mortimer."

"Yes, that was his name," answered Cornaro. "Well, an ambush was to be laid at a certain lonely spot, on the road between Fondi and Terracina. I hastened to give information to the commandant at the castle. and a troop of dragoons, with a battalion of infantry, were sent, under the command of Captain Lanfranco, to attack the brigands."

"I remember it well," rejoined Guiseppe;

"you need tell me no more. After a desperate engagement, our comrades were defeated and put to flight; many were killed, their leader, mortally wounded, with young Giovanni, were carried prisoners to the inn at Terracina. The one died, but the other—young Giovanni—effected his escape by the aid of Marco Bravo, Pepe, and other members of the band. You obtained your reward, did you not?"

"Yes; it was paid in full," answered Guiseppe. "But I did not long retain possession of it."

"Diavolo! were you robbed?"

"I will explain all," rejoined his companion. "Knowing that the chief would send his emissaries to assassinate me if I did not keep in close concealment, I disguised myself and took the name of Tomaso Manzo."

"Well, *camerado*, I took an humble lodging in an obscure street. I had my thousand piastres safely bound up in a strong goat-skin bag. It was my custom to place this under my pillow at night.

"One morning I awoke, after sleeping so heavily that I cannot help thinking the wine I had taken at supper was drugged. Imagine my horror and astonishment at finding a stiletto sticking in the wooden bed-post, close above my head. I will show it you."

He rose, and crossing the room, opened a box, and took out the weapon.

It was a long, murderous-looking knife, and to its handle was attached a slip of paper, bearing the following inscription—

"This from Marco Bravo. The next will find a sheath in your heart!"

"I was paralyzed with fright. I sought for my bag of gold. It was gone."

"*Cospetto!*" ejaculated Guiseppe. "I cannot imagine why he spared your life."

"For the same reason that a cat plays with a trembling mouse—to prolong my torment."

"But had I been in your case, I should have escaped from the country altogether."

"I made the attempt," returned Cornaro. "I engaged the master of a felucca to take me to Corsica, and it was agreed that we should set sail at midnight. We had not sailed out into the bay above half a mile when the master and two of his men came to me.

"'Can you swim?' he asked.

"I was bewildered, but answered 'yes.'"

"'All the better for you,' he said. 'You are the traitor who sold your comrades for blood-money. We carry no Jonahs in this craft. Overboard you go!'

"I was seized and plunged into the sea. The felucca sailed away, and I had no help for it but to swim ashore. Again I was without a *grano* in my pocket—a man accursed!"

"Since then you have taken refuge here?" said Guiseppe.

"One night I begged a few *grani* and brought home a bottle of wine. I then again left the house to purchase some maccaroni. When I came back, I found this label on my bottle—

"'Beware! This wine is poisoned!'"

"Never mind, comrade," Guiseppe said. "Your turn has come round. Now for revenge on Marco Bravo."

CHAPTER XXXIII.

MICHAEL CORNARO started up from the table, his brow lowering, his cheek ghastly pale.

"Revenge!" he repeated, in a low, fierce tone. "I will do anything—risk anything to have my revenge upon the tyrant Marco Bravo. Only show me the way."

"He is in your power," rejoined his comrade. "You have but to lodge an information against him, and a battalion of soldiers will be sent to arrest him."

"But where is he to be found?"

"Here—in Naples."

"In Naples!" exclaimed Cornaro.

"Listen, *amico*," replied his comrade, laying his hand upon his arm. "I cannot well show myself in this business. You must remember that some time ago the government issued a proclamation, in which the promise of a free pardon and a heavy reward was held out to any of the band who would betray Marco Bravo."

"Yes; but if I recollect aright, several of the companions were excepted from this offer of grace, and placed under a ban."

"It was so, and my own name headed the list of the proscribed," answered Guiseppe.

"In that case, if you appeared, it would be like thrusting your head into the lion's den."

"Exactly so," responded his confederate. "But with you it is different. You have already received your pardon, and if you were to apply for help to the commandant at St. Elmo, you would be trusted and well received."

"Yes; the commandant has promised me his protection," rejoined Cornaro. "But how am I to venture forth into the streets, where I have reason to dread an enemy lurking under every pent-house to murder me?"

"You must find some disguise," was the reply. "I will accompany you. I have a pass from the chief, and if we should meet any of the band, they will let us go on our way unmolested."

"But should our plan succeed," objected Michael Cornaro, "how can we hope to escape the fury of the band?"

"I am not without money," returned Guiseppe, "and as soon as you have received your reward, we will get away to Portici, where I have a kinsman who owns a smuggling craft. He is fond of money, and if we pay him well, he will carefully convey us to some place of safety."

"Done!" said Michael Cornaro. "I can endure this hunted life no longer."

"Spoken like a man!" replied his comrade, approvingly. "And now I will show what I have brought you to wear."

He threw aside his mantle, and produced a parcel which contained the robe and hood of a begging friar.

Cornaro put them on, and when he had pulled the cowl over his face, Guiseppe, with a laugh, declared the disguise complete.

"I will go with you as far as the hill of St. Martino," said Guiseppe. "There is a tavern there, where I will await your return from the castle."

"Agreed," replied the other; "and on our way you shall tell me when and where Marco Bravo is to be found."

Upon quitting the town, they commenced the ascent of the steep hill of San Martino, the summit of which is crowned by the majestic pile of the Castle of St. Elmo.

Upon reaching the castle the two brigands parted.

Michael went forward on his mission of treachery, and Guiseppe retired to a little wayside inn, there to await the return of his companion.

Two hours passed in this way, still Michael Cornaro did not come.

Guiseppe began to feel some degree of uneasiness.

Had his comrade been detained?—had he been disbelieved?—or had he played false with his confederate?

To his intense relief, he saw the bent form of a monk descending the hill from the direction of the barbican of the fortress.

He knew at a glance that it was Michael Cornaro.

He hastened to meet him.

Upon approaching Guiseppe, he looked nervously around him, then whispered in his ear—

"It is done; to-night Marco Bravo will sleep in yonder dungeons."

Guiseppe gave a leer of malignant satisfaction.

"It is well," said he; "La Catarina has proved a true prophetess; her word will be accomplished."

"Would it were all over, and that we were safe out of the country," rejoined the other; "but now, comrade, take my advice, and do not linger here. The soldiers are about to leave the castle—hark!—you hear the trumpet that calls them to the muster. Get you gone."

"But you——"

"I am to meet the commandant at a certain house in the Toledo," answered Michael.

"But where shall we meet again?"

"At my lodgings near the Mercato."

"And when?"

"At midnight."

"Till then, farewell," replied Guiseppe, as he waved his hand. "Success to your enterprise."

And with that he hurried away, for a glittering line of soldiers was now seen defiling down the hill.

CHAPTER XXXIV.

THERE are some men who, emboldened by impunity, put no limit to their daring, and venture on the rashest acts with a light heart.

Such a man was Marco Bravo.

Nothing daunted, he re-assumed the character of the Count Di Ancona, and presented himself at the palace of Sir Raymond Mortimer.

The protracted absence of Ralph Wildhawk had occasioned the greatest alarm in the household of the English baronet.

Violet Melville was greatly terrified and distressed at his disappearance, and she suffered the more keenly as she felt herself obliged to disguise her feelings.

Joe Moody and Matilda Sparkes were, each in their way, sincerely concerned about Ralph Wildhawk.

"It's no more than I expected," grumbled Joe; "Master Ralph was always so wenturesome a-hexplorin' of ruined cities as was built afore the flood. A-sailin' over the bay in them cockle-shells the maccaronis calls flukers"—feluccas he meant—"and clambering them awful chasms like a cat-a-mountain; shouldn't wonder but what he has tumbled into the crater of Mount Vesuvius."

"No, Joseph," replied Matilda, solemnly shaking her head; "the poor young gentleman has fallen into the clutches of them dreadful brigands. Miss Violet thinks the same, and is half dead with grief."

But Joe would hearken to no tales about the robbers, whom he affected heartily to despise.

Sir Raymond showed more emotion at Ralph's mysterious disappearance than might have been expected, considering that his manner towards him had always been cold and constrained.

There was only one in the family who, in secret, felt a grim satisfaction at what had happened.

This was Edmund Mortimer.

In the midst of all this commotion, the Count Di Ancona made his appearance.

The arrival of Ralph's bosom friend, in whose company he had last been seen, occasioned no less astonishment than delight.

Eagerly questioned, the artful villain told a very plausible story.

He mingled truth and falsehood in such an ingenious way, that even Violette Melville was completely deceived.

He told how he and Ralph had embarked on their madcap expedition, and had penetrated into the heart of the mountains.

How they had been captured by the brigands and had been separated the one from the other. That while Ralph had been carried off by the robbers to their fastness, he, the count, had been confined for the night in a shepherd's cabin.

The shepherd had proved to be a man in his employ, and at the count's entreaty had set him free.

"Can it be possible," said Sir Mortimer, "that even the feeblest of governments can permit itself to be laughed at and set at defiance by a mere handful of desperadoes? If I can secure the liberation of a youth who so well deserves the interest I take in him, I will quit this country for ever."

The count shrugged his shoulders.

"Signore, you are reputed to be very rich," answered the Italian. "It is only a question of money."

"If that be so," replied Sir Godfrey, "I must find some means of putting myself in communication with the brigands."

Soon after they separated.

The count returned exultant to his residence in the Toledo.

He found Generoso awaiting him.

The fellow looked gloomy and careworn.

"I am glad you have returned, signore capitano," he said. "Isaco il Nero, the king of e gipsies, has been here."

"Well, amico, I am sorry I was not at home to receive his majesty," replied the count, gaily, for he was in high spirits; "was it a visit of ceremony, or did he come on business?"

"On very important business," replied the brigand.

"Indeed!" said the count, lifting his black eyebrows. "Pray, let me hear what he had to say."

Generoso cast down his eyes.

"It is time we left Naples," he muttered.

Marco Bravo threw himself down upon a gilded couch, laughing heartily.

"Never believe it," was the buoyant reply of the elated chief; "I do not intend to leave Naples until I have pouched three thousand guineas in English gold."

"What would it avail you if you could pocket ten times ten thousand guineas, if one little pellet of lead were sent through your heart or brain?" grumbled his follower.

"'Every bullet has its billet,' they say," answered the count. "But if my good fortune will but last a few months longer, I shall be able to retire upon my laurels, and every man in the band will receive enough to make him comfortable for life."

"The saints speed that good time, signor capitano," said Generoso, in a doubtful tone; "but, remember, 'there is many a slip between the cup and the lip.'"

"Tush! how is this, companion?" returned the chief, bending his brows; "you appear to be changed of late. Your former courage seems to have evaporated; but let that pass. What said the monarch of Egypt?"

"He bade me warn you that there is peril at hand."

The count started.

"Ah! from what quarter does it threaten?" he asked, quickly.

"That I know not," replied Generoso; "but there is among the gipsies a certain Moorish astrologer, whom they call Muley Aben Hassan, who pronounces that the stars that rule your destiny are in evil conjunction, and that some danger hangs over you."

"The lying old juggler," sneered the brigand chief; "I defy him and the stars to boot. I am my own star, and am guided only by the light of my own genius."

"Be not too confident," returned Generoso; "there are many mysterious rumours abroad that there is a stir among the soldiers, and that some energetic movement is shortly to be made against the band."

Again the chief laughed contemptuously.

"I could have told you as much myself; I am the moving spirit of the scheme," he replied; "and I will lay such a trap for the chivalrous brigand-hunters as shall encage them all."

Then he produced his pocket-book, and took out a slip of paper.

"Look here, my trusty Generoso," he said, "here is a cheque for a thousand pounds, which I received from the English milordo. Now, it is always wise to take time by the forelock, and in case of accidents, I should like to have it cashed at once."

Generoso held up his hands in speechless admiration.

"Run at once to the bankers," continued the brigand chief, handing him the paper, "and when you have the money, bring it me."

"But these rumours, capitano ; is it safe to neglect them ?"

"Perhaps not," answered the count, carelessly ; "but I have other things of more importance to think of just at present. Make haste back, for I shall want you."

"Very good, signore."

"And by the way, Generoso," added the chief, as if taking a sudden thought, "there is that traitor, Michael Cornaro. I think we have played with him long enough ; he must die. Select one of the men to do that business. We must take the traitor's head to the mountains, to satisfy the band that justice has been done."

The villain spoke as coolly as if he had been asked to do some service of trivial account.

"Hark ye, *amico*," said the brigand chief, "to-night I shall visit the king of the gipsies, and test the truth and importance of the rumours you have reported."

Then rising, he waved his hand.

"Away, Generoso," said he, "and return as soon as you can."

Generoso bowed and left the room.

When he was gone, the count, still in excellent spirits, hummed a lively tune, and strode to and fro through the splendidly-furnished apartment.

Then he sat down at the table, and gathering together his writing materials, commenced writing some letters.

At times he would pause, and laugh at his ingenuity.

Once, he threw down his pen, and leaning his cheek upon his hand, fell into a moody train of thought.

"What waste of energy is this," he muttered. "I love that fair English girl, and for her sake, I would I had been assigned another and a better career. But *via !* out upon such craven thoughts ; in what am I worse than the conqueror who devastates half the earth, and is held in admiration?—than the sordid, rascally usurer, who coins the heart's blood of his fellows into gold ? Pshaw, I must attend to my work."

He recommenced writing, and bent all his energies upon the task he had in hand.

Silence reigned around him, broken only by the tick-tack of the ormolu clock upon the mantle-shelf.

So deeply was he absorbed in his employment, that he did not heed that the door of his chamber, which Generoso left ajar, was softly pushed open.

He was not conscious of the entrance of anyone, until he felt a hard grip upon his shoulder, and a stern voice rang in his ear—

"The game is played out ; you may as well throw up the cards. I arrest you, Marco Bravo, in the name of the law."

The detected brigand chief sprang to his feet.

Beside him stood a tall, determined-looking old man, with fine aquiline features, and an expression of the sternest determination.

He was very handsomely dressed in the uniform of a general, and held a drawn sword in his hand.

Marco Bravo slightly changed colour, but that was all, for otherwise, he was perfectly calm.

His hands instinctively clutched at his pistols, which lay upon the table.

The old soldier observed the motion.

With a sweep of his sword, he cleared the weapons off the table, and they fell with a clash upon the floor.

Marco Bravo turned a quick glance towards the door, but it was useless to hope for escape in that quarter.

A line of soldiers was drawn up in the corridor outside the chamber, and a young officer stood just within the threshold.

The brigand chief, in the coolest manner, turned towards the old general, and made a polite bow.

"*Monsignore commandanti*, this is unpleasant," he said ; "but you mistake me for someone else. You spoke of Marco Bravo ; surely, you must allude to the great brigand chief ?"

"Great or little, you are he," returned the commandant ; "and you are my prisoner."

The other laughed.

"Monsignore," he said, "this cannot be a jest, although it looks so like one. That I am not Marco Bravo I can easily convince you— all my dependents can swear to my identity— my papers, if you will condescend to examine them—my friends, amongst whom I have the honour to number some of the noblest names in the kingdom, all will prove as clear as day that I am no other than Silvio Berardino, Count Di Ancona."

The commandant smiled grimly.

"You are a clever fellow, Marco Bravo," said he. "But it is beneath one of your talents to attempt to keep up the deception any longer."

"Excuse me if I am utterly bewildered," replied the consummate rascal, with a shrug ; "at least I trust you will allow me to make some domestic arrangements, and to write a letter to my friends to let them know in what predicament I am placed."

"It cannot be permitted," returned the commandant, sternly ; "I am the bearer of an order of arrest, and you must come with me."

"Let me look at it," was the reply.

The commandant placed the portentous-looking document in the prisoner's hand.

He scanned it for a moment.

Then he returned it with a smile and a bow.

"I see it bears the king's sign manual," he said ; "there is no gainsaying such authority— yet take my word, this is nothing more than a mistake."

Then with the greatest courtesy he drew his sword, and presented it to the commandant.

The grim old gentleman took it and quietly handed it to the subaltern officer.

"And now, monsignore," said Marco Bravo, "I am at your service."

The commandant beckoned to the soldiers.

With steady tramp they advanced and surrounded the prisoner.

With a haughty air the latter threw his cape over his shoulder and cocked his hat fiercely upon his head.

"Remove his cloak and search him ; see that

he has no weapons concealed about his person," said the commandant.

The sergeant and one of his men proceeded to execute this order.

The prisoner offered no resistance, but on the contrary, not only submitted with a good grace, but of his own accord drew forth a stiletto that he wore concealed under his coat, and handed it to the officer.

The commandant took possession of his purse, his gold snuff-box, his jewellery, and other light articles that he had about him.

"Now bind his arms," said the commandant.

At this order the prisoner started, and turned like a roused lion.

"This is insufferable !" he ejaculated : " you have no right to put this indignity upon me ! I am a gentleman and a noble."

Seeing the sergeant hesitate, the commandant grew angry, and stamped his foot.

"Obey your orders !" said he.

A carbine was thrust under the prisoner's arm-pits, and his wrists were manacled in front.

The soldiers then shouldered their muskets and ranged themselves on both sides of him—

The commandant gave the word—

" March !"

The soldiers then conducted their prisoner from the room.

The frightened servants gathered on the stairs to watch his departure.

He looked towards them with a confident smile and an affable nod.

"Adieu, my friends," said he. "We shall soon meet again."

When they reached the street, they found a close carriage awaiting the prisoner.

The blinds were drawn down and the carriage was surrounded by a strong force of mounted dragoons.

The prisoner was put into the vehicle and seated between two soldiers with loaded pistols in their hands.

The commandant then got in and placed himself on the seat opposite to the prisoner.

The order to march was given, and the cavalcade started in the direction of the Castle of St. Elmo.

Meanwhile, the news had spread like wildfire through the city, that an important arrest had been made, and that it was indeed no other than the redoubtable Marco Bravo himself had been captured.

This report caused the greatest sensation among the idle and excitable populace.

The streets on the route to the castle were thronged with spectators, mostly of the lowest classes.

Some of these expressed the liveliest satisfaction at the capture of the mountain-wolf, and followed him with hootings and revilings.

Many, however, among the crowd, had a morbid admiration for the fictitious heroism of the desperate outlaw.

These greeted him with cheers and words of encouragement.

At different points on the route, throngs of the worst blackguards in Naples swept about the carriage.

"Viva Marco Bravo !" was their shout, and the soldiers had to charge into their midst and beat them back with the butts of their carbines.

The procession reached St. Elmo.

The turbulent rabble followed it to the very gates of the fortress.

The carriage with its warlike escort passed under the frowning portals, and the gates were closed upon them, baffling their eager curiosity.

The carriage stopped in a large courtyard surrounded by high and gloomy walls.

The place was full of soldiers, drawn up in lines, who presented arms to the commandant.

The door of the carriage was opened, and the prisoner ordered to descend.

Marco Bravo sprang out ; the old commandant followed him more slowly.

Conducted by his guard, the brigand chief entered a long arched corridor, at the end of which there was a flight of stone steps.

Mounting these, he was led into a spacious chamber, hung round with tattered, moth-eaten banners, and trophies of arms.

In the centre was a large table covered with green cloth, in the centre of which stood a lamp on the top of a pedestal, while at the upper end of it there was placed a large armchair.

At the lower end of the table sat two clerks in black serge cassocks, with writing materials set out before them.

They cast an inquisitive glance at the notorious brigand as he entered the room.

The commandant took his seat at the head of the table and proceeded to interrogate the prisoner.

First he demanded the prisoner's name.

"My name is Silvio Berardino, Count Di Ancona," returned the prisoner, firmly.

The commandant smiled grimly, and took a miniature from a small chest that stood before him. He passed it to one of the soldiers and motioned him to hand it to the prisoner.

The brigand turned slightly pale as he glanced at the little picture, exquisitely painted on enamel.

It was the portrait of a youth of about eighteen years of age, very handsome, with brown clustering curls, and dark hazel eyes ; he wore the uniform of a lieutenant of the Royal Guard.

"Do you recognise that portrait ?" asked the commandant.

"Scarcely," returned the other, smiling. "Yet, though a very bad likeness, I see that it is intended for me."

"Have you the effrontery to state that it is not a likeness, and a good one, being painted by one of the first artists of his day, of the Count Di Ancona ?"

"That is precisely what I mean," replied the prisoner, laying his hand upon his breast and haughtily bowing his head. "I am the Count Di Ancona."

"Per Baccho !" retorted the commandant, with a gruff laugh, "your audacity is admirable. Why, there is not the slightest resemblance between this youth and yourself ; his hair and eyes are of a soft, brown colour, yours jetty black."

"Oh, but your excellency must make allowance for the changes that time brings about. When I was a lad, my hair and eyes were of a much lighter colour than they are at present. Opinions may differ as to the goodness or badness of the picture, but it cannot be doubted that it was meant for me."

"Be it so," returned the commandant, grimly ; "you will shortly be examined before the podesta (the magistrate), and it will be well for you if you can convince him that you are not the famous Marco Bravo."

"Your excellency need have no fear on that score," was the reply. "I have abundant evidence to convince the most sceptical who I am."

The commandant rose.

"Remove the prisoner," he said.

The soldiers pushed the brigand.

He shook them off and turned upon them with a ferocious scowl.

"You cowardly rogues," he hissed between his clenched teeth, "if my arms were free, there is not one amongst you who would dare to lay a hand upon me."

"Silence, prisoner," retorted the sergeant, and brutally struck him in the mouth with the back of his hand.

Then two of the men seized him by the arms and thrust him out into a stone passage.

Dragged and pushed him along towards the head of a well-like staircase.

They descended a long, winding flight of stairs.

Upon reaching the bottom they found themselves in a black, dismal vault.

Crossing this, they passed through a heavy, iron-bound door, which was immediately closed behind them.

Again they were in a long arched passage, the granite walls of which oozed out with a dank, fetid moisture.

Here they were met by a rough-looking fellow, dressed in a leathern jerkin, while an enormous bunch of keys dangled from his belt.

This was the gaoler ; he carried a torch and lighted the way to the dungeons.

The brigand made no resistance, but kept his eyes wide open, keenly observing every turn in the way.

At length they reached the door of a gloomy cell.

The prisoner was led in.

He noticed that the gaoler had fixed the torch in a sconce in the wall.

The soldiers now unbound the prisoner's arms.

Marco Bravo stretched his benumbed limbs.

He gazed round his dismal cell, and could not suppress a shudder.

The gaoler now returned, accompanied by a blacksmith, a herculean, sullen-looking fellow, with his sleeves tucked up, exposing his bronzed and sinewy arms.

In one hand he carried a basket of tools, in the other, a pair of heavy shackles.

The brigand started.

"What is the meaning of this?" he asked, fiercely.

"We are going to put you in irons," said the gaoler, grinning maliciously.

"Put me in irons!" returned the prisoner. "Do you know who I am?"

"No. 47," returned the other with a leer ; "come, let us have no nonsense ; we must obey our orders."

The brigand quivered with rage, and glared around him with a look of hatred and vindictiveness worthy of a demon.

But surrounded as he was by armed men, resistance was, of course, out of the question.

He therefore submitted in sullen silence while the blacksmith riveted on the fetters.

The gaoler then took down the torch.

"There is your bed and your supper," he said, pointing to a corner where there was a heap of straw, a loaf of bread, and a pitcher of water.

"At least you will leave me a light," said the prisoner.

"Against orders," was the gruff reply ; "good night, Marco Bravo."

The soldiers, the blacksmith, and the gaoler quitted the cell.

The door clashed to, the key turned in the lock, and the captive brigand was left alone in chains and darkness.

CHAPTER XXXV.

GENEROSO, upon leaving the house of his master, the Count Di Ancona, hurried along the Via Di Toledo, in the direction of the bank at which he had been told to cash the English baronet's cheque.

"Diavolo," he muttered to himself, "I don't like the game the captain is playing, and I feel sure that it will bring some mischief. Fidelity is all very well, but if he chooses to run his head into a noose, I don't think that is any reason why I should sacrifice myself through his imprudence. I have half a mind to give him the slip while I have a chance, but whither should I fly to escape his vengeance? He would pursue me to the ends of the earth. Escape is not to be thought of."

His mind filled with the gloomiest forebodings, he hurried on.

He went into the bank, was received with great civility, and the money paid without demur.

He put it carefully into a bag and came out into the street.

"I have my fortune in my own hands," he said, mentally. "After all, Marco Bravo is but a man, and with all his cunning, he is not omnipotent! What is to prevent me from obtaining a passport and embarking on board some vessel bound for France or England? It is a great temptation."

Then he heard a loud hum of voices, the tramp of men's feet and the clanking of arms.

He turned his head and beheld a strong body of soldiers with their officers filing down the street, a mob of people following them.

"Basta !" he muttered, and felt his cheek grow cold ; "what is afoot now? The commandant himself rides at the head of the detachment—this is something unusual."

He had now entered the Toledo, and the soldiers, taking the same route, he mingled with the crowd that were following them.

At every step Generoso grew more and more alarmed.

"Santa Virgine!" he gasped; "where are they going to?"

A vague, yet chilling suspicion of the truth struck him to the heart.

"Marco Bravo is betrayed," was his thought. "I knew it would be so. La Catarina predicted it—her prediction is verified."

He still followed on like one in a dream.

He saw the soldiers stop before the residence of the pretended Count Di Ancona.

The commandant dismounted from his horse, as did also the other officers.

Generoso saw the commandant enter the house, followed by some officers and a score of soldiers.

It was enough.

Fear lending wings to his feet, Generoso turned and fled.

He instinctively made for the quarter of the city inhabited by the lowest of the populace.

He sought the old, weather-beaten house where dwelt Isaco il Nero, the king of the gipsies.

He gave a peculiar knock at the door, at the same time whistling a robber song.

There was a small iron grating in the oaken panel of the door, the shutter of which was slid aside, and a swart gipsy face appeared.

After exchanging a signal with the porter, Generoso was admitted into the house.

The man at once saw by his looks that something unusual had happened.

"Why, Generoso, how is this?" he asked, "you look as white as a corpse; what ails you?"

"I have no time to answer questions," returned Generoso, impatiently. "Where is Isaco il Nero? Quick; I must see him at once."

"He is holding a council with the elders of the tribe," was the reply.

"No matter, I must see him at once," rejoined the brigand. "The business I come on will brook of no delay."

"Follow me, then," answered the other.

He led Generoso along a gloomy passage panelled with oak as hard and dark as ebony.

He stopped by a door sunk in a deep embrasure of the wall.

"Stay here," he said, "I must announce you."

He gave three distinct knocks at the door.

It was opened by someone stationed in the inside for that purpose, who, as soon as he had entered, closed it behind him.

Generoso waited a few moments, and then the porter reappeared.

"All is well," he said; "you may enter."

Generoso, who was acquainted with the usages and etiquette of this vagabond court, doffed his hat with as much reverence as though he were about to enter the august presence of legitimate royalty.

He was ushered by a tall fellow bearing a white wand, who appeared to officiate as chamberlain, into a large and sombre apartment, wainscoted like the passage which led to it, in dark oak.

Around a long table were seated the gipsy senate, many of them aged men with venerable grey beards, and all having the prominent features and bronze complexions of their extraordinary race.

At the head of the table sat the gipsy king upon his chair of state, raised upon a platform.

He wore a patchwork cloak of many colours, and on his head a brass-gilt crown over a silk handkerchief, striped in bright scarlet and yellow.

Near the window sat the beautiful gipsy princess and celebrated opera dancer, La Zara.

She was busily employed in embroidering a jacket of rich blue velvet, with silver thread.

As Generoso entered, the gipsy king descended from the throne to meet him.

All the rest, who were present, turned towards him their inquiring glances.

Even Zara dropped her work and fixed her black eyes upon him.

"Welcome, Generoso," said the king, extending his hand. "You come at a busy time, but I trust it is to bring us good news."

"Per Baccho!" returned the other, gruffly. "The news I bring is bad enough. You will scarcely believe me when I tell it you."

"Out with it, man," returned the gipsy king. "There is nothing that I hate so much as suspense."

"Know then, that Marco Bravo is captured," said Generoso, "and by this time is laid neck and heels in the dungeons of St. Elmo."

There was a general cry of surprise and consternation.

"Marco Bravo a prisoner!"

"It is but too true," replied Generoso. "He must have been betrayed by some traitor to the band. He was seized at his lodgings in the Toledo, and conveyed under an armed escort to the castle."

"But how did you escape?" asked the gipsy king.

"Fortunately I was absent from the house at the time of the arrest," replied the brigand.

"I was returning homeward, when I saw the commandant riding with his soldiers down the Toledo. I guessed their intention and followed at a distance. When I saw the troop halt before the door of Marco Bravo's house, I knew that all was lost, and I fled hither for safety and protection."

"No one of Marco Bravo's companions shall be denied such protection as lies in our power to offer," answered the gipsy king. "But you must not remain here long, for no doubt, the *sbirri* (police) will soon be upon your track, and they have had several brisk encounters with our people lately, and are so enraged against us, that if they dared, they would lay sacrilegious hands upon our royal self."

"I ask your hospitality but for a few hours," returned Generoso. "I shall change my dress and make off to the mountains."

"Did you deliver him the message I sent?" asked the gipsy.

"I did," was the reply, "and urged other considerations for his immediate flight, but all to no purpose."

"Why, what answer did he make?" asked Isaco.

"He upbraided me with cowardice," replied the brigand. "It seems he had undertaken to lead a band of volunteers against the brigands, to exterminate our band and rescue the young Englishman he had captured."

"A daring plot, by Pharaoh!" returned the gipsy king, smiling. "But what young Englishman is he you speak of?"

"A fine young fellow," responded the brigand. "The secretary of a rich English milordo, who resides at Castellamare."

The king of the gipsies went to the table and opened a large book, a kind of ledger.

"Surely you don't mean the young cavalier who rescued my sister Zara from the violence of some libertine noble, who would have carried her off by force?"

"The same," returned Generoso.

The gipsy king turned over the leaves of his ponderous volume.

"I see his name is entered here," he said. "It is Ralph Wildhawk."

At the mention of this name, Zara rose, her cheeks deathly pale, and her hands clasped.

"He was made a free member of our brotherhood on July the tenth, that is three months ago."

"I know it," answered the brigand. "I was present at the initiation."

The gipsy king frowned darkly.

"This is not well," he said; "Marco Bravo has not kept faith with me. It was stipulated between us that all members of my brotherhood should be respected."

"Let me tell you this," returned Generoso, hastily. "The chief had no evil design against the young gallant, for whom, indeed, he entertains a sincere friendship. The orders given were that he should be treated well. He was seized only to keep him out of mischief, as he took a leading part in the movement against the brigands."

"So far so good," returned the gipsy. "But now that Marco Bravo is himself a prisoner, it will go ill with Ralph Wildhawk."

Generoso shrugged his shoulders.

"I am afraid you are right there," he replied. "When the news reaches the band that Marco Bravo is taken, they will hardly be able to restrain their rage."

"And will vent it upon their innocent prisoner, eh?" said the gipsy king.

"Perhaps so," returned the brigand. "I would not stand in his shoes for more than I can tell."

"You cannot answer for his life?"

"No," was the grave answer.

At this announcement Zara uttered an involuntary cry.

The gipsy king glanced towards her.

"How now, my sister," he said; "what has disturbed you?"

White and trembling Zara came forward.

"Can you ask?" she retorted with indignation. "I should be insensible and ungrateful indeed if I could hear, without emotion, that such deadly peril overhangs the gallant young cavalier to whose courage and generosity I owe so much."

A smile stole over Generoso's dark face.

"She is smitten by the young Englishman's handsome face," he muttered. "I can turn this to good account."

The gipsy king looked sorry and perplexed.

"Compose yourself, my sister," he replied.

"I am grieved at what has befallen your friend."

"Send to the band," returned Zara, "and demand his instant liberation; you know that there is more than one brother of our tribe among the garrison at St. Elmo, and that it is not quite impossible to find the brigand chief some means of escape."

"That is true," returned Generoso, eagerly.

Zara made an impatient gesture, and, without paying further heed to the remark, went on with increased earnestness.

"Consider, my brother," she urged, "this gallant youth is an adopted brother of the tribe. Remember your oath; you swore to protect him with your life, if necessary, and will you abandon him to his fate?"

"Zara," replied the gipsy king, "I will see what can be done."

Generoso here interposed.

"It will be possible to save the young Englishman, if you will use your influence with those of your brotherhood of St. Elmo, to bring about the deliverance of the chief."

"That I promise you, on my royal oath," returned the gipsy king.

"Alas! it may be too late," sighed Zara. "The poor young cavalier may have been already murdered."

"That is hardly possible," answered Generoso. "For though ill news flies fast, the tidings of Marco Bravo's capture cannot reach the distant glen, in the Abruzzi, for many hours to come."

"You must then hasten your departure," rejoined the gipsy king. "You may be in time to save him."

"I will tarry no longer than is needful to provide myself with a suitable disguise."

"I will take care to equip you with all that you require," returned the gipsy king. "When do you propose setting out?"

"As soon as all is ready," rejoined the brigand. "I will undertake to see that no harm befalls him. In the chief's absence the command of the band devolves upon me."

"I thank you," replied Zara, coldly. "But Marco Bravo has played me false. Let him look to it; it will be the worse for him if any mischief happens to his captive. We gipsies know how to avenge the wrongs of our friends."

And with that, she swept from the room.

"The signora is angry," said Generoso.

The gipsy king laughed.

"Heed her not, amico," he said. "But you must take care that you are not caught, for I doubt not the roads will be strictly guarded."

Then, after a pause, he added—

"I see now how it may be done; a party of my men are going as far as Itri; you can string a lute round your neck and pass yourself off as one of the crew."

"Excellent," returned Generoso. "The plan will answer well."

"At the same time I must warn you that I have taken that young Englishman under my guardianship," continued the gipsy king, "and that I shall consider any injury done to him as an offence against myself."

"I will take care of him," answered Generoso.

"It is well," said the gipsy king; "and now we must get you ready for the start."

By the orders of their monarch, two of the gipsy men set to work to disguise him.

One of them, an expert barber, shaved every vestige of hair from his face; the other brought him a basin containing some dark liquid, in which he stained his hands and face.

An old and seedy, but picturesque and Oriental-looking costume was put on, and a striped cloak thrown about his shoulders.

"Now take your mandoline," said the gipsy king, "and you are complete. The mother who bore you would pass you as a stranger."

Generoso laughed, and ran his fingers over the strings of the lute.

"Now come with me."

The gipsy king then quitted the presence chamber in company with his guest, whom he conducted into a stable-yard with folding gates, adjoining the house.

Here a motley crew were mustered.

There was the company of musicians, consisting of players on the flute, horn, pastoral pipe, tabor, drum and cymbals, and several groups of performers, acrobats and dancers, the Policinella, or Punch, and the bear leader.

The latter had a monstrous brute with him, a monkey dressed as an advocate, in cap and gown, seated upon his back.

Upon seeing Generoso, the bear gave a low, surly growl, and lumbered towards him.

"Don't be frightened, signore," the keeper said, smiling; "he will not hurt you; he is rather suspicious of strangers."

As he spoke, he gave poor Bruin a tremendous thwack with his heavy staff.

"Up, sir; shake hands with the signore," he said.

The huge, ungainly brute raised himself on his haunches and stretched forth his shaggy paw.

Generoso, however, showed no inclination to accept the proffered courtesy, but he laughed to see the monkey, squeaking and chattering, cling round the monster's neck.

"I should think, amico, you have some trouble to keep your unruly pupils in order," said Generoso.

"I get on well enough with this fellow since I have found him a new comrade."

"You allude to the monkey?"

"Yes; the last I had was a diavoletto—a little devil," laughed the bear ward. "And yet I was sorry to part with him."

"Why did you then?"

"Per Baccho! because he led the bear such a sad life of it."

"How so?"

"Always teasing him," returned the bear ward, pulling the bear back.

Then, after indulging in a hearty laugh, he went on in a grave tone—

"By San Gennaro, it is wonderful to observe the cunning and sagacity of monkeys. "One day I saw Jacko descend from his pole and creep quietly up to the bear and open one of his eyes, into which he peeped with a very knowing and inquisitive look."

"What did he do that for?"

A broad grin overspread the bear ward's face as he answered with a chuckling laugh—

"To see what he was dreaming about."

The conversation was here interrupted by a loud uproar in the street, and a gipsy came rushing into the yard.

His looks betrayed the wildest alarm.

"The soldiers!" he gasped; "they have entered our sanctuary, they are looking for some criminal, and are ransacking all our houses."

The bear ward crept close to Generoso, and whispered in his ear—

"It's you they are looking for."

Generoso sprang back, clutching the hilt of his dagger.

"Maledetto," he growled; "you know me then?"

"Signore, I know you well," returned the other.

"And would betray me?" retorted Generoso, in a fierce whisper.

"On the contrary. Take this bear's chain; you will pass unnoticed."

"Thanks," murmured Generoso.

Not without some feeling of trepidation, he took the chain.

The gates were thrown open.

The king of the gipsies entered.

He was followed by several officers of the sbirri, and a body of men-at-arms.

"My doors are open, captain," said Isaco. "Search the house, and if you find the man you are pursuing, diavolo, mine be his penalty."

"Bueno," returned the officer, coolly; "but if I find him here, you will have to accompany him to St. Elmo."

"Obey your orders," said the gipsy king.

"First, tell me," replied the officer, "what men are these you have here?"

"Zingari all, men of my tribe, musicians, conjurors, and so on."

"They seem preparing for a journey," replied the officer. "Where are they going to?"

"To the festa at Itri," answered the gipsy king. "To sell their wares, and amuse the public."

"Let me see the passports," commanded the officer.

Isaco produced the documents.

The officer ran his eyes over the long list of names.

One by one he called upon the men to answer.

They did so.

At length it came to Generoso's turn.

There was something in the fellow's look which raised the officer's suspicions.

"Stand forward," he said.

The brigand obeyed, dragging the bear by his chain.

"What is your name?" asked the officer.

The brigand stood mute and confused at the question.

But the gipsy king was at hand and at once came to the rescue.

"Speak up, Isaco," he said, slapping him on the back.

The officer turned fiercely upon him.

"No prompting," he said; "leave the fellow to me."

The gipsy king turned sullenly away.

"As you please," he said; "but if the man you are looking for is concealed by any of my people, you are losing time and giving him an opportunity of escape. Isaco is a dull-witted fellow, and it will take you some trouble to get much out of him."

He made a movement towards the house.

"Halt there!" shouted the officer angrily; "stay where you are."

The gipsy turned back with well-feigned reluctance.

The officer noticed this, and could not help thinking that the object of his pursuit might, after all, be hidden in the house.

He therefore interrogated him less severely than he had at first intended.

Generoso was cunning enough to take the hint given him by the gipsy king, and affected an air of stolid stupidity.

Still he was sufficiently acquainted with the language, customs and circumstances of the gipsy-tribe and made such good use of his knowledge, that the officer appeared satisfied with his replies.

He hurriedly left him and beckoning his men, entered the house.

With great apparent unwillingness, Isaco il Nero led the way, guiding them to all the rooms in the old dilapidated building.

They searched high and low.

They tapped the wainscots with the butt ends of their muskets, they removed the furniture to examine the floors for trap doors, and even fired shots up the chimneys, bringing down an avalanche of soot.

The gipsy king watched all these proceedings with inward glee.

He was glad to find the old house keep its secrets so well.

Not one of its numerous oubliettes and hiding places was discovered.

At length, deeply mortified, the officer and his men took their departure.

As soon as they were gone, the gipsy band, with Generoso the brigand, the occasion of all this fuss, took the road to the mountains—laughing at the defeat of the sbirri, whom they looked upon as their natural enemies.

CHAPTER XXXVI.

ALONE IN THE BRIGANDS' GLEN.

THE position of the adventurous young Englishman, Ralph Wildhawk, was one of terrible peril and uncertainty.

As yet he had been tolerably well treated, but he had seen nothing of Marco Bravo.

As every outlet from the glen, every post of vantage on the neighbouring mountains was strictly and constantly guarded, the prisoner was allowed to roam about at will within certain bounds.

This, however, had not been the case when he was first captured.

Having great faith in the word of an Englishman, the bandits at first tried to extract from him his parole not to attempt to make his escape.

Very wisely, Ralph Wildhawk refused to bind himself by any such promise.

He thought that some accident might happen which would give him an opportunity of slipping off, and so was reluctant of throwing away the chance.

Upon his refusal, he was removed to a deep and gloomy cavern, that formed a sort of dungeon for refractory prisoners, the food brought him was of an inferior description, and he was allowed to see nobody but his keeper, one of the surliest fellows in the band.

But this treatment only served to exasperate Ralph, and to harden his heart.

He maintained a sullen reserve, and when threatened, would tell his oppressors to kill him at once, as he had no fear of death.

At the end of a week, the brigands saw that their ill-usage began to have its effect upon the bodily powers of their victim, though none whatever upon his firmness of mind.

He grew pale and thin, sickened and pined, and showed symptoms of approaching serious illness.

The brigands grew alarmed.

They remembered how Marco Bravo had given the strictest orders that the prisoner should be treated with the greatest indulgence, and should be allowed as great an amount of freedom as was compatible with his safe keeping.

Ralph Wildhawk was, therefore, taken from his prison, regaled with the choicest fare, and permission was given him to roam at will within certain prescribed limits.

Ralph gladly availed himself of this privilege, and daily walked about the Brigands' Glen, and climbed the adjacent rocks.

One day young Giovanni Pizano came to him while he was at breakfast in a charming grotto which had been assigned to him for his dwelling.

The Italian boy's good-humoured face was flushed with pleasure, and he showed his white, even teeth in a smile of self-satisfaction.

Under his arm he carried a large portfolio and a small box.

"Good morning, Giovanni," said Ralph. "What have you there?"

"Something I have brought, you, *eccelenza*," replied the young brigand; "something which, I think, will please you."

And, with a gleeful laugh, he placed his treasures upon the table.

Upon seeing them, Ralph uttered a cry of delight.

"Excellent! You are the best fellow in the world, Giovanni," cried Ralph, shaking him by the hand. "Paper, paints, canvas, pencils, a box of mathematical instruments; these are indeed prizes. How much I thank you. But where, in wonder's name, did you obtain them?"

"Signore," replied the lad, "in another part of the Abruzzi, our band have a stronghold called Saracen's Tower. I brought them from thence. Having seen your excellency make drawings on the walls with pieces of charcoal, I thought the proper materials for the art might be acceptable."

"And pray whom did they belong to?" asked Ralph.

"To a French artist, signore."

"A prisoner?"

"Si, si—it is a sad story."

"'THERE IS YOUR BED AND YOUR SUPPER,' SAID THE GAOLER."

"Tell me about it."

"There's is not much to tell," returned the young Italian. "You see, this happened in the first year of my connection with the band. The Frenchman, who was a very young man, but little older than I am now, came to Italy to study our great masters. He took a tour through the Abruzzi, sketching the most striking scenery he met with. He was betrayed by one of the shepherds in league with our troop, and was captured by Marco Bravo. He was confined in the Saracen's Tower, and I was ordered to attend upon him. The chief demanded a thousand piastres for his ransom, but the poor artist was without money or friends. However, he wrote to the French consul, and the heads of several religious orders in Naples, imploring them to get up a subscription to satisfy the chief's demand."

"Well, and what response did he meet with?"

"Empty promises, nothing more," returned the young brigand. "Marco Bravo grew furious, and said that if by a certain day the ransom were not paid, the Frenchman should be shot. The next day letters came; they contained all sorts of condolences, but no money. Well, signore, the Frenchman only laughed and lit his cigarito with the papers, but the next morning, when I went to call him, I found him lying stiff and stark upon his bed, which was soaked with blood. He had opened a vein with a pen-knife which he kept concealed about him."

"Horrible!" muttered Ralph. "And he has left me this sad legacy."

"I am grieved, signore, that I have told you all this," said young Giovanni, in a kind tone. "But with you the case is different; the captain likes you very much, and whether or not your ransom is paid, I feel certain he will do you no harm."

"I cannot tell why he should take so much interest in me, or why he should make exceptions in my favour," replied Ralph, in astonishment; "I never saw the man."

"*Scusi*, signore," answered the Italian lad, smiling; "you must not make too sure of that. Marco Bravo goes everywhere and in all sorts of disguises. You may have met him, though you knew it not."

Ralph started violently; a painful and oft-recurring suspicion crossed his mind, that the Count Di Ancona and Marco Bravo were one and the same.

"Well, Giovanni," he said, "that will be settled very shortly, I trust. When do you think I shall see your captain?"

"In a few days, I think," returned the youth. "Stromba has brought news that Marco Bravo intends soon to return to the brigands' glen."

"And, meanwhile, what have they done with my friend, the Count Di Ancona?" Ralph inquired.

"I do not know, signore," was the gravely-spoken reply, "and if I did, I should not dare to tell you; it is as much as my life is worth to betray the secrets of the band."

"Enough, my boy," rejoined Ralph Wildhawk; "I shall not compromise your safety by asking any awkward questions. I thank you for your kindness, and, if ever I regain my liberty, it shall not be forgotten."

When he was alone, Ralph opened the portfolio, and examined the contents with much curiosity.

He found written upon the inside of the cover the luckless owner's name and address.

"Achille Renouf,
"No. 12, Rue St. Martin,
"Paris."

"So, then, if ever I get back to Paris, I shall know where to make inquiries about him," mused Ralph.

He found the portfolio contained a good many sketches, very cleverly drawn, but for the most part unfinished.

There were studies from the antique, sketches of the heads of lazzaroni, market girls, fishermen and brigands.

Among the latter there was one, a very striking portrait.

It was that of a brigand, consummately handsome, with black, eagle eyes, and clustering black ringlets.

He was gaily dressed in the somewhat theatrical costume worn by the banditti, profusely adorned with gold lace, the breast covered with orders, medals, and little gold crosses.

In the corner was written the name of the original of the portrait—

"Marco Bravo, *chef des brigands*."

Ralph fixed his eyes intently on this picture. His breath came short.

Every vestige of colour stole from his cheek.

"It must be so," he gasped out; "the likeness is exact. It is the face of the Count Di Ancona. He, then, the false villain, is indeed Marco Bravo. That accounts for his pretended friendship for me. My bitterest curse light on him. But, come the worst, I will have my revenge."

Calming himself, he again seated himself at the table and opened the box.

Walter found paints, brushes, palettes, instruments and everything that he wanted.

He, therefore, determined that he would at once set to work.

He rose, threw his capote around him, pulled his slouched hat over his brows, and went forth from the cave.

Some were employed in grooming their mules, others in burnishing their weapons, while not a few, relieved from their long night's watch, lay stretched upon their cloaks in every attitude of profound repose.

There were many females amongst them, whose elegant forms, and lovely, though sunburnt faces, would have maddened every swain.

Ralph passed through the crowds, who made way for him.

He strode on, his eyes moodily bent upon the ground.

"If I can get down to the banks of the river, I will take a sketch of the falls," thought Ralph; "they will form a splendid subject for a picture."

With this intent he was about to make an attempt to scramble down the almost precipitous face of the cliffs.

He was prevented, however, by a fierce shout.

"Ho, there! stand!"

Not without difficulty Ralph recovered his footing, and stood on the brink of the rock.

A tall, stalwart brigand advanced towards him with a menacing frown, his long carbine poised in his hands.

As he drew near, the robber levelled his piece at Ralph's head.

"Don't fire, *amico*," said Ralph. "Whom do you take me for?"

The fellow lowered his musket, but waved his hand impatiently.

"Back, signore," he said, "this won't do; you are trespassing beyond bounds. You should not have crossed the bridge."

"I suppose you are on sentry here?" asked Ralph.

"I am, signore," replied the other, "and Stromba, who has the command, gave me orders not to allow you to pass the bridge."

"Nonsense," returned Ralph. "I only want to get down to the bank of the river in order to make a sketch of the falls. You must perceive that it is impossible for me to wander far, as there is an outpost a few furlongs down the stream."

"That is no matter," answered the brigand, "I have my orders, and you must obey them."

"Here," said Ralph, placing some money in his hand, "here is a *buono mano*, something to drink my health. Only show me how to descend this cliff and allow me an hour for my purpose."

"I should be sorry to disoblige you," replied the brigand, in a softened tone. "If you would promise me to keep within sight, and not to wander beyond the stone cross you see glinting through yon thicket, I will let you pass."

"Thanks, *amico*," replied Ralph. "I give you my word of honour that I will strictly observe the conditions."

Then, casting a look down the horrid ravine, he added—

"But, tell me, is there any path by which I can descend?"

"Follow me, and I will show it to you," replied the brigand.

He conducted Ralph to a path which led in a steep descent, winding down the base of the cliff, through a covert of thick shrubs, to the banks of the river beneath the bridge.

The two walking abreast, with the foaming torrent on one hand, and a channel of water on the other, had soon reached the foot of the bridge.

Here the river was seen bursting through some pointed rocks.

On looking up they saw the bridge spanning the gulf at an immense height; and the cliffs, rising in perpendicular gloom on either hand, left but a narrow slip of blue sky overhead.

"An awful spot," said Ralph.

"Si, signore," returned the brigand; "we call it the Maiden's Leap."

"And why?" asked the young Englishman; "I suppose there is some legend connected with the place?"

"Oh, 'tis no idle story, but a fact which I myself witnessed," replied the bandit. "It is now three years ago. Stromba was in love with the daughter of a farmer, whose home-

stead is situated in the campagna, at the base of the mountains; her name was Margerita, and she was a very pretty girl."

"Well?" said Ralph.

"You see she would have nothing to say to Stromba—she detested him," pursued the brigand; "besides, she was betrothed to a young man who owned a vineyard in the neighbourhood of the village where she was born. The wedding-day was appointed. Stromba resolved to carry off the bride, and, on the eve of the marriage-day, he waylaid the young couple as they were sauntering together through a lonely glade in the wood. He stabbed the lover and carried off the girl."

"What a villain!"

"*Altro*, signore," returned the brigand with a shrug; "Stromba was passionately fond of poor Margerita, and grieved bitterly for her death."

"Her death!"

"You shall hear, signore," rejoined the brigand. "Struck with horror at the fate of her betrothed, poor Margerita seemed lost to consciousness. She tamely submitted to be led away by Stromba and his comrades. They set her on a mule and hurried her off to the mountains. They reached the bridge, the only access to the brigands' glen on this side. When they reached the middle of the bridge, she flung herself from the saddle, and with a heart-piercing shriek plunged into the abyss."

Ralph turned pale and bit his lip.

The man lowered his voice, and went on in an impressive tone—

"They say her phantom haunts this spot. I myself have heard the strangest sounds, as of human weeping and wailing, rising up from the chasm. This has happened at night while I have kept guard at my post above."

"Most likely, I have no doubt of it," returned Ralph, taking a malicious pleasure in encouraging the retributive superstition. "The spirits of the murdered often revisit the fatal spot where they met their doom. There are many well-authenticated instances on record."

The brigand looked uncomfortable.

"Madre Maria! I incline to your opinion," he answered.

"Did you ever see her?" asked Ralph, quite seriously; "I mean her spectre?"

"No, signore, the saints forbid," was the fervent response. "I do not account myself a coward, but such a sight would kill me."

Then, after a shuddering pause, he continued—

"You must not mention it to anyone, lest they ask you whence you gained your information; but Stromba once saw the spirit of Margerita."

Ralph nodded grimly.

"I can believe it," he replied. "But proceed."

"One night Stromba was on sentry at the bridge," resumed the bandit. "I was in the cave in which you lodge, playing at chess. Stromba rushed in; his face resembled that of a corpse rather than a living man's. The cold beads of sweat stood on his brow; he trembled like one who has just taken the tarantula; he could not speak; he fell on his knees before Marco Bravo."

Ralph smiled.

"And what said the chief?"

"Cospetto! he started to his feet, thinking the soldiers were upon us," continued the robber; "he was about to call the men to arms, but Stromba held up his hand, and by a great effort found the power to speak."

"What had he to tell?"

"But little. He stammered out something about having seen the form of Margerita gliding in mystic light over the dark bosom of the torrent."

"And what reply made Marco Bravo?"

"He cursed him for a coward and a fool, and smote him to the ground."

"Ha!"

"But, note you, signore mio," rejoined the brigand, "ever after that Stromba was exempted from the duty of keeping guard over the bridge. And all the wealth of Crœsus would not tempt him to approach it after nightfall."

"But I must leave you, signore. and return to my post. I warn you, I shall keep a sharp watch upon you, and if——"

He stopped and tapped his musket significantly.

"Spare your threats," rejoined Ralph, disdainfully. "I have given you my word that I will not abuse your confidence, is not that enough?"

"It is enough, signore," answered the brigand. "I will signal you from the bridge when time is up."

"Do so," said Ralph; "I shall be ready to answer your call."

The man waved his hand, left him, and shouldering his musket, strode up the narrow, rugged pathway, and disappeared behind an angle of the rocks.

Ralph settled himself down to his work. He selected the most effective point of view; he began making a sketch of the falls.

Nearly an hour had passed in this way, when his attention was aroused by seeing a dark shadow flit across the open page of his book.

He turned hastily.

Beside him stood the tall, majestic figure of a woman, who, though past the prime of life, still bore the traces of her former great beauty.

She was attired in the picturesque costume of a brigandess, and leaned upon a long carbine.

Ralph's heart gave a great throb.

There was something in the woman's manner and expression which inspired him with a strange and powerful feeling of awe and admiration.

"Pardon, signore," she said, with a pleasant smile, and an air of high-bred courtesy that was not without its charm. "I am afraid I have disturbed you in your work."

"No, signora, I am but too happy for such a pleasing interruption of a task I have set myself only to beguile an idle hour," he replied.

The glorious black eyes of the brigandess beamed upon him with a peculiar and irresistible fascination.

"But how comes it that your excellency has penetrated so far into the heart of the mountains." she asked, "and linger so dangerously near to the brigands' glen?"

"It is almost needless to assure you, signora, that it is not from my own choice that I am here," was the reply; "I have the misfortune to be a prisoner in the hands of the banditti."

"I am sorry for you," she replied. "The more so as it does not lie in my power to be of use to you, for though I am styled the Queen of the Brigands, my authority bears no comparison to that of Marco Bravo."

Ralph bowed.

"I think I have the honour of addressing the celebrated La Catarina," he said.

"I am La Catarina," she replied, "and in you I imagine I behold the young English gentleman lately captured by the band."

"I am indeed that most unfortunate person," was the response.

"You astonish me," replied the brigandess; "you speak our language like a native."

"That is not wonderful, considering that Italian is my mother-tongue," he rejoined, smiling. "My mother was an Italian, my father an Englishman."

La Catarina started and turned pale.

Then she pressed her hand to her forehead and drew a deep sigh.

"Had my son, my first-born, lived till now," she said, "he would have been about your age."

Ralph's voice faltered somewhat as he rejoined—

"Then he is dead."

"Alas, yes," replied La Catarina, sighing deeply. "My child died while still an infant. But it is useless to brood over the troubles of the past. Let us speak of other things."

She cast down her eyes, and for some moments she appeared to be lost in deep meditation.

Then she raised a wistful glance to his face, and asked, in a kind tone—

"Pray tell me, signore, how much does Marco Bravo demand for your ransom?"

"Signora," returned the young Englishman, "as yet, I have heard no sum mentioned, and strange to say, the brigand chief pretends to be my friend."

La Catarina laughed bitterly.

"Your friend!" she repeated in scornful accents; "oh, beware of his friendship, which is more dangerous than his hate."

But Ralph's words had evidently made impression.

"Your friend!" repeated La Catarina. "When and where have you encountered Marco Bravo?"

"I never saw him but once," returned Ralph. "It was when he and his gang so audaciously robbed the audience in the theatre at Castellamare, and even then his face was covered with a black mask. That was the first and only time I ever met him."

"Do not make too sure of that," was La Catarina's terse reply.

"Do you think that I may have met him in society when he has been under some disguise?" asked Ralph.

"Who knows?" was the tantalising reply. "Not I; but look, signore, Spado is calling you from the bridge. You had better leave me now."

Ralph turned his head and perceived the brigand standing in the centre of the bridge waving his hat.

Ralph answered the signal.

Then addressing himself to the brigandess, he bowed.

"Adieu, signora," said he; "I trust we may meet again."

"I hope so," returned La Catarina. "Meanwhile, consider me your friend."

She extended her hand.

Ralph raised it to his lips.

"*Addio*," said the brigandess. "There are other questions I would have asked you, but we shall meet again."

"I shall wait with impatience till that hour arrives," answered Ralph, with unconscious fervour.

He then closed his portfolio and hurried up the steep path to the bridge.

On the summit of the rocky bank he found the brigand anxiously awaiting him.

"*Cospetto*, signore, I am glad you have come."

"Why, *amico*, has anything unusual happened?" asked Ralph.

"Some of the band, who had gone on an excursion with Marco Bravo, have returned to the glen," was the robber's reply.

"What is that to me?"

"Only this, signore—I would not, for the world, have it known that I allowed you to pass the bridge."

"Be satisfied," returned Ralph Wildhawk. "Do not think me so ungrateful as to abuse your confidence."

"Well, signore, do you hasten back to the cave, and keep yourself close," returned the brigand, speaking very seriously.

"Why?"

"There is some mischief afoot," replied the other. "Our companions have brought bad news from Naples. What it may be I cannot tell, but upon their arrival there was a shout of anger and alarm."

"I thank you for your friendly warning," answered Ralph.

He crossed the bridge, and, with hastening pace, made towards the brigands' glen.

"I partly guess what is the matter," he said to himself as he hurried along. "My friends are coming to my rescue, and these brigands are terrified; yet I wonder that I have not yet been confronted with Marco Bravo."

On getting back to the glen, he found the brigands clustered together in groups.

As Ralph passed them, they greeted him with very different looks from those they had bestowed upon him when he left the glen on that morning.

Many of them scowled darkly upon him, and clutched the hilts of their stilettoes.

Pretending not to notice them, he walked on straight to the cave where he had been lodged.

Upon arriving there, he placed his portfolio upon the table, opened it, and added some touches to his sketch.

While he was thus employed, he was disturbed by the tramp of many approaching footsteps, commingled with the hubbub of loud and angry voices.

"Where is the Englishman?" was the shout. "Bring him forth. Let him die! Revenge for Marco Bravo!"

Ralph rose pale and dismayed, but not daunted.

"My time is come," he muttered to himself. "Some mishap has befallen Marco Bravo—perhaps he is slain or taken prisoner—and his gang intend to wreak their spite upon me. I am unarmed, but will meet them."

With this resolution he boldly advanced.

The ruffians drew back as he quietly approached them.

"What is the meaning of this?" he asked. "What do you want with me?"

Two score sets of white teeth gleamed, and as many pairs of rolling black eyes glared upon him in devilish fury.

Daggers were brandished and muskets cocked.

"Away with him; let him be shot!" chorused a multitude of voices, among which rang shrilly those of the women. "*A la morti!* Revenge for Marco Bravo!"

Ralph raised his hand.

"At least tell me why you are so enraged against me," he asked. "What have I done? In what have I offended you? Where is Marco Bravo? Let him be my judge."

"Marco Bravo is a prisoner in the dungeons of St. Elmo," was the fierce reply.

"Be reasonable, my friends," returned Ralph, calmly. "If you are sane and not mad, tell me in what way I am accountable for what has befallen your chief?"

"Do not listen to him," shouted the foremost of the vengeful crew. "Away with him to instant death!"

Several of the villains stepped forward from the crowd, and roughly seized him by the collar.

They dragged him along, while a number of ruffians closed around him with loaded muskets.

A rabble of men, women, and even children followed in the rear, heaping upon him the fiercest execrations.

A tribe of Red Indians dragging their victim to the death-stake could not have displayed more fiendish exultation and blind, insensible fury.

"Death to the heretic!" they yelled. "Let his head be sent to the commandant of St. Elmo."

Poor Ralph was hustled along until they reached a kind of *plateau* on the mountain side, at the extreme end of which there was a sort of curtain wall, of smooth, precipitous rock.

Fully assured that his last moment was come, Ralph muttered a prayer, and resigning himself to his fate, put on an air of coolness and dignity.

They sat him with his back against the rock.

Then half-a-dozen brigands, with loaded muskets, took their ground.

A man approached him, with a handkerchief in his hand, to blindfold him.

Ralph thrust him scornfully back.

"THE HUGE, UNGAINLY BRUTE RAISED HIMSELF ON HIS HAUNCHES."

"Go," he said, sternly; "it is only such guilty wretches as yourself that fear to look death in the face."

With a sullen growl, the fellow shrugged up his shoulders, and retired from the spot.

There was a breathless hush, as the execution party, at a word from Stromba, slowly and deliberately raised their guns to their shoulders.

Then came a slight reaction of feeling in the happy youth's favour.

He looked so calm, so brave, and handsome, many of the women shuddered, and turned away their heads, as if horrified at the approaching spectacle of blood.

"*Il povero!*" murmured some of them; "what a pity it is that one so young and handsome should be a heretic."

Meanwhile Ralph Wildhawk bravely faced his executioners.

"Fire, ye dogs and cowards!" he shouted, striking his breast. "I die with the assurance of a sweeping revenge."

The ruffians were about to take him at his word, when a clear voice rang out upon the calm mountain air.

The tall and noble form of the Queen of the Brigands glided between the executioners and the doomed man.

"La Catarina!" burst from every lip.

The executioners slowly and reluctantly lowered their pieces.

Stromba frowned, but nevertheless bowed respectfully.

"Why are you here, signora?" he asked. "This is no place for you."

"Slave!" returned La Catarina, her eyes flashing dark lightnings, while with startling suddenness she half raised her musket. "Dare you speak in this tone of insolence to me? By the Blessed Mother of Heaven, I have a mind to shoot you dead."

Then, striking the butt of the musket upon the ground, she added, in a fiercely derisive tone—

"Ye fools! what is this ye are about to do?"

"An act of justice, or at least of just vengeance, La Catarina," grumbled Stromba.

"Do you talk to me of 'justice?' Say rather of madness," she retorted; "an act which no one will resent more bitterly than Marco Bravo himself."

"Marco Bravo is taken, La Catarina," returned Stromba. "Perhaps you have not heard the fatal tidings. Our gallant chief is a prisoner in the Castle of St. Elmo."

"And likely to remain there if you take this young man's life," replied La Catarina. "While he lives, you may hold him as a hostage for your chief's preservation; when he dies, your power ceases."

"*E vero!*" murmured the brigands. "That is true."

"You shall hear what Marco Bravo has to say to this."

She turned towards two men who hung upon the skirts of the crowd, and beckoned them to draw near.

The brigands parted, and suffered them to pass.

One of them was a tall, dark, handsome fellow, of about thirty years of age; the other a mere youth, of slight, but graceful figure, and beautiful countenance.

Upon seeing the elder of these two, Stromba uttered a cry of delighted amazement.

"*Che diavolo?*" he exclaimed. "Can I believe my eyes? It is Generoso."

The two brigands cordially shook hands.

"Welcome, comrade," said Stromba. "We thought you also had been taken prisoner."

"I have had a narrow escape, I can assure you; but let me introduce you to a new companion."

Then taking the youth who accompanied him by the shoulders, he roughly pushed him forward.

"Come, lad, don't hang back so bashfully," he said. "Look your new friends in the face."

"Signore, you will find me ready to answer any reasonable question," was the reply.

"Generoso tells me you have joined the band."

"He tells the truth, signore. It is so."

His questioner laughed gruffly.

"*Basta!*" he exclaimed, "you a brigand! You appear more fitted to serve as a page to some fine lady."

The boy's delicate cheek flushed crimson.

"I am young yet," he answered, "but if your chief approves of me as a recruit, I cannot see that you have any right to complain."

"What is your name?"

"Angelo Sforza."

"And when did you join?"

"A week ago."

"Under what circumstances?"

"I will tell you, signore," was the reply. "I am the son of one of the gaolers at St. Elmo, where your chief is confined. Having been guilty of some slight breach of discipline, the commandant ordered me to be flogged. After my punishment, I made an inward vow to have my revenge."

Stromba nodded in approbation.

"A good and manful resolution," he said. "Well, proceed."

"First I obtained access to Marco Bravo," continued the youth. "I told him how cruelly I had been treated, and how I was determined to have my vengeance on the brutal commandant."

"Good, good!"

"And I promised that if he would accept me as a member of his band, I would contrive to find him the means of making his escape."

"Bravissima!" chuckled the brigand. "You are a hero; but did he consent to your terms?"

"He did, signore."

"And gave you the signs and passwords?"

"Yes."

Angelo gave the correct countersign.

The brigand then whispered some mysterious words in his ear, meaningless to all but the initiated.

Again the youth gave the right responses.

"Are you satisfied?" he asked.

"I am," returned Stromba. "Give me your hand."

"If more be necessary," continued the youth, "read this."

He placed a packet in the brigand's hand.

He hastily broke the seal, and read as follows—

"STROMBA,—I have initiated the bearer, Angelo Sforza, as a brother of our band. Receive him as such, and treat him accordingly. Beware that the young Englishman, your prisoner, is well used. All depends upon his being kept in safe custody till I have obtained my release or made my escape. The new brother will leave you on the day after you receive this, and will return to Naples. I hope to write you no more letters, but to be once more amongst you within a very short time. Generoso will tell you the rest.

                "MARCO BRAVO."

"This is indeed welcome news," said Stromba. "The captain's orders shall be implicitly obeyed."

"Is the chief at liberty?" asked one.

"No—but——"

A loud shout interrupted him.

"We will have him amongst us again even if our lives pay the forfeit."

"But you must be weary and half-famished after your long journey."

"I confess I am both," returned the youth, in a faint voice, "only I am so glad that I came in time to save the life of the young Englishman."

"All is well," rejoined Stromba. "Come with me. To-night you shall sleep in the cave; to-morrow I will find you a guide and provide you with everything necessary for your return journey."

"Grazia, signore, I thank you," rejoined the lad. "I have one other favour to ask of you?"

"Name it, my boy."

"As I told you, I am weary to death, not being used to mountain-travelling," was the reply, "and being a stranger amongst you, I desire that you may find me some quarters for the night where I may be alone, apart from the rest."

Stromba laughed.

"That shall be as you please," he replied. "But a town-bred, delicate lad like you will, I fear, soon get tired of the hard, rough life led by us brigands of the mountains."

While the above recorded conversation was passing between Stromba and the young Neapolitan, Ralph Wildhawk had been released from his perilous position.

He warmly thanked La Catarina for her generous interference in his behalf.

The brigandess smiled and laid her hand upon his shoulder with a soft motherly touch.

"Be of good cheer, *filio mio*," she said, kindly. "Do not spoil your good looks by useless care and anxiety. I will watch over you."

In the confusion and excitement of this appalling crisis of his fate, Ralph Wildhawk had not recognised in Generoso the former servant of his friend, the Count Di Ancona.

The rascal himself perceived this, and took care to slink out of his way, and keep himself in the background.

In moody silence Ralph returned to the cave.

He sent to Stromba, and asked permission to see the youthful messenger from Marco Bravo.

After some little delay, Angelo made his appearance.

The pretty boy's soft cheeks were dyed with ingenuous blushes.

He appeared strangely nervous and bashful.

Perceiving this, Ralph Wildhawk did all he could to reassure the timid lad and put him at his ease.

He asked him his name and history.

The boy hung his head and stammered out his reply, repeating the story which he had told to Stromba.

Ralph looked grave.

"Can it be possible that you have joined the brigands?" he said.

"It is quite true."

"Ah, my boy, you little know what a career of crime and terror you have embraced," said Ralph, sighing deeply. "Be advised. Free yourself from the trammels the villanous brigand chief would throw around you, before it is too late."

"It is already too late, signore," replied the boy; "those who once swear fidelity to Marco Bravo are his bondsmen for ever."

"It is a compact with the devil," replied Ralph, gloomily; "but you have done me a service, and I would gladly prove my gratitude. Do you return to Naples?"

"Yes, signore, to-morrow," was the reply.

Ralph's face brightened.

"Would you like to earn a hundred guineas in English gold?"

"Should I not!" returned the boy; "I wish you could show me the way."

"It is but to take a letter from me to my friends at Castellamare?"

The boy shook his head.

"If the letter were found upon me by the brigands, it would be instant death."

"But it need not be found on you."

"I will do it, signore, on condition."

"Name it."

"That the letter shall contain nothing that can compromise Marco Bravo or the band. As, for instance, you must not mention the place where you are confined, or give your friends any clue by which they may gain your enfranchisement except by the regular means—the payment of ransom."

"This I swear," returned Ralph.

"Well then, signore, I will be your messenger," replied the youth. "When shall I have the letters?"

"I will write them to-night, and if you call me betimes in the morning, I will give them to you."

"Very good, signore," returned the youth. "And to whom are they to be delivered?"

"One of them to Sir Godfrey Mortimer."

"The rich English milordi," returned the youth; "I know him by sight. And the other?"

"That is of still more importance. That I wish you to deliver secretly to none but the fair hand for whom it is intended."

The youth started.

"It is for a lady then," he said, in a low, trembling voice.

"For a lady—Miss Violet Melville, niece to Sir Godfrey," replied Ralph; "but how is this?—why do you turn so pale and press your hand to your side? Does your heart fail you?"

"No, signore it is not that," was the answer. "I am very tired and was struck with a sort of faintness. I will leave you now. Adieu till to-morrow."

And, turning round, he swiftly glided from the cave.

"What a strange boy," muttered Ralph. "How beautiful he is, and appears to have been delicately nurtured. He looks like a girl in masquerade. Well, my dear Violet's anxiety on my account will be relieved, and, perhaps, this poor youth preserved from perdition."

CHAPTER XXXVII.

MARCO BRAVO pined miserably in his dungeon at St. Elmo.

To him this imprisonment was death in life.

He grew pale and haggard.

The visit from young Angelo, however, in some degree raised his hopes.

One day it happened that the gaoler did not make his appearance, and even the night passed over and Marco Bravo saw nothing of him.

This was a fresh source of annoyance and anxiety to the imprisoned brigand.

The next morning, after a restless night, Marco Bravo arose with the first ray of dawn that penetrated through the grating of his dismal cell.

He rose from his couch of straw.

Stretching his fettered limbs, he dragged himself up and down his cold, dreary prison.

No one had broken his solitude for hours.

"How is it," he muttered to himself, "that I have seen nothing of that surly dog, the gaoler, since yesterday morning? What can be the meaning of it? Do they intend to leave me here to starve? Perhaps so. I wonder whether I can trust the messenger sent me by the king of the gipsies? What a pretty boy he was, and his face seemed well known to me, though where I have seen him before I cannot guess."

Then his thoughts flew back to the circumstances under which he had been taken, and he gnashed his teeth with fury.

"I am the victim of treachery," he mentally exclaimed. "That traitor, Michael Cornaro, is at the bottom of the plot. Oh, for the hour of revenge."

At last he heard a step in the stone passage outside his cell, accompanied by the jingling of keys.

"That is not the gaoler," he thought. "It is a strange footstep. Who can it be?"

The footstep suddenly halted on the other side of the dungeon door, and then came a clanking noise, as if the new-comer were selecting the right key.

"It is a fresh man," muttered the brigand; "I am glad of it. At least it gives me some faint chance, for he cannot be worse than the last."

The door was opened, and a short, thick-set swarthy fellow, with fierce black eyes and long black elf-locks, came in.

Upon seeing him the prisoner stepped backwards and stared him hard in the face.

The man made a motion with his hand as though to enjoin silence, and then, peering up and down the passage, to make sure that no one was near, re-entered the cell.

"Welcome, *amico*," said Marco Bravo. "I am glad to see a new face, but what has become of the former gaoler?"

"He is ill, signore," replied the man; "I do duty for him."

"So much the better," was the reply. "Any change is acceptable."

The man held up his hand and made a peculiar sign.

Marco Bravo at once recognised it, and his face cleared.

"Is it possible," he exclaimed, "you are one of the brotherhood?"

"Yes, signore," returned the man. "Do you not know me? I am Balthazar the Zingaro, and am sent hither to offer my services."

"Who sent you hither?"

"Isaco il Nero, the king of the gipsies," replied Balthazar.

"My faithful friend," rejoined the brigand chief, his black eyes sparkling. "He shall never repent this kindness; but in what can you serve me?"

"Do not deceive yourself," returned Balthazar; "the assistance I can render you is but small, and in offering that I subject myself to the most terrible danger."

"Have no fear," was the brigand's answer; "once free, I will take care to provide for your safety; but first let me know what position you hold in the castle?" said Marco Bravo.

"I am a soldier and belong to the garrison," he replied. "When the gaoler fell ill, I applied for the post, and was accepted."

"Well, what further?" said the brigand.

"To-morrow you are to be brought to trial," replied Balthazar.

"To-morrow!" retorted Marco Bravo. "I have received no intimation of the fact."

"You were purposely kept in ignorance," replied Balthazar. "But since the news came to St. Elmo, the guard has been doubled, and every outlet from the castle is strictly guarded."

"I care not for myself," rejoined the brigand. "If I can only get out of this dungeon, and have one last struggle for my life, I shall die contented."

"Nothing can be attempted until after nightfall, and I must leave you now, as I am bound to report myself to the captain of the guard; my delay may excite suspicion."

"Go then," returned the brigand. "But when will you return?"

"Within an hour."

"It is well," replied the prisoner; "I shall count the minutes till I see you again."

The gipsy took something from his pocket, and, with a smile held it towards the brigand.

"What is this?" asked Marco Bravo.

"Something to amuse you till I come back," was the reply.

Marco Bravo snatched it eagerly.

"A file!" he exclaimed, gleefully. "*Cielo!* you could have brought me nothing which I more wished to possess. Now, I shall soon taste freedom."

Balthazar pointed to the pallet of straw.

"Seat yourself on that," he said, "so that the noise of the grating, the fall of the shackles, may not be heard, and keep your ears open for the slightest passing sound."

He hurried from the cell and closed the door behind him.

The brigand seated himself upon his pallet of straw, and commenced his work.

At first he laboured with amazing vigour and good will, but was at last fain to pause, hot and breathless.

He stretched out his hand along the cold stone floor to reach the loaf and the pitcher of water.

Much to his delight, he found that Balthazar had placed there a leathern flask, containing spirits.

He drank a deep draught, and felt greatly refreshed, while his strength seemed renewed.

Setting to his task with renewed vigour, he had at length the extreme satisfaction of finding that he had succeeded in freeing himself of one of his shackles.

The iron fell to the ground with a slight clash that sent a thrill through his bosom.

In the course of another half hour, he had freed himself from the whole his chains, and stood erect with a feeling of relief so intense as to be almost painful.

"So far so good," he muttered to himself. "I will keep this instrument as a trophy, though, for that matter, I may yet find it useful as a weapon."

While he was thus engaged, his attentive ear caught the sound of an approaching footstep.

It struck a quick chord in his heart, and caused the blood to burn in his cheek, and checked the breath on his lips.

He instinctively clutched the file he still held in his hand.

"If he has played me false," he muttered, "the worse for him."

Presently the door was unlocked, and Balthazar entered.

"I am late," he said, putting down a bundle and a lantern.

The brigand smiled.

"Better late than never, my trusty friend," he said.

"True," replied Balthazar; "now follow me close, and I will conduct you to a little door that opens upon the water stairs, but I must forewarn you that you will have to swim the moat."

"That is nothing," replied Marco Bravo.

The gipsy then opened the bundle.

He took out a long coil of rope, and a black mantle.

"You will want this, signor capitano," said he, "for we shall be forced to make our way by a secret staircase that I have discovered, leading up to the ramparts."

"Be it so," replied the brigand; "but shall we not be disturbed by the sentries?"

"We must time it so that the guard will have passed on his rounds before you commence your descent from the walls," answered the gipsy.

"What kind of weather is it?"

"The night is as black as a wolf's mouth."

"The better for our purpose," rejoined the brigand chief. "Are you ready for the start?"

"One moment, signore," replied Balthazar. "As soon as I have set you at the foot of the staircase I mentioned, I must leave you, as I must go to the guard-room and make my report that all is safe for the night."

"But you, my brave and faithful fellow, what will you do?" asked the brigand.

"I shall know how to take care of myself," returned the gipsy.

"Let us lose no more time," said Marco Bravo; "I am impatient to be gone."

"This way then," replied Balthazar.

The brigand followed him with cat-like pace.

Balthazar led the brigand chief to a grim, stone passage, at the end of which was a door, deep sunk under a frowning archway.

They passed through the door, and found themselves at the foot of a spiral staircase.

"I must leave you now," whispered Balthazar. "When you reach the top of the stairs, you will find yourself in a small, vaulted chamber. On one side of it there is a large crucifix carved upon the wall, and beneath it an inscription engraved upon a slab. Press your foot hard upon the right side of this stone, and you will find it give way under the pressure. It turns upon a pivot. Descend into the gap, and you will find yourself in a narrow tunnel, so low, that you will be obliged to creep upon your hands and knees. When you get to the end of it, you will find a small iron door, easily opened by a spring—bolted on the inner side—this will give you access to the ramparts?"

"And then?"

"Then, signore, let yourself down to the moat. You must swim across it, and as soon as you are safe on the other side, make your way to the house of Isaco il Nero, who will be ready to receive you, and to provide you with a suitable disguise, and all needful means for escaping to the mountains. Do you understand all you have to do?"

"Thanks, my task is easy," replied the brigand.

"Go then, signore, and success attend you."

"I will not forget your faithful services. The worst of his foes have never accused Marco Bravo of ingratitude. Farewell, amico. Should the stars prove propitious, and all go well this night, you may consider your fortune made."

"So you escape, I shall be sufficiently rewarded," answered the gipsy, waving him away.

"But surely some motive——"

"The motive is a simple one," returned the gipsy, with a smile. "I do this for the love of Zara."

"Of Zara?"

"Even so. I adore her so much, that I would run through fire and water for her dear sake. I have but one return to ask you for this service."

"Name it."

"Save the life of the young Englishman you hold as your prisoner; such is her wish."

"Ralph Wildhawk. Ha! this is what I suspected. She loves him."

"'HO, THERE! STAND!'—THE BRIGAND LEVELLED HIS GUN AT RALPH'S HEAD."

This the daring brigand muttered to himself.

"Rouse yourself, signor capitano," said Balthazar; "is this a time for moody daydreaming? Away! Yet first tell me what message I am to take to La Zara. Will you give the required promise, or will you not?"

"I promise, I swear it," returned the brigand chief. "I will cherish the life of the young Englishman as dearly as though he were my twin brother."

"It is well, signore," answered Balthazar, his dark face lighting up with a radiant smile. "Give me some pledge or token that I may show to La Zara."

The brigand took a small gold crucifix from his breast, and placed it in the gipsy's hand.

"Be this the pledge and token," he said. "May the saints desert me in my utmost need if I prove false to my vow. But ere we part, *amico*, tell me one thing."

"Make haste to ask it, then."

"Who was that pretty boy that called himself Angelo, who visited me in my cell? He told me he was the gaoler's son, and that he wished to become a brigand?"

Balthazar smiled.

"Can you not guess?"

"I can," replied the brigand. "It was herself—it was La Zara."

Balthazar nodded assent.

"Fool that I was not to recognise her at the time," said Marco Bravo.

"Now, signore," replied Balthazar, "good night, and good fortune go with you."

Then he stopped short, for he was moving away.

"Stay, I had forgot," said he. "Here, take the lantern, but when you reach the rampart, take care to keep it well concealed beneath the cloak, least its gleam strike out in the darkness, and catch the eyes of the sentries on the rampart."

Then, with a final *addio*, he hurried out, and closed and locked the door behind him.

With flying feet, Marco Bravo mounted the dark turret stairs.

CHAPTER XXXVIII.

MARCO BRAVO, holding aloft the lantern, ascended the steep, narrow and broken staircase.

It was evident that this part of the castle was unused.

The steps were half in ruins, some of them had disappeared altogether, and those that remained were dank and slimy, and overgrown with lichens and mosses.

Marco Bravo's footsteps made the old tower ring with hollow and ghostly noises.

Ever and anon a scattering noise was heard, as of scampering rats.

In the fitful gleam of the lantern, Marco Bravo beheld his shadow wavering over the dripping walls in a weird and gruesome manner.

At length he reached the top of the stairs.

He found the small vaulted chamber, just as Balthazar had described it.

Upon advancing his foot, he trod upon a broken stone, and fell forward on his face.

He came into violent collision with the hard stone floor.

For a moment he was partly stunned.

Upon recovering his footing, he found, to his horror and dismay, that the lantern was extinguished, and that he was left in darkness.

Deep and dreadful darkness was around him.

A hand of ice seemed passed down his back, his limbs trembled with cold.

For some moments he dared not stir, for the ground was so uneven, through several of the paving stones having become displaced, that he was afraid to move, lest he might again stumble and fall.

He sat quietly pondering over his situation.

It was a terrible one.

He was immured, as it were, in a living grave, the outlet from which he could scarce hope to find in such Stygian darkness.

Certainly, he might return by the way he came, and, by his shouts and outcries, attract the notice of the guards and gaolers within the fortress.

But with what result?

Only to be dragged back to his dungeon, with pitiless scoffs and revilings, and thence to the place of execution.

The thought of such humiliation was too revolting to his haughty spirit to bear a moment's reflection.

Besides, it would be no easy matter to descend the narrow winding stair through the darkness, for, as we have said before, there was no handrail for protection, while the steps themselves were broken and slippery, so that anyone attempting to descend them, without a light, would run an imminent risk of being precipitated down the well, and crushed to pieces below.

The brigand dared not move.

Cold, dank wafts of foul air swept past him, the quick rattle of rats along the slippery floor startled him.

He stretched out his arms only to cleave the black gloom.

He could not see them.

He was buried alive!

For the moment he wished himself back in his former dungeon; but the daring villain soon recovered his nerve and presence of mind.

"If I could but find the means of relighting the lantern," he mused, and then remembered that on leaving the gipsy, he had thrust in his pocket some loose matches.

With trembling fingers he lit the candle, and replaced it in the lantern.

He could hardly restrain himself from shouting for joy when he beheld the candle burn up, and the light penetrate the gloomy turret chamber.

"Now let me see if I can discover the secret passage that leads to the ramparts."

Holding aloft the lantern, he searched the vaulted cell.

He found the crucifix as Balthazar had described it, carved in bold relief upon the wall.

He pressed his foot upon the stone, and after some exertion of strength, forced it down.

It swung heavily on its iron pivot.

Marco Bravo crept into the aperture.

Upon reaching the tunnel below the floor, he found himself obliged to crawl along upon his hands and knees.

The place was so confined that he was almost stifled, while showers of dust and mortar fell upon him, as he painfully dragged his limbs along.

Upon reaching the end of the narrow tunnel, he found the iron trap of which Balthazar had told him, and with some difficulty succeeded in drawing the rusty spring bolt.

With a loud beating heart he stepped out upon the parapet.

Remembering the gipsy's warning, he enveloped himself in the black mantle, which had a hood that he drew over his head, and concealed the lantern beneath it.

He found himself upon the ramparts overhanging the moat.

The storm had cleared off.

At this moment he was startled by a loud, stern shout from the battlements.

"Who goes there?"

"Diavolo! I am discovered," gasped the brigand. "It is the sentry; by good luck the trap is yet open. I must slink back and conceal myself till he has passed."

Again the voice hailed in a threatening manner—

"Who goes there? Speak, or I fire!"

Marco Bravo had crept back into the tunnel.

He crouched down and listened breathlessly.

Tramp, tramp.

A heavy footstep approached.

It passed by.

The sound returned, and then died off into silence.

The sentry was gone.

The brigand, however, did not quit his hiding-place.

"I will not venture just yet," he muttered. "I will wait till they have changed the guard."

The event proved that the brigand was right in proceeding so cautiously.

The sentry returned almost immediately, and passed the embrasure where Marco Bravo was lurking in the black shadow.

The man halted abruptly, and poised his musket.

Footsteps and the clatter of arms announced that the patrol was approaching.

Marco Bravo saw the glimmer of lanterns as a company of soldiers advanced.

Then he heard the sentry shout the stern challenge—

"Who goes there?"

"Rounds," came the answer.

"What rounds?"

"Grand rounds."

"Advance, grand rounds, and give the countersign."

The signal was given in a whisper, and the sentinels changed.

Then the guard passed on.

The sentinel thus left alone appeared to be in a dull and thoughtful humour.

Throwing his musket over his shoulder, he cast a moody glance around him, and paced up and down his beat, muttering to himself.

At length he halted, and gazed dreamily over the moonlit bay.

"*Maldito!*" cursed the brigand, "I hoped to have been spared this trouble; but there is no help for it now. It must be done quietly and with despatch."

He waited for a few moments, during which the sentry still remained leaning heedlessly upon his gun, and lost in thought.

Then Marco Bravo took a handkerchief from his pocket, and tied a knot at either end.

Clutching it tightly at either end where the knots were tied, to prevent the handkerchief from slipping through his hands, he crept behind the soldier.

In an instant he had thrown the handkerchief over the poor fellow's neck, and tightened it with a fierce and cruel turn of his powerful wrists. The poor fellow staggered back.

He tossed up his arms, and let the musket fall with a clash upon the stones.

His eyes started from their sockets, his face grew black, his fingers convulsively clutched at the air.

Marco Bravo tightened his grasp.

The struggles of the poor murdered wretch grew fainter and fainter, and at length he dropped to all appearance stone dead.

"It was done well," the brigand muttered to himself. "The worst part of the business is over. Freedom and revenge are before me."

Marco Bravo crept to the verge of the battlements, and looked about for a suitable place where to fix the rope.

He succeeded in fastening it securely round a large slab of masonry, and gazed below, previous to making his descent.

It was a fearful venture.

The wall was at least a hundred feet high, and its base was washed by the black and sluggish waters of a broad, deep moat.

But not one moment did the daring villain hesitate.

He boldly threw himself from the summit of the tower.

Straight as a sinking plummet he shot down the rope.

On reaching the bottom, he splashed into the water.

As he did so, he beheld the lurid reflection of torches and lanterns dancing about him on the dark surging waters of the moat.

Then turning his head, he cast a glance backwards and upwards at the vast, frowning fortress.

Lights glanced from window to window, and soldiers were seen rushing along from turret to turret.

Then he heard shouts.

"Alarm, alarm! The prisoner is escaping."

Flash, bang.

A shower of bullets splashed into the water, some of them passing close to his head, as he swam with all his might to reach the opposite side of the moat.

It was plain he was discovered, but he did not relax his efforts.

Then his quick ear caught the sudden splash of oars.

A boat had been launched in pursuit of him.

Buffeting the water with his strong arms, the brigand reached the low wall which formed the boundary of the moat.

To his consternation he found that the wall

was so steep and smooth as to render it impossible for him to clamber up it.

The only landing-place within his reach was a flight of narrow steps which descended to the water's edge, and was used as a landing-place for boats.

Unfortunately, it lay right in the direction from which the boat full of soldiers was approaching.

Still Marco Bravo had no alternative but to dash on.

He reached the steps just as the boat had come within a dozen yards of them.

"Halt there," shouted the governor of the castle, who stood erect in the stern sheets of the boat ; "stop, Signor Bravo, or I will give you no quarter."

The brigand took no heed of this threat.

He ran up the steps, and posted himself for an instant on the verge of the parapet.

Then he turned his face towards his pursuers, waved his hand and laughed derisively.

The musketeers in the boat fired a volley at him.

But the robber seemed to bear a charmed life.

The bullets sped harmlessly by him.

Then he turned and fled.

Meanwhile, the castle bell rang out its tocsin of alarm ; shots were fired, and a loud buzz of voices was heard from the walls of the fortress.

The soldiers gave chase, but the brigand, Marco Bravo, escaped in the darkness.

CHAPTER XXXIX.

SIR GODFREY RAYMOND sat in his library.

Joe Moody stood at a modest distance, silently awaiting his master's orders.

He was booted and spurred, and held a heavy riding-whip in his hand.

His clothes were covered with dust, and his face was hot and flushed as though he had just left the saddle after a long, hard ride.

Such was the fact ; he had but a few moments before alighted at the gates of the palace of the English baronet, at Castellamare, after riding from Naples, whither he had been dispatched to discover whether any fresh tidings had been received of the brigands and of his young secretary, Ralph Wildhawk.

"So the intelligence is confirmed," said the baronet ; "Marco Bravo escaped last night from the Castle of St. Angelo. Tell me, Joseph," he continued, looking up at his servant, "on your way hither did you hear anything further of this transcendent rascal ?"

"Only this, Sir Godfrey," answered Joe ; "the brigand chief is supposed to have got clear of the town, although every outlet was guarded to prevent his escape."

"The authorities must be asleep," returned his master, angrily.

"If you please, Sir Godfrey, I met a man on the road, a wild, gipsy-looking fellow, who told me of a queer report as had got abroad concerning poor Master Ralph."

"Ha ! what was it ?" asked his master.

"I calls it hadding hinsult to hinjury anyhow," returned Joe, in profound contempt. "... is actilly reported as Master Ralph, to sa'... life, has turned robber."

"What ?"

"That he has j'ined the band of rapscallions, and now scours the roads and passes, and calls upon travellers to stand and deliver, just like a kind o' furrin Dick Turpin. But Master Ralph is too good and honest a young gentleman to take to sich a gallows-bird sort of life."

The baronet started.

"I don't know, I don't know," he muttered ; "the lad has some wild blood in him. It was strange that the brigand chief should have taken such a violent fancy to him, as he clearly manifested when he spared his life and refrained from robbing him on the occasion of the extraordinary escapade in the theatre at Castellamare."

"Oh, that stands for nothin', Sir Godfrey," answered Joe ; "no doubt this bravo feller had his motive for acting in the way he did, which I must say his plunderin' the whole audience was a clever job, and the most horiginal way of bespeaking a benefit as ever I heered on. No, Sir Godfrey, I'll lay my head agen one o' them washy water melons as these frowsy Italians is so fond on, that Master Ralph would never so demean himself by jumpin' from behind a hedge and frightening poor peaceable people, and soilin' them white fingers with which he writes and paints so beautiful, by prigging what isn't hisn ; he'd scorn the haction, sir."

The baronet, for a few moments, paced moodily up and down the room.

Then turning to his servant, he pointed to the door.

"That door is open, close it," he said, "and come hither ; I don't wish any of the servants to overhear our talk."

Joe Moody obeyed his orders, and, approaching the table at which his master had seated himself, awaited what was to follow.

"Joseph," he said, "you have lived for many years in my family, and I have ever found you a trusty fellow, and, moreover, I give you credit for a considerable amount of shrewdness."

Joe bowed, and remained silent and attentive.

"I wish to talk with you about my son Edmund," he said. "I understand that he has been in the habit of attending the Neapolitan gaming-houses, and other disreputable places of resort, and that he is heavily in debt."

"Why, as for that, Sir Godfrey," answered Joe, "you can't put old heads on young shoulders ; but there's no doubt as Master Edmund will settle down, when he has sown his wild oats."

"Pshaw !" retorted the baronet, "I am ready enough to make every allowance for the indiscretions of youth, but for a son of mine to give way to such a mean and base a vice as gambling——"

He checked himself, as though conscious that he was speaking too freely to a servant, but the next moment his anger and vexation overcame his scruples.

"But for this infernal affair—the capture of young Wildhawk—I would at once return to England," he muttered to himself. "Edmund knows my wishes, my commands, in regard to

Violet, and until lately he appeared to be devotedly attached to her; but since we have been in Naples, he has treated her with neglect."

Hearing this, Joe Moody felt it his duty to advise Sir Godfrey of Edmund's love for the gipsy girl La Zara.

"Well, Sir Godfrey, the fact is that Master Edmund is over head and ears in love with La Zara, the gipsy dancing girl," answered Joe, "and now the murder's out."

This announcement appeared to fill the baronet with rage and consternation.

"Madness!" he exclaimed. "What, under my very eyes, the boy to form a *liaison* with such a creature. I cannot believe it."

"But it's true, though, Sir Godfrey," was the blunt retort.

Sir Godfrey paced the room in great perturbation of mind.

"This must not go on," he muttered.

"Your son must be terribly in love, when he has turned so generous and open-handed all at once, and makes such wal'able presents to the little black-eyed Romany as has bewitched him."

"Presents! Has it gone so far as that?" returned the baronet. "What presents?"

"Jewels of fab'lous value," returned Joe. "One bracelet alone, as came to my knowledge cost him two thousand pounds, which he paid for with money won at the gaming-table."

"And she, of course, accepts them? From a mere boy, too."

"No, she don't, and there's the miracle," Joe answered, dryly.

"What! she rejects them?"

"Sends the parcels back unopened and without one line of writin'."

"Is it so?" replied the baronet, his eyes kindling with admiration. "The brave, noble girl. How I have wronged her; but I will remove him from the influence of his enchantress," answered the baronet. "He shall return to England. And now tell me, how fares Mistress Violet?"

"Well, Sir Godfrey, if what 'Tilda tells me be true," answered Joe, "she takes on sadly about poor Master Ralph."

"Tush!" retorted the baronet, "I must see her. And now you may go, Joseph; let what has passed between us remain secret."

"Have you any more orders for me, Sir Godfrey?" asked Joe.

"Not at present. But I would have you keep a sharp eye upon Edmund."

"You may rely upon me, sir," returned Joe. And he made his exit.

The door had scarcely closed when it was opened again, and the pretty, saucy face of Matilda Sparkes appeared.

"What do you want?" asked the baronet.

"I came to look for my lady, Sir Godfrey."

"She is not here. And let me tell you that it is my wish you should be more staid in your behaviour. Your flighty manner has not improved your mistress. You must leave my service."

Matilda Sparkes fell on her knees before the baronet.

"Oh, Sir Godfrey!" she said, "I know not what harm I have done."

"Not any harm, perhaps, but you have neglected many opportunities of leading your mistress's mind in the direction you know I would have it led. Now go—leave me."

Left alone, Sir Godfrey pressed his hand upon his forehead.

"Ralph turned brigand, and Edmund reputed a gambler and a libertine," he muttered. "This is a pretty state of affairs. As for Ralph, I have good hope that he is belied, though time works strange revenges. The hand of destiny seems manifest in all that has befallen him since we set foot on Italian soil. But my present care must be for Edmund."

CHAPTER XL.

RALPH WILDHAWK, languishing a lonely captive among the brigands, began to find the time hang heavy on his hands.

Ever since the time when the news of the capture of their redoubted chief had been brought to the brigands' stronghold, a marked change had taken place in the robbers' behaviour towards their unfortunate captive.

Still, he bore all hardships and indignities with a manly fortitude beyond his years.

He was still allowed a considerable amount of liberty.

No objection was made to his roaming about the glens and passes within certain well-defined limits, but as these places were strongly guarded, there was but little chance of his making his escape.

It was his custom, when the weather permitted, to start out with his paint box and portfolio, and amuse himself for hours in making sketches.

One of his favourite resorts was the romantic waterfall near which he had first met with La Catarina.

One morning, he had taken up his position on a bank of the stream, just below the falls, and had made preparations for commencing work, when his attention was attracted by a woman's voice lilting a merry song.

He looked towards a rugged pathway that ran along the summit of the overhanging rocks.

"It is Marta," said Ralph to himself. "What a splendid voice she has, and with a light heart she carols her mountain-song — she, a brigand's daughter, and a brigand's wife."

He looked up and beheld the subject of his musings descending the rock, and approaching towards him with a free, bounding step.

On her head she poised a milk pail, while she led by her hand her child, a little girl of six or seven, with a face surpassing for expressive beauty, as Ralph thought, the face of any child he had ever seen.

"*Eccola, signore,*" she said, placing a luscious bunch of grapes before him. "See what Violetta has brought you, so nice, so nice."

Ralph expressed his delight at the gift in such an extravagant way that the little Italian maiden made the rocks ring with her silvery laughter.

"Ah, *madre mia*, is not the signore a funny man?" cried Violetta. "He does make me laugh so, and see what pretty things the signore is making."

And the little girl pointed wonderingly at Ralph's sketch.

"Eccelenza will find her troublesome," said Marta, drawing the child to her side.

"On the contrary," replied Ralph, "her artlessness and beauty are delightful; how beautiful she is. Will you permit me to sketch her face? 1 will afterwards make a painting of it, and give it you as a slight return for the many kindnesses you have showed me.'

"Do not speak of that, signore," replied Marta, her black eyes kindling; "I wish I could give you the help you need, for I pity you from my heart; but be of good cheer; your friends are rich, and your ransom will arrive soon, then you will be set at liberty."

Then she added, with childish eagerness—

"But if eccelenza will really paint the dear one's portrait, I shall be so delighted, and so will my good man, Felipe."

Ralph sighed.

"The sweet child," he said; "what a thousand pities that her spring-tide of innocence and unconsciousness should be passed among such frightful scenes as those by which she is now surrounded; what a frightful prospect lies before her."

The tears shone in Marta's fine dark eyes.

By way of diversion, he took little Violetta by the hand, and leading her to a flowery bank, made her sit down, and bade her be very good and quiet while he made the first rough sketch for her portrait.

The mother looked on admiringly, while the young artist, with rapid and masterly hand, made a half-length sketch of his pretty model.

While they were thus engaged, a tall, stalwart brigand joined them.

He wore a large leathern bag, slung across his shoulder, and carried a gun under his arm.

Upon seeing him, Marta ran to him and laid her hand upon his shoulder.

"Oh, Felipe, come and see," she said, "the good signore Inglese is painting such a pretty picture of our Violetta."

The brigand laughed, and patted the cheek of his pretty little spouse, and then linking his hand in hers, he strode up to Ralph, and looked down over his shoulder.

The robber was pleased with the sketch, and watched attentively till Ralph had finished and closed his portfolio.

"There, that will do for one sitting," he said, getting up and leading Violetta back to her mother. "Your little one is the most docile of subjects. We will have another turn to-morrow."

"Thank you, signore," answered Marta. "I will take care to dress the child in her best attire."

"Felipe," said Ralph, turning to her husband, "I thought you were in Naples; but I am glad to see you returned safe and sound."

"Thanks, signore," replied the brigand. "I returned yesterday from the city."

"And what news of your chief?" asked Ralph.

"Good news," replied the robber; "Marco Bravo is still a prisoner in the dungeons of St. Elmo, but an attempt will be made to aid him in effecting his escape. If the plan succeeds, we shall have him back to the mountains this very night."

"I shall not be sorry to confront him face to face," answered Ralph; "then my fate will be decided one way or the other. I am prepared for the worst, and anything is better than this terrible suspense."

"I trust that our chief's return will bring you freedom," answered Marta; "and now farewell, signore. I am going to yonder valley to milk the goats."

"And I into the woods in search of game," rejoined Felipe.

Then kissing the child, he added—

"Go you with the mother, *piccola mia*."

"*Addio*," said Ralph, waving his hand, "till we meet again."

Felipe mounted the rocks and clambered upwards to the shaggy, overhanging woods overhead, and was soon lost to sight among the crags and stunted bushes that covered the mountain-side.

Ralph watched, with a painter's eyes, the graceful form of the brigandess, as, with her child in her arms, and the milk-pail poised on her erect, stately head, she crossed the narrow, yielding plank that spanned the foaming cataract.

So dizzy was the height and so perilous the means of transit, that Ralph's heart stood still, and the blood ran cold in his veins as he watched the mother and child pass over the gulf of death.

Ralph drew a deep sigh of relief as the mother and child disappeared behind the rocks on the opposite side of the ravine.

"God have mercy upon them, poor creatures," he murmured, "and release them from their wicked, dreadful bondage. How strange, yet beautiful it seems that the domestic affections will bud and blossom in the most unfavourable soil, even as these flowers, that spring up among the crevices of these hard and barren rocks!"

He seated himself on a mossy stone, and having eaten the delicious grapes given him by Violetta, he recommenced his work of sketching the cataract.

CHAPTER XLI.

WHILE Ralph Wildhawk was sketching, his attention was called off on a sudden by a trill of childish laughter, sweetly and clearly echoed by the surrounding rocks and woods.

Looking across the stream, he saw a pretty little white kid come springing forth from a clump of bushes on a ledge of rocks on the opposite side.

Bleating and bounding along, it took the direction of the bridge.

It was instantly afterwards followed by the light, sylph-like form of Violetta in hot pursuit.

Ralph became alarmed when he saw the goat bound upon the bridge and come to a standstill on the very centre of it.

He soon found that he had just cause for apprehension.

The child pursued the bounding animal, and followed it on the narrow, rickety plank.

Ralph was beside himself with terror on the poor little one's account.

He stood silent and paralysed.

He dared not cry out, lest the child, being suddenly startled, might make a false step.

Violetta, laughing gaily, sprang on to the bridge, quite unconscious of the danger into which she was running.

In breathless suspense, he watched her till she reached the middle of the bridge.

Violetta, with a merry laugh, stretched out her arms, and, calling to the animal, tripped towards it, as though with the intention of seizing hold of it.

The goat swerved aside.

Violetta's foot slipped.

Ralph's blood seemed to freeze as her piercing scream rang through his ears.

The place where she had stood was void.

Sick and faint with horror, Ralph beheld the light, fairy form come drifting down the smooth, strong surface of the cataract.

The next instant it reached the torrent below, and came whirling along, amid the seething waters and cruel rocks of the swift, rushing stream, as it dashed past the bank on which Ralph was standing.

Without a moment's hesitation, Ralph threw off his jacket.

Keeping his eyes steadfastly fixed upon the poor child, as she was impetuously hurled onwards by the powerful current, Ralph sped along the banks.

At the distance of two or three hundred yards from the foot of the falls, the mountain stream widened and deepened.

Reaching this place, Ralph watched for a good opportunity, and boldly plunged into the torrent.

So violent was the force of the current, that Ralph found it a difficult matter to keep himself from being swept away.

Striking out fiercely, he at length came within arm's length of the drowning girl.

He made a clutch at her dress.

In vain.

The rushing waters bore her away.

Ralph swam after her, or rather just using his arms to keep himself afloat and to steer his course, he allowed himself to drift upon the bosom of the torrent.

His second attempt was more successful than the first had been.

He managed to seize the now insensible child by her floating hair.

In another moment, he got his arm round her slender waist, and held her in a firm grasp.

It might be supposed that Ralph's first object would have been to swim to the bank.

He would gladly have done so, but the thing was impossible.

The banks on either side of the stream were, in this part of its course, hemmed in by rocky banks of considerable height, and steep as walls.

As he was thus whirled on, his unconscious burden drooping over his arm, his ear caught a loud, terrified cry.

The voice was a woman's.

Turning his head in the direction from whence the sound proceeded, Ralph beheld Marta racing along the bank.

Her hands were clasped, her eyes uplifted to Heaven, and she appeared to be invoking the aid of the saints for the deliverance of her darling child.

Rousing his energies, Ralph answered her with a cheery shout of confidence and encouragement.

Then, tightening his hold upon the child, he swam on with renewed vigour.

The stream, though still very rapid, now became less violent and dangerous.

Enclosed on either side by dark, frowning rocks, the mountain river flowed over a channel comparatively smooth.

Looking before him, Ralph perceived at some distance abreast of him, a small, rocky islet, covered over with a growth of low bushes and tangled ground vines.

Towards the islet Ralph Wildhawk directed his course.

The current dashed around this rocky barrier with such force and velocity that Ralph was in momentary danger of being swept away.

He contrived, however, to seize hold of a long tendril of the ground-bine, which hung from the rocks and trailed upon the surface of the waters.

Not without a desperate effort, cumbered as he was by his light, but inconvenient burden, Ralph succeeded in clambering on to the summit of the rocky isle.

As he did so, he heard a joyous sound from the right hand bank, and perceived Marta springing from crag to crag across the rocky ford and making towards the island.

Half dead with exhaustion, Ralph sank upon one knee and pillowed the rescued child upon his throbbing breast.

He parted the dank, clinging hair from her brow.

He chafed her little cold hands, and pressed his own against her soft white bosom.

To his intense delight he felt a slight pulsation.

A trembling hand was laid upon his shoulder.

He cast an upward glance to behold the distracted mother bending over him.

"Speak, signore," gasped Marta in a quick, hoarse whisper; "tell me the worst; my child, my precious one."

"She lives," was Ralph's reassuring reply. "Compose yourself; all will be well."

The mother flung herself upon her knees, half-delirious with joy, and poured out a torrent of thanksgivings to the saints.

Then she took the child from Ralph, and clasping it to her bosom, smothered it with kisses.

"Brave, noble signore," she faltered, while her dark eyes brimmed over with tears, as she turned them upon Ralph with a look of ineffable gratitude. "Do not blame me, do not think me ungrateful if I cannot yet thank you for what you have done. Give me time, give me time. Ah, *Vergin Madre*, you know not a mother's heart."

"Never mind me, nor thanks," answered Ralph, smiling. "Look to your dear little one. By Heaven, look! her rosy lips part—she breathes—she opens her eyes—she lives—Hurrah!"

And Ralph's enthusiasm found vent in a hearty British cheer.

"She lives, rendered back to me from the

very jaws of death, and by you, dear, generous stranger," she sobbed, kissing Ralph's hand. "Ah. what will Felipe say, when he knows of it. Marco Bravo is a great captain, a terrible man, but he shall not harm one hair of your head. Felipe and I will save you ; command us ; we will risk our lives in your service."

The child now recovered her consciousness, and staring about her, commenced to cry.

The fond mother alternately caressed and scolded her.

"There, there, *vita mia*, don't cry," she murmured, rocking the little one in her arms. "All is well now ; you are safe, thanks to this brave, kind signore. Kiss him and be good."

But poor little Violetta was too frightened to obey.

"Naughty child, how dare you leave my side ?" cried Marta. "How often have I told you not to leave me for one moment. I will never bring you abroad again ; and to go on the horrid bridge, too. I declare I have a good mind to whip you, but there, my eyes, half-my-life, mamma's not cross now. Kiss me and we'll not tell father. Hush thee, *mi anima*."

Ralph's heart swelled, and he felt a strange qualm as he gazed upon the woman.

"My mother was good and kind, but she did not love me thus," he thought. "Yet she was an Italian."

Then taking Marta gently by the hand, he said—

"Come, come, you excite yourself too much ; get home with the little one. As for myself, I have strayed beyond my bounds, and my absence will cause an alarm ; I shall be pursued."

They crossed the ford, and returned to the bank.

They had scarcely set foot ashore, when they heard someone shouting, and saw Felipe come running towards them.

His looks betrayed the greatest terror.

When, however, he clasped the child in his arms, his delight and his gratitude to her preserver knew no bounds.

The simple, impulsive fellow flung himself at Ralph's feet, and swore that he would willingly lay down his life for him.

"Enough," said Ralph, "say no more ; let us return to the brigands' glen."

"Stay one moment, I beseech you, signore," replied the brigand ; "I have something to tell you that concerns yourself."

"Let me hear it."

"As I crossed the bridge on my way hither," rejoined the brigand, "I heard the sound of voices, and looking behind me, saw about twenty or thirty fellows belonging to the band."

"Ha ! they are in quest of me," replied our hero.

"No doubt of it, signore," rejoined the brigand. "At their head strode a man taller than the others ; by his stature, the feathers in his hat, and his long red cloak, I knew him to be Stromba."

"That rascal owes me a grudge," returned Ralph ; "for what reason I know not. Come, let us go and meet them."

"Signore, I am afraid your life is in danger," answered Felipe ; "Stromba has returned from Naples with secret orders from the captain, that, I'll warrant, bode you no good."

"I cannot help or hinder my doom. If I am to be murdered, I will meet my fate bravely," replied Ralph, with a sigh of resignation ; "I am wholly in their power."

"Unless you might seize the present opportunity of making your escape," was the reply.

"Escape !" repeated Ralph ; "how is that possible ?"

"Not far from hence is a large cavern that has many windings and many deep recesses," answered the brigand. "Its very existence is unknown to all but myself, Marta, and a few others. My wife will lead you thither, and at nightfall bring you such garments as are worn by the shepherds of the Abruzzi ; put them on, and I will join you at the first peep of dawn. I will then conduct you to the inn at Terracina, where you will be safe, and from whence you may hasten to your friends at Naples."

Ralph Wildhawk was struck with admiration at this generous proposal.

"But should you be discovered, your life would pay the forfeit for mine," said Ralph.

"I accept the risk," answered the brigand ; "you saved my child."

"And you, Marta ?" asked Ralph, turning to the brigand's wife.

"Go, signore, and may the blessed saints guide your steps," she said. "Trouble not yourself on our account ; trust to my woman's wit to hoodwink Stromba and the rest of them —even Marco Bravo himself."

"Well said, *mia vita*," rejoined Felipe ; then he went on, addressing Ralph—"Fly at once, signore ; you have not a moment to lose. Stromba and his men will be here presently, but I will undertake to throw them off your track."

"My kind, generous friends," returned Ralph, with warmth, "and do you suppose that I will allow you to imperil your lives for my sake ? Perish the thought. Besides, there is another reason which prevents me from accepting your offer—I am on *parole*. I have pledged my word, in consequence of the fair treatment and other privileges I enjoy, not to attempt to escape."

"*Altro*," returned the brigand, shrugging his shoulders, "if your excellency has sworn an oath to that effect, a few piastres, and it may be a slight penance, will readily purchase absolution for a fault so small, if fault it be."

"And more," put in Marta, "the good signor is a heretic—the saints enlighten him." She stopped to cross herself, and went on with perfect good faith and simplicity—"And so you know, one sin more or less, can make no difference either one way or another."

Ralph laughed heartily at this somewhat Jesuitical argument.

Nevertheless, he adhered to his resolution.

"It cannot be," he answered, firmly, "heretic or not, no man of honour would break his plighted word. No, my friends ; while they give me the length of my chain, I will await with patience until such time as my ransom-money arrives, or that it please Marco Bravo to set me at liberty."

"If you wait for that, signore, you will stay longer amongst us than you think for," returned the robber, grimly ; "you had better embrace an opportunity that may never occur again."

He had scarcely ceased speaking, when the low, soft notes of a bugle were echoed from the distance.

"Hark," said Marta, "that is Stromba, who sounds his horn to collect his men, who are no doubt scouring the woods in pursuit of you, signore."

Felipe, without remark, scrambled on to a rock, and gazed in the direction from which the sound proceeded.

He immediately returned.

"*Diavolo!*" said he, in an excited tone, "they are making this way, and are close at hand. Now is your time to decamp, signore, now or never; decide at once."

"I have decided," returned Ralph. "I will go forward and meet them."

Then, without stopping to listen to any further entreaties, he strode away.

He had not proceeded very far before he perceived a number of the bandits running towards him.

They all carried carbines and had pistols and stilettoes in their belts.

They were led on by a tall, stalwart fellow in a red cloak, which, with the feathers in his steeple-crowned hat, fluttered briskly in the mountain breeze.

Upon seeing Ralph Wildhawk, he gave a triumphant shout, and pointed out our hero to his companions.

They responded to his cheer.

Several of them brought the butts of their pieces to their shoulders in such a way as to cover him.

Retreat was now impossible.

"Hold! stand, or we fire upon you," thundered Stromba.

Ralph preserved his composure, and though his heart beat violently, he walked calmly forward to meet them.

Felipe, with Marta, bearing the child in her arms, hurried after him, anxious to act as peace-makers between him and Stromba, for they were well acquainted with the latter's savage and ungovernable temper.

Stromba came rushing up to Ralph Wildhawk, and seized him by the collar.

Ralph clutched his wrists and flung him backwards.

"What do you mean, you ruffian?" exclaimed Ralph, his whole frame quivering with anger; "do you think that because I am unarmed and unprotected, I will endure your brutality without resentment?"

Stromba recovered his footing, and with the snarl of an enraged wolf, drew his stiletto and sprang upon our hero, but Ralph's English blood was up.

With a stinging blow, directed straight from the shoulder, our hero struck the miscreant full between the eyes, and sent him reeling backwards.

Stromba's burly frame came full tilt against the man behind him.

The pair came to the ground together, and blinded with passion, rolled over and over, kicking and cursing each other.

At last, being separated by their comrades, both rose to their feet.

Stromba's rage was terrible.

Snatching up the carbine which had been knocked from his hand at the commencement of the fray, he levelled it point blank at the captive.

It was a critical moment for Ralph.

Felipe interposed just in time to save his life.

Throwing himself before Stromba, he pointed his gun at him.

"Lower your piece, Stromba," he shouted, "or by San Gennaro, I will put a brace of bullets through your head."

Stromba perceived that his comrade was in earnest, and, with a sullen frown, he grounded his carbine.

"*Maladetto!*" he growled, "what right have you to interfere? I'll tell you what, Felipe; the prisoner has broken his parole, and you, I suspect——"

"You may suspect what you like, comrade," replied Felipe, in a tone of indifference, "but you know, as well as I do, that the chief has left express commands that neither insult nor violence should be offered to the prisoner. As for the young signore having passed the bounds, he did so to save the life of my child, who must have been drowned but for his bravery."

Marta here stepped forward and showed the child with her wet clothes to the robbers, and in a few words related the story of her rescue.

When she had finished, a murmur of admiration ran round.

"Well done!" exclaimed the bandits; "the young Englishman is *un galant uomo.*"

Stromba, however, was not so easily appeased.

He still scowled darkly upon the prisoner.

"This is all very well," he said, "but I am responsible for his safe-keeping, and I will take good care that he shall not have another opportunity of leading us such a chase; from henceforth he shall be confined under lock and key in the tower, and if he proves the least refractory, I will have him put in irons."

Ralph's eyes flashed with indignation.

"Is that your resolve?" he asked, fiercely.

"It is, as you will soon be convinced," returned the ruffian, with a cruel leer.

"Then hear what I have to say," returned Ralph, drawing himself up to his full height, and looking his persecutor full in the eyes, "I pledged my word that, if I were allowed a certain amount of liberty, I would make no attempt to escape; but since you have thought proper to break the conditions, I, on my part, shall consider myself no longer bound to keep my pledge, and I give you warning that I shall break my prison at the first opportunity."

Stromba burst into a laugh of derision and snapped his fingers.

"*Basta!*" he growled. "I think you will find the old Moorish stronghold a harder nut to crack than you think for. Try it. Succeed if you can."

Then, turning to his companions, he went on—

"You hear what he says, comrades. He openly defies me, and declares his intention to escape if possible. *Bueno!* We will take care not to give him a chance."

Then, turning an evil look upon Felipe, he added with a sullen frown—

"As for you, Felipe, I regard your conduct as very suspicious ; the captain shall know of it."

"Do your worst," retorted Felipe, with supreme contempt ; "but have a care that you yourself do not offend our captain by exceeding your duty."

"That is my affair, not yours," returned the surly ruffian.

"Bind him, comrades," he continued, pointing to Ralph, "and away with him to the fortress."

Ralph was immediately seized, a stick cut from a neighbouring tree was thrust under his arm-pits, and his wrists were tied before him.

The brigands then closed around him in military order.

Two of them, with loaded carbines, placed themselves on either side of him.

Then Stromba gave the order.

"Forward."

The brigands marched their prisoner up the rugged defile and across the bridge over the falls.

They reached the brigands' glen.

Ralph was led into the old Moorish fortress.

At a sign from Stromba, one of the brigands raised a large and heavy slab from the floor by means of an iron bolt.

Ralph recoiled with a start. A black pit yawned at his feet.

It looked like a grave.

"Bring the torch from yonder sconce in the wall, and light it," said Stromba, to another of the gang.

The man obeyed.

Striking a match, he set fire to the flambeau, and held it over the dark shaft.

"Descend," growled Stromba, shaking his fist at the captive.

"You villain," retorted Ralph ; "whither would you take me ?"

"What do we do with wild beasts when we catch them ?" retorted Stromba, with a harsh laugh. "We keep them in dens. You have shown yourself so formidable that we must have you under lock and key. Descend, I say."

But Ralph showed no disposition to obey this mandate.

"Here, Pietro ; give me the torch," said Stromba.

He took the link and descended a few of the stone steps of a spiral staircase which appeared to penetrate into the very heart of the rock on which the tower was built.

"Now, drag him after me," growled Stromba, his voice rumbling like thunder in the echoing shaft ; "if he resists, pitch him head first over the parapet."

The brigands made no reply, but two of them laid hold of Ralph and pushed him before them, and pushed him down the stairs.

Ralph stumbled, and having his arms bound, found it difficult to balance himself so as to keep his footing.

He was forced to keep close to the wall.

Stromba led the way, holding aloft the torch to guide the steps of those that were following him.

Upon reaching the foot of the staircase, they found themselves in a small vaulted chamber of octagonal shape, in the walls of which were eight recesses, surmounted by arches of the horse-shoe pattern so common in Moorish architecture.

Entering one of these alcoves, Stromba thrust forward the torch, and showed a narrow door which appeared to be made of solid iron.

"Stefano," said Stromba, turning to the brigand he had spoken to before, "you have charge of the keys ; where are they ?"

"In yonder chest," answered the robber, pointing to a large coffer that stood in one of the alcoves.

"Bring them here," said Stromba, "and open this door."

The man went to the chest, opened it and took out a heavy bunch of keys, of very curious manufacture.

Selecting one of the keys, he thrust it into the lock, and, after some trouble, succeeded in turning the rusty bolt in its socket.

He thrust open the door, which sprang back with a loud, harsh clang.

Ralph was then pushed into a small cell, so low-roofed that there was barely room for him to stand upright.

Ralph was quite appalled at the narrowness and wretchedness of the dungeon to which he was confined.

The cell was not more than eight feet square, and appeared to have been hewn out of the bare rock.

It was lighted by a narrow slit through which one solitary ray of sunshine struck in.

In the wall opposite the little aperture that admitted the light, was a massive ring, from which hung part of a rusty, broken chain.

The atmosphere within the cell was close and offensive.

Ralph looked round him with a glance of horror and disgust.

"This is a living tomb," he gasped.

Stromba grinned maliciously.

"You are right there," he said. "It is the ante-chamber to purgatory. Yet one poor devil contrived to exist in it for more than five years."

"Five years !" he repeated, abstractedly. "Is it possible that anyone could drag out such an existence, and for so long a period ?"

"Quite possible," returned the brigand. "He was an instance of the possibility. What was strangest of all, during the whole of that time, he never left his cell."

"And was he alone all the time ?"

"Why, no ; for the last twelvemonth he had one companion."

"And what was he ?"

"A toad."

"A toad !"

"Yes," rejoined the brigand. "Cospetto ! I never saw such a monstrous reptile. Trust me, he was a noble fellow, as big round as the brim of my hat, and the prisoner was mighty fond of him."

"Ugh !" gasped Ralph, with a shudder of loathing.

"I pity that poor animal," continued the brigand. "He learned to know the prisoner, who fed him with crumbs ; he would come at a call. But one day our late chief, being annoyed that the ransom did not come, entered the cell, and seeing the strange pet squatting at his master's feet, set his foot on it, and crushed it."

"It was the action of a fiend," sighed Ralph.

"At any rate, it was rather hard upon the prisoner," replied Stromba, who appeared to take a cruel, mean-spirited delight in torturing Ralph. "Poor devil, he did seem to take it to heart, for he sickened and pined, and refused his food."

"And he died here?"

"Why, as for that, Stefano can answer your question better than I can."

He beckoned the grey-haired, wrinkled old bandit to approach.

"Come hither, Stefano," he said. "Finish the tale; tell the signore how Villanova came to his end."

The veteran gave a shrug, and answered sullenly—

"I was sorry for him. But it happened in this way. Our late chief grew tired of waiting for the ransom money, which never came, so one day he sent me to the cell with orders to put the prisoner to death. I did not relish the job, I can tell you, but I dared not disobey the chief's commands, so I was glad when, upon entering the cell, I found him lying fast asleep upon that pallet. I crept softly up to him, and sent my dagger straight home to his heart."

"Horrible!"

"I don't know. He died an easy death, and out of respect to his memory, I paid masses for the repose of his soul, buried him decently under yonder slab, and carved a cross upon it."

Ralph turned away in speechless disgust.

"Stefano will be your gaoler, signore," said Stromba, addressing our hero. "You will find him an amusing fellow; he can tell you a hundred such pleasant tales as that he has just related. But I forgot, you fully intend to escape. If so, do us the favour of leaving the old tower behind you. I think it needful to give you this hint, as, being such a Samson, you might have an idea of carrying it off on your shoulders."

With this jeer, he left the dungeon, followed by all but Stefano.

"Corrogio!" said the ruffian, clapping him on the shoulder; "if your ransom is paid, you will soon be released; and if not, there are plenty of toads here, and rats, too, to keep you company. Let me unbind your hands."

Deeply humiliated as he felt, Ralph knew himself to be entirely in the power of the villains into whose ruthless hands he had fallen.

He made no reply, but held out his hands for his gaoler to untie them.

"Pity to spoil a good cord," said Stefano. "It may be useful some day. I am a conscientious man, and never like to do my work in a bungling fashion. A good halter saves a deal of unnecessary pain to my patients. I won't cut such a nice bit of rope."

Throwing himself upon his knees, he undid the cords with his teeth.

"Now," said he, grinning, "you are a man again. I see your clothes are wet through. Had you not better change them? I will bring you another suit."

"No, I do not feel the moisture. My clothes are almost dry," said Ralph. "I only wish to be left alone."

"San Gennaro! your wish will be gratified to your heart's content," laughed the gaoler. "But let me advise you to change your clothes."

"No, I tell you, no."

"But you will want something to eat?"

He pointed in a very significant manner to the silk handkerchief that Ralph wore round his neck.

Our hero at once saw what he meant, and took the kerchief from his neck and tossed it contemptuously to the ruffian.

The fellow caught it and slipped it into his pocket.

"Bueno!" said he, "I will bring you some bread and cheese."

"Very well, only leave me now."

Stefano moved towards the door, and then lingering, looked back at the prisoner.

"Perhaps you would like a bottle of wine?" said the gaoler.

Ralph mechanically thrust his hand into his pocket for some money; not that he cared about the wine, but was anxious to get rid of his tormentor.

But he suddenly bethought himself that the few piastres he had been allowed to retain in his possession, after his capture by the brigands, might by and bye be found very useful.

He turned to Stefano, and answered with a faint smile—

"Wine! that is a luxury beyond my reach; how am I to pay for it?"

"Come, let me see," returned Stefano; "I am always pleased to oblige a prisoner when I can; let me look at those buttons."

Now Ralph's mountaineer's jacket, of rich brown velveteen, happened to be laced with rows of very handsome gold buttons of filagree pattern.

"Good," said Stefano; "if you will give me half-a-dozen of them, I will see what I can do about the wine."

Ralph plainly saw the character of the man he had to deal with, and, though dying with heart-sickness and impatience, pretended to haggle with him.

"Half-a-dozen of them!" he retorted. "Why, you cormorant, each one of them is worth half-a-sequin."

"That's all very well," returned the ruffian, grinning, and playing with the hilt of his stiletto; "what is to hinder me from helping myself to the lot?"

"You dare not," replied Ralph; "you know that all booty goes to the general fund, and that you are only entitled to your proper share."

"Well, I won't be hard upon you," replied Stefano, in a milder tone. "Make it four, and I will go——"

"Go to the devil!" retorted Ralph, stamping his foot, "only leave me in peace."

"'WHY DO YOU TURN SO PALE AND PRESS YOUR HAND TO YOUR HEART,' ASKED RALPH."

"As you please, signore," grumbled Stefano, once more making a feint to leave the cell; "but if you want the wine, say how much will you give me for it?"

"I'll give you one of the buttons, worth half-a-dozen bottles of your trash."

"Not possible," replied Stefano.

Then seeing Ralph made no answer, he went on, bluffly—

"Come, let us split the difference; if you will let me have two of them, I will bring you a bottle of prime Rosolio, and throw in a fresh bundle of straw for your bed."

Ralph tore two of the buttons from his jacket and placed them in the fellow's hand.

"There," said he, "now are you satisfied? For Heaven's sake take yourself off. I wish to be alone."

Stefano chinked the gold trinkets in his hand.

"It's very little; it's not enough," he mumbled. "But small profits and quick returns was always my motto. I'll bring you the wine presently."

He left the cell, shutting the heavy door behind him; the sound of the closing bolt shot through Ralph's heart, and for the first time he felt all the bitterness of captivity.

He seated himself on the straw pallet and buried his face in his hands, a prey to the keenest emotions of wrath, anguish and despair.

CHAPTER XLII.

"HAVE a care, Edmund; do not provoke me too far," said Sir Godfrey Mortimer; "you little think how one word from me could blight your prospects for ever. And above all, sir, never again let me hear you speak slightingly of Ralph Wildhawk. He has suffered injustice at my hands, but it is not too late for me to make him ample reparation, and then where would you be? He would occupy the position you now hold. You would take his place."

Edmund Mortimer bowed haughtily.

"Your pardon, sir," he answered, coldly. "Heaven forbid that I should show any lack of the filial reverence and submission which are your due; but since you threaten me, I am bound to tell you this—that I can never fill the post of secretary to my own father."

The baronet and his son stood confronting each other in the library of the palace of the former, at Castellamare.

"You are a fool, Edmund," retorted the baronet; "a rash, ungrateful fool! You know not what sacrifices of honour and peace of mind I have made for your sake."

Again Edmund bowed coldly, and answered in a sneering tone—

"I grant, sir, that you have not forgotten what was due to the credit and dignity of the ancient house of the Mortimers."

"I will not bandy words with you, sir. You must cut your acquaintances, boy," replied his father; "they are no good to you. Whatever their rank, they are nothing better than a pack of profligates and gamblers."

Edmund's face grew scarlet.

"Why are you tongue-tied?" asked Sir Godfrey. "Why do you not speak?"

"I know not how to answer, sir," stammered Edmund; "I trust you do not insinuate that I am capable of acting dishonourably."

"Very good, sir," was the cool rejoinder. "Then at once discharge your gambling debts, and beware how you incur fresh ones."

"I shall do so," answered Edmund, "as soon as I receive the monthly allowance you are good enough to grant me."

"So on Monday next you expect to draw upon my bankers for the sum of two hundred pounds," returned Sir Godfrey; "and that will suffice to meet all demands upon you?"

"Why, not exactly," returned Edmund, evidently cowed; "my most pressing demands."

"I am sorry to hear you say so, knowing the assertion to be false," answered Sir Godfrey. "Now sit down, Edmund. Tush! bring your chair nearer to the table, and let us go into your accounts."

Edmund obeyed mechanically, feeling very uneasy, and wondering what was to come.

"Some traitor has betrayed me," he muttered to himself; "I'll lay my life it is that rascal Joe."

"Are you ready, sir?" asked Sir Godfrey, sternly.

Edmund folded his arms with affected indifference, and bowed his head.

"At your service, sir," he answered.

"Let us begin then," said the baronet.

He turned over the leaves of the note-book.

"Let me see," said Sir Godfrey. "Yes; first we have the French marquis."

"De Laval!" cried Edmund Mortimer, starting up from his chair, quite disconcerted.

"You are right," said his father, quietly, "the first on the list, as you say, is M. Le Marquis De Laval. Very good. How much do you owe the marquis?"

"Well, really, sir," stammered Edmund, "I don't know the exact sum, but——"

"I do," returned his father, coolly; "the marquis holds your note of hand for the sum of five hundred guineas lost at cards on or before the seventh of last month."

"The perfidious scoundrel!" gasped Edmund.

"Do you admit the debt?" asked Sir Godfrey.

"Indeed, sir——"

"That is your handwriting, I believe?"

He turned the paper to Edmund.

"I cannot deny it."

"Very well," said Sir Godfrey. "Five hundred guineas to M. Le Marquis De Laval."

And he jotted down the sum in his note-book.

Then he looked up once more, and fixed his keen eyes upon his son's face, now pale and confused.

"Oblige me by giving direct answers to my direct questions," he said; "it will facilitate our progress."

"Very well, sir," answered Edmund, sullenly.

Sir Godfrey placed the Marquis De Laval's account on one side.

Then he took another slip of paper from the fatal pocket-book.

"Whom have we here?" said he. "Oh, the

Prince Visconti; to him you lost six hundred guineas at *rouge et noir*. Is that right?"

Edmund bowed his head.

"Six hundred guineas," said Sir Godfrey, entering the sum. "Five and six, Edmund?"

"Five and six are eleven, sir," blurted Edmund, trying to look defiant, but failing miserably in the attempt.

"Now," said his father, looking at another paper, "Captain Monteleone, one hundred guineas; Count Di Villanova, two hundred; Signor Bastiano fifty; but enough. Edmund," he added, putting the papers back into the pocket-book; "I will go no further into these accounts just now. Suffice it that I know you have involved yourself to the extent of ten thousand pounds, which I, of course, shall have to pay. But there is something else, however, to which I wish to call your serious attention."

"And what is that, sir?" asked Edmund in a humble tone.

"Your *liaison* with La Zara, the opera-dancer," replied his father.

Edmund turned deadly pale.

"Shame and ruin!" he muttered to himself. "He has discovered all! What a villanous set of spies I must have had about me!"

Sir Godfrey rose from his chair, and coming to Edmund, laid his hand upon his shoulder.

"Mark me, my boy," he said; "I do not wish to quarrel with you, but upon one point I am resolved. You must never again see or communicate with La Zara. If you disobey me the consequences will perhaps be very terrible."

"There is little fear that I shall see La Zara again," answered Edmund; "as I am given to understand that she has left Naples."

"I am glad to hear it," answered Sir Godfrey; "I trust you will never even hear of her again."

"Sir, be satisfied," replied Edmund, with a deep sigh; "I shall never behold her again."

"Sit you down, Edmund," rejoined the baronet; "and give me your attention whilst I relate to you a true story, which I trust may serve as a warning to you."

Edmund bowed, and seated himself.

"There was once a man of my own rank, whom I knew as well as I knew myself," continued the baronet, "who, when a young, unmarried man, sojourned for some time in Naples. He fell in love with an Italian girl, of humble parentage, who, if possible, surpassed even the celebrated Zara for beauty and fascination."

Edmund smiled incredulously, and shook his head.

Without noticing this, the baronet went on in a calm, measured tone.

"My friend, as I said, became so deeply enamoured of this fair siren, that disregarding their difference in station, his own straitened circumstances, he formed an alliance with her."

"Do you mean, sir, that he married her?"

Sir Godfrey turned pale, and answered in some confusion—

"You go too fast; I have not said that, but it soon became necessary for him to break off his connection with her. He left the affair to the management of an unscrupulous man—the Count Di Beltrani, whom he suspected of having robbed him of the girl's affection; the count carried off the girl, and he—my friend, I mean—quitted Naples, and returned to England."

"And did he see his Italian mistress no more?" asked Edmund.

"Soon after his return to England," continued the baronet, "my friend succeeded to the title and estates of a distant relative. He became wealthy, and held his head high in the world. About this time he married a fair and amiable young lady, who bore him a son. The young wife being in a delicate state of health, my friend thought she might be benefited by a tour in Italy. They came to Naples, and mark what followed; the discarded mistress, who was thought to be dead, had married a brigand chief. She sought out her rival, and stabbed her to the heart."

"The murderess!" exclaimed Edmund, passionately; "and did she escape?"

"She did," returned the baronet; "she fled with the brigands to the mountains, but whether she still lives, is more than I can say."

"And pray, sir, who was the unhappy lady who thus fell a victim to the jealousy and revenge of this Italian fury?"

"She was your own mother."

Edmund started to his feet with a cry of horror.

"Good Heaven! is it possible?" he exclaimed.

"It is but too true," replied his father. "This terrible event has hitherto been kept a secret from you, and it was my intention that you should never learn it, but I have told it you as a warning, which I trust you will not disregard. But it must be kept a secret from everyone else."

Quite overpowered by a revelation so terrible, Edmund buried his face in his hands, and groaned deeply.

"Forget it, sir, I can never," he replied, "but I shall nevertheless obey your commands in maintaining silence upon a subject that is too painful to bear even a moment's reflection."

"It is well," answered his father; "and now I will leave you. As soon as I have negotiated with the brigands for the ransom of Ralph Wildhawk, we will hasten our return to England. Meanwhile, urge on your suit with Violet Melville."

So saying, the baronet quitted the room.

CHAPTER XLIII.

MEANWHILE Violet Melville had kept her room for weeks; anxiety and distress of mind had had a serious effect upon her health.

Her thoughts were constantly fixed upon Ralph Wildhawk, and she listened eagerly to the slightest report brought to her by her faithful though somewhat indiscreet attendant, Matilda Sparkes.

To her trouble was added the annoyance she experienced at being constantly importuned by her uncle and guardian not to delay her marriage with Edmund Mortimer.

"Oh, Matilda, how enviable is your condition in comparison with mine," she said to her maid.

"You are at liberty to bestow your affections upon the object of your choice, whilst I am being constantly urged to give my hand to one I cannot love."

"Ah, miss, sich is the wicissitudes of greatness," sighed Matilda; "I've read of one of our queens as envied a milk-maid. Still, miss, we all has our secret scorpins, and it's werry seldom we can find a congenial pardner. Look at my Joseph now, a good-natured fellow enough, but he has no more soul for poetry than any knife-grinder."

"He is not much the worse for that, Matilda," answered her young mistress.

Matilda smiled and simpered.

"Lawks! miss, perhaps he ain't no worse," she answered. "But certainly I do love the romantic and the picter-skew."

"The picturesque, I think you mean, Matilda," replied her mistress, who could scarcely refrain from laughing outright.

"Some calls it so, miss," rejoined Matilda, rather hastily, "but we were talking of Master Edmund; I believe you was betrothed to him whilst mere children."

"Yes," answered Violet, sighing. "My father, on his deathbed, expressed a wish that I should marry Edmund when I came of age, and I have been always brought up to regard him as my future husband."

And then, not caring to prolong a conversation with her maid, which she felt was growing too confidential, she dismissed the girl, and sent her on an errand into the town.

In the course of an hour, Matilda returned in a state of great excitement.

"Oh, Miss Violet, the most wonderful thing has happened!" she exclaimed. "I had been to the Mercato to order the gloves and ribbons as you told me, and the English serving man in the shop had been telling me of the horrid goings-on of those frightful brigands after the escape of their chief from the Castle of St. Elmo, when just as I was leaving the shop, a young Italian gentleman stepped up, touched me under the arm, and asked me if I could obtain him an interview with my mistress, the niece of the great English Milord Mortimer, for so he called Sir Godfrey; the young man spoke pretty good English."

"An interview with me?" returned Violet, in astonishment. "What can it mean? Was he a stranger?"

"Yes, miss. I had never set eyes on him before," replied Matilda.

"What kind of person was he?" said Violet.

"Quite a youth, a mere stripling, miss," returned her maid. "He had no more hair on his face than you or me, but I never saw such a pretty boy in my life; delicate complexion, chiselled features, and for all his cloak, which he kept close round him, though the weather is so hot, his form were a picter of youthful grace."

"For shame, Matilda," returned her mistress, colouring up, "I wonder you should notice. But there; what has this to do with me? You must know that I cannot receive this young gentleman without a proper introduction."

"Oh, yes, but you will, miss, when I have told you all," rejoined Matilda, her eyes twinkling. "He brings you letters."

"Letters from whom?" eagerly inquired her mistress.

"From Master Ralph Wildhawk," answered Matilda, lowering her voice to a whisper.

Every vestige of colour faded from Violet's soft cheek.

"Where is the youth?" she asked.

"He waits below in the westibule," answered Matilda.

"What shall I do?" Violet asked herself, reflectively. "Do you not think you could persuade him to deliver up these letters to you?"

"No, miss, I am sure of it," answered Matilda; "he declares that unless you will consent to see him, he will take them back."

"Well, Matilda," answered Violet, "since there is no alternative, I will see him at once, but you must remain with me, and let Joseph be within call."

"Very well, miss," answered Matilda, as she hurried from the room.

Violet had not long to wait, for almost immediately, a light, springing step was heard outside, the door was opened, and the mysterious stranger entered, ushered in by Matilda Sparkes.

Violet was at once struck with the youth's remarkable beauty of form and feature, which the romantic Matilda had in nowise exaggerated.

He bowed with much grace and self-possession.

Violet was quite startled by the sweetness and softness of the tones in which he addressed her.

"Signora," he said, "I crave your pardon for thus intruding upon your privacy, but there are reasons which prevent me from giving up the letters entrusted to me by Signor Wildhawk, now, unhappily, a captive among the brigands. He gave me special instructions to deliver them into your fair hands alone."

Violet blushed, and she felt her heart beat violently, but she answered as composedly as she could.

"Signore, I feel certain that Ralph is most fortunate in having found such a messenger, but I trust you will not deem me impertinent if I venture to ask your name, and the circumstances under which you met Mr. Wildhawk."

The youth's eyes flashed for an instant with a peculiar, half scornful expression.

"The heartless English prude," he muttered to himself; "can she speak thus coldly of the man she loves?"

Then he added aloud, with another bow of stately courtesy—

"I will tell you, signora; my name is Angelo Sforza. I am a student of Mantua, who, while sketching in the Abruzzi, was captured by the brigands."

"Alas, signore, and how did you effect your escape?" asked Violet.

"By very simple, not to say ignominious means, signora," replied the youthful stranger, with a smile; "in fact the only means by which it is possible to escape from the clutches of Marco Bravo. My friends paid the sum he demanded as my ransom, and I was set at liberty."

Violet shuddered.

"Why is such an abominable miscreant suffered to pollute the earth?" she exclaimed, indignantly. "It is a public calamity that the mountain wolf should have broken his chain, and escaped, as he did, to work more mischief."

"Perhaps, then, signora, you have heard of the fearful revenge he took upon the unhappy men who betrayed him?"

"No, indeed."

"They were both members of his own band," replied the young stranger; "one of them had before played the traitor; he subsequently passed under the name of Michael Cornaro, but his real name was Carlo Volti."

"Who was the other man?" asked Violet.

"Guiseppe Veletri," replied the stranger. "He had been one of the chief's most trusted lieutenants, but Marco Bravo having given him some offence, he took counsel with Michael Cornaro, to betray the chief, who was then passing himself off as the Count Di Ancona."

"True, under that name, he became a constant and welcome visitor in our family," answered Violet. "At first I was imposed upon by his specious manners, but afterwards I suspected him; but what of these two poor wretches, Guiseppe Veletri and Michael Cornaro?"

"You see, signora, our dilatory government failed to pay them the reward promised for the betrayal of their captain," replied Angelo; "part of the money, indeed, was paid, and it would have been well for them if they had left the country and not waited for the rest, but they did so. Disguised as shepherds, they took up their abode at a little village, not far from Itri. Meanwhile, the devil had broken loose. Marco Bravo escaped. With fifty of his band he besieged their hut, and then——"

"Dragged them forth, and shot them down like dogs," suggested Violet, seeing the youth pause and turn pale.

"Not he, signora," replied Angelo; "you do not know the demon-spirit that inspires that man. He had the doors barred on the outside, and the hut fired. When the poor, shrieking, half-consumed wretches broke their way out of the blazing ruin, imploring him to kill them, and put them out of their misery, he calmly ordered his fiendish band to thrust them back with their muskets, which they did, and the miserable creatures were burnt alive."

"Horrible!" returned Violet, covering her face with her hands; "and dear Ralph lies at the mercy of such a monster."

An expression of keen anguish crossed Angelo's noble features, but his black eyes softened, as he replied, in a low voice—

"Not for long. The signore has powerful friends, who will perhaps even risk their lives to save him."

Then, unfastening his cloak, he took the letters from his bosom, and placed them in her hands.

Violet took them with trembling eagerness.

"This is for my uncle, this for my cousin Edmund," she murmured, "and this for me."

Placing the other letters aside, she broke the seal of the one addressed to herself, and eagerly devoured its contents.

Angelo watched her keenly, and his countenance changed as he noted her glowing eyes and blushing cheeks; and when at length Violet turned aside, pressed the precious writing to her lips, and then placed it in her bosom, the young stranger uttered a faint cry as though smitten with sudden pain.

Violet started, and turned towards him, with a look of surprise and pity.

"You are ill," she said, gently; "how pale you look, how thoughtless and selfish I must be not to have observed it before. Run, Matilda," she added, turning to her maid. "Fetch assistance."

By a violent effort the stranger recovered himself.

He stepped to the door.

"Not for worlds," he said; "it was nothing —a passing faintness that at times overcomes me. The horrors I have lately witnessed have given a shock to my system, but I am myself now."

"At least, repose awhile and take some refreshment," returned Violet, "let me entreat you."

"No, signora, I must begone, I dare not remain here longer," answered the youth.

Then dropping on one knee, he kissed her hand.

"Farewell, signora," he said. "May the blessed saints have you in their holy keeping. May he whom you love be speedily restored to you, and may you enjoy to the utmost the greatest happiness that we may dare to hope for in this changeful world. Farewell, for ever, farewell."

He rose, bowed with matchless grace, and glided from the room.

"Stay, signore," cried Violet. "Do not leave me thus——"

But he was gone.

"Fly, Matilda, bring him back," said Violet, hastily. "I have much to ask of him, much to say to him."

Her maid hurried from the room, and presently returned in great haste, looking flushed and excited.

"Good lack, miss, if it isn't enough to make a blind man open his eyes with wonder," exclaimed Matilda, holding up her hands; "I've made a discovery, miss, a hawful discovery."

"What do you mean?"

"I mean no more nor less than this, Miss Violet," returned Matilda; "the young gentleman as was here just now was no young gentleman at all—he was a woman, miss."

A flash of jealous anger darted from Violet's blue eyes.

"A woman!" exclaimed she. "Who can she be? What motive could Ralph have in sending her hither? Was it to insult me? Yet—no! I do her wrong. Her noble, generous conduct ought to raise her above suspicion, and I know Ralph too well to believe him capable of baseness or treachery."

"Miss Violet, I have made another discovery," said Matilda.

"And what is that?"

"I know the name of the Italian heroine," returned Matilda. "Joe Moody told me that Master Ralph defended her with his sword against a whole host of ruffians that were

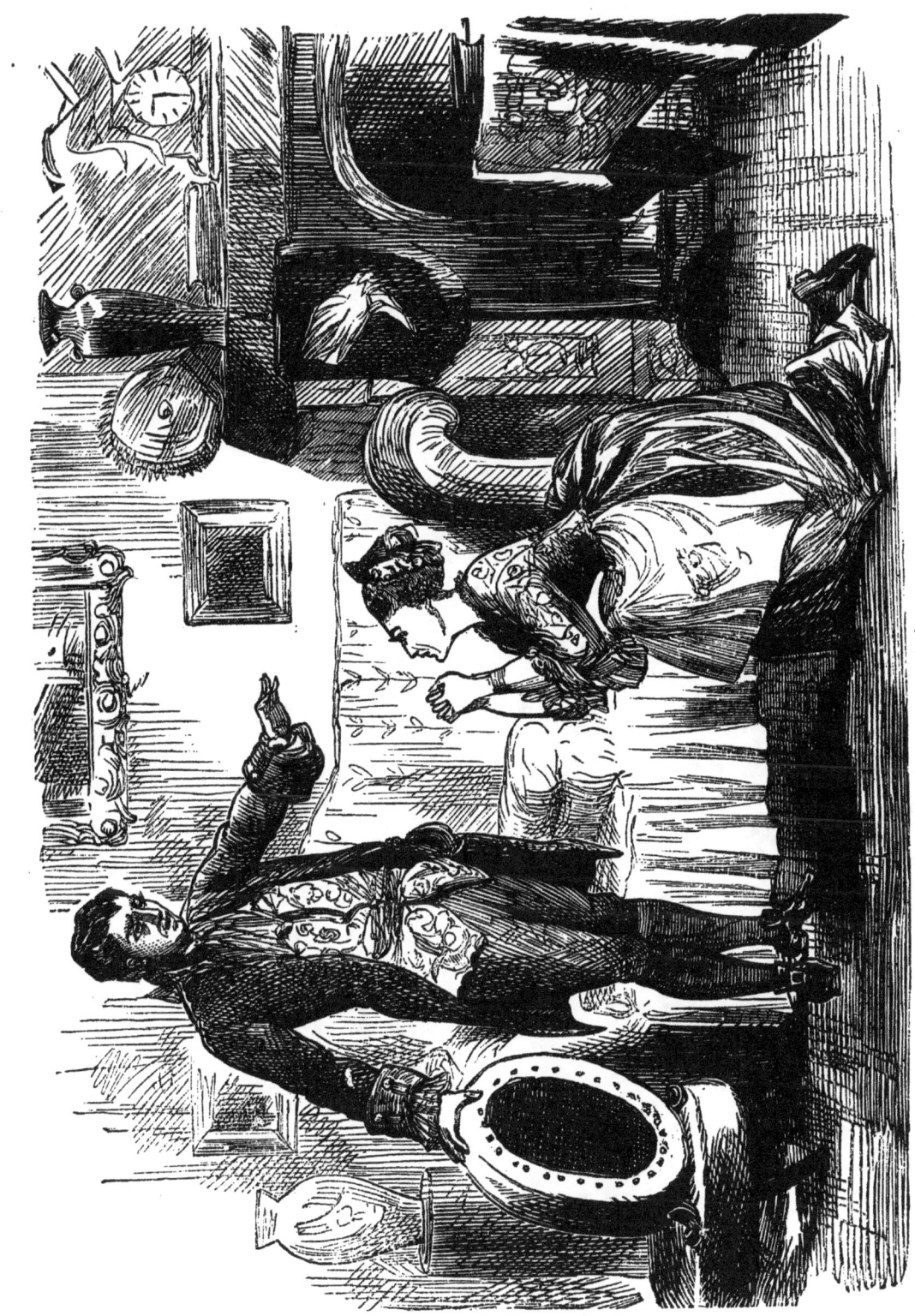

"'OH, SIR GODFREY,' SAID SHE, 'I KNOW NOT WHAT HARM I HAVE DONE!'"

going to carry her off. It is Zara, the opera dancer!"

At the mention of the name Violet fainted.

CHAPTER XLIV.

EDMUND MORTIMER, after his exciting interview with his father, hurried from the palace at Castellamare, and, mounting his horse, rode towards Naples.

The intelligence conveyed to him of his mother's terrible fate had stricken him with horror, and his first thought was how to shake off the gloomy impression.

He therefore left a note for his father, in which he stated that he was going to Naples for a few days, to settle some of his little affairs of business, which it was necessary to arrange before quitting Italy, but that, upon his return, he should be ready to follow his father's directions in every particular.

In a few hours, he entered the city of Naples.

It happened to be one of the numerous festivals of the church, and the streets were crowded with merry-makers in all varieties of picturesque costume, many of them wearing masks.

He put up his horse at an hotel in the Strada Di Toledo, partook of some refreshments, and then, having donned his cloak and a mask, he sauntered forth to take a stroll through the bustling streets of the gay town.

Passing unrecognised, in his disguise, he roved from casino to gaming house, not trusting himself to remain long in one place.

At length, drawn by some mysterious impulse, which he found it impossible to resist, he betook himself to the disreputable and dangerous quarter of the city, where he knew La Zara resided with the gipsy tribe.

"Some happy accident may throw her in my way," he thought; "there can be no harm in seeing her once more, and bidding her a long farewell."

Through narrow, tortuous streets, hemmed in by high, dark houses, he wandered, gazing wistfully at the few female passengers he met with.

Edmund was struck by the strange quiet that prevailed around him; no faces appeared at the windows, the doors were all closed, and as the rambler penetrated deeper into the recesses of the place, he seemed to be passing through a city of the dead.

He paused opposite a large house, which, though now crumbling to decay, bore the traces of former grandeur.

"If I am not mistaken," Edmund said to himself, "this is the palace of the gipsy king, and here dwells my peerless Zara."

The sound of a light footstep, which echoed along the pavement of the deserted street, caused Edmund to start and turn round.

He saw the slight and graceful form of a youth advancing rapidly towards the spot where he was standing.

The stripling, who was closely wrapped in his mantle, appeared unconscious that any one was near him, and glided on, lost in thought, his eyes bent upon the ground.

Not wishing to be seen, Edmund slunk behind a buttress of one of the houses, and watched the advance of the youth.

The latter suddenly stopped, and as if rousing himself from the moody train of thought into which he had fallen, glanced heedfully up and down the street, to make sure that he was unobserved.

Then apparently reassured, with quickened step he approached the palace of the king of the gipsies.

As he did so, he flung back his cloak, and revealed his face.

"Good Heaven!" muttered Edmund; "those features! They are Zara's."

"It is she, there can be no doubt of it," he murmured, in astonishment; "but why is she masquerading abroad in boy's clothes?"

La Zara, for it was indeed the gipsy girl disguised, having, as she thought, ascertained that she was unobserved, took a key from the little velvet satchel that hung by her side, and cautiously opened the door of her brother's dwelling.

She entered the large stone hall, leaving the door ajar.

When she had advanced a few steps, she stopped and listened, as though hesitating whether to close the door, for fear that the noise might disturb someone in the house.

All, however, was silent.

"Why does she slink home, and enter her own house with all the secrecy and caution of a night-prowling thief?" Edmund muttered, in jealous rage. "Where has she been to? Most likely to visit some favoured lover. I will extort the confession from her own lips."

Maddened by passion, Edmund lost all thought of the risk he was running; he gently pushed open the door, and entered the gloomy hall, still magnificent in its decay.

The door slammed behind him.

La Zara turned round, uttering a piercing scream.

Her face was white as marble with surprise and terror, and she trembled violently.

Edmund sprang forward and caught her by the hand.

"La Zara," he exclaimed, "do not alarm yourself, it is I—your devoted lover."

Zara wrested away her hand and gazed upon him with anger and dismay.

"Holy Virgin! What madness is this?" she ejaculated. "How, and why have you tracked me hither? But fly; this is no time for reproaches; escape at once—there is not a moment to lose. If you are found here, no power on earth can save you from my brother's vengeance."

"Perish the thought," returned Edmund. "I am about to leave Italy, it may be never to return, but e'er I go, I am determined that you shall listen to me. I love you, beautiful Zara, a thousand times better than my life, and though instant death threatened me, I would remain to die at your feet."

"You are demented," returned Zara, beside herself with fear and agitation. "Hereafter you will learn to repent the baseness and cruelty of this unmanly persecution. Oh, for my sake, if you would not destroy me as well as yourself, begone."

"Never, dearest Zara," answered the infatuated youth. "Why should we part thus? As for your brother, gold will conciliate him."

At this moment a fierce growl, as from some wild beast roused from his lair, was heard, and footsteps resounded down a long passage that led to the entrance hall.

"It is Balthazar; if he finds you here, he will kill you," cried Zara, struggling to release herself from his clasp. "Let me go, madman and ruffian," she went on, trying to bite his hand. "Will you not?—then your blood be upon your own head."

As she spoke, the red glare of a torch shone along the passage.

The next instant, a stalwart, ferocious-looking ruffian rushed into the vestibule.

In one hand he carried the flaming torch, in the other he grasped a hatchet.

Somewhat daunted by the appearance of the savage gipsy, who sprang towards him, brandishing his murderous weapon in the air, Edmund released the girl, and retreated towards the door.

Zara seized Balthazar's arm.

"Do not strike," she cried, imploringly; "I will explain."

Balthazar lowered his axe, and stared first at Edmund and then at Zara, in stolid amazement.

Edmund would now have gladly beat a retreat.

It was too late.

The door was burst open, and five men rushed in.

Their dark, tawny skins, their prominent features, their rolling black eyes, and long, black ringlets proclaimed that they belonged to the gipsy tribe.

They were all armed with bludgeons, pistols, and stilettoes.

The tallest and fiercest-looking of the group was their chief, or king, Isaco Il Nero.

His features were distorted with rage.

Confounded at an attack so sudden and unexpected, Edmund sprang back, and drew his sword.

"Rash fool!" hissed the gipsy king through his clenched teeth. "Have you dared to carry your insult so far as to beard the lion in his den? Your insolence, I suppose, despises my race, my power, and you think to escape with impunity, but you are mistaken. Within these precincts my will is law. You shall die."

"Signor Isaco," said Edmund calmly, "you are enraged without cause. It was by mere accident that I am here."

"It is true, my brother," rejoined Zara. "Do not be angry. All is well. Hear me speak."

"Silence, wanton, shame and curse of your race," retorted the gipsy king, stamping his foot. "Why did you suffer this libertine to dog your steps, and introduce him into my very house?"

"I did not so, my brother," returned Zara. "Restrain your blind fury, and listen to my explanation."

"Wretch, will you plead for your paramour?" growled Isaco, raising his fist; "beware lest you share his fate."

Then, turning to Balthazar, he demanded, fiercely—

"What do you know of this?"

"Per Baccho!" replied the gipsy, shrugging his shoulders, "I know no more than this. I heard La Zara shrieking for help, and rushing to her assistance, found her struggling in the stranger's arms."

"A la morte! down with him!" chorussed the gipsies, as they pressed upon Edmund.

Brought to bay, Edmund set his back against the wall, and swept round his sword.

Isaco broke through the little knot of gipsies, and beating down Edmund's guard, plunged his stiletto into the English youth's breast.

Zara uttered a piercing shriek, and sank to the ground.

Edmund let fall his sword, clutched at the blood-streaming wound in his breast, and with eyes glaring horribly upon his assassin, rolled at his feet.

"Ah, my mother, we perish by the same cruel fate," he murmured.

Then, feebly raising himself upon his arm, he added, in a husky whisper—

"Isaco, I alone—I was to blame. Your sister is innocent, as I hope for mercy."

Then his head fell back, and with a deep groan, he expired.

Balthazar bent over the body of the murdered youth, and laid his hand upon his heart.

"Diavolo!" he said, "this is a pretty business. He is dead."

Balthazar lifted the insensible Zara in his brawny arms, and bore her away.

The gipsies gathered round poor Edmund's corpse, and gazed upon his ghastly, white face, not without some expression of remorse and of pity.

Balthazar now returned.

"How fares my sister?" asked the gipsy king.

"She is still insensible," replied Balthazar; "I left her in the charge of Naomi."

"Better so," returned the gipsy king, gloomily; "and hark ye, Balthazar, at your own peril, do not allow Zara, or for that matter, any other of the women, to leave the house until I rescind the order."

"Good; I will lock the door in the passage that leads to their apartments," replied Balthazar.

"It would be well for you to decide quickly then," returned Isaco, "before our comrades return. The fewer who are made acquainted with such a secret as this, the better."

Then turning to the others, the gipsy king added—

"I need scarcely impress upon you the necessity of keeping your counsel about this awkward affair. Do not speak of it even to your nearest relatives, your most intimate friends."

"Not a word, Isaco," replied the men. "We will keep the secret."

"Good," said the gipsy king; "and now let us consider how best to dispose of the body of this English youth."

"If I may be allowed to offer a suggestion," said Balthazar, "ought we not to bury this body in the vaults beneath the house?"

"That will never do," was the reply; "as soon as he is missed, no doubt a rigorous search will be made for him—he may be traced hither, therefore our object must be to remove suspicion from ourselves."

"Even so," returned Balthazar. "But may I ask what brought you home so early, and in such an evil hour?"

"I will tell you," answered the gipsy king. "As I was crossing the Strada Di Porto, I recognised my sister disguised as a boy. As you are all aware, I have been alarmed and anxious at her prolonged and mysterious absence from our midst. Well, I resolved to watch her movements. So calling together four of my comrades, in case I might want their aid, I tracked her to this place. I need not tell you the rest."

There was a moment of embarrassed silence, and then the gipsy king resumed with a sigh—

"This is a bad business, but we must look it in the face. As soon as night falls, the body shall be placed in a covered carriage, and conveyed to the piece of waste ground near the Porta Nolano, and there left."

"So that it may be thought that he was killed in a duel," replied Balthazar, "as that is the spot where the gentry decide their quarrels by the sword."

"Not so; that would only cause inquiry," replied Isaco. "The blame of the deed must be thrown upon the robbers and cut-throats by whom the city is infested. To that end, we will strip the body of money, jewels, and other valuables, so that the motive may appear to have been robbery."

"But we gipsies never plunder the dead," rejoined Balthazar; "such has been our law since the times of the Magi, from whom we are descended."

"No, no, we will touch nothing belonging to a dead man," chorussed the others. "Evil will come of it."

"There will be no need to appropriate such things to our own use; they may be buried or destroyed," returned Isaco; "but it shall be done as I have said, and now carry the body into the vaults, and let it lie there until after sunset. Meanwhile, Balthazar, lose no time in washing out these bloodstains, and removing all traces of the fray. I will caution my sister, and once more I conjure you all to keep close our fatal secret."

CHAPTER XLV.

RALPH WILDHAWK still remained a prisoner in his close and narrow cell, below the old Moorish tower in the Brigands' Glen.

He wondered that he had received no answers to the letters he had transmitted to his friends by the hands of Angelo Sforza.

As time wore on, he became broken in health and spirits, and plunged into the deepest gloom of despair.

He almost wished that an order might arrive from the chief for his immediate execution, as he was tired of life, and longed to be put out of his misery and suffering.

The only visitor who broke the tedium of his solitude and captivity was the hoary-headed old ruffian, his gaoler, Stefano.

One day, as Ralph was pacing drearily up and down his cell, the door was suddenly opened, and young Giovanni Pisano entered.

Ralph seized his hand.

"Welcome, Giovanni," said he; "I cannot tell you how glad I am to see you once more.

I am afraid to think how long it is since I looked upon any countenance besides that of the brute who keeps me here mewed up, a wild hawk as I am—the detestable scoundrel, Stefano."

"Hush, signore, do not speak so loud," returned the young brigand, looking back. "He is close at hand. It is not safe to offend him."

"To the devil with him; I fear him not," returned Ralph; "but your news—is it good or bad?"

"That depends upon yourself, signore," answered the boy. "Marco Bravo is arrived."

"Marco Bravo!" repeated Ralph Wildhawk, with a start. "Has he then escaped from his prison at St. Elmo?"

"He has, signore."

"This is news, indeed."

"It is but old news after all," answered Giovanni, with a sickly smile; "for ten days have passed since the signor capitano broke his prison and returned to the mountains. Since then he has not been idle, I can assure you; he has taken a terrible revenge upon his enemies."

"The villain appears to lead a charmed life," answered Ralph, bitterly; "but have you any intelligence to give me that concerns myself?"

"Much, too much, signore," answered the young brigand, shaking his head. "It is ill news; can you bear to hear it?"

"I can bear anything. I am prepared for the worst that can befall me," replied our hero. "So keep nothing from me—let me know the truth."

Giovanni had certainly a terrible tale to tell.

In the first place, he narrated how the body of Edmund Mortimer had been found near the Porta Di Nolano, murdered and weltering in blood.

"The body was found stripped of everything of value, signore," continued the young brigand, "even to the cloak, hat, and sword. The crime was charged to our band, but without just cause, for I have reason to know that none of our troop, from the captain to myself, had a hand in the murder."

"By whom then could it have been perpetrated?" asked Ralph.

"By some of the thieves and bravoes in the city, who have no connection with us of the mountains," answered Giovanni. "But I have worse to tell you."

"Impossible; nothing could be worse," returned Ralph, burying his face in his hands. "It is true that Edmund Mortimer loved me not, but for all that, I was drawn towards him by some mysterious impulse, and felt towards him the attachment of a brother. But go on with your story."

"Well, then, signore, since you will have it, listen with what patience you may," rejoined the young brigand. "Driven to distraction by grief and rage at the murder of his son, the English milord laid his complaints before King Ferdinand, and clamoured for revenge upon the brigands whom he supposed to have been guilty of the murder. Well, signore, a large force was sent against Marco Bravo; an engagement took place, and though many of our comrades were slain, the royalist troops were defeated."

"Well, Giovanni," urged our hero, turning pale, and trembling. "Go on with your story; do not hesitate, whatever you may have to tell."

"Know then, signore," replied the young Italian, "that our chief attacked the carriages of Milordo Mortimer on the road between Naples and Castellamare, took the lord, his family, and servants, all prisoners, as also about half a dozen of the soldiers who formed the escort."

Ralph was thunderstruck.

"Great Heaven !" he ejaculated, "and where has he disposed his prisoners ?"

"He has brought them here to the mountains," answered Giovanni.

Ralph staggered backwards and raised his clenched hands to heaven.

"Distraction !" he ejaculated. "Violet, can she be in the hands of those fearful miscreants ?"

"The Signora Violetta with her maid are among the prisoners."

"Horrible !" gasped Ralph, turning quite sick and faint. "But I will save her or perish."

"Signore, listen to me," answered Giovanni, in an impressive manner. "I like you much, and should be very sorry if any harm befell you."

"You are kind, Giovanni," answered Ralph, in a despairing tone. "But I care not what happens to me now."

"Do not give way to despair; there is hope for you yet; you have more friends in the band than you think," replied the young brigand. "Only let me beseech you not to provoke Marco Bravo; you might as well take a lion by the beard as to dare him in his present humour."

"But Violet."

"Not all the gold in the treasury of King Ferdinand or the pope would ransom her," rejoined the youth. "Marco Bravo loves the beautiful Inglesa, and has sworn to marry her and make her queen of the banditti."

"I would rather see him plunge a knife into her heart," returned Ralph, savagely.

"At all events, beware of him in his present mood," returned Giovanni. "He is in one of his tigerish passions. Only just now, the English milordo taunted him with insulting his unarmed prisoners, and declared that old as he was, if he had our chief hand to hand, and foot to foot, he would rid the world of him."

"And did the ruffian accept the old man's challenge ?" asked Ralph.

"He did," replied Giovanni, "and declared he would fight him within the hour. But you must go with me, signore; I am ordered to bring you before the chief, and in my anxiety to put you on your guard, I have lingered too long on my errand. Come at once."

They left the dungeons.

Giovanni leading the way, they mounted the stairs, and passing through an open door, emerged from the old Moorish tower.

CHAPTER XLVI.

Upon reaching the plateau at the entrance of the Brigands' Glen, a strange and terrible spectacle met our hero's view.

Guarded by a strong detachment of the brigands were the prisoners.

Amongst them our hero recognised Violet Melville, with her faithful maid Matilda Sparkes, together with honest Joe Moody and several other men-servants belonging to the household of the English baronet.

But he glanced at them only for a moment, his attention being called off by the exciting and tragic drama that was being played upon an open space around which the brigands and their captives were grouped.

Marco Bravo and Sir Godfrey Mortimer stood face to face, each with a drawn sword in his hand.

It was evident that they were about to commence a duel.

"Do not interfere," Giovanni whispered, "it would be worse than useless."

Ralph broke away from the young brigand, and was about to rush forward to Sir Godfrey's help, but was dragged back by four brigands who were near.

In an agony of breathless suspense, Ralph was forced to watch the combat, which had now commenced.

The combatants were not so unequally matched as might at first be supposed, it being rather a trial of skill than a conflict of mere brute force.

Of course, Marco Bravo was a much younger and more powerful man than his opponent, but then, Sir Godfrey Mortimer was a consummate master of fence.

While at Oxford, Mortimer had practised under the tuition of an Italian fencing-master, considered the best swordsman of his day, and the pupil acquired such skill that few could hold their own against him.

The conflict was long and doubtful, Sir Godfrey Mortimer fighting with an agility and desperation that could scarcely have been expected from a man of his time of life.

Marco Bravo appeared no little astonished at the skill and determination of his elderly antagonist.

The brigand chief fought warily, acting upon the defensive principle.

At length, the robber having somewhat rashly exposed himself, Sir Godfrey Mortimer lunged in and wounded him in the left shoulder.

Marco Bravo sprang back, clapped his right hand to the bleeding wound, and dropped his sword.

The brigands uttered a shout, and levelled their carbines at Sir Godfrey, who glanced round upon them with a quiet smile of cool contempt.

But Marco Bravo picked up his sword, and waving his hand to the brigands to lower their muskets, they did so, and with glaring eyes and close-set teeth watched for the issue of the fatal contest.

The duel recommenced with greater ferocity on both sides.

"'WITH A STINGING BLOW, OUR HERO STRUCK THE MISCREANT FULL BETWEEN THE EYES.'"

Marco Bravo now seemed to give full rein to his temper, and fought with almost frantic desperation.

At length Sir Godfrey grew exhausted, and gave his antagonist the opportunity he had so long and keenly watched for.

Parrying a well-delivered thrust, the brigand chief made a furious lunge and passed his sword through Sir Godfrey's body, the hilt striking against his ribs.

The old man uttered a sharp cry of anguish, threw his arms aloft, and staggering backwards, rolled upon the ground.

Violet uttered a piercing shriek, and rushed to the side of the dying man.

At the same moment Ralph shook himself free from the brigand's grip, and kneeling beside the wounded baronet, lifted his drooping head.

"Dear Sir Godfrey, I will avenge him," muttered Ralph Wildhawk, as the brigand wiped his sword.

With a sob of pity and compassion, Violet threw herself upon Sir Godfrey's body.

Marco Bravo sheathed his sword, then striding forward, he attempted to raise Violet from the ground.

His loathsome touch appeared to revive her. She wrested away his hands, and slunk back.

"Wretch, murderer," she exclaimed, "complete your work ; kill me as you have killed my best and kindest friend."

"He provoked his fate, signora," returned the brigand, gloomily ; "I took no advantage. What has befallen him might have befallen me. It is but natural that you should feel embittered against me just now, but time will change your sentiments ; meanwhile, respect my power and obey my will."

Violet made no reply.

Overcome with horror and despair, she had fainted in the arms of her attendant.

"Take her away," said Marco Bravo, addressing his myrmidons. "Let her and her maid be lodged in the apartments formerly occupied by the Countess Di Carrara ; but on your lives, let her be treated with all tenderness and respect."

The brigands promised obedience, and Violet was borne off in the arms of Pepe.

Matilda followed, weeping and wringing her hands.

Then, for the first time, Marco Bravo took notice of Ralph Wildhawk.

Our hero still remained supporting Sir Godfrey's head upon his knee, and trying to staunch with his handkerchief the copious flow of blood that gushed from the bosom of the dying man.

Marco Bravo came close to Ralph, slapped him on the shoulder, and said in a voice of forced cheerfulness—

"What, signor, look up. If you have lost one friend, you have found another, and a truer one, as I will convince you when time and opportunity shall serve. I am sorry you have met with rather rough usage during my enforced absence. But, believe me, it was by no fault of mine, and I will make such reparation as lies in my power. Come, have you no word of welcome for your old companion, the Count Di Ancona ?"

Ralph looked up, his eye on fire with scorn and defiance.

"Perfidious villain, touch me not," he exclaimed. "I scorn your friendship, and resent it more than your hate and cruelty. If you have the manliness and courage to fight me. I am ready to measure swords with you now."

Marco Bravo frowned darkly.

"This is not the language to use to your chief and commander."

"My chief ?"

"Aye, you must join the band."

"I—I become a brigand ?"

"Even so."

"You jest."

"Do not trust to that. I am resolved that you shall be one of us."

"And the alternative ?"

"Death."

"Welcome death a thousand times rather than such disgrace," returned Ralph, fiercely. "I would rather die in torments, than live your bondsman."

Marco Bravo turned red with passion, and half drew a pistol from his belt.

But he instantly thrust it back.

"No," said he, "I have promised."

A look to his followers sufficed.

They gathered round our hero, and dragged him to his feet.

They glanced at their captain as though awaiting his orders.

Before Marco Bravo had time to speak, a brigand, whose showier dress proclaimed that he held a post of command, appeared.

It was Generoso.

"Signor capitano," said he, "I bring you ill news. Our scouts have come in with the report that a large body of troops are on their way hither. They have already passed the gorge on this side of Fondi, and we must prepare to resist them."

"There is some treason," rejoined the brigand chief. "Who could have betrayed the position of our fastness ?"

Again his dark, evil eyes fell upon Ralph.

"I bear you no malice," he said. "But your life rests in your own hands. I give you time to reflect upon your position. I shall return before dawn, and shall expect your answer—yes or no ; either you shall become a brigand like the rest of us, or you shall die."

"Miscreant, I have already given you my answer," retorted Ralph. "I am in your power. Do your worst if you are not man enough to fight me."

"Away with him," cried Marco Bravo, waving his hand. "Let him be re-conducted to the cells under the Moorish tower."

Ralph was dragged away, and, he found himself once more a miserable captive mewed in a horrible prison.

CHAPTER XLVII.

RALPH WILDHAWK had reason to thank his favouring stars that he was not long left to brood in chains and darkness.

The door of his cell was thrown open within half an hour of the moment when he was thrust back into the dreary dungeon, where he had passed so many dismal days.

Giovanni entered, accompanied by Felipe.

"Rouse you, signore," said the young brigand; "I come to release you, and bring you to La Catarina and the English milordo."

Ralph sprang up.

"Tell me," said he, "does Sir Godfrey still live?"

"He is dying, signore," answered the young brigand. "He wishes to see you before all is over with him."

Giovanni conducted our hero to a cave in one of the stern, frowning cliffs that formed the sides of the Brigands' Glen.

Here he found Sir Godfrey stretched at length upon a pallet of straw, and evidently at the last gasp.

Beside him knelt La Catarina, who busied herself in wetting his lips with wine, and wiping off the death-dews from his cold, pallid brow.

Upon the entrance of Ralph, the queen of the brigands uttered a wild, joyous cry.

She sprang towards Ralph, and flung her arms about his neck.

"My son, my son!" she moaned, "speak to me, your mother—your unhappy mother."

"My mother!" exclaimed Ralph, in utter bewilderment. "How can that be possible?"

Sir Godfrey raised himself upon his arm, and beckoned Ralph to approach.

Our hero flew to his side.

"Ralph, it is true; I am your father," he said. "La Catarina is my wife, and your mother. Would to heaven that I had life enough left to tell you our sad story. It is too late now; but I have consigned the documentary proofs of my marriage and of your legitimacy to my lawyers, and you will be righted. Fra Domenico, who came hither with La Catarina, knows all. Let him accompany you to England; his testimony will be of the greatest use to you. And now, give me your hand; tell me I am forgiven, and I shall depart in peace."

"My father!" murmured Ralph, grasping his clammy hand.

"Cherish your mother; I have done her wrong," said Sir Godfrey. "Her rival died by violence, but not by your mother's hand. La Catarina came to recover you, her child, and Lady Margaret was murdered by the brigands. She has had her revenge. May Heaven pardon my sins, and protect you from the perils that environ you."

Not many more words spake the dying man. The hand of death was upon him.

Muttering some incoherent phrases of remorse, he sank upon the bosom of La Catarina, and expired.

For some moments Ralph Wildhawk stood gazing upon the pale, dead face in awe and silence.

But the sound of distant musketry roused them, by reminding them of the danger of the situation.

Young Giovanni rushed into the cave.

His looks betrayed his excitement.

"Fly!" he exclaimed: "escape! Not a moment is to be lost! Hark, they are shouting!"

A loud cheer from the brigands rang upon the air.

"What means this?" asked La Catarina. "Is Marco Bravo once more victorious?"

"Yes, signora," replied the youth. "Stromba has just returned, and brings tidings that Marco Bravo has worsted the troops sent against him; but it is said that fresh troops are on the march from Naples."

"*Va bene*, it is well," said La Catarina; "Marco Bravo is a valiant man, but he has had his day."

Taking Ralph by the hand, she added quickly—

"Let us begone, *mio figlio;* all is prepared for our departure. There is a secret outlet from this cave, known only to myself, in the valley below. We shall find mules awaiting to carry us to Fondi."

La Catarina bent over her dead husband, and pressed a kiss upon his brow.

She led them on into the recesses of the cavern till she came to a large mass of stone that appeared to block up a disused entrance.

She bade Ralph and the two Italians, Guiseppe and Felipe, try their strength upon it.

They strained every muscle to hoist it from its place.

They would never have succeeded but that the mass of stone was poised upon a sharp point of the rock under it in such a way as to be removable when great force was applied to it.

The stone rolled over, disclosing an opening in the rocks through which the green, shimmering leaves of the forest were visible.

They found mules ready saddled, and attended by four of the brigands, who were trusty attendants of their chieftainess.

Ralph and his companions mounted, and the cavalcade wound its way down the steep and precipitous path that led to the valley below.

As they passed a small ruined fort, Ralph descried two blackened skulls stuck upon iron stakes on the top of one of the nodding walls of the ruin.

He pointed them out to Giovanni, and asked whose heads they were.

"The heads of the two traitors—Guiseppe Veletri and Michael Cornaro, who betrayed their chief," replied Giovanni.

"Let us hope that the time is not far distant when the arch-villain's own head will figure on the battlements of St. Elmo," said Ralph, vindictively.

"I wish no harm to Marco Bravo," replied Giovanni, "but I am glad to be once more free."

"Then you have fully made up your mind to leave the brigand gang?" asked Ralph.

"Yes, signore, for ever," he replied, and his eyes sparkled with an expression of hope and animation which was quite new in him.

"I am right glad to hear you say so," replied Ralph; "but will you not be afraid to show your face in Naples?"

"No, signore," answered Giovanni; "Fra Domenico, whom we are to meet at yonder shepherd's hut, has obtained for me a free pardon on condition that I should quit the territory, but there are more states in the peninsula than Naples, and I can live happy anywhere, with my dear Lisetta by my side."

"I am glad to see you in such high spirits, my brave lad," answered Ralph; "I owe you much, and believe me that while life endures, you shall never want a friend."

"Ten thousand thanks, signore," answered Giovanni.

They had now arrived at the shepherd's hut, where they found the good old monk awaiting them.

He received La Catarina and Ralph Mortimer, to call our hero by his right name, with every demonstration of joy and affection.

"My son," said La Catarina, sadly, "we meet but to part again. I shall never leave Italy. As soon as I see you placed in the position you have the right to hold, I shall bury my remorse and regret in the seclusion of a convent, and spend the brief span of life remaining to me, in penitence and prayer."

Ralph thought it best to waive for the time any attempt to persuade his mother to alter her resolution.

Ralph was anxious to hurry forward to secure help to rescue Violet, for without her he felt life would be a burden to him.

At a small town they were informed a strong body of troops, dragoons and infantry, were stationed, and Ralph much wished that he could join them as a volunteer, and take part in their foray against the detestable brigands.

The little cavalcade jogged on unmolested, until they entered a belt of forest at the base of the mountains.

Here they were brought to a standstill by the distant sounds of strife.

They heard cheers, shots, the clattering of weapons, and the galloping of horses' feet.

Leaving La Catarina and Fra Domenico in the charge of two or three, Ralph and Giovanni climbed up some high rocks to reconnoitre.

They were both armed with guns and stilettoes.

It was only consideration for his mother and the good priest that caused Ralph to restrain his ardour, and prevented him from plunging into the midst of the fray.

A running fight was kept up between the robbers and the military.

The former were evidently getting the worst of it.

They retreated from rock to rock, and bush to bush, keeping up a fierce fire upon their pursuers.

Hastening their pace, they had nearly reached the end of the ravine, when they saw a number of brigands, in full retreat.

Upon seeing the party of travellers, some of the foremost of the ruffians opened fire upon them, in mere spite and wantonness.

The bullets whizzed past Ralph, who had rushed forward, but La Catarina uttered a faint cry, and pressing her hand to her heart, sank to the ground.

Ralph flew to the spot and raised her in his arms, at the same time calling on Giovanni and the priest for assistance.

La Catarina raised her eyes with a languishing expression of ineffable tenderness, and fixed them with a last fond look upon her son's pale and dismayed countenance.

"Mother, my dear mother, this last cruel blow is more than I can bear," cried poor Ralph, in tones of anguish. "Was it for this that we were so late restored to each other? Look up, my dear mother, speak one word of comfort to your unhappy son; you are wounded, but not seriously, I hope and pray."

"I have got my death wound, *caro mio;* but grieve not for me," she answered faintly. "My fate is a just retribution for the guilty life I have passed. It is better that I should thus die in your dear arms, whilst we are yet newly united, than that I should live to be looked upon as your shame and disgrace, the stumbling-block in your path. Kiss me, child, and take my dying blessing."

Ralph knelt by her on the ground.

"The Virgin Mother of Heaven bless and preserve you, my child," she murmured, "and receive my spirit. Pray for me."

Her head fell back.

A convulsive shiver ran through her frame.

Her limbs stiffened.

La Catarina, the queen of the brigands, was dead.

CHAPTER XLVIII.

BEFORE Ralph and his companions had time to recover from their amazement and consternation at the sudden and fatal event recorded in our last chapter, they were alarmed by the sound of voices and footsteps approaching towards them.

"Save yourselves," said Ralph, turning to his companions, "the brigands are upon us. As for me, I will not stir a foot; I have my murdered parent to avenge."

He had scarcely ceased speaking when a large body of cavalry and infantry were seen entering the glen.

"Holy St. Francis be praised," exclaimed the monk; "it is the soldiers."

"They may mistake us for brigands," said Giovanni; "go forward, holy father, and speak to them, to prevent accidents."

This hint was not lost upon the priest, and proved a well-timed caution.

The soldiers of the advanced guard had already perceived the travellers and pointed their carbines at them.

Fra Domenico threw himself in their way, and shouted to them not to fire.

Upon seeing him, and observing his monkish attire, they lowered their weapons.

Then their officer, a handsome young gallant in shining accoutrements, came galloping up and interrogated the monk.

Fra Domenico explained matters to the officer's satisfaction.

The young cavalier immediately hurried up to Ralph and held out his hand.

"I congratulate you on your escape, signore." said he. "Have you forgotten me? I had the honour of making your acquaintance in Naples."

Ralph grasped his hand.

"Monsignore the Count Di Roso," said Ralph, "this a most fortunate meeting."

In as few words as possible he narrated what had happened to himself and his party since their escape from the brigands.

The news of the deaths of Sir Godfrey Mortimer, and of the famous La Catarina caused a profound sensation among the soldiers.

They gathered around the rigid form of the brigand chieftainess as she lay stretched in death, and commented on the austere, classic beauty of her features, and the stateliness of her tall figure.

"I have no doubt, signore," said the young captain of dragoons, addressing our hero, "that you will guess what brings us to the mountains?"

"You are in pursuit of that fiend, Marco Bravo," returned Ralph. "I see you have some led horses——"

"Yes; their riders, poor fellows, have been tumbled from the saddle by the bush-firing of the robbers," returned the officer.

"I must mount one of the spare horses and go with you," said Ralph. "I will strike at least one blow at the accursed wretches who have caused me such dreadful loss and misery, and rescue Violet."

"I cannot refuse a request so natural," answered the captain. "Even women forget their weakness and timidity in the desire to wreak vengeance upon the murderous gang, witness the brave lady who accompanies our troop."

"What lady?" asked Ralph, in surprise.

"See, she comes this way," answered the officer. "Let her speak for herself."

Ralph was astonished to behold riding towards him a young and very beautiful lady, dressed in a black velvet riding-habit, and a black hat and plume.

She was mounted on a beutiful white palfrey.

There were pistols in her holsters and a sword hung by a baldrick at her side.

"By Heaven! it is the beautiful Countess Di Carrara," exclaimed Ralph. "What motive can have induced her to exhibit herself in this Amazonian guise?"

"Revenge for her lover, Captain Lanfranco, slain by the brigand chief," replied the officer. "You English can scarcely understand the intense passions, whether of love or hatred, that stir our women's hearts in the southern clime."

Ralph thought that he had already seen some striking examples, but he held his peace.

The countess now rode up, and uttered her surprise and delight at seeing our hero restored to liberty.

"Now let us advance, for I fear some evil may fall on Violet from the wretch Marco Bravo," said Ralph.

"Let there be no delay," answered the countess. "Signore," she went on, speaking to Ralph, "like some distressed damsel of romance, I appoint you my champion."

She took the sword from her side, and hung it by the belt over Ralph's shoulder.

"Take this sword," she said. "It belonged to poor Captain Lanfranco, whom the brigand killed at Naples. Use it valiantly. The saints nerve your arm. It may be you will encounter Marco Bravo himself; bring me his head."

At a sign from their captain, the trumpeter of the troop blew a long shrill blast.

The soldiers cheered, and formed in marching order.

A horse was brought to Ralph, who sprang lightly into the saddle.

"*Addio, signori*," cried the countess, waving her hand. "I shall go back to Fondi, and there await your return, and pray that you may bring back a good account of the brigands."

The troop dashed off at a rattling pace.

As they ascended higher up the mountain side, the distant volleys of musketry gave token that a furious battle was raging between the brigand and the troops in advance.

Excited by these sounds of strife, the Count Di Roso and his men, together with the English volunteer, found it difficult to curb their fiery impatience.

Before they had got very far, they found to their extreme mortification, that the road became so difficult, as to necessitate dismounting and proceeding the rest of the distance on foot.

They left their horses in charge of some of the troopers, and began clambering the steep and rugged rocks.

Ralph, who by this time had become thoroughly accustomed to mountain climbing, outstripped his companions, and was the first to set his foot upon the stretch of table-land whereon the battle was raging.

A desperate conflict was being waged between the brigands and the soldiery.

The robbers had been overtaken and brought to bay.

They now made their last stand, and fought with all the valour of despair and desperation. Shots cracked, swords clashed, and cries and shouts made the rocks re-echo.

Almost beside himself with fury and vengefulness, Ralph looked around him in search of some foe on whom to vent his wrath.

A flash and a sharp report close by him, caused him to look up.

He saw a tall, handsome figure, in the picturesque brigand costume, perched on a rock within a few paces.

His carbine, still smoking from its discharge, was poised in his hands, and his black eagle eyes were fixed upon an officer in a showy uniform, whose head drooped on his horse's neck; the next instant the unfortunate soldier fell from his saddle, and the charging dragoons rushed trampling over his body.

The brigand uttered a fiendish laugh of triumph, and sprang down from the rock.

Ralph rushed forward and confronted him.

It was Marco Bravo.

Upon seeing our hero, he started back.

"You!" he exclaimed. "So you have escaped. Well, I am not sorry for that. We have been friends, why should we fly at each other's throats? My career is over. I have been betrayed. Treachery, the cursed treachery of those I have served so well, has been my ruin. But at least, I shall die as becomes a chief of the free banditti, and for generations the peasant at his toil, the muleteer on his journey, the improvisatore surrounded by his rapt listeners on the shores of the bay, will sing the exploits of Marco Bravo."

"No, villain and murderer, a wiser, purer generation will arise who will execrate such crimes as those you boast of, and brand you as a rascal," answered Ralph, furiously. "Murderer of my father, defend yourself. One or both of us must die."

"Your father," said Marco Bravo, pausing and regarding him curiously. "Why, then I was not wrong in my suspicions. I know your story. Well, avenge yourself. My carbine is discharged; fire upon me, my breast is bare."

He flung down the musket and threw open his gold embroidered jacket, and confronted Ralph with a cool dauntlessness worthy of a better nature.

Ralph instantly flung away his musket.

"I will take no advantage," said he. "Draw your sword, villain, as I draw mine. Yet, no, not mine; this is the sword of Captain Lanfranco, whom you murdered."

"*Altro*," returned the brigand chief, "I killed him in fair fight as I killed your father, and as I mean to kill you, boy. Come, as you say, one or both of us must sup with Pluto. Prepare thou to go from this world."

A few rapid passes were exchanged, but Marco Bravo had already received a gun-shot wound, and overcome by weakness, he fought wildly and recklessly.

Ralph took quick advantage of the brigand's wildness, and soon passed his sword through the body of the redoubted chieftain, who fell at his feet.

Marco Bravo gently raised himself on his elbow.

"Wildhawk, you are the victor, yet one word, *amico*," he gasped. "The beautiful English signora; I loved her. She is in the hands of Stromba and Generoso—save her. They are on the road to Frosinone. Now, farewell. I die by your hand, but if the power had been given me, I would have taken your life in this fair fight."

He drew his mantle over his brows, and died like an ancient Roman.

Ralph had no time to waste over the dying brigand.

A body of dragoons rushed past him, charging and slashing down the brigands, who had expended all their ammunition, and were now forced to fight with their knives.

Informing the Count Di Roso of the death of Marco Bravo, and the last words he had spoken, Ralph urged the officer to lead his troops on to the stronghold of the brigands.

The Count Di Roso, detaching a certain number of his men to pursue and kill such of the brigands as had not surrendered, went with the rest of the troops to the rescue of Violet and the other prisoners.

Guided by Giovanni, they reached the old Moorish fortress, which they found in flames, the brigands having set fire to it, as it contained ammunition and provisions which they thought the enemy might take possession of and use against them.

They found Generoso and Stromba, with the rest of the band, preparing for their flight, having their prisoners bound ready for the start.

A desperate conflict ensued.

Joe Moody, who had escaped from the brigands, and was hiding in a cave, came forth and joined the attacking party.

He fought like a dragon, and bore off Matilda Sparkes from Generoso, killing that miscreant with his own hands.

From that hour Joe was a hero in the eyes of his romantic sweetheart, and never again did she accuse her sweetheart of a want of sensibility.

Ralph's first act was to seek for Violet.

Under young Giovanni's guidance, he entered the apartments to which the fair captives had been consigned.

But the birds had flown.

Greatly terrified, Ralph hurried from the tower, and discovered that a fight was going on for the rescue of the prisoners.

Ralph's fury was roused when at last he caught sight of Violet struggling in the hands of the ruffian Stromba, like a fluttering dove under the talons of a hawk.

Ralph aimed with his pistol, but dared not fire for fear of hitting the girl.

Ralph saw Violet's dress gleaning among the bushes, as the brutal ruffian dragged her shrieking up the mountain.

Our hero sprang up the rocks, and struggled painfully through the thorny bushes, guided by the cries of Violet, and the blustering oaths of the robber.

He overtook them.

Stromba, upon seeing Ralph, levelled his carbine and fired.

The ball whizzed past Ralph's hat, but the brave young fellow, nothing daunted, sprang upon Stromba, and closed with him.

Ralph, the brigand, and Violet were now hustled together upon a narrow path along the face of the cliff, little more than a foot wide.

The despicable ruffian, Stromba, tried to push the poor girl over the precipice.

Violet clutched at the branch of a solitary tree that overhung the abyss.

"Hold on for your life, dear Violet," panted Ralph, still wrestling with the brigand; "hold on till I can come to your aid."

Stromba had drawn his stiletto, and struggled desperately to plunge it into Ralph's heart.

Our hero, however, gradually got his adversary nearer and nearer to the verge of the precipice, and at length succeeded in extricating himself, and hurling him into mid-air.

Ralph looked over the giddy brink, and beheld the brigand lying heaped and motionless, dead among the rocks, far below.

The defeat of the brigands was complete, the band broken up and almost exterminated.

With numerous prisoners, the victorious troops returned in triumph to Naples, and the next day the head of the redoubted brigand chief, Marco Bravo, was set up on the battlements of St. Elmo.

Our story draws to an end. Not without some trouble, difficulties occasioned by the "law's delays," our hero, Ralph Mortimer, proved his right and title to the baronetcy and estate of the late Sir Godfrey.

As soon as he came into possession of his property, he set about bestowing suitable rewards upon those from whom he had received kindness in times of trial and adversity.

To Giovanni and Lisetta, he gave a considerable sum of money to purchase a vineyard, and set themselves up for life.

He used his interest to obtain a free pardon for Felipe and his wife, whose little daughter our hero so gallantly rescued from drowning.

Felipe started a fresh life as an hotel-keeper at Palermo, and flourished exceedingly.

A few months after their return to England, our hero led the beautiful Violet to the altar, amongst the heartfelt rejoicings of his tenantry and dependents on his estate, to whom Ralph had endeared himself in boyhood.

Joe Moody and the romantic Matilda were married on the same day as Sir Ralph and Lady Mortimer, in whose service they remained for the rest of their happy and prosperous lives.

In after years, Sir Ralph Mortimer would often entertain the brilliant circle of distinguished guests, assembled in his fine and hospitable manor house, by relating the adventures he had met with whilst alone among the brigands.

www.ingramcontent.com/pod-product-compliance
Lightning Source LLC
Chambersburg PA
CBHW080832250626
47160CB00008B/2906